2-98

AMERICAN WOMAN

AMERICAN WOMAN

R. Garcia y Robertson

A TOM DOHERTY ASSOCIATES BOOK
New York

AMERICAN WOMAN

Copyright © 1998 by R. Garcia y Robertson

Part of this work appeared in somewhat different form in *Fantasy and Science Fiction*, December 1995, as "Happy Hunting Ground."

This book is printed on acid-free paper.

A Forge Book
Published by Tom Doherty Associates, Inc.
175 Fifth Avenue
New York, NY 10010

Forge® is a registered trademark of Tom Doherty Associates, Inc.

Design by Helene Berinsky

Library of Congress Cataloging-in-Publication Data

Garcia y Robertson, R.
     American woman / R. Garcia y Robertson.—1st ed.
          p.   cm.
     "A Tom Doherty Associates book."
     ISBN 0-312-86146-X
     1. Little Bighorn, Battle of the, Mont., 1876—Fiction.
2. Indians of North America—Wars, 1876—Fiction   3. Custer, George
Armstrong, 1839–1876—Fiction.   4. White women—West (U.S.)—Fiction.
I. Title
PS3557.A71125A83 1998
813'.54—dc21   97-40293
                                                        CIP

First Edition: February 1998

Printed in the United States of America

0 9 8 7 6 5 4 3 2 1

For my mother and father
John Garcia and Dorothy Inez Robertson

THE WINTER MEDICINE BEAR LOST HIS MEDICINE

1873

Do not write down my words. People reading them in a book will not believe them—but I saw what I saw.
> —Pretty Shield (Crow Medicine woman
> and wife to Custer's scout Goes Ahead),
> telling about her vision of a yellow-haired,
> blue-eyed spirit woman

The Yellowstone

CRAZY HORSE LOWERED THE BINOCULARS, HANDING THEM TO my husband, who passed them to me. I could already see the cavalry column coming on, wavering in the heat, a great blue-coated snake, coils rising and falling with the prairie. Brings-'em-close-glasses broke the dark snaking line into men and horses marching in pairs, raising clouds of yellow-white dust that covered the rear of the column. One look had me working hard on my Medicine, making myself small and invisible. For a young white woman to sit unnoticed in the middle of a Lakota war party is big Medicine indeed. But invisibility is like God's Grace or a clean conscience. You have it or you don't. That day on the Yellowstone I had the Medicine. No one questioned it. Not even me.

I had done my damnedest to be transparent. My blond braids were wrapped in otter pelts. Yellow Legs had painted my face that morning—nothing garish, just dull gray with a black-and-white streak across the eyes, the colors of a fire burned down to ash; peaceful raccoon colors that keep a pale face from showing in the shadows.

We were on a bluff above the Yellowstone, hidden by a stand of lodge-pole pines that had never known an ax. Below us rolled the river, brown and muddy from the rains. Upstream, tourists camped in Yellowstone National Park. Downstream, a column of U.S. cavalry was about to get a Crazy Horse welcome. And I was in the middle, scared rigid and straining to stay invisible, molding myself to the back of my Nez Percé pony, my bare toes curled into her belly hairs.

All around me sat half-naked men on horseback, silent as the grave and set to do mischief, wearing war paint and animal masks, carrying guns, bows, graceful Sheyenna lances, and the murderous spiked clubs and eight-foot

hatchets favored by Lakotas. I could smell the fear and sweat on their thickly painted bodies—for the day was hot, and some of them would die. These were not Loafers, the Hang-About-the-Forts that tourists see, wrapped in blankets, bumming whiskey. They were the original article: Hunkpapas, No Bows, Oglalas, and wild Sheyenna whose grandfathers had known yellow-haired white women only in Medicine tales. Sitting Bull once told me how the Oglalas first brought a white woman into a Hunkpapa camp. Like most Sitting Bull stories it was half truth, half flattery. She was much admired. Men called her Real Woman, offering many ponies for her. But when Sitting Bull saw Real Woman did not want to be a real Lakota he sent her home, and the excitement over Wasichu women ebbed. What was the use of having a woman who did not want to be a Lakota?

Crazy Horse slid backward off his pony, a golden buckskin with broad white patches. His movements were always sure and decisive, a man with much Medicine. Sandy hair, light skin, and soft features set him apart—the fair-haired boy-general of the Lakotas. Scooping up gopher dust, he sprinkled himself and his pony.

We women do not need to dirty ourselves with gopher dust to be invisible. Warriors getting ready for battle would as soon not see a woman—we have been known to weaken a man's Medicine enough to let a bullet in. Unless we are singing encouraging songs, braves prefer us silent and unseen. I knew some pretty encouraging tunes, but bursting into a few bars of "Amazing Grace" or "The Star-Spangled Banner" did not fit the occasion.

Instead I shut my eyes, barely breathing, silently willing the horse soldiers to go home.

With eyes closed, feeling the heat and the horse between my thighs, I could hear the hum of insects and smell hot gunmetal under the clean pine scent. Summers on the Yellowstone are living things. In the Moon of Black Cherries, noon shadows shrink down to ink spills; bluestem and grama grass breathe up a blanket of air as warm and thick as a buffalo robe. Sweat pooled under my doeskin riding dress, collecting above fringed leggings. Sheyenna women's calfskin underwear always made me perspire, but it was not the moment to scratch a personal itch. Luckily I never needed their rope chastity belts.

When I opened my eyes the cavalry column was gone. My Medicine felt pretty big. For a heartbeat it seemed we could all go back to camp alive and happy. Then I saw they had not vanished. The column was curling up in the grassy bottom near where the Tongue and the Yellowstone run together—it being the time of day when snakes hide from the sun. Now there was no way to stop the killing.

Crazy Horse remounted and the men readied themselves. My husband unrolled a doeskin bundle scrawled with Medicine signs. He took out his warbonnet of twenty-eight black-tipped eagle feathers—feathers that told his enemies he had touched them in battle, then ridden away, leaving them humiliated. Yellow Legs had a special pair of leggings, cut from blue cavalry breeches, with a yellow officer's stripe running down each pants leg. The seat and crotch were cut out because Sheyenna men find normal pants too confining. He was tall and dark-eyed, with a lean build and clean brown complexion, and his face was painted to match his pants, blue from the eyes up and yellow below. The effect was barbarous—but at the moment this painted-up savage was the center of my shaky world.

Beyond him, Medicine Bear broke the silence, humming a bullet song, rattling his shield trimmed with bear claws. This shield had been stretched by Ice. Aside from the Buffalo Hat Keeper, Ice was the biggest Medicine man among the Northern Sheyenna. No one made bullet Medicine better.

Medicine Bear had on a wildly extravagant outfit. From his bear-faced headdress to his high-beaded moccasins, hardly an inch of him went undecorated. He wore grizzly teeth, weasel bones, red body paint, pony beads, human hair, a cheap crucifix, a dozen silver three-cent pieces, and a tiny metal portrait of Queen Victoria. Most braves go similarly decked-out into battle, proclaiming their identity in hopes that death will go looking for the anonymous victim. Anything might have the magic, even a little nailed-up Jesus or thirty-six cents in change.

But Crazy Horse wore only a feathered hawk skin tied in his hair and plain blue leggings. His skin was barely painted. A few white hail spots made him as pure and dangerous as lightning on a sunny day. Crows claimed Crazy Horse had a never-miss Medicine rifle, and in battle he was as bulletproof as doubled boiler plate—ever since Chips gave him a tiny stone to tie behind his ear. That winter Chips had given Crazy Horse another stone to tie under his horse's tail, making his mount immune. Big Medicine indeed. But all Medicine is big beforehand. Below us, hundreds of carbines were set to test the bullet Medicine.

Crazy Horse outlined the attack in a flurry of hand signals. Despite winters of camping together, Crazy Horse's Lakotas and the Sheyenna Lakota Eaters spoke completely different languages, sign-talking to each other as though they were hard-of-hearing. Crazy Horse made the two-handed sign that means go ahead, touching his breast to say he would lead. Like a team captain choosing sides, he picked five men to go with him. I saw him wave a little finger, then strike his index fingers together, which meant "First Coup," my husband's Lakota name. (It was part of Yellow Legs's Medicine

that he counted only first coups, just like Crazy Horse never took scalps.) I
guessed Crazy Horse would want Yellow Legs with him, but I wished he had
picked another brave.

Crazy Horse made the rolling spiraling sign for Medicine Bear, followed
by three Lakota names less familiar to me. Then he circled his right hand,
passing it under his left, telling the others to hide. Twice he pushed his flat
right hand down and forward. He wanted no mistakes. Everyone else was to
wait. Here sat living proof of the thinking Indian. Despite his Medicine
gun and bullet Medicine, Crazy Horse never liked to go into a fight unless
he had already won the battle in his head. Those Wasichu who call Lakotas dumb and lazy have not seen Crazy Horse on the hunt or warpath. A real
go-ahead brave. The army would never feel secure until he was behind bars
or lying on his burial scaffold.

Silent as noon shadows, the warriors and their ponies vanished into the
timbers, leaving me wishing to God this was not happening. But no one had
consulted me, silent and invisible. No one had consulted anyone. Crazy
Horse merely said he was leading; braves were free to stay or follow. His
Crow Owners kept hot heads from attacking too soon, but no one was forced
to fight.

I could have stayed, with my mare for company, hearing the shots and
wondering. But that would have been unbearable—I *had* to know what was
happening. Raven says that I am as curious as a lovestruck antelope, a trait
she considers unhealthy. I suppose it is, but my husband would be staking his
life on the bullet Medicine. If he was killed, I did not aim to hear it from ·
some arrogant warrior, watching to see if I dishonored the death with a
weak Wasichu reaction.

Dismounting, I had a thorough talk with my pony. I told Keeps-the-Fire
that she was to stay still; no matter how wild the shooting was, no matter
how handsome the big American stallions were. "One of us has to show
some foresight." My mare stared back, saying nothing, her skin flicking sideways in the heat.

Yellow Legs had given me his army Colt for "protection," but I left the
huge revolver tied to Keeps-the-Fire with a loop in the drag rope. The pistol was heavy enough to hammer nails; and crawling about with a capped
and loaded revolver would be more of a menace to me than to anyone I met.
Daddy taught me poker at a tender age, saying, "Daughter, play the cards you
are dealt—don't cling to a kicker." If you aim to be at peace with the world,
you can't go carrying a big gun; it's a plain advertisement for trouble.

With my husband's binoculars banging against me, I blundered into the
undergrowth, taking care to make a fair commotion. Which is easy for a Wasichu, and safer than trying to sneak about—this being the time of day

when snakes hide from the sun. A rattler can kill you as sure as a carbine, but if you give them fair warning, rattlers will go their own way. They prefer our company about as much as we prefer theirs.

There were no rattlers, not so much as a bull snake, but little eyes did watch me wiggle through the plum thicket. A ground squirrel chattered, telling the world I was coming. Then suddenly he fell silent, stock-still, staring upward. A lone eagle circled a thousand feet above the bluffs, scaring this squirrel more than all the armed humans sneaking about. A pair of black specks began to mob the eagle, wheeling and diving, driving the hunter away.

Smelling coffee on a wood fire, I poked my binoculars over the edge of the bluff. Several of the soldiers below were sleeping. One lay stretched out in his underwear, with a red flannel shirt for a pillow, as relaxed as if the wilds of Montana were Central Park, Manhattan. I took a long salacious look, since I did not often get to ogle handsome white gents in their underwear. He was slim, with a whip-hard body, reminding me of Crazy Horse.

Binoculars brought the soldiers almost within reach, and I kept feeling I was seeing dead men who walked and talked without knowing they were dead. I did not want them to die, but I did wish they would go away— because right now they were shopping for a cheap funeral. I missed an immense list of things from home—hot baths, ice cream or just plain cream, piano music, and any type of pastry. But I did not miss men with guns and uniforms.

Men with guns were overcommon in Lakota Country, and growing up in Pennsylvania I had seen my quota of uniforms. Our farm lay a dozen miles from the Mason-Dixon line. One hot July day when the corn was waist high, my sisters and I sat on our split-rail fence, watching thousands of boys in butternut gray stream past our house, filling the Chambersburg Pike. Barefoot Rebels plucked primroses for their hatbands, asking our names— saying if we did not tell, we were Yankees. We yelled back to them that they did not need to know our names, but to be careful, because the real Yankees were somewhere over Herr Ridge, past Black Horse Tavern, where the Pike crosses Willoughby Run before going on into Gettysburg. A black man marching with the column stopped to beg water for his master. Fetching a bucket from the well, we asked what he thought of Pennsylvania. "Hits a free country," he drawled, "but she don't measure up ta Virginia."

For three days the guns banged south of the Lutheran Seminary, shattering peach trees, while men and horses trampled down the wheat. Then the Rebs staggered back broken and bleeding. Mother turned our farm into a field hospital that served both sides. We were Quakers, and aimed to be friends and neighbors to all.

Courtly southern officers took our plow team to pull their guns, and left us their poor relations to moan and bleed until men in blue uniforms came and got them. The local militia had fled the county, and the Culps lost a boy fighting on the "other side," killed on the hill named for his family. Jennie Wade, the girl the Culp boy courted, died too, shot in her kitchen by a stray bullet. Adams County saw more war in a week than the entire Sheyenna nation sees in a century. I once tried to tell some Sheyenna that, but the warriors scoffed. What do Wasichu or women know about war?

I did know the bluecoats below had no more business in Lakota Country than men from Maine and Texas had coming to shoot up Adams County. From the Black Hills to the tops of the Big Horns, this was Unceded Indian Territory—outside the United States. Under the Fort Laramie Treaty, no white could set boot heel here without Lakota consent. I was tolerated for my husband's sake, and because Lakota braves naturally assumed treaties did not apply to agreeable young women.

It was still a thorny business being a Wasichu among wild Lakota and Sheyenna. And now the army was coming, scouting for a railroad nobody needed or wanted. First the cavalry, then the Northern Pacific, with neither a please nor a thank you. Some folks think Indian braves are like children, who don't know right from wrong—the fastest way to find out different is to wrong one and see what happens. These soldiers had been warned politely away. Now Crazy Horse planned to put more vigor in the request.

I winced as the air filled up with shots and yells. Crazy Horse, Yellow Legs, and the other bulletproof men came wheeling out of the timbers, taunting the soldiers, trying to stampede the big American horses. Seeing Yellow Legs at war was like seeing a stranger. As a husband he was exceptionally tender, never striking me or offering intentional insult, being as honest as his savage lights allowed. Yet he had trained since boyhood to fight, and had been killing white men, off and on, since I was a small girl. When his war Medicine was working, he claimed nothing could touch him, not an arrow, not a bullet—not even me.

The sleeping soldier leaped to his feet, game as a bulldog, grabbing a rifle and leading a countercharge, wearing only socks and underwear. Crazy Horse retreated before this novel attack—but that was his plan, to lead the Wasichu into arrow range of the timbers.

Pulling on his pants and red flannel shirt, the soldier swung atop a fast-looking horse and led a small body of troopers forward, following the bulletproof braves at a trot. Within rifle shot of the timbers the troopers stopped. The officer in red and a couple of others kept advancing at an easy canter. Crazy Horse hooted. Yellow Legs urged the soldiers on in English, daring them to show some courage. My skin prickled as he used words that I had taught him. Even intimate words. Crazy Horse, no great student of American letters, shouted "Sons of bitches" in clear Wasichu.

My husband got down, pretended his pony was lame, acting helpless. The man was a born thespian. All these antics were meant to bring the troopers closer to the trees. Lying flat on my belly, I steadied the binoculars. I could see the soldier in red's drooping mustache. Beside him rode a cavalry scout, with an eagle feather in his hair and the stern brown face of a Corn Indian. Sweat itched down my leg, but I was too paralyzed to scratch. My least movement threatened to throw the world into bloody chaos. Hundreds of warriors hid in the timbers, honing their scalp knives. Four score soldiers were strung out between them and the river, ready to be rolled over when Crazy Horse gave the command.

Digging the fingers of my free hand into the grass roots, I whispered, "Go back—this is going to be a massacre."

I prayed to Jesus, to my father's miraculous Virgin, to my mother's rational, peaceable God, and to the Great Medicine. To anyone that might stop the soldiers short of the timbers. The troopers were a nuisance, but I did not mean to see them strewn hacked and naked in the sun-bleached grass, their white bodies feathered with arrows. Quakers believe the worst use you can make of a man is to kill him.

Never doubt the power of prayer. Even in Montana, God or the Great Medicine can show pity. The officer in red drew back. I heard the Sheyenna massed in the woods chanting a name: "Long Hair, Long Hair." Hunkpapa Lakotas also called out a name, shouting, "Bloody Knife."

I shifted the binoculars. Sheyenna poured out of the timbers, whooping to beat the devil. Behind them came the Hunkpapas, led by a huge warrior named Gall. Crazy Horse's Crow Owners and Last Bull's Coyote Society could no longer hold the braves back.

Sheyenna had charged too soon, ruining Crazy Horse's ambush. The red-shirted officer took one swift look, turned his thoroughbred, and raced for the river. The Indian scout galloped behind him, drawing a rifle from his saddle scabbard. Troopers threw themselves from their mounts, putting their backs to the muddy river, disappearing into the tall grass growing along the bottoms.

I don't fault them for running. A full-out stampede by painted-up braves, waving spiked war clubs and blowing their eagle-bone whistles, is a terrifying spectacle. Fit to send stout hearts screaming for cover. But these troopers met the hideous onslaught with cool discipline. As the warriors came on, filling the air with heathen cries, a line of soldiers rose up out of the wheatgrass. Smoke from their carbines blossomed like a cloud of bright white yarrow, covering the firing line.

⌐ Even before I heard the crash of gunshots, the oncoming wave split and scattered. Few warriors will ride full-tilt into gunfire. Most braves believe war should be fun; unless they feel especially bulletproof, or suicidal, they never press a charge. If General Pickett had led a division of Oglalas at Gettysburg, he would have charged alone. Real bang-up disasters require more discipline than Buffalo Indians will stand for.

Braves put on displays of trick riding for the troopers, laying alongside their mounts and firing from under the horses' necks, or rising up and showing their backsides, daring the Wasichu to come out of the long grass. Yellow Legs and Medicine Bear made a game of teasing the firing line, galloping neck and neck, then breaking in opposite directions at the same instant. That took the bounce out of me—setting me back to praying, begging for the bullet Medicine to hold.

Twice they rode right up to the soldiers' line. The first time, the bullets parted and they rode safely away. The second time, two figures rose up out of the grass. One was the officer in the red shirt, the other was his Indian scout. Both fired.

I thought maybe they had missed. Then the impossible happened. Medicine Bear tottered and fell from his horse. Bullets were not supposed to bring down Medicine Bear; they were supposed to bounce off him or be caught by his bearhide shield. Sheyenna groaned aloud in disappointment.

Yellow Legs must have heard. He reined in, turning back toward where Medicine Bear sat clutching his belly. My own stomach gave a heave. Forgetting to hide, I leaped up, my heart pumping in panic. Twisting the binoculars into focus, I saw my husband swing down, braids and bonnet tail bouncing on the ground. Shots clipped the grass around his head, stripping feathers from his warbonnet. Another instant and a bullet had to strike.

Then he straightened up, with Medicine Bear in his arms. Braves whooped in admiration. This was war Sheyenna style—one brave risking life and limb on a whim, doing the impossible, even if it did no damage to the enemy beyond embarrassment.

Even without Yellow Legs's hand on the reins, his pony turned and trotted back into the timbers, carrying double. We Wasichu think that horses cannot reason, but they are insightful enough to hate gunfire. (Lieutenant Edward S. Godfrey of the 7th U.S. cavalry once told me that nearly every retreat starts with troopers being carried off by runaway mounts—which shows that cavalry mounts can be smarter than the men on their backs.) Yellow Legs made it a point to always discuss his battle plans with his ponies.

Troopers kept firing furiously, long after he was out of range. Enough, I thought. No longer caring about rattlers, I thrashed back through the plum thicket to where my mare was tethered. I had to ride down and see that Yellow Legs was truly unharmed—and to keep him from further mischief. Thanking Keeps-the-Fire for her patience, I mounted up, and we plunged over the dusty bluff into the trees.

The Iron Road

THE AIR IN THE TIMBERS WAS ELECTRIC. CARBINES SNAPPED. Warriors moved through smoke drifting up from the box elders by the river. My insides quaked and my limbs felt loose and hollow. Surrounded by war and men's Medicine, it was a comfort to know the Lakotas considered me a prize of sorts. A moon ago, I had heard them taunt white squawmen living with the Crows—"Come get some Lakota women, if you can." Keeping me from the enemy was at least a minor coup—not to be compared with a scalp or captured weapon, but a useful anecdote to dress up a kill talk.

Of course, women can be too valuable. Civilized officers have told me that as a general practice it is prudent to shoot white women rather than leave them to savages.

Medicine Bear sat propped against a tree, holding a red mackinaw trade blanket tight about his middle. Blood was turning the blanket a deeper, darker crimson. He was gutshot, but looked too mean to die, muttering, "My Medicine is not broken—the bullet did not go through me." Cheered by that observation, he sat back and bled some more, satisfied to find his Medicine intact.

Yellow Legs was holding a hatchet, looking lamely about for a sapling. I had been half angry at him for that terrifying display of horsemanship, but now I was just happy to have him alive. Seeing me, he smiled. "Get down, wife."

I smiled back. This sentence is not as curt in Sheyenna as it sounds in English. "Get down" is a greeting. If a Sheyenna brave is not happy to see you, he would just as soon that you stayed on your horse. And to Yellow Legs, "wife" was a term of endearment more tender than any of my names. I've been called Mandan, white squaw, even a half-breed whore—but that

18

is mere ignorant opinion. I was born Sarah Kilory, youngest daughter to a going-to-meeting Quaker, and a charming Bog Irish drunkard. But not even my husband bothered with my Christian name. Birth names were for babies. Who cared what meaningless sounds my parents cooed over me when I was weak and formless? The Sheyenna kept hanging names on me, hoping one would stick. Not all were flattering. To some I was "That One." Or *Enutah*, "the Foreign Woman." Most commonly I was "American Woman," a name borrowed from Lakota. Only Yellow Legs could call me "wife."

"This man needs a travois." Yellow Legs cocked his head to indicate Medicine Bear, sitting against the tree, bleeding busily. It was part of my husband's Medicine that he never said the word "bear." He would refer to a bear as "that animal," and if a man had "bear" in his name, Yellow Legs would say "this man," or "that man." We generally knew what he meant.

Sliding off Keeps-the-Fire, I took over the task of making a travois. Yellow Legs was uncommonly skilled at domestic tasks, but he could be as clumsy as any man when his war Medicine was up. Taking his hatchet I set about cutting a pair of long poles, wanting to be close to Yellow Legs but far from the fighting—a geometric impossibility like squaring the circle. Next best was having something to do. Work gave me a place, something to fix my thoughts on. Armed braves raced about with homicidal intent, their mental states ranging from happy excitement to hysterical dementia. Many were still deliberately not seeing me, not straining their Medicine. Work put a peaceful frame around the picture. She is a woman and a Wasichu, but she is working. What could be more normal?

Comes-in-Sight, a popular Sheyenna with a hideously painted face, knelt beside Medicine Bear, assuring the wounded man that he had missed nothing. "These Long Knives do not want to fight. They just sit in the grass and shoot at us. Sitting Bull, the Hunkpapa, has set fire to the grass—but the wind is blowing up from the river."

Sitting Bull was a font of clever ideas, not all of them practical—any woman could have told Comes-in-Sight that. But I cut my saplings, saying nothing. Comes-in-Sight was a sort of brother to me by marriage, which made us taboo, too closely related to freely converse. Sheyenna firmly believe words lead to action. A smile, a greeting, a simple "How's the war going?" and we could get carried away in this shooting and confusion— and end up fornicating under a bush. It was safer not to see each other.

Comes-in-Sight complained to Yellow Legs, "I wish these Wasichu would stop coming. They are spoiling war for everyone." My husband agreed, saying People should have only sensible enemies, like Crow and Pawnee—"People" is how the Sheyenna refer to themselves, everyone else being an afterthought in creation.

I finished my crude travois, tying the two poles I cut across Keeps-the-Fire's crupper, stretching a bed of buffalo hide between the ends that dragged on the ground. Yellow Legs stripped off his pants and warbonnet, putting them back in their doeskin bundle, then he passed the bundle to me. Its borders were beaded blue and white, with long tasseled fringes—Raven's work.

Comes-in-Sight had brought back Medicine Bear's shield, snaring it with a lariat from under the guns of the soldiers. Yellow Legs needed to be sure that his tasseled Medicine bundle, with the warbonnet and leggings inside, did not touch the bearhide shield. He was convinced beyond reasonable argument that a fellow Sheyenna's shield could do him more harm than hundreds of hostile bullets—many times he had told me that he was not brave in battle, just invulnerable. Understanding his reasoning did not make his taboos any less comical, but by giving me his war Medicine he was putting his life in my hands, so I felt pride mixed with amusement.

"This fight is finished?" I observed hopefully. Giving up his Medicine meant more than if my husband had given up his weapons. Yellow Legs sometimes went into battle unarmed, but never without his Medicine.

"It is finished," he declared, though bullets still hummed merrily overhead. "I could not coax the Long Knives into a real fight." He had given the cavalry a chance to fight fair, and they refused. Yellow Legs was adept at long-range shooting, but saw no honor in it. How could a target-shoot show who was braver?

He looked at peace. Blue and yellow paint gave his face a savage power—which is why he wore it—but underneath he had relaxed. His real face showed through the paint: kinder, happier, with a high forehead, sharp chin, and laugh wrinkles around his eyes. Bowlegged from a life on horseback, he was still taller than me, and taller than Crazy Horse, though not so tall as Touch-the-Clouds. He exuded a hardy confidence, the perfect portrait of a warrior, wise in the ways of weapons, horses, and Medicine—able to handle everything but bears and women.

I ached to touch him, knowing his skin would feel soft, softer than a white man's, almost like a girl's. I was just past twenty, and desperately in love. He was only the second man I had ever known—and the first had discarded me like damaged goods. Yellow Legs was over forty, but I was only his second woman, and he always treated me as something precious. Public rectitude and ease of divorce make the Sheyenna seem like casual lovers—which is in no way the case. Behind the stern warrior facade Yellow Legs had a craving for affection as bottomless as mine. A lifetime of living by his own rugged Medicine made him desperately afraid of desertion. In that way he was like a woman, expected to be everything, but secretly wanting someone to care for him.

Holding him, even for an instant, would have reclaimed him from his war Medicine. But that too was taboo. And he took his superstitions seriously. Yellow Legs was as God-fearing a husband as you could want. He never lit a pipe, bent a bow, sat down to eat, or mounted me without invoking the Great Medicine—the ultimate mystery that enfolds us all.

He lashed Medicine Bear onto the travois, while I tied his war Medicine to Keeps-the-Fire's back. Without bothering to bid the war party good-bye, we rode up the bluffs, out of those gloomy timbers onto rolling shortgrass prairie. Smoke and death fell away as the sky opened overhead. Towering clouds ran from one edge of the world to the other. Fear faded, and I felt brim-full of power, seeing America in the raw just as God or the Great Medicine made her.

We tried to follow a gentle trail, to spare Medicine Bear some pain. Riding a travois, looking into the tall Montana sky, must be a fairly decent way to die. Travois poles form a V with the point resting on the horse. The poles dragging along the ground become long flexing springs, absorbing shocks with a gentle swaying motion. The same cannot be said for an ambulance wagon, which shakes an injured person to death over rough ground. That was why officers of the Army of Northern Virginia left their men in my mother's care, trusting enemy women more than their own ambulances.

As Medicine Bear sang songs to his belly, I reached over and took my husband's drag rope, drawing him closer. Free of the fighting, he came to me. Soon we were riding knee to knee, almost touching.

With his leggings off, Yellow Legs was nearly naked, wearing nothing but breechcloth and moccasins I had sewn for him. His body was a long flawless stream of brown skin stretched over tight muscle—no arrow, no bullet, no war knife had ever touched him. I knew, because I had made a thorough study of him, going over his body by candlelight in my tipi at night, touching every sweaty inch. Marriage is more than saying "I do."

Looking me over, he asked, "You have ridden the Fire Wagons that roar along the Iron Road?"

"The railroad brought me here," I reminded him. We talked half in Sheyenna, half in English, still learning each other's tongues. When we first met we had made do with pidgin Lakota and sign-talk, acting out words, laughing at our antics.

"I am glad you are here." He thought for a moment, then added, "I once rode the Iron Horse. It was like being dead." Most Sheyenna treated death as a transition—they were awed by it, afraid of it—but they thought it not much different from being alive. "Land and air rushed by faster than birds fly. I lost the earth, fearing I would fly away as well. When the Fire Wagon stopped I wanted only to touch the earth, to be alive again."

"The Iron Horse excited me." I tried to make the locomotive less terrifying. "It took me west, to places I had never seen." I wished that I had not said "west." To Yellow Legs the land of sunset is the land of darkness and death. "It took me to you."

He smiled. "There is only one Light-Haired Woman. The Iron Road will never again bring anything as good as you." *E-hyoph'sta*, Light-Haired Woman, was his Medicine name for me. No other Sheyenna used it, saying it had too much Medicine for a Wasichu to wear. "To the south there is a river, called the Fat River, because it was fat with game, a good place to hunt and get fat for winter. My old man chief said, 'Let the Iron Road come, the world is big enough for Wasichu and Sheyenna to pass over it.' But when the Iron Road came, the land died. The animals went away. No People live by the Fat River now."

Only Wasichu—but he was too polite to say it. I did not try to defend the Northern Pacific Railroad. He was right, the Iron Road would kill his world. Mine too. I had been happy as a chickadee, enjoying life with the man I loved. There had been peace of sorts on the high plains, as long as the army stayed clear of Unceded Territory, letting wild Lakotas live as they pleased. Now the Northern Pacific bore down on me, a railway to nowhere. Another brilliant government giveaway. Congress had no right to sell Unceded Indian Territory, so they gave it to the railroad for free. Crows and other friendly Indians were forced to surrender great swaths for pennies an acre.

I tried to explain this to Yellow Legs. He understood treaty violations, but could not make sense out of courts and Congress. Who can? Ignorance of the law is as American as the Constitution—the very essence of republican government. If we threw the crooks and fools out of Congress, how could they claim to represent us? Daddy used to say, "In a true Democracy the majority is always drunk."

To be agreeable my husband summoned up an example of his own, saying, "The Great Chiefs in Washington seldom hear what is said in Sheyenna. The winter when I first came north, Long Knives rode into the Burnt Thigh camp where I was staying. Some Minniconjou had killed a Wasichu's cow. They threatened the Burnt Thigh chief, whose name contains that animal." I supposed this was Old Conquering Bear, a relative of Crazy Horse.

Speaking of "bear" names, Yellow Legs looked over his shoulder, to make sure our patient had not fallen off the travois. We were leaving flecks of blood on the grass tops.

He turned back to me. "This chief laid five sticks before the Long Knives, explaining that he was a Burnt Thigh, and that the man who killed the cow was a Minniconjou." Five sticks meant he offered five ponies for the lost cow, a poor trade, but chiefs are expected to beggar themselves to keep the Peace of the Camp. "Determined not to listen, the Long Knives blew up the chief with a wagon gun. Angry Burnt Thighs rubbed them out."

He laid a reassuring hand on my thigh. "I took no part in this fight, though the Long Knives were rude—and in the wrong." His triumphal innocence was amusing. "We went with the Blue Clouds to talk to our agent, offering to make peace—if he would give presents and make everyone feel better."

"What presents?" I had learned to be wary of stories told with a smile on his face and fingers on my thigh.

Yellow Legs looked wounded. "The Long Knives had blown up an old man chief over a cow. We could not calm the Burnt Thighs with a few blankets. Or with pairs of Wasichu pants—that pinch at a man's private parts and get in his way when he makes water."

I told him his private parts had never felt pinched. "So what *did* you ask for?"

"In the spirit of peace and forgiveness, we asked for a thousand Wasichu wives."

We both laughed. One more Indian request that Washington never saw fit to act on. I looked forward to making love to him, but that had to wait until the fourth night after the fight, when his war Medicine was totally gone.

His joking and touching should have warned me; he was getting ready to leave. "Light-Haired Woman," he told me, "I want to feel the land." And he meant to do it alone.

I let him go. Keeps-the-Fire and I could hardly get lost. This country north of the Yellowstone was only moderately dangerous. Crows claimed it as a hunting ground, but only a moon ago hundreds of Oglalas and Sheyenna had gone up the Yellowstone to drive back the Crows. Besides, I had my husband's heavy revolver tucked beneath my lap blanket, a handsome weapon, presented to Yellow Legs by the Department of the Interior after the Medicine Lodge Peace Council—for being a good Indian and helping keep the peace.

And like a silly ass, I was ashamed that Congress had been bribed into giving his land away. It was not *my* Congress—I could no more vote than he could. To safeguard our freedom, the vote was denied to children, lunatics, Indians, and women. Still, I felt guilty. Gandy dancers had not driven a single spike into Lakota Country, but already the Iron Road was coming between me and my husband.

He cantered off, leaving me with the wounded Medicine Bear, a thundering bore even in the best of health. Medicine Bear must have had equally little use for me, but fortunately it was beneath him to take notice of another man's wife.

With my man and his Medicine gun gone, the prairie filled up with animals unworried by a woman on a travois pony—buffalo, pronghorn, and white-tailed deer put color and movement into the landscape. Living in the wilderness makes you realize that truly wild animals have no special fear of people. Birds and small animals often ate from my hand. On lazy afternoons like this, Keeps-the-Fire and I had ridden with the herds, rubbing up against buffalo, luring antelope into reach by waving a Medicine feather. Like so many Wasichu, I came west out of desperation; only later did I learn to love it. I had hated factory work and found domestic service degrading. The only thing left was to teach, get married, or go west. I ended up doing all of them.

Before coming west, I got all the usual advice about Indians—to cut my hair short, or invest in cyanide pills, "just in case." Not being particularly nervous or excitable, I did neither. I was coming to teach and do good, and assumed that put me in the hand of God. I ended up at the Red Cloud Agency, doing an indifferent job of teaching the Bad Faces things they did not much want to know. They in turn taught me some very useful Lakota.

Then one day a well-born Bad Face jokester named Woman's Dress asked if I wanted to meet a real wild Sheyenna. Someone who knew Crazy Horse and Sitting Bull and had seen the Spirit World. Seeing no harm in it, I let Woman's Dress introduce me to Yellow Legs.

From the very first I was impressed. Instead of the usual Medicine man mumbo-jumbo, I met a smart, no-nonsense savage who knew much more about my world than I knew about his. He entertained me royally, and we had a grand time talking in signs and halting Lakota, mostly about the strange ways of the Wasichu. Suddenly I saw it was getting dark and rose to take my leave. "Medicine stories may only be told at night," my host informed me. I left anyway—not sure how much I wanted to learn.

Next morning the gifts began arriving at my makeshift lodge. First some fine fox furs, then a buffalo robe, then a live prairie hen. When I found out I was being courted I was shocked.

Trying to return the gifts did no good. Attempts to discourage him turned into added chances for Yellow Legs to exercise his barbarous charm. Besides being sharp and good-looking, the man could be alarmingly persuasive. I was still under army protection, but not even the cavalry would shoot an Indian just for flirting. And the Bad Faces treated it as an uproarious joke. Who but a Sheyenna Medicine man would want a wife who could not sew a tipi or mend a moccasin?

Finally one morning my horse disappeared, replaced by two fine ponies (including the mare I was presently riding). Enough, I thought. Giving the mare her head, I let her take me to Yellow Legs. A big mistake. This time I stayed to hear the Medicine tales. By sunup I was lying naked under a buffalo robe watching Yellow Legs make us breakfast. The "visit" stretched on into a long week of lovemaking, followed by a fairy-tale honeymoon along the Yellowstone, where Sitting Bull threw us a wedding feast. Yellow Legs had enough Contrary in him to put the wedding last. All that was two years ago, and I had yet to get back to Red Cloud's camp.

I stopped at a creek to wash the paint off my face. Cold clear water felt reassuring. Several times I had dreamed that the paint would not come off, leaving me all Indian. These were just panic dreams, like imagining you were naked at Sunday Meeting. But Yellow Legs kept pushing me to take bizarre dreams more seriously—they are a Medicine man's stock-in-trade.

Looking up, I was startled by an oversized coyote eyeing me from the far bank. He was big and bold, but otherwise nothing special, having the usual shabby dirty-yellow look coyotes like to affect. I was not afraid. After seeing armed warriors shot from the saddle, no four-footed scrounger was going to scare me. I glanced over at Medicine Bear, to make sure he was not attracting scavengers. The man lay easy as you please on his travois, placidly eating ants. Sheyenna will dine on all manner of vermin, but ants are especially prized. The busy little insects are supposed to clean out your insides.

Without warning someone spoke—and it was not Medicine Bear, whose mouth was full of bugs. The words were as clear as stream water, partly in Lakota, partly in Sheyenna, but all in my head: "American Woman. Why are you lugging this great burden about? Put it down."

My immediate thought was hallucination—I had been up all night with a war party, supping on berries and water—my whole being felt hollow. I turned to stare at the coyote. He grinned back, with a smile as crooked as a six-card hand. I must have looked awfully snakebit, staring wildly about, but I could not believe the beast had spoken—though the Sheyenna consider talking canines fairly common. Yellow Legs regularly listened to coyotes, even talking back, claiming he learned their language from a Snake boy who was raised by wolves.

If the coyote could speak, he had said his fill. With a flick of his tail he drifted off, as silent as windblown smoke.

Medicine Bear moaned for water. It was pointless to ask if he had heard the coyote talk—no one can pry a straight answer out of a dying Sheyenna. I wet a rag, wondering why I *was* lugging this big useless burden about.

Taking the rag to him, I dampened his lips then let him suck, just enough to wash down the ants. Before coming west, I worked as a maidservant in the employ of a medical doctor, one William Warren of Manhattan. Dr. Warren never mentioned the medicinal value of ingested insects, but he did tell me there is nothing more fatal to a gutshot man than too much water—no matter how much he begs for it.

Medicine Bear licked ants off bloody fingers, and we got going again. Soon the game disappeared, replaced by clumps of ponies grazing amid garbage and dog droppings. Sure signs we were coming into camp. At the head of a long coulee I saw a young warrior standing on a buffalo skull, turning slowly to follow the sun, looking for a vision. To me it seemed a good way to go blind. This is as close as the Sheyenna usually come to posting a lookout, but he certainly did not see us ride past. His eyes were in the Spirit World.

Spring Grass

TOPPING A RISE, I SAW THE TRIBAL CAMPS, TWO OPEN CIRCLES of peaked tipis, surrounded by yellow-brown grass that bowed and waved in the wind. We were camped at the upper end of the coulee. Crazy Horse's Oglalas were a little way downstream, closer to the Yellowstone.

Sheyenna claim their camp circles are the human spirit in physical form, and that they can feel the camp Medicine rotating with the day, changing with the seasons. That day I felt it riding in, a tight curtain closing about me, strong and secure. J. S. Mill says our "mental chemistry" mixes the new with the familiar, and the smell of cook fires took me back to my mother's hearth with its smoky warmth and security. Just seeing so many lodges made me feel safer. Behind me, men stalked and killed each other—but here women dug tubers and tanned hides, while their children played in the sun, wearing nothing but smiles.

Sheyenna men turn war into a lethal game of "Dare Base," using scalp knives to keep score. Step into the camp circle and you are safe. Catch you on the prairie and you die. If a Crow warrior can make it peaceably into camp, the Sheyenna feel compelled to feed him. The hair of women and children may trim his scalp shirt, but his worst punishment would be hard looks that might disturb digestion. Such is the way of the Sheyenna.

Personally, though, I know few Crows who would put their Medicine to that test. Prudence dictates that when calling on enemies you leave your spare hair at home.

Medicine Bear's women met me at the gap that lets sunrise into the camp circle. Easing him off my travois, they carried Medicine Bear to his tipi, a great twenty-skin lodge sitting near Old Bear's. None of them spoke. These women traced their descent from generations of strong shrewd

27

women; and they set the standards for camp production, fashioning the finest lodges, robes, parfleches, and possible-sacks. I was a mere Wasichu with no blood-kin closer than Cleveland, the wife of a southerner who had married into the band.

Not that I felt insulted. No, ma'am. I was grateful to get rid of Medicine Bear before he died on me; volatile Medicine hung over him, and I wanted none of it raining on me.

I tethered Keeps-the-Fire in front of my tipi, a tiny twelve-skin lodge pitched a little back from the camp circle, behind Raven's bigger one. It was just big enough for me and my husband—when he came to call.

Black Shawl came up from the Oglala camp to ask for news of Crazy Horse, bringing their daughter, They-Fear-Her, a thoughtful child with her father's way of mixing up the Medicine. She had made a pet of a spotted skunk. There was a plague of these little pests that summer, as playful as kittens, always demanding you indulge them, since they had the power to make life insufferable. Her beast loved to tyrannize my tipi, conducting a constant search for handouts.

With them was Given-to-Us, a large friendly woman, and the only other full-blooded white woman in camp. Aside from her white skin, Given-to-Us was pure Lakota. A warrior named Black Bear had found her parents succumbing to cholera on the prairie. Her dying father gave the infant girl to Black Bear, along with money and a letter instructing him to deliver the child to relatives back east. Lakota males on the prairie are liable to do almost anything, but they are not a baby delivery service. Black Bear spent or lost the money, but he preserved the baby and the letter of instructions. He gave the girl to female relations to raise; and when Given-to-Us was reasonably grown, he married her. The Lakotas abhor blood-incest and sexual relations with their parents-in-law, but a right-thinking brave will use any excuse to increase the number of women in his lodge. Sisters-in-law, brother's widows, other men's wives, transvestites, attractive adolescents, and foundlings are all fair game.

Despite her strange history, Given-to-Us never doubted that she was white, and in her mind that made us sisters. Black Bear had told her that Wasichu women took tea together, so Given-to-Us never missed a chance to visit. Her open good nature assured that we got along famously, and she liked best those tea parties where I translated her dying father's written instructions into Lakota. To her, the forty-year-old scrap of paper was a Medicine message from her white father in the Spirit World. His plan for her civilized upbringing in the Land Beyond the Sunrise was a fairy-tale fate that her husband had saved her from.

Right here you can see how the Lakota Eaters got their name. Not by being cannibals, but by living close too, and eating *with* the Lakotas. I never met a Sheyenna who was a cannibal, at least not seven days a week. They do play jokes on the Lakotas, like telling uninvited guests that the meat in the pot was Pawnee. A strict code of hospitality does not preclude a sense of humor. And we Wasichu like to tell similar stretchers. Longfellow wrote a poem about Rain-in-the-Face eating General Custer's heart. Having known both Rain and the General, I can say the poem was mostly trash. But I did once meet a Hair Rope Sheyenna who had dined on Pawnee. A woman had served him buffalo heart, breaking his taboos, threatening to get him killed in battle. So he cut the heart out of a dead Pawnee, cooked it, pounded it, and ate a pinch—since anyone who ate human flesh would hardly be harmed by a buffalo heart. He claimed that pinch of Pawnee was the worst thing he ever tasted.

I told Black Shawl I had seen her husband in battle. Spiraling two fingers before my brow, to indicate Medicine, I made the striking motion that means both strong and brave. His Medicine was with him. What other comfort could I give? She knew Crazy Horse would be riding close to the enemy.

But Medicine is not always enough. In the center of camp Contraries were hard at work, trying to cure Medicine Bear. They had set up a contrary lodge—an inside-out tipi with the lodgepoles on the outside and the entrance facing sunset instead of sunrise. Contraries did everything backward; saying "yes" for "no," riding rump forward, bathing in dirt and drying with water. A man in a woman's dress, dyed red with dock root, sat against the lodge, head on the ground and legs in the air. An old woman backed out of the lodge and walked backward to Medicine Bear's tipi. She was painted stark white and wore nothing but a man's breechcloth. For a Sheyenna woman to walk across the camp circle in a breechcloth was about as common as a white woman going dressed that way to church. But Contraries were allowed to clown about and break taboos. Whether or not they cured the sick, they lightened the camp Medicine.

One sure advantage of Sheyenna Medicine is it seldom does the patient much damage. My former employer, Dr. Warren, had been an enthusiastic teacher, who took it on himself to see to my sexual education. Between bouts of lovemaking on his big feather bed, he once described the death of President Washington, a disturbing tale doctors tell in private. The father of our country succumbed to medical care at age sixty-six. He had returned from riding with a cold. Doctors opened his veins, letting out five pints of blood; probably more than Medicine Bear had lost. His last words to his physicians were, "Pray take no more trouble with me"; had they been his first words he might well have lived to the promised three score years and ten. A Medicine man tooting on a bone whistle, while an unblemished virgin

burns sweetgrass over you, is trivial compared to a massive hemorrhage—
your only worry is that some brave might have gotten past the virgin's crotch
rope, endangering your cure. Even an old woman backing into your tipi
with her behind painted white is a shock most invalids could likely recover
from.

Good luck to you, I thought. I did not have much hope for Medicine
Bear, but the fewer dead this fight produced, the sooner the soldiers would
be forgotten.

Suddenly Given-to-Us stood up. A lone Oglala rode back and forth,
raising dust near the Lakota camp. More riders gathered on the hill above
him, wearing fresh paint and their favorite feather arrangements. Oglala
women emerged from their lodges, calling out to their husbands and heroes.
Braves began to descend the hill, the boldest and most admired coming
first. Each man circled the camp while women shouted out his deeds.

Black Shawl grabbed up They-Fear-Her. Crazy Horse did not play this
game, where successful warriors were called in by their women. But Black
Shawl knew the warriors would not be showing off if Crazy Horse was shot,
and she wanted to be waiting when he returned to her lodge. She and
Given-to-Us gave me a Lakota goodbye, going with barely a word. The
skunk toddled after them, sensing a feast.

I would not have minded a feast myself, but a dutiful Sheyenna wife
does not skip off to a neighboring camp circle to mix with returning
braves—not when the band has dead and wounded to worry over. Instead
I made a small meal of fry bread, prairie greens, and pounded meat. At dusk
the Caller came around, saying we would move camp in the morning, heading up the Yellowstone. Yellow Legs and I had spent last night together, riding with the war party, so tonight we would sleep apart. Night drums beat
in the Oglala camp. Crazy Horse's people had a fight to celebrate, and went
at it like hottentots on holiday, not caring how much they disturbed the
neighbors—but last night's ride, followed by a harrowing day, left me able
to sleep through a twenty-one-gun salute.

I saw Medicine Bear again a few days later. We were moving camp, headed
upriver. In the heat of noon we came to the broad bottom where the Yellowstone and Bighorn run together. The whole Sheyenna dog and pony
show spilled down the bank, travois loads bouncing loose, littering the slope
with parfleches and possible-sacks. Stones and earth rolled ahead of us,
muddying the river. Horses shied at the swift water; pack dogs dashed past
to drink, wetting their loads—all under a burning sun.

We paused to collect children and valuables. Amid the bustle I saw Medicine Bear seated on a travois by the riverbank, lashed upright with lariats and cut sticks. He bore the delay without complaint, though he had gotten dirty in the descent and no one would dust him off. Sheyenna think that death is catching. Warriors count it a first-class coup just to touch the enemy dead—a feat more honorable than the actual killing. But Medicine Bear aimed to be back. Before dying, he had given detailed instructions for his res- urrection; what songs to sing, what prayers to say. The man had an incur- able ego, that not even death could daunt.

Right now, though, he was sure enough dead, no matter how much he refused to admit it. Blank eyes stared at me, expressing extreme disapproval.

I looked away. Young people on painted ponies dashed into the current, showering us with spray, racing each other to the far bank. Women tied lodge poles in bundles, piling infants and other prized possessions on the most trusted ponies. Many had regular bull boats. Yellow Legs was loafing somewhere ahead, but I was able to rope my two ponies together using my lodgepoles to make a crude raft. Keeps-the-Fire could be trusted to lead Carries-the-Lodge, my pack pony.

The water flowed as fast as a trotting pony, turning the crossing into chaos. Children squealed. Dogs leaped from sinking travois to strike out for the far shore. Several old or overloaded hounds were swept away down- stream, but not a horse or baby was lost. On the south bank, families rallied around lances held aloft by the old women, calling after animals gone astray. The sun dried us, and we went on up the Big Horn, toward the Greasy Grass, stopping where we found the circle of chiefs—Old Bear, Little Hawk, and Ice—smoking to mark the campsite.

That night drums beat in the dark where the two rivers came together as men put Medicine Bear into the water, still sitting upright, and weighted down with rocks. He would sit for four days at the bottom of the Yellow- stone, then on the fifth he would return to the living. Or so he swore. I took no part. Raising war dead was men's Medicine—taboo to women—and I was too heavily involved in this death already. But Yellow Legs stood vigil, which meant four more nights before we could make love.

On that fourth morning, I lay in my lodge, watching clouds drift past the smoke hole, taking stock and thinking of the night to come. My tipi was neat and adequate. No children brought disorder to my lodge, nor was it cluttered with weapons and men's possessions. Buffalo robes were rolled and stacked. Trade blankets and cooking utensils hung from the lodgepoles; my precious store of books and notebooks lay behind my willow backrest. The fire pit was "square with the world." No ashes spilled over the edges. The very picture of primitive luxury.

Light slanting through the lacing holes made a dotted pattern that crept along with the morning sun. I could tell which stitches were mine and which had been threaded and tied by other women. Mine had the huge, gaping holes that let in the light; Raven's or Black Shawl's stitches were so tight and exact that I could not tell one woman's work from the other's. Quilling sororities held feasts where women counted off the tipis they had covered and the hides they had decorated, like old warriors at a kill talk. No one invited me, but so far I had nothing to boast of. I was noting how my stitches improved as they progressed around the tipi when someone scratched at the lodge entrance.

Scrambling up off the fresh grass floor, I grabbed a half-finished moccasin. No one needed to know I had been mooning about on my back, studying clouds through the smoke hole. The women I worked with were all accomplished artists, pleased by my progress, never liking it when I took work lightly.

Poking my head out the entrance, I saw Raven pouring coffee from a kettle. She was a sturdy, powerful Sheyenna, with round brown arms, and hips and shoulders twice the width of mine. Coarse badger-tail braids framed bright blue-white beadwork stretched across her breasts. I got a drinking horn and joined her. The coffee was brown and weak, but it was coffee. There was no cream to be had in camp, and barely a pinch of sugar. The Lakota Eaters think most of our virtues are indecent, but they consider a few of our sins holy. Coffee to them is "Black Medicine," and whiskey is "Medicine Water." I often wonder how they got drunk at night or roused themselves in the morning, before we came.

I sat and sipped, not bothering to thank Raven. Buffalo Indians did not have, or need, a dozen different ways of saying "much obliged." Raven was Yellow Legs's Sheyenna wife, and sharing coffee was as normal to her as sharing a husband.

When I first came to camp, I was a wide-eyed Wasichu, always thanking people for everything, trying to *make friends*. Raven was the one who pointed out that gushing over people for doing right implied their natural impulse was to do wrong. Gratitude assumes a giver, not a sharer—and comes more easily to a Wasichu than to a Sheyenna. Raven drank her coffee from a chipped china cup, my spur-of-the-moment gift during that embarrassing pause after we discovered we were married to the same man. Yellow Legs had a way of letting the Medicine work itself out, and did not manage to communicate that he had another wife until he and I arrived in camp. By then I was deep in Unceded Territory, hardly likely to stalk off in a huff. Of course, Raven got no warning either. He had not told her, "I'm going to Red Cloud Agency to pick up a couple of pounds of coffee and a thin blond wife." Her first hint that I existed was seeing me ride into camp side by side with her husband. She had yet to thank me for the cup.

Being married to the same man had not made us all that close. Raven was a respected Lakota Eater, sister to Calf Road and Comes-in-Sight. A skinny yellow-haired stranger was not a fit object for jealousy—it was beneath her dignity to quarrel with me, or to accept anything but proper respect.

Yellow Legs came down to brush and braid my hair. Whether or not he slept with me, he spent every morning in camp brushing my hair with a porcupine-tail brush beaded along the back. This beautiful morning ritual always made me feel loved, and tonight his taboos would be lifted. He painted my hair red at the parting, to show the whole camp how proud he was of me, then went off to water our ponies.

Raven was already at work, briskly pounding chokecherries to mix with meat and make pemmican—a trick learned from Lakotas. A glutton for labor, she openly prided herself on being Yellow Legs's "working wife." I was plainly one of those silly indulgences that successful warriors wasted time with—like a parade pony, painted and primped, but only ridden on special occasions.

A young woman joined us, whose name meant something like Spring Grass. She was very much the white man's fantasy of how a Sheyenna maiden ought to look: tall and stately, with midnight-black hair past her hips, and a savage dignity that would have sat well on a dutchess. Like Yellow Legs, Spring Grass was a southerner, accustomed to proper clothes and Kiowa silver. Today she wore a green print dress over red leggings with little silver slides that sang as she walked. She spoke pure Sheyenna, unmixed with Lakota, and clearly considered the Lakota Eaters to be barbarous dressing in skins and pounding pemmican.

Spring Grass had no husband, but she did have a son named Yellow Bird, and her affection for him was unusual, even for Sheyenna, who spoil their children more than a civilized parent could endure. I knew nothing about Yellow Bird's father, except that boy had pale skin and curly hair and reminded the Oglalas of young Crazy Horse. Men seemed to think Spring Grass was free to marry, and younger Lakotas courted her—but young males are forever optimistic about the availability of pretty females. Sheyenna women take their virtue more seriously.

As we worked, we told stories. Mostly camp gossip. It was too fine a morning for Medicine tales. Tired of having the Sheyenna work ethic rubbed into me, I told them about factory work. There is no Sheyenna word for "factory," so I described a lodge taller than a pine and wider than the camp circle. "Every day they rang a bell. In summer the bell rang at sunrise, in winter it rang in the dark. We all ate the same morning meal, then went into the big lodge to weave and spin on giant looms. In summer we worked until sunset, in winter until after dusk."

Spring Grass grimaced. "When did you see the sun?"

"Twice a day, when we left the lodge to eat. Four days out of every moon were Medicine days when we did not have to work."

"Those were your woman's days apart?" Raven meant for menstruation.

I shook my head, saying there were no women's holidays from factory work. Raven shivered. Everyday life among the Wasichu is as familiar and inviting to a Sheyenna as the dark side of the moon. My stories were easily more outlandish than Spirit Tales.

Being in a mood to really amaze, I added, "And many men worked with us." Raven rocked back laughing, assuming my story was an elaborate joke told for the sake of this absurd ending. Women working together in a great whirring lodge filled with machines was possible; men spinning and weaving from before dawn to after dusk was not.

Spring Grass merely smiled. I suspect she knew more about the ways of Wasichu.

Raven sobered up, saying, "We have these men-women too." Men-women were Sheyenna males who wore dresses and did women's work. Like coffee and whiskey, transvestism was a sin the Sheyenna thought was holy. Pipe, a popular man-woman, not only joined the quilling sororities but went mule stealing with Old Bear.

"These were men-men," I assured her. "We were locked up at night to keep us safe from them." Raven had heard of doors and locks, but assumed they were for punishment. I made the sweeping "no" sign, brushing aside the idea. "No one was being punished. We were rewarded every seventh day with silver."

Raven stayed skeptical. "You worked summer and winter in this big lodge—so where is all the silver?"

I laughed. "I've asked myself that many times."

By midmorning the pemmican was mixed and in its rawhide cases. Raven went to dig tubers, never my favorite task. I lingered, talking to Spring Grass. Tipi manners do not encourage idle personal questions, so I had no idea why this long-haired, dark-eyed young woman who had rejected half the men in Crazy Horse's camp seemed to be courting me—I just tried not to scare her off with too many Wasichu questions.

Calf Road, Raven's younger sister, came up, wearing a buckskin dress dyed blue with berry juice. She was strong-limbed, with a warrior's body, but still unmarried. Behind her trotted her favorite pinto, as faithful as a dog. Speaking past me, she asked if Spring Grass wanted to swim.

By our standards Sheyenna are filthy brutes. The mess in camp would defeat a brigade of chambermaids, and for anyone not used to green hides and dog droppings, a deep breath on a hot day could be an education. Despite this, they are firmly convinced that it is Wasichu who are dirty. Like most wild things, the Sheyenna fuss over their bodies, spending spare moments washing and preening. Each morning men strutted down to the nearest water to bathe; women had to be more inventive. I was careful to bathe often, or there would be wrinkled noses and comments about distinctive Wasichu odors.

When Spring Grass passed the invitation to me, Calf Road snorted, saying I would slow them down.

My foot felt an urge to kick. Calf Road was my active enemy, and never ashamed to show it. She had a hate as plain as face paint, that went deeper than my white skin. No one else was so openly rude—most being content to ignore me—and now she meant to show me up in front of the one Sheyenna woman who had sought me out.

I rose up, thanking Spring Grass. "Let us get our horses and race to the river." Without a word to Calf Road, I casually cut Keeps-the-Fire out of the pony herd. This was one insult Calf Road was going to have to eat whole. Spring Grass fetched a blaze-faced mare for herself, saddling her with a high-bowed Spanish saddle trimmed with brass tacks. Calf Road and I rode bareback.

In a moment we were off. Calf Road took the lead leaving camp, scattering the pack ponies. Her pinto was fearless and fast on his feet. I held back until we came to the long stretch of rising ground where the Big Horn cut a gap in the bluffs. As soon as I saw the pinto slow, I laid my head down in Keeps-the-Fire's neck, shouting for her to run. She took off like a stung whippet.

My mare was a Nez Percé pony, given to me by Yellow Legs because he loved seeing me mounted on the best he could steal. Her full name was Keeps-the-Prairie-Fire-Behind-Her, and when I urged her to run, she never wanted to see another horse ahead of her. Half the reason I was so bold on the prairie was that I could not imagine another rider catching me. Certainly not a heavy trooper on a big American horse.

Calf Road was no strawfoot trooper. She was a wild Sheyenna, born on horseback, but once Keeps-the-Fire caught the spirit of the race, my pony's second wind carried us into the lead. The hammering hooves, the wind in my hair, the mane whipping my face, made me feel like an unmarried girl again, with no responsibilities except to please myself—and to teach Calf Road not to be so pissy.

When Spring Grass and Calf Road caught up, I was at the riverbank, idly giving my pony her reward—a drink and a rubdown, brushing her black flanks and white rear with handfuls of grass, using long, loving strokes. Warriors will mark their favorite mounts: a handprint means a man has touched the enemy, hoof marks record successful raids and horses stolen. I could make no such boasts, so I decorated my fast pony with phases of the moon.

Calf Road eyed Keeps-the-Fire with more respect than she ever showed me, saying, "This pony is wasted on a Wasichu."

I snorted. "Just see that you do not borrow her without asking this Wasichu." Keeps-the-Fire lifted her tail and farted lightly. Without Raven around we could be as rude as we pleased.

Hobbling our horses in a coulee, the three of us headed downstream, avoiding a swift spot where the current cut past a small island. Calf Road showed us a calm stretch suitable for swimming, not far from the burial pool where Medicine Bear sat. Stripping quickly, she dived in, unbothered by ghosts and men's Medicine. She had long brown limbs and a thick tangle of hair between her thighs.

Spring Grass followed. I unlaced my leggings, then in one movement I drew my dress over my head, and dived in. This was when I felt most different. My forelimbs were tanned as dark as a light-skinned Lakota. I could draw a blanket over my hair and cover my face with paint. Wasichu had walked right past me, seeing only a squaw in her blanket. But with my dress off, my white body betrayed me.

Calf Road called out, "Look, a white-tailed deer, I saw the flick of her rump." Not a new joke.

The water was frigid. Even in the Moon of Black Cherries, when the world is hot and ripe, the only warm waters along the Yellowstone are those that boil up from deep beneath the national park. So we swam hard and fast to keep our blood flowing. Downstream we came to a grassy bank and climbed up to dry off, stamping out a circle in the warm grass. Water gleamed on our bodies, a cool blanket keeping off the sun. It is wonderful to be young and feel the world in summer, and Sheyenna make the most of it, knowing that old age and winter would surely come. Only the Spirit World has endless summer.

Burned dry, we headed back upstream to get our clothes. Bluestem and wheat grass grew head-high along the banks. Lagging behind, I saw nothing but cloudless sky and waving grass tops, until Spring Grass brought me up sharp.

I nearly stepped on her. She was down on hands and knees, curled into a motionless brown ball. Giving me an anguished look, she held her right hand up, then brought both hands slowly down, making the motions just like a white woman would—the signs for "Stop, get down quietly" being more or less universal.

I dropped to my knees. Calf Road crouched a couple of paces ahead where the grass thinned, naked and motionless. Her fingers were hard at work prying a flat, heavy stone out of the ground. Standing between her and the riverbank was a man with his back to us. Calf Road could have stretched out a bare arm and touched his cartridge belt. He was Wasichu. A red, sunburned neck showed between his wet black hair and yellow bandanna. Hatless, bootless, and dripping wet, the man was dressed in a blue shirt and cavalry pants and had just swum the river, since he clutched a cable made of lariats connected to the far bank. I could count the beads of water on his wrist and the buttons on his cuff. A yellow stripe like my husband's ran down his pants leg; lieutenant's bars peeped over his shoulders. This was a U.S. cavalry officer, fit and full of energy, certainly a real go-ahead type, standing alone in Lakota Country on the south bank of the Yellowstone.

Long Hair

*Long before people had guns and horses a handsome man lived alone
in a lodge his mother made for him. Many women wanted to marry
him. He refused them all, until a beautiful black-haired woman
came to his lodge. He liked her and married her. Later another
woman came to his lodge. She had yellow hair and he married her
too. The first woman was really a buffalo cow and the second
woman was really an elk cow, but no one knew this, for they had
human form.*

— Sheyenna (Cheyenne) lodge tale

HAD THE HORSE SOLDIER TURNED HIS HEAD, HE WOULD HAVE
seen three nude women, one of them white, crouching behind him. Some
surprise—which shows how you have to be ready for anything on the
prairie. Then it would be Calf Road's rock in hand against his holstered revolver. Stone Age vs. Industrial Society—at the most savage elemental
level. My insides wobbled as I watched Calf Road's fingers curl around the
stone. But he did not turn. He was too busy looping the lariat cable around
his arm, letting the slack in the line draw him upstream.

The three of us slipped back into the tall grass. We had nowhere to go.
Our clothes lay by the bank, in clear sight of this man, if he turned to look.
Half a mile of shortgrass prairie separated us from the coulee where our
horses were hobbled. Under less trying conditions it would have been com-
ical, crawling along with my nose a few inches from Spring Grass's behind.
But none of us were laughing.

Calf Road found a fold of ground where we could lie flat and see without being seen. Parting the grass tops, I saw that the officer's line led to the

wooded island we had avoided earlier. He must have started swimming from the island and been swept downstream by the current, just as we were. The island had seemed empty. Now I could make out cavalry troopers and Indian scouts crouching in the plum tangle at the center of the island.

Calf Road made the wing-beating motion that means Crows. Spring Grass made a corn-husking motion, asking with her eyes if there were Rees on the island as well. Calf Road bowed her finger, "Yes." She had seen an Arikaree among the Crows. Wild Sheyenna distinguish army formations not by unit numbers or commanding officers, but by the wolves who scout for them. In this case it made absolute sense. If they saw us, the Crow scouts could cross the river and ride us down before the cavalry rightly knew what was happening. We were the sort of lucky find Crow warriors dream about.

The lieutenant on our bank paced about, totally alone, with nothing nearby but broad river and open prairie; no trees, nothing but grass for cover. If the fool had a dram of sense he had to be as scared as I was. Pony tracks and travois ruts gouged the south bank, sure signs that hundreds of lodges had passed this way. Crazy Horse's Oglalas and Sitting Bull's Hunkpapas had crossed a few days behind us. But the army sent only one man over.

As I watched him pace, the lieutenant's dilemma dawned on me. There was nothing to anchor his lariats to. The cavalry crowding the island were halted by the current. An army regiment staffed with West Point engineers was having the utmost difficulty crossing the Yellowstone—the river we forded a few days before, carrying lodges, old people, and papooses.

My fears subsided. Big American horses were shying from the swift-running river—a cavalry mount was not so crazy as to plunge into a treacherous current carrying a well-fed trooper with a hundredweight of gear and weapons. And there were packhorses, mules, and even cattle to consider. After some entertaining confusion, the Crows left the island for the far bank and started fashioning bull boats, but it was already clear they were never going to get across. The lieutenant on our bank gave up and dived back into the river. A strong and brave swimmer, he eventually reached the far shore.

Seeing no other sign of scouts or soldiers on the south bank, we wriggled down through the grass and got our clothes. Once dressed, I was set to dash back to our ponies—but I discovered Spring Grass gone. Seeing the grass tops sway, I realized she was headed back upriver, toward the island. Cursing in Wasichu, I crept after her, not wanting to go off with just Calf Road for surly company.

When I caught her, Spring Grass was lying patiently at the edge of the grass, studying the men across the river. She stretched her hand, making the sign for "long," then touched her hair and added the signs for "Long Knife Chief." She was looking for an officer called Long Hair.

"Long Hair" was not likely to be on the West Point rolls. But it was what the Southern Sheyenna had shouted when the officer in the red shirt approached the timbers. I scoured the island, wishing I had brought the binoculars. Finally I spotted his shirt. Crooking my finger I pointed him out, tugging on Spring Grass's sleeve and pretending to paint my face—red being the most common shade of face paint.

Spring Grass refused to leave as long as the officer in the red shirt was in sight. Sheyenna often act bizarre around soldiers, but seldom with such quiet intensity. She seemed consumed by his identity. "His hair is not so long now, but it looks like him," she whispered. "Was he leading in the fight when you first saw him?"

I signed that when I first saw him he had been sleeping, but that once he woke up he had led the soldiers against Crazy Horse.

Spring Grass considered. "It is hard to know. His brother looks much like him. And both are brave." Whoever he was, there was no doubting this was the soldier in red, and the Corn Indian scout was with him—the one Calf Road called a Ree. The men who shot Medicine Bear had returned, only to be held back by the stream he sat in.

Eventually Long Hair and the Ree scout left the island to confer with the Crows. As soon as he was out of sight, Calf Road and I dragged Spring Grass to the safety of the coulee and the horses. I was so scared I scolded her.

Spring Grass barely noticed my breach of conduct, looking stubbornly back to where Long Hair had been. But Calf Road was quick to correct me for being foolishly dramatic. According to her I was never in danger, since the Wasichu would not harm one of their own. (That was nothing but blind savage ignorance. Calf Road had not been at Jennie Wade's funeral, or seen the acres of dead at Gettysburg. We killed each other faster and easier than the most fanciful Sheyenna might imagine.) Besides, she insisted, the soldiers would never cross the river. "They have no women to carry their lodges. See how they picked the worst place, where the river runs fast and narrow by that island. No woman would try to cross there."

I was beyond arguing with Calf Road. Certainly the U.S. army had looked unimpressive, splashing about and getting nowhere. But the Crows would have crossed at once if they had seen something worth coming over for. I never wanted to run naked across the prairie with Crow wolves howling after me. Spring Grass kept looking back over her shoulder, while Calf Road cantered along in high spirits, barely smothering her laughter. "Tell American Woman about Long Hair," she suggested with an evil snicker.

Unwilling to be goaded by a northern savage, Spring Grass spoke slow and easy, like Yellow Legs telling a southern tale. "In the Winter When Spotted War Bonnet was Killed, my village was camped on the Lodgepole River. My father was a chief, and followed Black Kettle, our old man chief, in everything. They touched the pen together at Medicine Lodge, and went south like the Wasichu wanted, to camp in Indian Territory. He went with Black Kettle to the Long Knives, asking to camp under the walls of the Wasichu fort, even offering to return a Wasichu woman we bought from the Kiowas. But the soldier chief would not let us camp by the fort, nor would he take back the woman, though she was very upset and did not want to be with us."

That I could hardly credit. "The soldier chief said he did not want the woman back?" What officer would not help a white woman in distress?

Spring Grass gave me a haughty look, not pleased to be contradicted. "A Sheyenna had bought her from the Kiowas for five horses. Father could not just steal a woman from a warrior's lodge. He suggested the soldier chief pay the five horses. But the Long Knives said that any Wasichu woman who had been in the hands of the Sheyenna was not worth five horses."

Calf Road was quick to agree at my expense. "Five horses would be way too much to pay for a Wasichu."

Spring Grass snorted. "A warrior once gave eleven horses for me. But the man was insolent. I shot him in the knee and left his lodge." Divorce among the Sheyenna was simple and direct; disputes were more likely to involve Medicine men than lawyers. "My father sent his eleven horses back, having more honor and dignity than this soldier chief."

As usual we had veered away from the story of Long Hair, but Spring Grass found the trail again. "The morning after my father returned from the agency, Long Knives attacked the camp. My father died fighting. I was with child and could not escape, so my aunt hid me until the soldiers stopped shooting and started taking captives. Then she presented me to the Long Knife chief who led the attack. This was Long Hair, the one the Wasichu call Custer."

Long Hair I had never heard of, but everyone knew General Custer; a hero among heroes, the youngest general in the Union army, the commander who took the first rebel battle flag, whose men killed J. E. B. Stuart, and who accepted Lee's white flag at Appomattox. I had read about his battle with the Sheyenna on the Washita, never knowing it was Spring Grass's village.

With a few brutal strokes Spring Grass painted a horrible picture: snow stained with blood, women and children killed, men's bodies mutilated, the screams of dying horses—all the time acting as if it were only the occasion for a unique introduction. She concluded by saying, "Angry warriors swarmed up the Lodgepole like wasps from a broken hive. Not just People, but also Apaches, Blue Clouds, and Kiowa. Long Hair escaped with me and half a hundred other captives. But he had to shoot the ponies he captured and leave some of his men behind."

It sounded ghastly. Spring Grass had seen all this when she was young and pregnant. No wonder nothing seemed to touch her now. "Do you hate Long Hair for this?"

Calf Road burst out laughing, spinning her pony in little circles. My question had capped the comedy. Spring Grass ignored her antics. "No, I do not hate him. Long Hair is my husband. He is Yellow Bird's father."

I knew Sheyenna could carry a grudge for generations, then toss it aside when the mood suited, but this seemed far too forgiving. "But your father died in his attack?"

She gave me a lofty look. "I still hate the man who shot my father—but he is dead. He stumbles through the Spirit World searching for his scalp and penis, which were taken by a Sheyenna. When I miss my father I laugh at this man's fate. But why should I need to hate Wasichu? I do not hate you. I do not hate my husband. More than most Sheyenna I have learned to live with Wasichu. When I became a captive I expected that some man would take me—honor demanded this man must be the soldier chief."

And there are still people who claim that Indians are not practical. Spring Grass had clearly made the best of a bad hand. She described their impromptu wedding in the shattered camp. "As soon as the shooting died, I put my hand in his, saying the words that made us married." She sounded as happy and conceited as if the ceremony had been performed in St. Patrick's by the Bishop of Manhattan. "Of course Long Hair could not understand—but I knew from the way he held my hand and looked at me that he wanted to copulate. Wasichu cannot hide their desire the way a warrior should. They are all like boys in that respect."

I wondered what the Wasichu Mrs. Custer had thought of becoming a sister-wife, and whether General Custer knew he was only a river away from his Sheyenna wife and son. Spring Grass might look forward to a family reunion, but I was just as glad to have the Yellowstone between us and the soldier in red.

When we reached camp, I found Raven set to butcher an antelope buck. I got down to help with the gutting, feeling guilty for going gallivanting and nearly getting caught by the cavalry. The antelope was still warm. That did not make him one bit livelier, but warm meat meant that Yellow Legs was nearby.

I went to work at once, driving my skinning knife in a red line along the buck's belly. I could never shirk from gutting, since I was well known to be the biggest sissy in camp. The slippery, steaming innards, with their warm sensuous aroma, reminded me that I had hardly eaten. Growing up on a farm, I had often butchered animals, but raw entrails had never made me hungry back in Pennsylvania—I would put the bloody mess in my mouth only when my sisters dared me. But life with the Sheyenna dared me every day. On the hunt or march, it was eat raw liver or miss lunch. After forcing down entrails in fits of hunger, I found I actually craved them. This sounds impossible, but any number of things sound impossible until they have happened.

Yellow Legs insisted that eating the whole animal showed respect. Maybe so. I did notice that savages who ate the whole animal were less troubled by scurvy than cavalry troopers living on hardtack and salted beef. God knows the Sheyenna got their share of other diseases. I suppose if you plan to live like an animal, you had better learn to eat like one. The trick is to take small bites, picking at your entrails while you cook.

Word of Custer's return swept through the camps like a grass fire. Lakota and Sheyenna women flocked around Raven's tipi, hardly leaving room to work. Calf Road boasted about finding the cavalry, while I hid in the shadow of my big sister-wife. My Medicine had dumped me back in the community of women, but not the way I would have wanted. Bent on keeping busy, I worked until my hands were slick with blood. All the while the buck's brown eyes seemed to reproach me.

Raven did the detail work, cutting small strips of meat, slicing with the natural contours—Sheyenna hate crosscut meat. Their method is slow, but produces thin savory strips that will not rot in the sun. Calf Road, plainly excited by the prospect of more fighting, picked a more vigorous task, breaking marrow bones between two flat stones. Whenever she wanted to make a point she brought the top stone down with a special clap.

Raven complained, "No matter how many times our men beat the Long Knives, more keep coming. Which is strange, for they do not seem to enjoy war the way our men do."

Calf Road clapped her stones together. "This is the Long Knife chief who came to get Wasichu women from Black Kettle and Medicine Arrows." She made the sign for Wasichu by drawing her finger across her brow and flicking it my way. No one could miss the implication. Custer was coming for me.

I set down my skinning knife, staining the grass with its edge, signing that the Long Knives were scouting for the railroad, making the signs for Iron Horse and Fire Wagon, so these women would know I was not to blame. Custer's cavalry betrayed the government's guilty conscience; knowing they were in the wrong, they expected trouble.

The women found Calf Road's theory more convincing. Railroad right-of-ways were strange abstractions; stealing females was something they all knew well. Women dreaded the notion of enemy men breaking into the camp circle, our one haven in the hostile prairie. Irritated by the buck's blood on my hands, I pulled up some grass, trying to wipe the blood away so I could sign with clean hands.

Calf Road pressed her advantage. "Women seem to draw Long Hair like honey draws a bear." She reminded everyone how I had been there a week ago when Long Hair first appeared. Calf Road took it for granted that I had broken Medicine Bear's bullet Medicine and had brought Custer down on them—a neat bit of superstitious logic; idiotic, but utterly convincing. She shot me a triumphant look. "It is like the day on the Arikaree Fork, when a foreign woman broke Ice's bullet Medicine and Spotted Warbonnet was killed. Ask Yellow Legs—he was there."

Raven stopped work to sign as she spoke, her firm brown hands pressing down the argument. "The Warrior with the Spotted Warbonnet was not killed because of a woman. White Contrary got him killed. All women know that. And if Long Hair comes after our women, he will die. There is a curse on him if he attacks the People again."

I suppose she thought that might comfort me. Too angry to care, I sat fuming in silence, digging the blood out from under my nails.

Spring Grass backed up my sister-wife, saying she was there when Medicine Arrows invited Long Hair to smoke with him. "He told Long Hair that if he smoked with a bad heart, Long Hair would die with all his men. Long Hair smoked, and passed the pipe to Brave Bear. Brave Bear knocked the ashes of the pipe on Long Hair's boot, to make the curse stick."

I could sense the weight of the curse, and Spring Grass's sorrow. Feeling defeated, I searched for something to do. The buck's hide looked like it would be worth tanning, and I certainly needed the practice. My leather-work was never up to Sheyenna standards. My efforts were always so obviously Wasichu, the sort of work a man or a Ute might have done. As I set to work the buck's eyes stared up at me, reminding me of Medicine Bear sitting beside the Yellowstone. Taking Raven's stone mallet from among her tools, I smashed at the buck's head, hitting him again and again, until his skull broke and his brains dribbled out into the sunlight. Lakotas had taught the Sheyenna that every animal's brains held enough oil to tan its own hide. Raven had passed this bit of wisdom on to me.

Seeing my hand shake, Spring Grass took the stone hammer from my trembling fingers. "Do not worry," she told me, "the curse is not on you. These killings happened on the Lodgepole, winters ago and far away. I feel nothing but gratitude toward you."

"Gratitude?" Spring Grass seemed to be carrying forgiveness a mite far. What had I ever done for her?

"Of course," she replied. "I owe you a great debt. Yellow Legs was at the Lodgepole River. The hair of the Wasichu who killed my father is on your husband's scalp shirt."

I had finally found a Sheyenna willing to say "Thanks," but I was too stunned to say "You're welcome."

Bloody Knife

AT DUSK THE CALLER CAME AROUND, SAYING LONG KNIVES were just over the river. Mere lung exercise by now, but I suppose he took his calling seriously. I stayed bent over the staked-out antelope skin, working out my frustrations. I had a fine flesher, a gift from Black Shawl, made out of an elk antler and an old saw blade. The best fleshers are flattened gun barrels, which have the weight and hold an edge—but it is hard to get men to give up their guns.

Footsteps approached. I recognized beaded Medicine leggings I myself had mended. Not in a mood to greet anyone, I kept working, applying a steady even pressure. Fleshing is hard and exacting. Gouging the hide leaves thin spots in the leather.

The leggings folded and Yellow Legs sat down. "I see you, Light-Haired Woman."

Even my Medicine name did not amuse me. This was to have been "my night." But with the cavalry so close, war Medicine was bound to come between us. His hunting trips, Medicine rituals, nights with Raven—and my days apart—left us with depressingly little time together. I had taken to tagging along on war parties just to be with him.

"You make a very good wolf. No one else knew the Long Knives were chasing us."

Being caught bare-assed on the prairie by the U.S. cavalry seemed no rare feat, but I was new to scouting; perhaps Crazy Horse got started that way. I thanked him, dropping fatty rags of flesh into the cooking pot. Hide-scraping soup is a Lakota treat. He made admiring sounds, bending sideways to look into the pot. Fat globs floated in lukewarm water. "Tasty," he declared. "Too bad we are feasting with the Hunkpapas tonight."

My flesher nearly went through the hide. If the big fool meant to cheer me, he should have begun by inviting me out. Pushing hair out of my face, I looked up. There were smile wrinkles in the corners of his eyes. A night out and a free meal was the first decent news in days. I hung the fleshing frame on a pole so dogs would not dine on my work, then dived into my tipi.

My sweat-stained buckskin working dress was too plain for a call on Sitting Bull. I changed to my best blue calico, over a pair of dress leggings, with bells on the laces and beaded fringes that trailed behind me like foxtails on a warrior's moccasins. Yellow Legs sat outside, tapping his knee with a short feathered coup stick, saying that the Hunkpapas would enjoy my finery more if we arrived while there was light.

I wrapped my braids before the mirror, using white ermine skins from beyond the Backbone of the World, letting their black tips hang down over my breasts. A silver Kiowa belt tied the costume together. Part Wasichu, part Sheyenna, with a touch of Kiowa. Half of the joy of living in the wilds was dressing so extravagantly. Everything is open to exaggeration. Outright lies were dishonorable, but hyperbole in dress and actions was expected.

I scooped up horn spoons and a pair of wooden bowls—Lakotas expect guests to come prepared—then stepped out. Yellow Legs smiled in smug approval, clearly proud of his show pony. "Living up here among the wolverines, the Hunkpapas forget what beauty is. You will open their eyes."

He was wearing a touch of Kiowa himself, silver earrings, silver hair clips, and a blue print shirt over his beaded leggings. Living in Lakota Country I had to work hard on my wardrobe just to stay even with the men. When our husband dressed this way, Raven would tease him, saying we had married a Kiowa or maybe a Mescalero. I snuck a look to see if she was coming with us.

Raven was bent over my antelope hide, finishing the fleshing. She worked with the spare, easy grace of a woman who had been doing this since girlhood, singing with each stroke. For all her strength and size, she had a beautiful voice, as clear as a strummed bowstring. I felt like I was skipping chores to play Indian with Yellow Legs. But it was "my night," and how often do you get to play Indian in Sitting Bull's tipi?

We did not have far to ride. Sitting Bull's Hunkpapas were camped just up the Big Horn, surrounded by huge pony herds. In the Moon of Making Fat, the northern bands had gathered in one great sundance camp—Hunkpapas, Oglalas, Minniconjous, No Bows, and Sheyenna had filled the bottoms along the Rosebud. Afterward the bands had separated. We had gone north of the Yellowstone with Crazy Horse. Sitting Bull lingered on the Rosebud before following the herds north. Now the threat of cavalry coming was drawing the camps closer together.

The air was still full of light; tipi ears looked black against the bright summer twilight. Hunkpapa lodges are taller and narrower than Sheyenna tipis, with wide flamboyant smoke flaps. Lakotas cannot even set up a lodge without making a show. Young men lounged about, arrogant as only Lakotas can be. I dismounted, letting the lacing bells ring beneath my dress, getting them to look up, savoring the tension of being an exotic presence.

Some of the smaller and poorer lodges had their poles planted butt-end up—Red Top's Santee Dakotas were camped with the Hunkpapas. It chilled me to see Santee tipis. The Santee Dakotas had been Corn Indians, churchgoing cousins of the Lakotas, living east of the Big Muddy. Like all Corn Indians, their story was gruesome. Santees and Wasichu had farmed side by side, until successive waves of settlement squeezed out the Santees. Massacres and countermassacres followed, worse than anything that had happened on the prairies. The Santees that survived were so poor they were called the "No Clothes." People claimed white captives still lived in Santee tipis. I had never seen any, though the longer you lived like a Lakota the more it seeped into you, like layers of old paint.

Sitting Bull's lodge always occupied the same spot in the camp circle; a seated buffalo painted on the north, "male" side of the entrance was Sitting Bull's personal mark, his promise to feed guests as freely as the buffalo did. It was feast night and the tipi overflowed with women and food. Kids and dogs dashed past, rib bones between their teeth. Other lodges were bigger. Many boasted more horses. But to my mind none was as important. Sitting Bull was the heart of the Hunkpapas, as close as the northern Lakotas came to having a leader. Without him, the Powder River bands were just a hodgepodge of anarchists, pony thieves, scalp hunters, and visionaries on horseback.

Mixed Day, Sitting Bull's mother, greeted us at the entrance to the lodge, a twenty-two-pole tipi that must have required as many cowskins to cover it. Once you have put together a tipi from the raw hides and living trees, you notice such things. As we entered, we separated. The south side of the lodge was for women and the north side for men. Yellow Legs sat down beside Crazy Horse, He Dog, and Black Bear, the only male Oglalas present. Given-to-Us made space for me next to Seen-by-the-Nation, Sitting Bull's senior wife, a tough hatchet-faced Lakota. Seen-by-the-Nation and I always got on well, admiring each other's husbands without being overly tempted by what the other woman had. Four Robes, Seen-by-the-Nation's younger sister and Sitting Bull's second wife, sat on the far side of her.

Two Santee braves immediately got up and left. They might have been offended by seeing a Wasichu, or just a strange woman. Maybe their Medicine just told them to be elsewhere.

Sitting Bull sat in back of the lodge, wearing a single eagle feather and stained leggings. He was no more than medium height, lean and muscular, about as old as Yellow Legs. His favorite daughter, Plenty Horses, sat next to him. Without seeming to notice the Santees leaving, he had started a new pipe to acknowledge our entrance. Filling the long red pipe with tobacco and red willow bark, Sitting Bull tamped down the mixture with blunt fingers—Crazy Horse would not smoke tobacco tamped with a stick or tool. A good host has to remember everyone's taboos. Sitting Bull's boyhood name was Slow, and he was deliberate in everything he did—each movement reminding you he was a Medicine man.

After offering a smoke to the earth, sky, and four directions, the Medicine man passed the pipe to his left, so it moved in the same direction that the sun moves through the sky. First to get the pipe was Gall, a Hunkpapa war chief, whose huge presence made me uneasy. Gall headed the anti–Sitting Bull faction in camp, and his presence meant this was not your normal Hunkpapa hoedown. The man was a mountain of raw energy, full of strength, intelligence, and barely suppressed fury. His nostrils expelled the pipe smoke like twin volcanoes. Gall's women claimed he was a calm and devoted father, but I never wanted to see this forbearance tested.

Gall passed the pipe to a Hunkpapa dandy whose name I did not know, wearing heavy arm rings, long beaded earrings, and painted buckskins trimmed with the hair of dead enemies. Most of the scalps were dark and straight; only a few were light and wavy, Wasichu or maybe Mandan. The dandy passed the pipe to a tall warrior in yellow paint, with a proud hatchet face.

Next to smoke was He Dog, an Oglala Bad Face. He Dog was a nephew of Red Cloud and a boyhood friend of Crazy Horse, a likable warrior who got on well with anyone, even Wasichu. He was a true sagebrush diplomat, able to talk the hide off a buffalo if the need arose. People loved, feared, or hated Crazy Horse; but most just liked He Dog.

Crazy Horse took the pipe from his friend. Except for the star-shaped scar on his face, Crazy Horse looked at peace. He was most relaxed when war was in the air. First in battle among the Oglalas, he never performed at scalp dances or spoke at kill talks. The easy way he surpassed others made him many friends, and more than a few enemies. He passed the pipe to Black Bear and Yellow Legs, where it turned around and went back to Sitting Bull. At a full-dress feast, the pipe never crossed the fire to the women's side of the tipi. We valued these smokes as a time to do quiet tasks, or to slip away and talk among ourselves.

The warrior in yellow spoke first, saying his name was Rain-in-the-Face, pointing to his nose and making the sign for falling rain. He added that he was also called Takes-the-Enemy, and that he had killed two Wasichu in the latest meeting with the Long Knives. I was sorry to find that we had entered in the middle of a kill talk. To me an evening spent listening to men's war stories was an evening wasted. I much prefer warriors like Crazy Horse, who never bore and disgust you with constant descriptions of their deeds. Already I could see Rain-in-the-Face was prone to soliloquy. He told how he had taken two good horses from the men he murdered, a big bay and a black Mexican pony. He had given the bay to his brother, Iron Horse, indicating the dandy next to him. The black pony he presented to an old woman with no horses to carry her lodge. The men all said that was good. What else could men say to such courage and generosity?

Iron Horse eagerly backed his brother's story. Everyone had seen the old woman leading her new pony around camp, but the big bay was not here. Big American horses cannot be ridden like tough Lakota ponies. Chased by the cavalry, Iron Horse had ridden the bay until its sides heaved and its heart burst—but he had cut fine meaty steaks from its dead flanks. I hoped none of that bay had made it into Mixed Day's pot. Ridden-to-death horse-meat rates just above rattlesnake, and well below dog.

There were no scalps because one Wasichu wore his hair short and the other was old and bald. Right from the start I thought Rain was embroidering his case. No scalps, no big American horse, and most of all no guns. Had these two fierce, balding Wasichu been unarmed? One small Mexican pony was not much to carry a fighting name like Takes-the-Enemy. Takes-the-Pony would have been nearer the truth.

I contained my anger. Making uninvited comments at a Lakota kill talk was as welcome as a whiskied-up Medicine man speaking out at a Women's Christian Temperance Union convention. I hoped to hear my husband put the homicidal braggart in his place—there were two freshly painted crosses on Yellow Legs's shirt, letting the Lakotas know he had rescued a fellow warrior while on horseback. But he claimed to have done nothing special, pretending that diving under a hundred carbines to pick Medicine Bear off the ground did not rate with butchering two helpless Wasichu.

Gall spoke up, saying that Grabber—a half-breed wise in the ways of Wasichu—had heard the Long Knives making war music across the river. Also four Hunkpapas had gone to the south bank, seen the soldiers, and recognized the Arikaree scout called Bloody Knife. Now I now had a name to go with the dark face of the scout who was always at Custer's side.

And to hear Gall tell it, Long Hair was in damned poor company. Gall launched into a longish discourse on the sins of Bloody Knife and the unwholesomeness of Rees in general, calling them treacherous corn eaters who copulated with their sisters, daughters, and mothers-in-law. To illustrate his lecture, he stood up and let his robe slip off his shoulder, exposing white scars on his massive chest. "One winter, Bloody Knife led Long Knives to my lodge. When I came out, the Wasichu shot me and pinned me to the ground with a long knife." Gall made a thrusting motion to show how he had been bayoneted.

"They left me to die in the snow. But a Medicine woman saved me. Seven Wasichu have died for this—but I have not yet killed Bloody Knife." He went on in that jolly vein, making cheerful references to death and dismemberment. Rain-in-the-Face had been absurd and disgusting, but Gall was just plain terrifying. When he talked about Bloody Knife his eyes went wild with hostility.

The guests growled their approval. Then He Dog the diplomat spoke for the Oglalas. "Our aim is always the same. Wasichu who come as friends are welcomed as friends. Wasichu who come as enemies are welcomed as enemies." He Dog did not look toward the women's side of the lodge, but Given-to-Us and I were living proof of this policy, each in our own way proud to be Wasichu, yet living alongside the wildest Oglalas.

None of the Lakotas had an unkind word to say about Long Hair. For all the Hunkpapas cared, Bloody Knife might have commanded the 7th cavalry. General Custer was strictly a Sheyenna concern, being both a sworn enemy and a member of the tribe by marriage.

Having heard his guests out, Sitting Bull rummaged through his Medicine pouch, producing a folded scrap of yellow paper. He passed it to Yellow Legs, who handed it over the fire to me, saying, "Light-Haired Woman, will you read this talking paper?"

I saw that I was going to pay for my supper. The men on the far side of the fire fell silent, waiting to hear what the talking paper had to say. Keeping my eyes off them, I unfolded the paper. Sitting Bull had a passion for old newspapers and circulars, but this was the absolute pick of his library, a railroad handbill, full of choice bits that even mentioned him in the text. Medicine men are as vain as any other newspaper readers, loving to find their names in print; unless like Yellow Legs they think writing is bad Medicine. Some of the words and concepts were difficult to translate, but I did my best, starting with the bold lettering.

"SAFE, PROFITABLE, PERMANENT" was printed across the top in huge capitals. "LARGE tracts of FERTILE LAND ready for SETTLEMENT" was in slightly smaller print. This broadside was months old, but it said that the Northern Pacific would soon cross the Missouri to meet another line of track coming out of Washington Territory, forming a railway empire sprawling over an area larger than New England, with a climate as mild as tidewater Virginia. Whoever had written the handbill had never huddled in a Sheyenna lodge during the Moon of Frost in the Tipis. However, the author did comprehend that millions of acres would have to be pried away from unwilling savages, and closed with a comforting quote from the Superintendent for Indian Affairs in Montana: "Should the wandering Sioux under Sitting Bull persist in their efforts to interfere with the progress of the Northern Pacific Railroad, the interests of civilization and common humanity demand that sufficient military force will be sent against them to severely punish them—even to annihilation, should that unfortunately be necessary."

Civilization and common humanity, indeed. If this broadside sounds the least bit foolish to you, imagine reading it at a Lakota kill talk. The largest military force for hundreds of miles sat camped around me—close to a thousand Hunkpapa, Oglala, and Sheyenna warriors. Any immigrant who arrived in Lakota Country looking for a balmy climate and army protection was in for a fatal shock. The Northern Pacific had named its latest settlement "Bismarck," to attract colonists from as far off as Central Europe, so you may guess just how unprepared some new arrivals were.

I was close to crying. The only comforting thing about reading this broadside was that none of it made much sense to my audience. Instead of falling into a savage fury and "unfortunately" annihilating me with a war club, they found that part about "sufficient military force" as puzzling as the section comparing the climate to the Virginia coast. The Hunkpapas were in fact rendered speechless—no mean compliment to the power of the pen, since a smoked-up Lakota is normally as talkative as a Maryland minister drunk on moonshine and salvation.

Yellow Legs filled the silence, speaking simply and forcefully. "Fire Wagons will bring more Wasichu than an honest man can count. (Sheyenna believed that anyone who used numbers higher than a thousand had not counted the objects in question, and was most likely lying.) With them will come walking soldiers, and the men who gamble all of the time, and the women who copulate for money. They will shoot the buffalo for their hides, or just for the joy of seeing them fall over. All this happened when I lived in the south. Ride down to the Fat River and see how thin it has become."

The Hunkpapas shifted uneasily. Rain-in-the-Face's petty killings and Gall's feud with Bloody Knife paled before the image of the Yellowstone strung with railroad camps like beads on a trade necklace. "Hell on Wheels" was what temperance preachers called the railroad towns—they did not like them either. Crazy Horse followed up Yellow Legs, saying everyone must fight together, swearing that if no one ruined the Medicine surround they'd knock off soldiers like ninepins. The warriors all agreed. "Hoka hey," as the Lakotas like to say.

Not one of them had a harsh word for me. If that seems odd, remember braves had no objection to Wasichu cooking their meals and warming their sleeping robes. If the Iron Horse had brought only trainloads of young women, from factory and finishing school, braves would have turned out in all their feathers to greet the carriages. They would have helped lay the tracks. Most Lakota considered Wasichu obnoxious and ill-mannered, but few actually hated us. Hate was something they reserved for enemies they understood, like Crows and Pawnees. Rees were northern cousins to the Pawnees, which might explain Gall's low opinion of them.

Four Robes brought out platters of buffalo ribs swimming in fat, along with boiled tongues and strips of jerky. I stopped listening to the war talk, trying to to ignore the men's smoker, and just enjoy the company of Sitting Bull's women—who did not blame me for Medicine Bear's death, or Long Hair's coming. I hated having to read that handbill, realizing that Sitting Bull and my husband must have arranged it all ahead of time. Lakotas are spoiled by their sense of freedom. To keep several thousand touchy individualists happy, Sitting Bull had to bribe, wheedle, and flatter like an Irish ward boss on election day. But this time he had outdone himself, giving the type of show that made him a Medicine man.

Sitting Bull also knew what Medicine would take away that sting. When his guests had left, he motioned for Yellow Legs and me to sit on either side of him and share a private pipe, saying, "You must forgive me. I am a wild Lakota who wants to live as the Great Medicine made him—I will not sell my birthright for sugar in my coffee."

He packed a plain pipe using a feathered tamping stick; neither Yellow Legs nor I shared Crazy Horse's taboo. As he worked the stick he started on a story. "I would just as well not fight the Wasichu—nor the Rees either. Bloody Knife was born among us, but his mother was a Ree and took her sons to live with her people. When Bloody Knife came back, hands were raised against him. He was mocked, and beaten with ramrods and coup sticks. But I would not let people kill him."

Seen-by-the-Nation said this was so—*Hetchetu aloh.* Bloody Knife left camp alive, when many wanted him dead. Sitting Bull took the Peace of the Camp seriously, going about sparing people that the less tenderhearted hoped to see gutted. She added that Bloody Knife's sister still lived with the Hunkpapas. Having enemies in camp was common. Sitting Bull's halfbrother, Fool Dog, was born to a Ree.

The Strong Heart Chief passed his pipe to Yellow Legs, who passed it to me. Women did not usually smoke with men, but Sitting Bull liked to show me he could make the rules. Not being much of a smoker, I tapped the pipe and returned it to Yellow Legs.

Mixed Day took this moment to chide her son for taking too many chances in war. "If you don't wish to fight the Rees and Long Knives, you must hang back more. Let the young men show their bravery, those who have no women and children to feed." Sitting Bull had over sixty major coups in battle, and like Yellow Legs, had reached the age where a warrior no longer had to constantly prove his courage.

Her son grinned broadly at his mother's warning. Everything about his face was big—a big forehead, a big nose, large luminous eyes. "The Great Medicine did not make men and women the same, and I cannot claim much power over women."

I gave him a look of polite disbelief. Women laughed. It was plain that Sitting Bull loved women. His tipi was always full of them—mother and sister, wives and daughters. He was well-known for his gallantry, even to Wasichu women. Real Woman owed her freedom to him. Annie Oakley had nothing but good to say about him. Years later I was not surprised to find a white woman sharing his tipi. He always made it clear that if I tired of Yellow Legs, there was a place for me in his lodge. The love of his youth, who died in childbirth, had also been called, "Light-haired Woman."

"Yes, yes." He made the sign that means both yes and good. "I have had a few wives, but I have never managed them. Once I brought a new wife into my lodge. Each night she would seize an arm and leg, while my first wife would grab my other arm and leg. Far from enjoying two women, I had to spend my nights flat on my back, staring up the smoke hole."

Mixed Day rocked with laughter, so I suppose the story was true.

Then he turned serious, saying directly to me, "If the Iron Road comes up the river, we will all be tested. Yellow Legs and I are men; we will be tested in battle. But it is the women who will test you. *You betcha.*" That bit of English was his favorite Americanism.

Riding back, I heard the heavy beating of Oglala drums. Braves were singing a simple refrain to the Crow scouts across the river:

> *Crows,*
> *We will see you*
> *In the morning.*

Yellow Legs came home with me. On a warm summer night like this we might have made love or gone visiting, looking for a lodge filled with people where we could eat Lakota fry bread or Sheyenna candy, talking into the night. Men would loosen up and women would joke. I could tell tall tales about the strange ways of the Wasichu, while children played tickle games in the dark. But this was not a night for telling funny Wasichu stories, not with Crows and cavalry waiting across the river. Already I could feel war Medicine coming between us.

I sat by the fire pit, poking at the dying embers, watching sparks fly upward, following the spiraling lodgepoles through the smoke hole and into the Spirit World. Having half a husband was not as bad as you might think. Having Yellow Legs come every other night to my tipi was more dignified than my slipping up the servants' stairs when Dr. Warren's wife was away. On my nights alone, what I really wanted was something neither man had given me. I wanted a child, a baby who would be with me every night. You would think a Harvard doctor or a Sheyenna Medicine man could have performed that ordinary medical miracle—but so far it had been all fun and no family. Dr. Warren was knowledgeable enough at his trade not to get servant girls pregnant, and Yellow Legs sometimes had damned little Medicine left for me. Far from being steeped in sin, the Sheyenna are so set against idle fornication that most couples in camp led lives that a Presbyterian divine can only aspire to.

I told him how I was afraid. "Already women think I broke Medicine Bear's Medicine."

Yellow Legs waved impatiently. "Such talk is foolish. The man himself said his Medicine was not broken. Who would know better?" Who indeed?

"But what if he does not come back tomorrow? What will they say then?"

My man smiled. "Are you asking me to see into the future? That would take much Medicine, and I am tired."

"A simple opinion will suffice." I did not need any Medicine man flimflam. These Medicine Dreamers and Owl Prophets never come up with anything useful, like next season's winners at Narragansett Park.

He considered. "It is not easy to know, but this man assured us his Medicine would bring him back from the Spirit World. He is not worried, and he is the one most concerned. It would be wrong for us to worry more."

There you have it. I was more worried than Medicine Bear, and I did not much like the man. Of course, to feel comfortable, I had to succumb to that crazy logic, putting my faith in Medicine Bear's ability to raise himself from the dead. As a girl I had watched a Hagerstown preacher from over the Maryland line try to bring back a drowned boy. The boy stayed drowned. But the preacher was drunk; perhaps it had not been a fair test of resurrection.

Yellow Legs took off his shirt and leggings and slipped under my sleeping robes, the Sheyenna way of saying our talk was at an end. Wasichu are not so easily satisfied. Shedding my dress, I crawled in beside him. Pressing against his large, dark form, I started to stroke him, down low where it would do the most good.

He reminded me to show respect for his war Medicine.

But I was sick of his taboos and damned well determined not to be like Raven, who would sit up half the night crooning some godforsaken chant, just for the good of his Medicine. He wanted a Wasichu wife, and he was stuck with me. "This is stupid," I told him. "It is arrows and bullets you must fear, not my body. Withholding yourself from me will not make you one whit safer." Already I could feel my love Medicine losing out. What I wanted was physical comfort, not to argue superstitious behavior with a savage.

He refused to be swayed. "As long as I keep my Medicine strong, I need not fear bullets and arrows."

Even with naked bodies touching I could feel the gap between us, the great chasm between the civilized and the savage. He must have felt it too. Did he even want half-Wasichu children? I was afraid to ask. If he did not want children with me, I could not bear to hear him say it. Instead I begged him not to cross the river in the morning. Custer had already proved that the cavalry could not ford the Yellowstone. If I could just keep my husband on the south bank of the river he would be safely out of the fight.

Yellow Legs nuzzled my neck, as though he were comforting a nervous foal. "Light-Haired Woman, do not worry. Nothing will break my Medicine. Crazy Horse has planned this fight well. It will be an antelope surround. We will cross upstream and downstream, trapping Long Hair on the north bank with the river at his back." He made it sound so minor, nothing to worry a woman. Only these antelope would shoot back.

I told him I was sick of fighting. "War Medicine is making me sad and miserable. You do not need to cross the river to defend what is yours."

"There is also the railroad," he reminded me. "If we do not stop the Iron Horse, he will trample us beneath its steel hooves."

I pulled him tight to me. "Killing soldiers will not stop the Iron Horse. Kill them all and more will come. When I was a girl I saw the Long Knives kill more Wasichu in three days than the Lakota and Sheyenna ever could. And we fought among ourselves for four years."

Yellow Legs sighed. "You are right. Bullets will not stop the Iron Horse. For your sake I will not cross the river." Unlike most men, he was not immune to logic—one of the many reasons why I loved him. For a long moment he lay silent. Then he added softly, "There is strong Medicine in you, stronger than you know—and wisdom too. But it is a wild and untamed wisdom, like a child that always must have her way."

What was so wrong with having my way? Nothing that I could see. I gave him a gleeful hug, happy to have won.

He accepted it, then moved to make space between us, saying, "These are not the old days when our grandfathers fought with bows and lances. Wasichu wisdom has given us bullets that fly across the river. I will need my war Medicine, even if I stay on the south bank."

Garryowen

The 7th cavalry can lick all the Indians on the Plains.

—Gen. George Armstrong Custer

AT DAWN WE ALL WENT DOWN THE BIG HORN TO SEE LONG HAIR and his men rubbed out. Morning tasks were set aside; women, children, and old men gathered on the bluffs to cheer on the warriors. To the Sheyenna, war was not something you marched off to—sometimes it came to you, like it came to Adams County. Braves traded insults across the river, asking after friends and relations on the far side. Lakotas wanted to see Two Bodies, a French-Lakota scout who had married a Crow. Crows called back that he was hunting upriver, too busy to scalp a few Sioux.

Uncomfortable with the carnival mood, the cavalry increased their fire, driving the Lakotas back from the bank. Nothing makes an officer more nervous than casual chats between "his" Indians and the ones they are supposed to be killing.

As the game turned deadly, parties of warriors crossed the river. Crazy Horse led the Oglalas and Sheyenna across upstream. Gall crossed downstream with the Hunkpapas and the Santee Dakotas. They were soon out of sight. When I saw the soldiers turn their backs to the water I knew the Medicine surround had begun. Somewhere on the far bank a wagon gun was firing. Shells rattled over the bluff, sounding exactly like a fast express passing overhead. None burst anywhere near us.

Lying in the buffalo grass atop a high bluff, I focused my husband's brings-'em-close-glasses on the nearest soldiers. Three troopers had taken cover right at the riverbank, and one of these was a dead shot. A couple of hundred yards is comfortable range for a cavalry carbine, but on the long side for the sawed-off muskets and magazine rifles most Lakotas carried. This sharpshooter killed a warrior close to the river, then wounded two more coming

58

to get the body. For a Lakota or Sheyenna, death does not end a relation-ship. Lakotas will brave gunfire to recover a friend's corpse, and Sheyenna delight in cutting up a dead enemy.

Yellow Legs sat on a blanket not far from me, smoking with Sitting Bull. Both men were wearing paint and warbonnets, but they acted as if this were a Sunday in the park. Sitting Bull wore rainbow face paint and a bright red breechcloth; my husband had on his scalp shirt and cavalry pants. With them was White Bull, Sitting Bull's nephew, wearing a red warshirt, a bone breastplate, three eagle feathers, and yellow paint. Thank the stars none of them needed to prove his bravery today. Exactly a year ago, I had seen all three of them sitting and smoking under fire at the mouth of Arrow Creek. A mob of young braves had gone down to confront the cavalry, and Long Holy put on an indifferent display of bullet Medicine. Several braves were hit and bleeding, when Sitting Bull suggested they call off the show. Long Holy told him not to be so "mouthy."

To put Long Holy in his place, Sitting Bull had picked up his pipe and stalked out onto the prairie in full sight of the soldiers, saying, "Anyone who wants a smoke, follow me." Yellow Legs, White Bull, and a couple of others went with him. In a cool, terrifying display of Medicine, they sat down like old friends at a feast, passing the pipe from right to left while bullets whipped through the protective smoke. When they were done, Sitting Bull carefully cleaned out the pipe, then put the pipe and cleaning stick back in his to-bacco pouch, while bullets kicked up puffs of dust around him. Then they all got up and returned to safety: Sitting Bull limping from an old war wound, Yellow Legs and White Bull being more brisk about it.

That was last summer. This time my husband did his deed alone. With-out warning Yellow Legs passed the pipe to the Hunkpapas, picking up his Medicine gun, a Henry repeater trimmed with black eagle feathers. I could tell at once something awful was about to happen.

Cradling the Medicine rifle, Yellow Legs sauntered down to the river, as if he were moderately thirsty. I saw what a prime fool I was, thinking I could keep Yellow Legs away from danger. He would have been far safer riding back and forth on the far bank with Gall, Crazy Horse, and hundreds of other braves. Instead he was walking deliberately down to the river where the army sharpshooters were posted.

Yellow Legs knelt by the bank, taking careful aim at the marksman on the far shore, drawing fire away from the braves who were not so bulletproof. Warriors scurried about, recovering the dead and wounded. I alternately prayed that the bullet Medicine would hold and cursed the idiotic superstitions that made him so bold.

My husband and the cavalry sharpshooter fired together, repeater and carbine speaking at almost the same instant. Only one of them had the bullet Medicine. Sand kicked up next to Yellow Legs's knee. The soldier on the far bank slumped back, disappearing into the brush. I did not see him again, and the cavalry fire lost a lot of both accuracy and daring.

It had to be either magic or an absolutely lucky shot. A magazine rifle had no business hitting at that range. As he got to his feet, Yellow Legs reached down and picked a bright object from the sand. I saw a glint of brass in the sunlight. Crows claimed that the Medicine guns carried by Yellow Legs and Crazy Horse never missed. Maybe so, but I knew Yellow Legs had only six brass rimfire shells for his rifle, and until he reloaded the shell in his hand only five could be fired. If Yellow Legs had more shells, and believed that killing alone would win battles, there would have been many more dead cavalry.

Calf Road rose to her feet, cheering her sister's husband, giving a long Sheyenna ululation, while I shook with relief. Raven must have heard my knees knocking; she looked over at me, saying, "For a woman who goes out with war parties you get easily alarmed." Raven had been married to our reckless man for a number of years and was better used to waiting about, wondering if he would return.

Women on the bluffs echoed Calf Road's ululation, yelling like they do at an antelope surround. Calf Road called out to Medicine Bear:

> Take pity,
>   Your time to come back
> Has come.

Others shared her hope, turning toward the pool where Medicine Bear sat. He had been four days and nights in the drink; today was the day when he vowed to return. I did not see so much as a ripple, but Calf Road swore she could see his spirit winging over the water like a sandhill crane, coming to our aid. Southern Sheyenna chanted Brave Bear's curse against Long Hair—some of them must have been in Medicine Arrows's camp when it was first delivered.

As though stirred by the chanting, the soldiers across the river started to move. A line of dismounted troopers climbed up toward the crest of the far bluffs. Firing increased around a small knoll downstream. Gall and Crazy Horse were closing in on the Long Knives pinned against the river, completing the antelope surround. My binoculars turned the toiling blue ants across the river into living men, climbing in ragged lines toward the puffs of firing at the top of the knoll. Every so often a man would falter and go

down, sometimes to stagger up again, sometimes not. Mounted soldiers
formed up for a charge.

On our side of the bluffs women grew reckless, ignoring the rattling
shells to push forward and get a better view. Spring Grass was hopping about
beside me, stretching her graceful neck, trying to catch sight of Custer. Yellow Bird was with her, wearing blue leggings, and a dead bird tied in his hair,
his body dotted with hail spots. He clutched a hunting bow and some buffalo hair braided to look like a scalp. How could I not have seen that this was
the son of a famous major general? Had Spring Grass told him his father was
on the far side?

Yellow Legs was back with Sitting Bull. They calmly sat and talked, as if
they were only moderately interested in the goings-on, but it was part of
their Medicine to show no special excitement at times such as this. Aside
from the odd howitzer shell, the shooting was not aimed at them. Crazy
Horse was the one having his bullet Medicine tested.

Music began to float across the Yellowstone. First a series of bugle calls,
then a whole brass band was playing. I stood up, utterly amazed, not be-
lieving it was really band music until I recognized the tune—one of those
quick Irish drinking songs that my father used to sing riding home from
Black Horse Tavern. I hummed along, just to be sure, moving my lips in time
to the music:

> Let Bacchus' sons be not dismayed
> But join with me each jovial blade;
> Come booze and sing, and lend your aid
> To help me with the chorus.

The Southern Sheyenna fell silent. They too had heard the tune. Spring
Grass turned to Calf Road, "It is Long Hair's Medicine song." Word went
around that this was the war music Grabber had heard coming from the
Long Knife camp. The light beat sounded like a cavalry canter:

> Instead of water we'll drink ale,
> An' pay no reck'ning on the nail,
> No man for debt shall go to jail,
> While he can Garryowen hail.

Through the binoculars, I saw the cavalry sweep over the ridge, their
split-tailed guidons streaming and bugles blowing. Soon they were out of
sight. "Garryowen" faded and people sobered up, realizing we would not see

Long Hair rubbed out. Instead of Crazy Horse and Gall storming over the crest and pushing the cavalry into the river, Custer had countercharged. Music and firing proceeded merrily into the distance. The fight rapidly headed elsewhere, as Lakota and Sheyenna ran from the Long Knives.

There was naught to do but straggle back to camp. Taking a last look at the pool covering Medicine Bear, I saw nothing. No stirring in the water. No sign of life. What else would a sane person expect?

The Arikaree Fork

To the south, where Union Pacific trains ran daily into the sunset, the schedules and newspapers read 1873, but up here by the Big Horns, in the land of moons and winter counts, years were not numbered, but named. Each year is named for its winter—for without winter's freezing snows the summers would all run together, like they do in my memory. This particular winter has many names. I favored the Minniconjou winter count that marked 1873 by the death of a Medicine man named Little. When his wife died, Little sat down, saying, "This woman and I have lived long together. I do not care to live on without her." He placed a chip of dried buffalo dung on the ground and sang his death song. His soul flew out out of his mouth in the form of a prairie owl, landing on the buffalo chip. When the owl flew off, Little was dead.

But among the Lakota Eaters the year was most often remembered as the Winter Medicine Bear Lost his Medicine.

We left Medicine Bear propped on the bottom of the Yellowstone and went up the east bank of the Big Horn, deeper into Greasy Grass country. In our tight little community Medicine Bear's loss was keenly felt, and I moved like a ghost among the grieving Sheyenna, a living symbol of their sorrow—the Wasichu who broke the bullet Medicine. Ridiculous but real. Talking stopped as soon as my shadow fell on the speakers; my Medicine was strong enough to stop People's mouths, whether or not I willed it.

Crossing over to the Little Big Horn, we camped below Ash Creek, where there was shade and grass beneath a long sinister line of bluffs. On the second day in camp we saw strange pony tracks. And that night Last Bull killed a Flathead. I was awakened by gunshots and shouts of "Kill the Crow!" (Crows and Flatheads are hard to distinguish in the dark.) Last Bull was vis-

63

iting with a wife and crawled into an old woman's tipi to borrow a pistol. (What Last Bull wanted from his wife had not required a weapon.) He shot the man, who had tried to make off with a mule. The Flathead mule thief was at fault, but the Peace of the Camp had been broken—to me that made the Little Big Horn an unlucky campsite.

Four days after the fight, Yellow Legs invited me to ride with him over the bluffs east of camp, searching for a fat buffalo cow or even a skinny antelope—fighting the Long Knives had burned powder and shot without putting meat on the drying racks. I was delighted to leave the dreary camp. Raven was busily ignoring me, grunting and heaving over her digging stick, hunting out a rather tasteless root that grows by the Big Horns. I did not disturb her with any Wasichu goodbyes.

Yellow Legs and I crossed the Little Big Horn at the base of Medicine Tail Coulee, where there is a swift pony ford, a few feet deep and pebbled at the bottom. Then we mounted a grassy bluff sprinkled with blue flax and wild sunflowers. Atop the dry divide separating the Little Big Horn from the Rosebud the afternoon turned from sultry to intolerable. Alkali dust burned my nose, and the shrunken creeks were too bitter to do anything but mock my thirst. Thunderheads released hot sprinkles of rain—but never enough to wet my lips. Patience evaporated in the noon heat. Ready to eat even Raven's root porridge, I prodded my husband to give in. Yellow Legs insisted he hunted best on an empty belly, but here there was plainly nothing to hunt. Buzzards circled above us, hoping to see a kill. Otherwise we were alone. No buffalo, no antelope, not so much as a prairie dog.

He agreed to rest the ponies, pointing his bow at a far-off green speck. It looked like a bush, but was more likely a treetop peeking out of a draw. Following his bow tip we found a cottonwood hollow, an island of shade in the yellow haze.

My husband dismounted, but I sat and admired the green coolness. The grass grew, thick and supple, a sure sign of water seeping underground. Flies buzzed about.

"Get down, wife." His wry smile should have warned me.

I smiled back. "The world looks wonderful from here."

"Your pony needs rest." Even in the shade, Keeps-the-Fire dripped sweat, her taut black-and-white hide twitching each time a fly touched it. Reaching up, Yellow Legs lifted me out of the saddle. "You are so light," he observed as my moccasins met the ground.

"And so white," he added, holding tight to my buckskin dress, pulling it up past my thighs and belly, marveling at the swell of creamy flesh. Wild Sheyenna do not often see Wasichu as white. They see us as tanned, or dirty, or sunburned; but they seldom see creamy white skin. He once said my belly had the cool warmth of snow in midsummer.

"My wife has skin like buffalo fat." To be compared to any part of a buffalo is a compliment, especially an edible part, but he was making fun of me. Knowledgeable Sheyenna enjoyed making up double-meaning metaphors that sounded absurd to Wasichu. He yanked again. The dress went up to my shoulders. So this was what we were here for. I had nothing beneath the dress but short buckskin leggings tied off at the calf. It was a sweaty day, and I thought I was safe with just my husband. Now I was naked from knees to shoulders.

Some rest stop. Some buffalo hunt. Telling him to wait—in Sheyenna and English—I sat back in the grass, struggling to get my dress all the way off. Men have it much easier. They need only loosen their breechcloths to be ready. Our horses stood watching like big inquisitive children.

Summer wheatgrass felt scratchy against my skin, but he knew how to distract me. His hands slid down and in, spreading my thighs, stroking, massaging, searching out the right rhythm. I closed my eyes, lying back, breathing deeper, feeling his mouth on my breasts, then my belly. His wet tongue brushed the blond hairs between my legs, then the fleshy bud beneath them. A moment later he had me arching and moaning, gripping at the grassroots with my fingers.

I am happy to say I taught him this bit of civilized behavior. Wild Sheyenna know neither prostitution nor pornography and are mostly virgins when they first marry. My training was more thorough. Dr. William Warren had been an avid student of female anatomy at Harvard, a progressive young physician dedicated to putting knowledge to use. I learned a lot as a maidservant under him. But once Yellow Legs was convinced that learning my secrets would not harm my Medicine, he too turned into an avid student. Having proved himself as a warrior, he was not afraid of the male taunt, "Your face smells like vagina."

He stopped to ask me, "You enjoy this?"

"Of course, you silly savage." I had dug little holes in the sod with my heels.

"That is strange." He propped himself on an elbow. "The first time I did this with Raven, she hit me. Me, the husband who puts meat in her lodge."

I laughed, though that "meat in her lodge" joke was ancient when we Wasichu first arrived on the plains. "And what did she do the second time you tried it?"

"That is a secret between husband and wife. But I did discover that Wasichu and Sheyenna are not so different beneath a buffalo robe."

Reminiscing about nights with Raven must have given him new notions. Mumbling a swift prayer to the Great Medicine, he mounted me. Smooth sweaty friction gave way to galloping pleasure, strong and insistent. Reaching around, he grabbed my bare buttocks with both hands, bucking and heaving inside me. After so many Medicine days, and Raven's nights, making love felt like a fleshy explosion under the Montana sun.

By the time that sun touched the cottonwoods, I was lying in the long grass on an empty belly, telling Yellow Legs that he might at least have put down a blanket. I had finally rid myself of the dress, but I still had on the leather calf-length leggings. Looking the perfect French postcard version of a frontier wife.

He ran a hand down the back of my bare hips. "If you want children, it is better to copulate directly on Grandmother Earth."

I had not heard that bit of Sheyenna wisdom before and assumed he made it up on the spot, since being a Medicine man is more than half flimflam. It is always wise to be wary of anything a man says when your dress is up and his breechcloth is down. I cocked an eyebrow. "Making children? Is that what this is about?"

He feigned surprise. "Do you Wasichu have a different way?"

"Do you want half-Wasichu children?" There were aspects of this that scared me. Having a baby would mean no going back; "half-breed" was not a nice name among my people.

"Yes, I want a daughter that looks just like you." The lines in his face deepened. He had thought long and strong about this. "A girl with hair like grass in summer, and eyes like the sky."

His fingers slid farther back, slipped into the moist flesh between my legs. Checking to see if his seed was planted? Rolling over, I sat up and reached for my dress. A woman can let herself be handled only so much, even by her husband. The thought of having to go back to our surly camp had gotten me out of sorts. Shaking the dust from my dress, I told him, "Sometimes I hate your Medicine."

He looked suitably shocked, sitting up and speaking earnestly. "Medicine is the wind about you; it is the water in the streams. Who can hate that? Learn to live with it, and your Medicine will care for you, here and in the Spirit World." The Sheyenna assumed it was never too soon to start preparing for the Hereafter.

"I am careful with my Medicine," he admitted, "but I want to make children with you. On a warm night, when you have kicked off the sleeping robes, moonlight falling down the smoke hole shines on your sleeping body, turning your hair into a silver torrent. Do you think it is easy then, to hold in my Medicine? To look, but not to touch?"

I pulled the fringed buckskin over my head. "Men's Medicine can be very convenient, always striving to find just the right times to hunt, fight, and fuck. Raven spent her afternoon breaking sun-baked earth with a digging stick. Tonight in her tipi, what will you say to her about your hard day of hunting?"

He stretched and stood up. "I will tell her I stuck my lance into a sleek white buffalo cow, but could not bring her down—she had too much Medicine." He was clearly pleased with the day's hunt, even though it had not put meat in my lodge, except in the figurative sense.

"If you want to be a man," he told me, "you should go live with the Crows. Did I tell you about the Big Belly woman who became a Crow war chief and had four wives of her own?"

I snorted, swinging myself up onto Keeps-the-Fire's back. Sometimes Yellow Legs had too many stories. We were not far from Mountain Crow Country. From atop my mare I could see the black, pine-covered foothills of the White Rain Mountains, known to Wasichu as the Big Horns. The Greasy Grass country had belonged to the Crows until Sitting Bull pushed them back beyond the mountains.

What he really said to Raven I do not know, since a silence had descended between me and my sister-wife. Which was sad. Difficult as Raven might be, I missed the jokes we used to share about Yellow Legs. On winter evenings we would trap him in involved conversations about bears, bearskins, and people with Bear names. Soon the "that mans" and "that things" would become thoroughly confusing. Women enjoyed making veiled fun of men's Medicine—but bear jokes were no longer funny among the Lakota Eaters.

Even pretending to argue over him had been a much-needed release. We used to have mock fights in front of him, over who could put up with him better, or which of his worst traits we loved most. Now there was no humor. No arguing. No release. At each new camp our two tipis were pitched farther apart.

Raven's silence and Calf Road's accusations gnawed at me. Our last night on the Greasy Grass was one of "my nights." Near to morning I braved myself to ask Yellow Legs about the fight on the Arikaree Fork when a warrior with a spotted bonnet was killed. He took his taboos seriously, and I had to know if he secretly believed I could be responsible for Medicine Bear's death.

He sat up, sleepy and surprised, pulling the robes around him. "Yes, I saw that fight, but I did not take part. I hid behind a hill." His tone was flat and inflectionless.

"Was that warrior killed because of a woman?" A couple of winters back we had camped with the Minniconjous, and I had seen one of Long Holy's bullet Medicine shows go sour. Braves had blamed their wounds on a menstruating woman. Could Yellow Legs really be that stupid and unreasoning? He absolutely lived by his silly taboos.

Yellow Legs glanced up the smoke hole to see if dawn light was coming down yet. No Sheyenna liked to tell Medicine stories unless it was pitch-dark. Sunup was still a ways off, so he brought out his short black pipe, carved from an antelope leg bone, packing it with tobacco and willow bark, adding some dried hemp to give it more of a kick. Cut-down pipes are a sign of disgrace among the Sheyenna, but Yellow Legs never connected his small pipe with any wrongdoing.

Lighting the pipe from the fire, he offered a smoke to the earth, sky, and four directions, then puffed and handed it to me. I took a couple of pulls, for form's sake. I don't care for smoking, but the ritual relaxed me, expelling anxiety with the smoke.

"This warrior died during the Moon of Red Plums," he explained, "just before the leaves turned yellow, three winters before we met. The winter is called When Spotted Warbonnet was Killed, because this warrior wore a spotted bonnet made by Ice. Wasichu named him Roman Nose, so that is what I will call him. He had a name among the People that means the little creature that flutters through dark caves and cannot be hit." Yellow Legs was very particular about not naming the dead. By using Roman Nose's American name, he figured the warrior's Medicine would be less offended.

Taking back the pipe, he tapped the ashes into the fire. "This was the summer after the Medicine Lodge Treaty. I remember what a great thing the signing was—a thousand lodges were strung out along Medicine Lodge Creek: not just People, but Kiowa, Blue Clouds, Southern Snakes and Iron Shirt's Apaches. There were no northerners there, no Lakotas or Lakota Eaters; all this happened far away, Where the Warm Winds Come From."

I lay against my backrest, breaking twigs and tossing them one by one into the fire. This was going to be one of those southern stories. The story of the southern village that Yellow Legs grew up in always came to me in bits and pieces. I had read Henry M. Stanley's report of the Medicine Lodge Peace Council when it appeared in the *Herald*, but I had never heard Yellow Legs tell the story. Even during the darkest winters he would never tell me the tale of his old village straight out. His southern stories always came threaded to one another in peculiar ways. This one was supposed to be about a Northern Sheyenna named Roman Nose.

He began to refill his pipe. "For me it was very difficult to make peace. There was revenge to think of, my first village had been rubbed out; friends and family had been killed. More than revenge, there was war, which had been my way of life for many winters. Once I had been afraid of death in battle, but now I had my Medicine gun and bullet Medicine. It would have been easy to go on killing Wasichu. I wrestled with my spirit many times before I decided to touch the pen."

"Why?" He had never talked so directly to me about his old fighting days.

"Because in my dreams I saw what the future would be if the fighting went on. So when my old man chief touched the pen, I touched it too. We were given many fine gifts, so many that we could not carry them all. Women refused to pack and unpack so much property, saying the steel axes and heavy kettles broke their travois. I myself got a very good pistol."

I produced the pistol, which had been taking up space in my tipi. "Here, you can have it back. I too find it cumbersome to carry."

He laughed as he took the gun, feeling its weight. "It is good to still carry it, otherwise the Medicine Lodge Treaty might be no more than a story. Touching the pen changed nothing. The soldiers building the Iron Road still shot at us. Wasichu came in even greater numbers to kill the buffalo, while we sat waiting with slack bellies for the food promised at Medicine Lodge."

"The treaty was signed," I told him softly, "but it must pass the Senate and be proclaimed before it is law. After that, Congress most appropriate money to carry out the terms."

Yellow Legs dismissed the constitutional process with an irritated wave. "For me, peace began when I touched the pen. From that moment I stopped fighting and expected the Wasichu would do the same. People cannot wait years or even months for food. When it came time to hunt and raid, many young men said, 'It is not so bad that there is no treaty; now we may do as we have always done.' Our old man chief tried to stop them, saying we were at peace. Young men galloped north anyway, back to our old hunting grounds, saying they would raid the Kaws and Pawnee. But everyone knew Wasichu lived there now, not Kaws and Pawnee. Snakes and Kiowas rode south into Texas, saying peace with the Americans surely did not include Texans."

"Texas is part of America," I reminded him.

"So I have heard. Someone should tell the Texans."

"What did you do?" Maybe the Civil War was still going on in Texas—I wanted to know how my husband had kept his peace.

"I could neither raid nor stay in camp watching the People starve. Instead I rode north, past the Flint and the Smoky Hill Country, up to the river we call the Pawnee. There I met Dog Soldiers returning from a raid. They lived in a large village, with many Burnt Thighs and a few Blue Clouds. These northerners had not touched the pen and could fight as much as they wished."

He stopped to take another pull on the pipe, the warm glow turning his face fire-red. "There was a man in this camp who was tall, strong, and absolutely fearless. He wore a spotted bonnet with a feathered tail that swept almost to the ground. Ice had painted dragonflies on the bonnet, making this northerner as hard to hit as the little insects that flit forward and backward, raising dust as they fly." We had finally gotten to Roman Nose.

"Even the Wasichu knew him, calling him a chief. People began to think that perhaps he should be a chief, if it would please the Wasichu. But Roman Nose refused, saying that he was too much of a warrior and that he might put fighting above the good of the camp."

Yellow Legs rested the smoke-blackened pipe on a buffalo chip—I kept bits of that holy dung in my tipi, for holding pipes and feeding the fire. "On my third night in camp we were feasted by the Lakotas. A Dog Soldier noticed that a Lakota woman was turning the fry bread with a metal fork. The Medicine in the spotted bonnet was very particular. Roman Nose had to abstain from women and eat his food from wooden sticks."

"Did she know she was breaking his Medicine?" I needed to know if women could be blamed for things done in innocence.

He dismissed the point as unimportant, "Knowingly or not, his Medicine was broken. Tall Bull, the Dog Soldier, advised Roman Nose to renew his Medicine at once. The rituals needed by the spotted bonnet were long and difficult, and many times his bonnet made Roman Nose late to battle. Before he could even begin, Wasichu were seen headed toward the camp. We met these Wasichu in a dry fork of the Pawnee River, called the Arikaree Fork." That was somewhere near the headwaters of the Republican River in Colorado.

"The stream bed there is wide and sandy, bordered by lazy hills. The Wasichu hid on an island in the dry river bottom, covered by plum bush and cottonwoods. At first Roman Nose refused to fight, telling people that his Medicine was broken. But the Wasichu had many-firing guns and braves began to fall, and Roman Nose could not stay away. He rode out to the fight, but stayed behind a hill. I was with him behind that hill."

A most sensible place to be when many-firing guns are speaking. I wondered why Yellow Legs had been so careful, but I let him tell the story.

"White Contrary rode up saying, 'Here is the man everyone relies on, sitting behind a hill.' Roman Nose explained that his Medicine had been broken. White Contrary replied that others had already died, adding that they had not hid behind a hill. Roman Nose was angered, saying, 'My food has been touched by an iron fork. I will die.' Painting himself, he put on the spotted warbonnet and rode right at the enemy. A Wasichu hiding in some tall grass shot him through the back. He crawled away from the fight and braves brought him back to camp, but by sundown he was dead."

"Do you think it was the woman's fault?" I myself was furious with White Contrary, who had pushed another man into getting killed for no purpose.

Yellow Legs thought for a moment, then decided, "Clearly there is only one person who can be blamed." He started fiddling with his pipe again.

I grew impatient. "Who is that person—White Contrary or the Lakota woman."

Yellow Legs looked startled. "No, the person to be blamed is Roman Nose. He was proud and foolish to ride into battle with his Medicine broken, just because a Contrary told him to. Contraries cannot help talking backward, but that does not mean we must listen and obey."

"And women cannot help cooking," I added. "It is a comfort to know no one blames the Wasichu who shot him."

Yellow Legs stared as though I had said something silly. "But Roman Nose rode through Wasichu bullets many times. If the Wasichu had the Medicine to kill him, surely they would have done it sooner."

Their cockeyed Medicine made the Sheyenna immune to cause and effect. No wonder everyone assumed Custer and Bloody Knife needed my help to hit Medicine Bear. There was no answer to this logic, so I asked, "Did you ride out, or did you stay behind the hill?"

"I stayed behind the hill." He said it evenly, without a hint of shame.

"Was your Medicine broken also?" I knew how carefully he kept within his taboos.

"My Medicine was strong, too strong for me to fight."

"Too strong?"

"It was so strong that I had brought the Medicine Lodge Treaty with me. I had touched the pen. I found that even where there was war I could not fight. So I left the northern camp. They did not need a warrior who carried peace around with him. I went back to be with my family and my old man chief."

"You cannot still be carrying the Medicine Lodge Treaty around with you?" I remembered how he had looked riding and fighting beside Crazy Horse.

"No, all I have left is the pistol the Wasichu gave me. I lost the Medicine Lodge Treaty that winter, on the Lodgepole River."

Spring Grass had told me all about Long Hair's surprising the Sheyenna on the Lodgepole—I did not have to hear any more hideous details from Yellow Legs. But I was still stewing over women being blamed for men's fatal mistakes. "We do things differently," I told him. "We have laws in writing that hold people innocent until actual harm is done—even then you must intend harm to be truly at fault." I was giving him the *essence* of the law, as J. S. Mill would have it, not as imperfect men administered it. "Our laws are against robbery and murder, not against bleeding every month or serving fry bread with a fork. That's the civilized way."

Yellow Legs sounded shocked. "What you say is impossible, even for you Wasichu." When he used words like "you Wasichu," I knew I had touched a hard core of bitterness, from deep infected pain. His contempt for the written word came out swift and keen. "In camp there is peace. On the prairie there is war. Those who cannot keep the peace must take their war Medicine out onto the prairie. Old Man Coyote does not say to the mouse, 'I eat you because you robbed the seed sack.' Coyote eats because he must, not to make the mouse a better animal. At the Lodgepole I saw women and children trapped against the river, shot down because they flinched at the icy water. What written law had they broken? Was Long Hair punished for killing them?"

I had to admit Custer was probably rewarded.

"He should be honored. He is brave. But I will kill him before he can enter this camp. I left the Medicine Lodge Treaty by the Lodgepole River. I no longer believe in touching the pen, or words on paper."

With all that had happened, how could he still love me? And how could we stay together when there was only war between our peoples? Quakers meant to be friends to all mankind—but sometimes mankind made it damned difficult.

Sensing my sadness, he slipped his buffalo robe about my shoulder. It was an old soft winter pelt, feeling like furry velvet; his skin beneath was warm and smooth. He touched my cheek, answering my unvoiced question. "I love you, because you have brought me peace." His uncanny habit of reading my thoughts was one of his best Medicine tricks.

"How can I have given you peace?" War was all around us, even threatening to invade the camp.

"You are Light-Haired Woman, the giver to all, the Jesus woman who will not take sides. There is bravery in refusing to fight. The first time I saw you in Red Cloud's camp teaching the children of armed enemies, my heart said, 'This is a Wasichu without fear.' When I fought the Long Knives they were always afraid—having no bullet Medicine to protect them. Even when they rode through our camp on the Lodgepole, firing their many-shooting pistols and carbines, they looked afraid. They never seem to enjoy war."

He smiled ruefully. "Your Jesus woman bravery has brought me peace. Now I am the one who cannot enjoy war—not even with bullet Medicine to defend me and a Medicine gun to kill with. But I still do not have your fearless friendship for all. I am not so brave. If enemies come, I will kill to defend what I have."

Happy to have him at least halfway off the warpath, I burrowed in beside him, letting the murmur of the Little Big Horn flowing over the pony ford lull me to sleep. During that last sleep on the Greasy Grass I dreamed the cavalry came falling down my smoke hole. Ironshod hooves scattered embers from my fire pit and trampled my possessions. Led by the soldier in red and his brown-skinned scout, they burst out of my lodge and into camp.

Crazy Woman Creek

FINDING NO BUFFALO ON THE LITTLE BIG HORN, THE BANDS separated. Crazy Horse's Oglalas decided to cross over the divide to the Rosebud, while we aimed farther south, headed for the forks of the Powder. At our last camp together, Crazy Horse came and bid Yellow Legs goodbye, with They-Fear-Her and her pet skunk tottling after him. The lines on Crazy Horse's face were as deep as the pistol scar on his cheek. Sitting on his heels, he told my husband, "This time there is no one to blame but me." He meant no one had spoiled his attack on Custer, no one had broken the Medicine surround.

Yellow Legs was working on some Medicine of his own, reconstructing his spent rimfire cartridge by leaching phosphorus from match heads. Such primitive handicrafts were his specialty, along with horse stealing and storytelling. The army did its damnedest to keep him from trading for rimfire ammunition, but the Interior Department assumed matches were a harmless taste of civilization. Only Yellow Legs knew a deal more about civilization than either the army or the Interior Department suspected. Most of modern life he rejected outright as pointless or indecent, but parts of it had earned his admiration. He had taught himself to hand-build cartridges by reconstructing the priming, repacking the shell with powder, then molding a new bullet to fit it. Very laborious, but Yellow Legs was meticulous about his ammunition. If a shell misfired, he had himself to answer to—it was part of what made the Henry a Medicine gun.

Without stopping work, he told the Oglala, "Any blame lies with the Long Knives. They come where they are not wanted."

Crazy Horse began to build a tiny stick and bark tipi for his daughter, saying, "Long Knives will come in summer, like cold winds come in winter. But we should have beaten them. This time no one failed me."

"I did not see the fight on the far side," my husband admitted. Neither of them looked at me.

"They had many guns," Crazy Horse told him, "and fired them faster than a blue jay can speak. When they charged, they charged all together, playing their Medicine songs. Our strength turned to water."

My husband tried to put the best blanket on things. "But they could not cross the river. Our camps are still safe."

Crazy Horse took a stick he was sharpening for his daughter's bark tipi and stabbed it into the ground. "To be beaten honorably leaves you with honor. To be beaten by fools who cannot even ford a river makes you less than a fool. A river will not always run between us. We must have more guns, more powder, or we will see women taken and lodges burned." Crazy Horse always took a stern view of the future, but I had never seen him so distraught.

Yellow Legs held up his partly rebuilt shell, turning it in the sunlight, studying it for flaws. "All the People working together could not make a single bullet like this one. But the Wasichu have machines that make more than a man can count." My accounts of factory work had amazed and horrified him. "Guns and powder will never be enough. We must trust our own Medicine." Given his prejudices, my husband's words made superstitious sense.

Crazy Horse stood up. "Then we need the Medicine that stops the bullets. We needed more bulletproof braves on the far side of the river." He left, too polite to say more.

You did not need to be an Owl Dreamer to know who got to Yellow Legs after he smoked the war pipe—who kept him from crossing over. During the whole exchange Crazy Horse had not had a word for me. Nor had Black Shawl dropped by, not since the day of the fight. She was a One-Man Woman, and had once told me that despite the bullet Medicine she dreamed that the Long Knives would someday slay her husband. If my Medicine could kill Medicine Bear, why not Crazy Horse as well?

I missed the companionship of Black Shawl and They-Fear-Her. And now that the Oglalas were leaving, I would lose even the silly comfort of tea parties with Given-to-Us. Worse lay ahead.

South of the Greasy Grass we crossed into Carbon County, Wyoming, a vast empty place, three times the size of New Jersey, with a population of 460 according to the 1870 census. Of course, that was 460 Wasichu, and did not include me or Given-to-Us. The Lakota Eaters alone numbered over 400.

Now that we were in Wyoming I could vote, though the polls were a good ways off and 1873 was not an election year. Even before coming West I had read about Wyoming's experiment with female suffrage—*The Nation* declared the damage done by women voters would not be great, since Wyoming had so few white women, and most were whores anyway. (The Democrats tried to take the vote back when they found out how many whores voted Republican.) I could also hold property and sit on a jury, though I could not marry a Negro or Mongolian. (That prohibition was passed over the Republican governor's veto; the Democrats refused to let women just run wild out here in Wyoming marrying whomever we liked.) But Yellow Legs was not a Negro, nor a Mongolian except in a distant sort of way. And Wyoming had no law against marrying Indians. Wasichu males were not stupid. There were only a handful of marriageable white women in the entire territory—and thousands of Indian women. The Democrats might feel comfortable condemning blacks and Chinamen to celibacy, but they were not going put the law between themselves and ninety percent of the marriageable females.

We struck buffalo on the Crazy Woman Fork of the Powder. By the time I arrived the air was black with crows and the ground was dotted with shaggy brown mounds waiting for the butcher knife. Raven and I found the kills feathered with Yellow Legs's arrows, then she set to work butchering, while I cut forked poles for drying racks. Hunting is not sport for the Sheyenna, but hard work—and buffalo hunts are the worst. Even without his Medicine gun, using just a bow or pistol, Yellow Legs could kill buffalo faster than Raven and I could gut, skin, butcher, and tan.

That first camp on the Crazy Woman Fork was a dirty sprawling factory, smelling of wet green hides and rancid meat, ringed by whitened bone piles—not at all like the lazy summer camps we had been living in. While we stitched and mended, making robes, clothes, tipi covers, and high winter moccasins, I could feel the summer dying around me. Nights were noticeably longer. Cold winds blew out of the sunset.

I did not have Raven's love of labor, but finding buffalo meant that food, clothing, and shelter were there for the taking. This was the wonder of living in Lakota Country, where none of life's necessities cost a penny. (Which made money nearly worthless—I saw coins used for jewelry, and hundreds of dollars in greenbacks turned into play tipis.) Bursts of concentrated effort could be followed by long periods of leisure—if you planned things right.

Until I came into camp, the Wasichu women seen up close were mostly captives, set to work at strange tasks in an unfamiliar tongue, and none too pleased about it. A captive Crow or Snake will start to work at once, unless

she wants to goad her captors into killing her—but the last thing most Wasichu aspired to was earning a permanent place in the camp circle. We got
a reputation for working little and complaining a lot. (A Crow woman typically registered her complaints with a bone needle or a skinning knife—the
sort of gesture a Sheyenna warrior could readily appreciate.) But I came
freely into camp, having already lived and worked among the agency Lakotas. Which made me a genuine oddity. Visitors would walk all the way across
camp just to see a Wasichu hard at work, doing something comprehensi-
ble—not building senseless structures or tearing up the landscape. They
would stare from a safe distance, then turn and walk away. Sort of like seeing the Elephant. My willingness to work stirred up the Medicine, but who
could argue against hard labor?

With the fall hunt done, men grew restless. They began to drift away,
aiming to take a last whack at the Crows or Blackfeet, or planning to winter at the Lakota agencies, where they could eat government beef and tell
winter tales about a summer of hunting and fighting along the Yellowstone.
Agency women were always impressed by a man returning from the wilds
with fresh coup feathers and stories to tell. I know—Yellow Legs first caught
my attention because he was a "wild Indian," who did not live on government handouts. He went to the agency, spun a few stories, and came back
with me.

Yellow Legs left as well. Not to raid or to impress more women at the
agencies, but to hunt for elk and deer in the Big Horns. The moment he rode
away I felt abandoned. Women would not speak to me, and the man who
had brought me into camp was gone. I pitched my tipi close by the creek,
away from the center of camp. There was hardly any company to miss.
Raven gave me rigidly what a second wife deserved, not a weaselskin more.
No Sheyenna law said wives had to like each other, or even get on. If a wife
does not like her husband's choice of mates, she can toss his goods out of her
tipi or return to her family. Husbands can resort to friendly persuasion or
physical violence at their own risk. I could not see myself asking Yellow Legs
to beat Raven into a better opinion of me.

The Moon of Black Cherries became the Moon of Red Plums, and I
found myself missing something besides the company of women. Raven's
time apart came and went. Mine did not. My menses was long overdue, and
the faintest whiff of rotting meat or dog shit made me sick in the mornings.
Once I would have been overjoyed, but now I found the notion of being
pregnant fairly terrifying. How could I have a baby living like this? When
the child came, would they hate her too?

And rearing over everything was the Iron Horse. The railroad would
bring hordes of settlers. It was no secret what these newcomers would say

about a white woman with a half-Sheyenna baby. America, wild and free, was shrinking. Civilization was closing in just as savagery was rejecting me.

When people won't speak with you, sitting around cross-examining yourself becomes a prime temptation. What was a grown woman, maybe a mother-to-be, doing playing Indian? Out here I needed no wages and paid no taxes, but what if I left this wild island for the Wasichu world? To be a serving girl was degrading; to be a factory worker was boring beyond belief. Nor could I go back to teaching Lakotas at the agencies; with a half-breed baby on my hip, most folks would figure I had already educated one Indian too many.

Could I find a new husband? No decent man would have me. Rape was excused—even downright expected—but giving yourself freely to an Indian was one of those peculiar unpardonable crimes that only women could commit. "White squaw"—like "Wyoming woman voter"—was another word for whore. Some nights I cried, others I lay awake feeling for new life within me.

Spring Grass was the only Sheyenna woman who would waste time on me, considering herself far above the fears and worries of the Lakota Eaters. We went together to cut wood and pick buffalo berries, partly for company, partly for protection. This was the western limit of Lakota Country. A Crow warrior could always slip out of the hills, set on proving his manhood by scalping some Sheyenna woman. Of course, my hair was much too pale to be paraded about on the tip of a Crow scalp stick. Crows were "peaceful" Indians, and a blond scalp would draw embarrassing comments from visiting tourists. The worst I could expect from a Crow was an arrow in the back.

When the wood was cut and bound to the backs of our ponies, we sat and snacked on plums and pounded meat. It was a warm fall day, the sort the Santees call a "gopher's look back." What we Wasichu would call Indian Summer. I told Spring Grass about my loneliness, saying nothing about expecting a baby.

"You could leave." She said it simply, without the hostility that Calf Road would have packed into the suggestion.

"I could. But I have nothing to go back to. Here I have a husband, or half a husband."

She gave me a thoughtful look. "Many Wasichu would think sharing a man was reason enough to go."

I gave her the Sheyenna woman's pat answer. "Better to share a good man than to have a bad one all to yourself."

"Of course, but it is surprising to hear a Wasichu admit it."

"Yellow Legs is strong and honest and treats me better than any man I

have known." By Sheyenna standards he was near perfect—too old for the
warpath, content to be a deadly hunter and a hardworking horse thief. Eager
to put meat in my lodge. An easy man to maintain, especially with Raven
to help make his meals and mend his moccasins. But . . .

"You will laugh if I try to explain."

Spring Grass looked up from her plums and meat. "Keep speaking. This
talk could use some laughter."

I stammered out the short history of my life since leaving home. "I hated
being locked in a factory all day and a boardinghouse at night, so I did domestic work for a man who made me into a second wife, with no standing."
Spring Grass said nothing, but I suspected she was familiar with that aspect
of Wasichu civilization. "Teaching paid less than factory work, or being a
serving girl and gentleman's whore, but I thought there might be some pride
in it. I heard about the Quaker work among the Lakotas. Supposing that the
Lakotas would know nothing, I figured even the little I could teach would
be a blessing. So I came west, aiming to make them into Wasichu." Other
than Yellow Legs, she was the only wild Sheyenna I had dared say this to.

Spring Grass grinned over her meat, but did not laugh outright. "And
then you met Yellow Legs?"

"Yes. He came down to the agency, to cadge free meals and be amused
by the Wasichu." I hefted her ax. It was a steel one, handed out by the Interior Department to "tame" Indians. The heavy metal rippled like water in
the sun, so different from the soft earth and yellow leaves. "See what a
piece of work this is? How hard it is, yet how easily it takes an edge? Imagine my surprise when I met a man with a keen mind, a man with much Medicine, who thought there were only two good things that the Wasichu had."
Two things worth having in all of Western civilization. "Tools like this—
and me."

Spring Grass's grin spread into a smile.

"In the textile mill I learned to rate myself beneath a bolt of cloth. As a
servant, I was cook, maid, and concubine for four dollars a week. Yellow Legs
stood my whole world on its head, rating me above everything, above even
the metal ax and the many-speaking rifle. It was dizzying."

"Did you know he had another wife?"

That question brought me back to earth. "Not at first. I suppose he told
me, but I misunderstood. He has a way of telling the truth without telling
everything. But I had shared my last man with another woman. I was young
enough to think it would be more tolerable with a man I really loved. I
come from a Quaker-Catholic marriage. My mother married an Irish gambler who never did a day's work except by accident. He taught me poker,

while my mother cooked and plowed. One day he just disappeared. Yellow Legs looked like more of a stayer." My father's affection and desertion left me an easy mark for any attractive desperado. Yellow Legs had begun by stealing my horse, and ended up winning my heart.

I said most of this in Sheyenna, so I am not sure how much made sense. Most Sheyenna knew nothing about Quakers and Catholics, assuming we Wasichu were all Christians—just as most Wasichu would not know the difference between a Blackfoot Lakota and a Piegan Blackfoot, though that was a life-or-death distinction in Lakota Country.

Spring Grass did understand loving a handsome stranger. She told me about her life with General Custer. "I was like you, lost among strangers. But I found the Wasichu better than I had expected. They did not want me to cook, tan hides, mend tipis, or gather firewood. Wasichu chiefs make their men do that, or they have paid women." Dark eyes flicked my way; seeing I was not insulted, she went on. "To be Long Hair's wife was all fun and little work. For a Wasichu he is very handsome, lean and strong, with cold blue eyes, a fierce nose, and hair the color of frost-burned grass. I rode at his side during the day and shared his canvas tipi at night, visiting our villages, telling People it was hopeless to resist him. You saw how easily he swept Gall and Crazy Horse aside."

"How did the other Wasichu treat you?" It was hard for me to picture the proud Spring Grass as a cavalry officer's concubine.

She laughed. "At first it was easy, living in a world of men, married to their greatest chief. Who would dare insult me? Wasichu chiefs can have their men beaten for trivial reasons—for getting up late in the morning, for slipping off to lie with a woman. Long Hair even had some of them shot. Men have no freedom among the Wasichu." Sleeping with Custer had not softened her savage prejudices.

"What happened when Yellow Bird was born?" The fate of half-breeds wore on my mind.

Her laugh turned bitter. "By then it was over. His Wasichu wife had come, and I was nothing. He treated our marriage as a joke, afraid to tell her about me—quaking before his woman. My son is all I had left of my husband."

Not an advertisement for mixed marriages. I took her hand. "Did that make you despise him?"

Spring Grass swept the suggestion aside. "I hate *her*. She is my enemy. She treated me like a little savage to be pitied. I would kill her if I could."

I felt her fingers tighten, as though she were clutching a war club. Mrs. Custer was lucky to be miles away. "Did she know you were his wife?"

Spring Grass studied the keen edge of the ax. "It is hard to know. She hides things well, and even the cowards who hated Long Hair would have been afraid to tell her."

"Afraid of Long Hair?" General Custer had authority over his men, but what about officers?

"No, afraid of her. She is a worthy enemy, with a strong mind and a cutting tongue. She sees the world the way she wants it to be. Any man who told her Long Hair had another wife would be her enemy, and she would know how to hurt him. Her pity cut me more than a knife would."

I did not ask her if she had ever been knifed, just for the sake of comparison. Spring Grass was a strong woman herself, who also saw the world the way she wanted it. I merely told her that when Dr. Warren hid our love from his wife it made him seem weak.

"Long Hair is not weak," Spring Grass insisted. "But Wasichu do not let their men be strong. If Long Hair were of the People, or even a Lakota, he could be whole. Who would stop him from having two wives, one a Person and one Wasichu? He could challenge the Wasichu chiefs who hate and envy him, using a warrior's weapons." I pictured General Custer swaggering into the next Republican Party convention, wearing a warbonnet and scattering the party faithful with a coup stick. Spring Grass's plans were not as practical as she supposed. She had seen civilization, but remained a hopeless savage.

I could not hope to match her reckless confidence—I had been brought up to take a civilized view of things, and there is no cure for that. But my case was not so bad as hers. I had a husband. Half of one anyway. And he had no intention of throwing me away.

For company I cultivated one of the camp dogs, a half-starved, overly friendly bitch—we seemed to have a lot in common. I never bothered to name her, but we got to know each other well; her chief joys were eating, sleeping, and plaguing the local rabbits. But Keeps-the-Fire remained my favorite confidante. She alone had the patience and undivided affection that I needed. I would sit stroking her black-and-white muzzle, singing my Medicine songs to her:

> De long tail filly, an' de big black hoss,
> Doo-dah, doo-dah.
> Dey fly de track, an' dey both cut cross,
> Oh, doo-dah, day.
> De blin hoss sticken in a big mud hole,
> Doo-dah, doo-dah.
> He can't touch bottom wid a ten-foot pole,
> Oh, doo-dah day.

With Yellow Legs off in the hills, I felt like one of those crazy old women who live on the edge of the camp circle in cut-down tipis, fighting the dogs for scraps. I had even seen one or two who might have been born white. People either left them alone or did them favors, but it did not seem to be much of a life. Crazy Woman Creek was named for one of these female hermits.

One morning I found my meat racks tipped over and my green hides torn. My new friend was lying on her side, legs and paws stiff, her skull crushed by a club. Some public-spirited individual had gone out of his or her way to ruin my meat, rip my hides, and beat my dog to death. I stared stupidly at the pattern of spattered brains and splintered bone. My enemies were getting bolder—but not brave enough to leave some identifying sign. The bitch had not been mine in any strict sense, but the blow was clearly aimed at me.

Until that morning I had not felt physically threatened—which may sound daft, but I had trusted in the Peace of the Camp, thinking that proper and modest behavior would keep me safe. Most whites assume that in a camp full of armed savages there would be a couple of murders each morning before breakfast—but generally a woman is safer in a Sheyenna camp circle than on the streets of the world's most civilized city. Rape was practically unknown in camp and severely punished, often by gangs of women. An abusive husband indulged himself only at the risk of being set upon by his wife's friends and relations. A woman could be excluded from camp protection and taken out on prairie, where men would do what they wished with her—but I had done nothing to provoke that. I had done nothing to provoke anything.

I went back inside my lodge and had a good cry, then I heated a pot and slow-cooked the dog. All morning she simmered in the pot. By noon Yellow Legs returned. The flanks of his pack ponies were black with blood; their backs were bent with fresh meat. He wore a proud hunter's grin, assuming the dog feast was for him.

My Medicine looked a whole lot better. Cooking that dog was my first ritual that worked just right. I cannot say for sure that the smell brought him down from the hills, but he dearly loved cooked canine. As did a lot of Sheyenna—you seldom saw a sullen or mean-spirited dog in camp. Not for long anyway.

When I told him how the dog had died he shed his grin, but still insisted on eating, inviting me to share, saying, "So we have an enemy in camp." The man could be a master at understatement; I felt more like I did not have a friend. Picking at my boiled pooch, I told him how hardly any of the women would talk with me. Yellow Legs chewed thoughtfully. "That is women's Medicine. There is little that I can do."

I said nothing about being pregnant. Nothing about Raven's indifference. One crisis seemed plenty. That night it was enough to have him in my tipi, sleeping next to me. For the nights when he was with Raven, I found another dog to tie outside my lodge. And not some friendly bitch this time. He was a big hulking male, alert and untrusting.

One cold dark dawn, when the Moon of Red Plums was waning, I heard my new watchdog yipping and barking, as though the sun were coming up blue. Frightened by the commotion, I sat up, keeping my robes wrapped tight about me. The lodge was still black and cold. Whatever was happening, was happening outside.

Bending over the fire pit, I blew life into the embers. The stream of air going in and out of my lungs calmed me, like puffing on a Medicine pipe. I had instinctively grabbed for my skinning knife. Now I put it down, feeling safer without a weapon. I would give my enemy no excuse for breaking the peace.

The fire flared up, filling the tipi with light. Cautiously I opened my entrance flap. In the half-light from the fire I could see the dog, still tied to his stake, leaping about, very much alive. Stepping out, I quieted him. A strange whimpering came from where Keeps-the-Fire was tethered, as though she too were frightened. Feeling my way over to her, I patted her black shoulder, saying, "Do not worry, sister, I am here."

My arm came away wet with blood. I wanted to scream, but before I could cry out, Yellow Legs was there, holding me. In his free hand was a pine-knot torch—he had been better prepared for trouble in the night. Seeing the bright red blood in the torchlight sickened me, shattering the secure little world I had imagined for myself. Nothing could ever be the same.

My poor, slashed pony could still walk. The cuts were on her back and flanks. Together we took her to Raven's big tipi, where Yellow Legs kept his stock of Medicines. She did not seem mortally wounded, but she was in terrible pain. I brought fresh water up from the creek, while Yellow Legs gave Raven the inner bark of oak and aspen to pound. He soaked a mixture of white pine, wild cherry, and red medicine root, molding the mess into a plaster, then pasting it over the wounds—explaining that the bark of young, growing trees caused flesh to knit and mend.

Beyond being polite, I confronted Raven, demanding to know who had done it. She sat there, big and stubborn, pounding tree bark, refusing to face me. "People want you to leave. Names do not matter."

Wasichu that I was, names mattered very much to me. "Who accuses me? What have I done?"

She brought her pounding stone down hard, reminding me of Calf Road. "They say you will bring Long Hair again."

"It is the Iron Horse that brought Long Hair." I was tired of repeating this fundamental fact. True, I had secretly wished for Crazy Horse's ambushes to fail, but those private prayers had nothing to do with the Northern Pacific.

Raven would not relent. "Until you came, the Iron Horse was only talk. Twice in one moon Long Hair found us; both times you were there. Women say that if he comes again you will remember that you are Wasichu and go with him. You wear our clothes and paint your face, but in your heart you are still Wasichu. And no one knows what a Wasichu will do."

My eyes blurred, but I could not wipe them without getting bark paste all over my face. Instead I damned her for daring to say what half the camp had to be thinking. Fortunately most of my cursing was in English, a language Raven would not deign to learn. Sheyenna was too polite and formal for how I felt. "Could it have been Calf Road?" I demanded. "You know your sister hates me."

Raven went defiantly about her work, banging rocks with a will—staying stubbornly in the Stone Age. "My sister loves her family. Her sister married a good provider and brave warrior. Calf Road might have become that brave's second wife, living with her sister, married to her brother's friend. Instead Yellow Legs took a Wasichu stranger, splitting her family, throwing Calf Road away."

What lunatics these people were. I had swallowed my pride, staying with Yellow Legs though he had a Sheyenna wife; now that was held against me. All I had done was be an innocent accomplice to bigamy—and keep him from marrying his sister-in-law. Somehow that was a crime. No wonder a hard core inside me insisted the Sheyenna were strangers. "Wasichu" did not mean white skin; it meant a way of living. I could paint my skin, live in a lodge, sleep with Yellow Legs, even have his baby, but I could not change the way I thought. Two winters ago my only relation to these people had been an idiotic desire to lead them into the Christian life. Now I was sitting in a tipi arguing with my sister-wife, a heathen relationship that I had been vaguely aware of but never dreamed I'd experience.

Raven snorted. "You play at being a Person, like They-Fear-Her plays at being a woman. The rest of us do not play at being People. We do not go with war parties. We do not smoke with men in Hunkpapa tipis. To be a wife and Person is too little for you. American Woman must mix in everything—but when things go bad, she wants no blame to stick."

By "Person" and "People" she meant Sheyenna. Sitting in a skin hut, pounding roots with a rock, Raven remained convinced she lived the way we were all supposed to—if we aspired to be Sheyenna. During this whole exchange our husband had sat staring like a cigar-store statue. Now he sighed and broke his silence. "Sometimes one camp is is too small to hold two men's Medicine. My Medicine and this other man's have mixed into a storm."

His Medicine? Another man? Had Yellow Legs been listening? This was between me and the Sheyenna women. Calf Road hated me. Raven thought I had ruined her family. The others all feared me. I managed to croak, "What other man?"

"The man I may not name," Yellow Legs explained. "The man shot by Bloody Knife and Long Hair."

He meant Medicine Bear. I was stunned. We had left that cantankerous brave sitting in a rock pool where the Big Horn flows into the Yellowstone, mixing his Medicine with no one but the fishes. I could not tell if the sight of his wives fighting was making Yellow Legs assert his maleness or if it had merely unhinged him.

"There is nothing for me to do," he concluded. "I must go before I break the Peace of the Camp." He started getting his things together.

I got up too. Yellow Legs was not going to get out of camp a pony's nose ahead of me. Keeps-the-Fire's condition was bad, but no matter what, she must travel. Even if we stayed, the camp would be moving. My pony would be safer traveling with Yellow Legs and me than staying with the camp that held her attacker. Raven could come or go as she pleased.

My sister-wife decided to come. Privately I damned her devotion; by now I thoroughly wanted our man to myself. Yellow Legs helped us take down our tipis. The three of us pulled up pegs and folded lodge covers as fast as I have ever seen it done. From the way we worked, you'd have thought Custer *was* coming.

First light lit the camp. Men and boys padded past on their way to the creek to bathe. Women emerged from the lodges to watch us work. Soon all our pack ponies were loaded. There was still a pile of parfleches, possible-sacks, cooking kettles, and lodgepoles. Keeps-the-Fire of course could carry nothing, so Yellow Legs went to collect his ponies. He came back trailing a delegation of warriors including Comes-in-Sight and Young Two Moons— all trying to talk him into staying. Making no attempt to answer their arguments, Yellow Legs lent us his trail ponies to carry the remaining tipi furnishings, keeping only his war horse and his best buffalo pony.

No one tried to talk me out of leaving. Which was fine. For all I cared, the Lakota Eaters could hold a victory dance and rename the year—the Winter We Got Rid of Our Wasichu. Only Spring Grass came up, offering a parfleche filled with pounded meat for the trail. That was enough to start me crying, though it was only a parting gift, not an invitation to stay.

Yellow Legs turned his back on the dawn gap and Morning Star, leading us out the rear of the camp circle, saying nothing about a destination. Normally I might have looked for a hint from Raven, but we had not spoken since tearing down the tipi. Dawn light touched the white tops of the Big Horns. Black pines covered the slopes below like a blanket of dried blood. We were headed west, into the direction of death and sunset, toward the White Rain Mountains where Sheyenna only went to fight or die. Ahead lay the favorite killing ground of Bad Lodges, Northern Snakes, and Mountain Crows.

Medicine Wheel

MEDICINE—*Hold right hand close to forehead, index and second finger extended and separated; move hand upwards, and at the same time turning hand from right to left so that extended fingers describe a spiral. . . .*

Indians use this sign to signify the mysterious and unknown. God is the Great Mystery rather than the Great Spirit as is usually translated. We have no word that can convey the meaning of "Medicine." Sometimes it shadows forth holiness, mystery, spirits, luck, visions, dreams, prophecies, at others it signifies the concealed and obscure forces of nature, working for good or ill.

—Capt. W. P. Clark, *Indian Sign Language*

KEEPS-THE-FIRE COULD TRAVEL AS LONG AS SHE CARRIED NO weight. I rode Yellow Leg's best buffalo pony, keeping my wounded mare close alongside me, telling her how no more harm would come out of the night, how the hurt she bore was meant for me. She limped along, her back smeared with dried blood and bark paste.

By noon we had crossed Clear Creek. By afternoon, yellow-green foothills reared up in our path. Behind them the black-forested Big Horns rose tier upon tier into the clouds, home to grizzlies, mountain lions, and two-legged hunters. I rode up even with Yellow Legs, asking, "Where are we going?"

"We are going to the Spirit World." He said it as evenly as if the Hereafter were some familiar campground. He had not bothered to paint himself and was wearing plain leggings, a soiled buckskin shirt, and a single eagle feather—a shabby outfit to meet your ancestors in. Did he want to die? Death would be a rather extreme reaction to being driven out by the Lakota Eaters. Raven rode behind him, dutiful and silent.

We turned north, along the line of the old Bozeman Trail, now reduced to the faint remains of wagon ruts, vanishing beneath prairie grass and clumps of sage. Yellow Legs led us up to a flat-topped rise, half surrounded by an open amphitheater of higher elevations. The hilltop was crowned by a sizable rectangle of charred and broken timbers. There he dismounted, sitting down alongside the ashes for a silent smoke. Ragged strands of rain hung over the open prairie.

I fetched fresh water and cut grass for Keeps-the-Fire. The shattered structure on the hilltop was obviously Wasichu and could only be the wreck of Fort Phil Kearny. When I was a mill girl working in a textile factory, Phil Kearny had been Fort Perilous, the westernmost army post in Lakota Country and the scene of daily battles. Seamstresses had tucked folded notes into fresh blue blouses, for unknown soldier boys to open and answer. Now it was a lonely wreck above an abandoned trail. I could just make out the remains of barracks, stables, storehouses, a laundry, a hospital, and a powder magazine—all burned to the ground by Old Bear, Two Moons, and Little Wolf, with the aid of Red Cloud and Crazy Horse. Already it seemed like ancient history.

These days Red Cloud had his own agency on the Lakota Reservation. I had even heard him address the Cooper Union in New York City. Dr. Warren had taken me, passing me off as a niece from Boston, and introducing me to the Oglala chief. The Bad Face leader deeply impressed me, the first Lakota I had seen up close, a tall tomahawk-toting nightmare, with a fierce hook nose and tight lips—but his fingers were extremely graceful when he signed. Watching him made me vow to learn sign language.

His speech in Manhattan was eloquent, invoking the Great Mystery and our common humanity. "We want to keep the peace. Will you help us? You have children. So do we. We want to rear our children well. Will you help us?" I went right up after the speech and offered my services, saying I would come west and teach Lakotas the Christian way. His gratitude was earnest and animated. Still hopelessly green, I did not realize that truly wild Lakotas have as much use for God's "Good News" as they have for French table service. Most braves looked for something altogether different from friendly wide-eyed young blondes.

Crazy Horse did not come to the Cooper Union. As far as I know he never made a moccasin print east of the Big Muddy. He was out there on the prairie, camped by the Rosebud, wanting to be nothing but a wild Lakota.

I had yet to get earnest and animated thanks out of Crazy Horse, but then I had never had the courage to lecture him on the Christian Life.

Yellow Legs stood up and knocked his pipe clean, adding a tiny ash pile to the charred remains of Phil Kearny. We remounted and he led us north, up over Lodgepole Ridge, part of the divide between the headwaters of the Tongue and the Powder. Raven hung back like the good Sheyenna wife she was set on being. Looking about, I asked our husband, "You were here with Crazy Horse?"

"Yes"—he nodded—"I had to see it again, to touch the past, since I fear the future."

"The future is what we make it."

He smiled at me for the first time in that whole bleak day. "A very Wasichu thing to say. But true. Together we will shake the blanket and unfold the future."

Beyond Lodgepole Ridge the land fell away; large rocks dotted the slope where the trail dipped down into a hollow. I could feel the chill of evening coming on. Shadows crept up out of a wild tangle along the creek beds. Yellow Legs leaned forward, drawing his Henry rifle, resting the weapon across his pony's withers. His horse snorted at the cold hard touch of gunmetal. I feared Yellow Legs sensed some danger down in the brush, then I saw he was just remembering. He tapped the stock of his rife. "Here is where I got this gun." I looked down at the rifle decked with feathers.

"It was in the Moon of Popping Trees, many winters ago. Red Cloud and Little Wolf had called everyone together to drive the Long Knives out of Lakota Country. There was a huge winter camp at the headwaters of the Tongue, the biggest I had ever seen—Bad Faces, Oglalas, Sheyenna, Minniconjous, Hunkpapas, No Bows, Burnt Thighs, and Blue Clouds. Red Cloud even took the war pipe over the mountains to the Crows. The Crows listened. Young Lumpwoods and Fox warriors wanted to smoke the pipe and drive the Wasichu away; but Blackfoot, Plenty Coups, and the other Crow chiefs said no. Instead they offered to fight beside the Long Knife chief in the fort."

He straightened a bit in his saddle, turning his head to indicate the blackened fort behind us. "The Long Knife chief sent the Crows away, telling them he had wagon guns and did not need bows and war clubs to protect him. As the Crows rode home, some stopped in our camp to eat and smoke, saying someone should teach the Long Knives what clubs and arrows could do." We were uncomfortably close to Crow Country, so it was heartening to hear of such happy exchanges between hardened enemies.

"The Wasichu chief even gave us a tour of his fort, firing off a wagon gun.

Two Moons told him, 'It is good the Great White Father gives big guns to his children'—all the while laughing behind his eagle-feather fan." Sheyenna do not think that war should be left to children, however well armed.

"What happened then?" I had heard of the Phil Kearny massacre, but not from him.

"The Lakotas made Medicine. The Minniconjous had a man-woman named Dreamer. Wearing a woman's dress, he rode ahead of the Lakotas, zigzagging up the hills on a sorrel horse, blowing on his bone whistle. He came back holding his hands away from his body, like a gambler hiding the gambling bones, saying in a high-piping woman's voice, 'I have caught ten men, five in each hand. Do you want them?' The war chiefs laughed and drove him off, saying, 'Throw them away. See how many we are—ten enemies are not enough.' Twice more Dreamer zigzagged up the hill, coming back with twenty, then fifty enemies. Each time the war chiefs whipped the man-woman's horse, saying, 'Go back. Get more.' Finally Dreamer returned for the fourth time—the Medicine time. He fell off his horse and struck both fists on the ground, the way a gambler does when he plays for the last stick. 'I have fifty enemies in each hand; answer at once: Do you want the hundred in my hands?' Warriors yelled, striking the ground around the man-woman's fists with their coup sticks, saying that a hundred enemies is what we wanted."

He pointed his rifle down toward the thickets by the creek. "Red Cloud's warriors waited in those trees, while Crazy Horse and I rode up to the fort. I was on an fast Appaloosa. He rode a bald-faced, white-footed bay. The Long Knives chased us. A hundred of them came over this ridge and down this hill, drawn like antelope to a Medicine feather, moving and shooting. Here on this slope we rubbed them out. That is how I got this gun."

I shivered as though it really were the Moon of Popping Trees. He seemed to be reliving the past, preparing to die.

When we got to where the pines grew thick, Yellow Legs told us to leave the lodgepoles and most of our supplies, taking only meat for the trail and my small lodge cover. He looked up at the clouds capping the peaks. "We must go as far and as fast as we can while there is still light. This is a dangerous place, but it is the nearest entrance I know to the Spirit World. The entrance itself is farther up, in the Land of Eagles, between the mountains and the sky."

"But why are we going?" Despite the picturesque Medicine talk, the whole business seemed pointless, and incredibly dangerous.

"We are going to take our problems to the Great Mystery. There is nothing else to do with them."

I would have been glad to give my troubles to the Great Mystery, or whoever else would have them, but my Medicine had bottomed out, and I figured we would find nothing in these mountains but grizzly bears and angry Crows. "Why are you taking me? I do not believe in the Great Mystery."

Undisturbed by my blasphemy, he explained, "The Great Mystery is beyond belief or disbelief. It is. You are coming because you are Light-Haired Woman, with more Medicine in you than you know."

I wanted to say I was just plain Sarah Kilory and he should lead me back to Pennsylvania because I was going to have a baby, but I was dead sure I would never see Pennsylvania again.

For three days we worked our way upward, through the foothills and into the peaks. Mountain Crow Country was no place to light a fire, so we dined on cold jerky beneath tall pines that hid the stars. When it was too dark to travel we slept under my lodge cover propped up by branches—not a proper tipi, but cover enough in this black-pine cave. Lying there, with Yellow Legs between us, I remembered Sitting Bull's story about lying between two wives who would not let go. It was not half as funny on a cold mountainside as it had been in a warm Hunkpapa lodge.

When I opened my eyes on the fourth morning, the Medicine morning, fog hung over the mountains. Pines faded into thin white mist. The jerky I had eaten at dinner did not want to stay down, but I knew this nausea was not morning sickness. During the night I had bled all over my Sheyenna underwear. Naturally it was a favorite pair, a southern cloth style Spring Grass had shown me how to fold. My pregnancy had been nothing but wishful thinking. My sole relief was that I had kept that happy fantasy to myself.

I crept about cleaning up, while Yellow Legs and Raven slept. There was no time to cry over something that had been mere heartache and imagination. In camp I would have taken a women's holiday; men would have avoided my tipi, and I would have cooked and worked to please myself. On the trail into Crow Country there were no holidays, no such thing as pleasing yourself.

My husband and sister-wife awoke to find me washing up in a frigid stream. Yellow Legs merely said it was lucky that his bullet Medicine was not bothered by women's blood. I knew his taboos too well to think he was making that up to please me.

Raven stripped and joined me. Yellow Legs moved artfully upstream. I knelt there, naked and shivering, staring straight at my sister-wife, no longer bothering to be decent. Raven sat like a big brown rock parting the swirling ice water sweeping past our calves, climbing up bare hips. She did not even wince. Once I had admired that immobility, wanting it for myself; now I found it infuriating. "I wish you Sheyenna would learn to listen."

"Why, American Woman?" Hugging her knees, she refused to return my stare.

"Because we could be sitting safe in camp if your People had listened to reason instead of blaming me."

She gave me a chilly smile. "Of course, the Wasichu always know better."

Damn it. We did know better, especially about railroads. All the Sheyenna knew about steam on rails was that they did not like it. "We could be doing something to stop the Fire Wagons, instead of freezing our rears in these mountains, proving our Medicine."

"Is that what we are doing?" Raven asked.

I pointed my chin upstream. "That is what he is doing. I am being dragged about for the thrill of it."

"Go back to your Wasichu," Raven advised. "You know them so well. Tell them we do not want the Iron Horse; they never seem to hear anything People say."

"And leave you with Yellow Legs?"

Raven looked toward the sullen peaks. "My home is on the plains. I hate these cold dark mountains; but if my husband says there is an entrance to the Spirit World here, I am willing to help him find it."

Most Buffalo Indians believed in some sort of afterlife. Skeptics like Sitting Bull adopted a wait-and-see policy, but a fair number claimed to have visited it already. An old woman named Picking Bones once told me how she found the Spirit World in a high place. Lying sick in her lodge, Picking Bones heard her dead mother calling. Thinking she too was dead, she got up and left the lodge, walking straight into the cold north wind, until her feet no longer touched the earth. She came to a big bluff that opened like a huge tipi. Inside the bluff she spoke with the dead and saw their camp circle. They thanked Picking Bones for her visit, but sent her packing. When she awoke, she was back in her lodge, fully recovered. But her brother Red Eagle had been sitting beside her the whole time, so her spirit journey was just a fever dream.

We dried and dressed, setting out again. As we climbed, the fog lifted, becoming a gray storm blanket spread over the peaks. A single slash of light to westward came from clear skies over the valley of the Big Horn.

By late afternoon Keeps-the-Fire and I were lagging far behind. We caught up with Yellow Legs just as the sun dropped through the clear space between the clouds and the western edge of the world. He was relaxing on a bit of bare shoulder in the last spot of sunlight. I collapsed next to him. For a time neither of us spoke. I could smell his wet buckskins and the buffalo grease in his graying braids.

Lighting his pipe, he nodded down at a long grassy meadow that we had crossed at noontime. "Wife, watch what happens."

All I saw was a grassy break in the pines, cut by a winding creek. Without warning, a doe and a yearling fawn dashed across the clearing. I waited. A little farther up the meadow a stag emerged from the timbers, crossed the creek, and disappeared into the trees. "Deer do not break cover without a reason," Yellow Legs explained. "Someone is coming up the trail. Watch where it crosses the creek."

I studied the spot where the trail forded the stream, seeing nothing but a bit of empty game trail and a thread of white water. Suddenly two dozen men emerged from the trees, splashing silently through the stream. Dark hair spilled over red-brown war shirts. Maybe half of them had guns. They did not look up, vanishing at once into the timbers.

Yellow Legs rose and put away his pipe. "It is good to know who you share the trail with, even if it is a war party of Mountain Crow. We must reach the entrance tonight. Even Crows cannot track us in the dark, but if we wait for dawn, they will catch us at the brink of the Spirit World." With thunderclouds above us, and Mountain Crow behind us, I was sure we would get to the Hereafter by one path or another.

Raven came down the trail carrying some dead branches, saying the coming rain might cover our tracks. She too had been keeping track of the war party. Only a Wasichu would be blind to happenings back on the trail and halfway down the mountain.

We kept climbing, reaching a high saddle between two peaks. Clouds blotted out the day. Lighting struck on both sides of the saddle, tearing silver rents in the dark sky, dragging thunder behind it. Yellow Legs roped the horses together. I followed by touch, feeling wet pine needles squish against the blunt heavy earth.

Yellow Legs came back down the line, telling us to hobble the horses—the gateway to the Spirit World was just ahead. "We are near, but that is all I know. There is a blackness that sits between me and the future." That I believed. It was too black to see a pine in front of your face.

Giving Keeps-the-Fire a goodbye hug, I hoped the Crow who got her would think her worth keeping. Then we stumbled up the rocky slope. Yellow Legs carried the dry wood Raven had collected, wrapped in a Medicine hide tanned white and scribbled with power signs. I still did not expect to see the Spirit World. I thought that if the Crows caught us we might die. That was bound to be unpleasant, but I was laying no bets on what would come afterward. My father gave me breezy lectures on heaven, where we would spend eternity harping and boozing—never setting eyes on an Englishman. Like most Bog Irish he thought he had done his time in hell. Between his foggy notions of an eternal Hoolihan and my mother's Quaker humanism, I faced death without fixed expectations.

The mountain flattened out. A vague web of white stonework covered the ground ahead; my first thought was of ruined walls or a gateway, but neither Crows nor Lakotas build in stone. Then a flash of lightning turned the world white. In that instant of illumination I saw a huge Medicine wheel sprawled over a hundred feet of open hilltop. Stone spokes radiated out from a central cairn, forming a crude rimless wheel.

I had seen Medicine wheels before, but never one as big as this, and never one in such a high and awesome place. Usually they lay in chains on the prairie with the spokes of one wheel pointing to others hidden beyond the horizon. Some were relatively new, others were as old as the pyramids. I could hardly judge the age of this one, seeing it only in short lightning flashes, like a series of brilliant photographs in stark black and white.

Yellow Legs led us straight to the center of the stone web. We walked single file—what back in Pennsylvania we called Indian style—taking care not to step on the spokes. I did not think there was real magic in the stones, but I was not about to stretch my Medicine, not with lightning striking all around us. Yellow Legs sat down near to the hub. Raven found a place on his right. I sat where my menstrual blood would not mix into his Medicine. This was bound to be an impressive failure, and I did not want any more spoiled Medicine laid in my lap.

Taking the sticks from under his Medicine hide, Yellow Legs started two small fires with the same government match. Crooning over the twin blazes, he tossed in dried herbs. Smoke from the right-hand fire smelled of sage and sweetgrass, while he sprinkled the left-hand fire with a dried weed bearing little yellow flowers. Lighting his pipe from the sage fire, he sat smoking, every so often holding his pipe aloft, letting the storm winds fan it, sharing his smoke with the sky.

Nothing happened. Rock spokes ran through the twin circles of firelight, disappearing into the dark. Somewhere close by in the blackness I heard a few sharp yips followed by a long high-pitched wail. Old Man Coyote calling.

Yellow Legs cocked his head, listening. Raven opened up some wet leather, producing several thin strips of raw meat. Yellow Legs spitted the meat on an arrow and held it over the flames, crooning a particularly monotonous Medicine song. Perhaps the coyote howl encouraged him. To the Sheyenna coyotes are sacred, more sacred than wolves or even mountain lions. Lions are admired for their strength, wolves for their loyalty, but coyotes are revered for their cunning. When we Wasichu first came to Pennsylvania our woods were famous for panthers and wolves. Now the panthers are a memory and the wolves have been pushed up into Canada, but coyotes are becoming common. Nothing curbs them, not guns, not traps, not poison. Old Man Coyote is the only sizable wild animal to increase in numbers and territory since the coming of the Wasichu—a trick the Sheyenna wished they could copy.

I felt sick and sad. Yellow Legs's singsong was putting me to sleep. My underwear was a mess, and my stomach rebelled at getting nothing but raw greens and jerky—making me wish my husband had picked a ritual that did not involve fresh roasted meat.

Lightning crashed close at hand, and a lone scavenger came padding in out of the darkness between the spokes, stopping at the edge of the firelight. The coyote had come up for a handout.

"Sit down," Yellow Legs spoke softly, tossing out a bit of the spitted meat. The coyote sat, expertly snaring the meat in his teeth. How rude, I thought, feeding some mangy animal while I sat salivating on an empty stomach. The beast in no way deserved such attention, being bigger than most, but with the usual dirty-yellow coloring and sly narrow snout. Wolves are so much nobler.

Gulping down his treat, the coyote cocked his head at me, saying, "*American Woman, even you should not grudge a guest.*"

The Bone Game

IT WAS NOT FATIGUE, HUNGER, OR MY MENSES MAKING ME HEAR things. Night and storm had not infected my senses. The coyote was talking. The words did not come out of his throat, which was busy swallowing meat; instead they formed inside my head—just as they had on the day I dragged Medicine Bear home to die. And in English, if you please. Somehow I would have been less surprised to hear the beast speak Sheyenna—but as Mr. Mill tells us, words are formed in the mind, not in the ears, since people hear quite clearly in dreams.

Yellow Legs was sharing my dream, because he told the coyote, "We come seeking a favor from the Great Mystery."

He spoke in Sheyenna, but the beast answered in English. *"Don't expect much of a favor for a stringy bit of meat."*

"The favor I need is big." Yellow Legs drew his doeskin Medicine bundle onto his lap. "And I will trade my bullet Medicine for it."

Things were happening far too fast. A talking coyote was unsettling, but acceptable. I am not overly credulous or superstitious. I believe what I see and hear, without covering my eyes and calling my ignorance science. But what my husband was saying was as alarming as any talking animal. He was going to trade away his bullet Medicine, which had saved his life time and again. Without his Medicine Yellow Legs swore he was a coward, fearing death in battle as much as any sensible man.

The coyote cocked his head and considered. *"What do you want to trade for? What could be worth so much to you?"*

Yellow Legs pointed his chin my way. "My wife has been driven out of camp. I want to find a way for her to come back."

Dumbstruck, I stared at Yellow Legs. I had thought this Medicine journey was just a point of honor with him, to show up the Lakota Eaters. The big idiot never said it was for me.

The coyote yawned, showing a long tongue and sharp teeth. *"Your Medicine means much to you, but very little to me. Bullets drove you Cheyenne across the Mississippi, into Indian Territory and Lakota Country. But bullets do not stop coyotes. We roam where we wish. Nothing stops us, not the Big Muddy, not the white farmlands beyond. All the whites have done is make the world better for me—cutting down the woods, opening up the country, replacing fast rabbits and tough buffalo with stupid sheep and helpless chickens. Save your bullet Medicine for someone who needs it."*

"I have nothing else that is worth so much." Yellow Legs looked weak and shaken.

"Too, too bad, old man." The coyote shook his snout, showing as much remorse as a tarantula. *"To be kind, I will take your Medicine—but only as a stake."* He bared his canines in imitation of a human grin. *"Beat me at the bone game and I will grant your favor."*

"No," Raven hissed. "He means to trick you. You will lose your bullet Medicine and get nothing." Raven was an expert gambler, able to spot a rigged deck as soon as it appeared on the table.

"We need not listen to women." The coyote spread his stubby forepaws. *"How could I hide a bone? You shall beat me easily."*

Yellow Legs held tight to his Medicine. "If winning is so simple, forget the game and just give me what I want."

The coyote smiled. *"There is a wholeness to the world. Nothing comes from nothing. We must not break the circle of creation."*

"Then I must beat you or lose my Medicine?" Yellow Legs wanted to hear all the rules ahead of time, knowing this game would not be played according to Hoyle.

The animal's eyes gleamed. *"Let us each play for ten sticks. But since I can hardly hide a bone, you must beat me or lose the wager. Let me hide first, to show you how easy it will be to win. If you do not like what you see, stop after the first ten sticks and leave this mountain, taking your Medicine with you."*

"I can leave after ten sticks, losing nothing?" The coyote nodded. My husband turned to Raven. "Wife, have you brought your bones and sticks? Nothing would tempt me to use Coyote's."

Raven reluctantly produced her set of four gambling bones and ten sticks. Gambling is a great addiction among Sheyenna women. Girls learn the games in their play; old women digging prairie turnips will gamble away all they have gathered. Sheyenna women will bet on anything, but the bone game is special. Raven's bones were cut from antelope shanks—one pair left plain, the other marked with black paint. The marker sticks were ten inches long, made of stripped white pine painted with red stripes. The sticks usually stood for ponies, but women will bet prized beadwork, the dresses off their backs, the covers off their lodges, and nights with their husbands. She slapped the bones and sticks down, saying, "Remember who you play with."

"If we do not like what we see," Yellow Legs reminded her, "we can walk away after the first ten sticks."

"Use your legs now," Raven replied, "and save your Medicine."

Laying all ten sticks on the ground, Yellow Legs gave the coyote a pair of bones, one marked and the other plain. He spread out his painted buffalo hide and sat down on it, to bring him the luck of the buffalo. "You hide first."

This was the simplest form of bone gambling, where one gambler hides the bones and the other tries to find the unmarked bone. At times I had seen teams play with two sets of bones, and half a camp circle screaming advice. When rival tribes competed, gambling became a battle. During the Winter with Two Truces, the Hunkpapas and Rees took a break from fighting to trade and gamble. Contests grew so heated that the peace of both camps collapsed; several braves ended up shot or stabbed, and Sitting Bull had to arrange a second truce so the women and children taken captive could be exchanged.

This game did not look so memorable. The coyote's attempts to hide the bones were pathetic. He patted them back and forth with his paws, unable to cover them completely. Yet Yellow Legs took each guess seriously. He sat on his knees, swaying and singing a Medicine song. Each time the coyote thrust his paws forward, Yellow Legs would give a grunt; slapping his left hand to his right shoulder, propelling the right hand forward. His right index finger would point to the paw with the unmarked bone. Good bone guessers can gain as much fame as a successful scalp hunter or horse thief, but Yellow Legs's picking took no particular talent. You could *see* the bones peeking out from under the coyote's forepaws.

After each guess Yellow Legs scooped up another stick. Soon he had all ten piled beside him. His opponent grinned. *"See, no need to make an enemy of me—I am so simple to beat. Now, wager your Medicine."*

"I won ten sticks. You must win all ten back to beat me?"

"If I miss even once you win."

"If he guesses all ten, then you lose your Medicine," Raven reminded him.

"Wife, we have no other choice."

"We have the choice of going home—back to the Lakota Eaters. Let American Woman go home to her Wasichu. You have risked enough coming to this high and dangerous place."

I was going nowhere without Yellow Legs, but I said nothing, trying to keep separate from any more sour Medicine.

My husband picked up the bones, tossed them into the air, and began to sing. Raven fell silent. Touching the bones meant he accepted the stakes. He passed one hand over the other, then put both behind his back. His song was filled with jumps, halts, skips; mixing meaningless phrases with hints and challenges, all in time to his hand motions. Bending down until his head grazed the ground, Yellow Legs hid his hands under his chest. When the bones were ready he straightened up, holding his closed fists before him.

The coyote pointed with his left paw at Yellow Leg's left hand. My husband opened both hands; the unmarked bone was in his left. The coyote reached out a paw and rolled one of the ten sticks back over to his side.

Not much of a loss. We needed only one stick to win, and we still had nine. Yellow Legs juggled the bones again, but when he brought them out the coyote guessed right again. Odds were my first arithmetic, and the odds on making ten straight guesses are about the same as turning a pair into four of a kind on a two-card draw. You have to play a long time to see that sort of luck from a straight deck.

But the coyote continued to guess bones as effortlessly as he spoke English. By the time the coyote had won his fourth stick I could see Yellow Legs was shaken. When the coyote collected his fifth stick, Yellow Legs stopped. He set down the bones, refusing to pick them up, turning instead to Raven. "Wife, these are your bones; they will not hide for me."

"Do not blame the bones," Raven replied with a snort. "Coyote has tricked you. Your Medicine goes for nothing, and American Woman has brought ruin on us all. We have been driven from camp, dragged into Crow Country, and you will have no bullet Medicine when the war party comes at dawn."

For once Raven was right. The coyote's guessing was uncanny, and it did not matter whether he could really steal Yellow Legs's Medicine, as long as Yellow Legs believed he could. Without faith in his Medicine, my husband could not fight. Come dawn the Crows would be stalking us. Our tired ponies could never keep ahead of them on mountain trails. Breakfast would be whatever the Crows cared to dish out.

Raven scooped up the antelope bones and slapped them into my lap. "Here, you brought us to this. Finish the game yourself." That was truly unfair. This whole mad trip up to the Medicine Wheel was Yellow Legs's doing. No one asked me where I wanted to be. But grief never changed the cards, and we had to play out this hand. I sat myself down on the painted buffalo hide.

The coyote sniffed at my crotch. *"I will not play with a bleeding woman."*

I looked at Yellow Legs. "Do you know this dog? He is being very familiar."

For the first time since the game began, Yellow Legs smiled. "The dog's name is Old Man Coyote."

I had guessed that. Who could winter in a camp circle without hearing hundreds of Coyote tales? Still it felt good to shove some deliberate Wasichu ignorance in his pointed face, to take the trickster down a notch. He might be a god to the Sheyenna, but he was a mere dog to me. "Play or forfeit. You said nothing about who would hold the bones."

Coyote gave me a look halfway between a snarl and a smile, his yellow gaze piercing down to the bone. *"Don't call me dog. You Wasichu think you own the world, but you don't own me."*

Yellow Legs sang for me, his energy renewed. I stuck the bones beneath my dress, shuffling them the way women do when men are not around. If Coyote disliked women's blood, well and good; let my bleeding help hide the bones. Slipping the unmarked bone into my right hand, I tried to blank my mind. Coyote could put English sentences into my head; perhaps he also picked thoughts out of my brain. I brought my clenched fists out of my dress.

Coyote pointed with his right paw. I opened my hands, and he took another stick. We had four left.

Yellow Legs sang again. This time I tried to lie, pretending to pass the bones, picturing the unmarked bone in my left hand while it stayed in my right. I held out my hands, knuckles up, bones hidden. Coyote gestured with his paw, pointing to my right hand, winning another stick. Now we had three left.

He had made seven straight guesses. The odds against that are well over a hundred to one. I looked down at the three painted sticks in front of me. The odds against three more correct guesses were a good deal less, about the same as pairing a lone ace with a two-card draw. Somehow I had to make those odds work for me. I had to hide that second ace. This time I paid no attention to the bones, concentrating on nothing. What my brain did not know, Coyote could not steal.

Coyote hesitated and licked his lips, yellow eyes looking me over. I hummed to myself, a song that had sustained me through mind-numbing months of factory work:

> *A penny for a spool of thread,*
> *A penny for a needle,*
> *That's the way the money goes,*
> *Pop! Goes the weasel.*

He pointed right. I opened my hands and there was the unmarked bone. Two sticks remained. I started shuffling again, resisting the temptation to follow the bone, losing track of it under my dress, singing to myself—becoming that little girl I had been, far from home, forced to keep track of hundreds of whirling spindles, twelve hours a day, six days a week:

> Potatoes for an Irishman
> A doctor for the measles,
> A fiddler always for a dance,
> Pop! Goes the weasel.

Again Coyote picked right. Again the bone was there.

Yellow Legs took our last stick and pounded it into the ground in front of me. This was something the losing side always did when they were down to one stick. He sang a song to the stick, calling it his pony, telling it to be strong, to carry us home. All the time I shuffled blindly. When I brought my hands out, Coyote hesitated even longer. I sang aloud:

> Round and round the mullberry bush,
> The monkey chased the weasel.
> The monkey thought it was all in fun . . .

I pulled back my hands, sticking them under my dress, shuffling again. I wanted to force Coyote into a quick pick, giving him no time to work his Medicine. My hands came out again. This time Coyote pointed right at once.

I opened my fist and Coyote howled. The unmarked bone had settled in my left hand.

> Pop! Goes the weasel.

I jerked the painted stick out of the ground, holding it tightly in my fist an inch from Coyote's pointed face. "We win."

He howled again. "I should never have played with a Wasichu. You did not play the game, you let the odds win for you."

I kept the red-striped stick clenched tight. "No rule says I had to know where the bone was. Now you must help us."

"It was blind luck. You did not beat me, the numbers did."

"Numbers are the way to win," I taunted him. "There is more to a game than a poker face."

"And there is more to a game than winning." He gave me a sly sideways smile. *"You won, but now remember, whatever you ask for you must live with."*

I considered. Whatever I asked for must be as all-embracing as possible. After all this effort I could not demand something small. Exhaustion and euphoria had washed away all my doubts. At that moment I thought Coyote could grant whatever I asked. Why not? Yesterday I had been fairly certain animals could not talk; now I was bargaining with one. Besides, Coyote seemed similarly confident. With history in my hands, I could imagine only one thing that would solve all our problems. "You must stop the railroad."

Coyote's eyes narrowed. Raven looked startled. Yellow Legs took my hand, saying, "I thought you most wanted to come back to camp." Raven had probably feared the same thing.

Holding fast to the painted stick, I told my husband. "If the railroad comes, we will all be ruined. Soldiers will come again next summer, and the next—I would be driven out again. No railroad means no soldiers. Once everyone sees that, I will be free to return." My Medicine felt so great, only a locomotive could stop it.

"All the railroads?" Coyote looked suddenly humble. *"There are so many."*

My enemy was the Northern Pacific. What did I care if the Union Pacific met its schedules, or if the Atchison, Topeka, and Santa Fe was ever completed? The eastern lines were no threat. The B&O and Reading Railroad could keep running. I felt a surge of generosity toward the many thousands who held railroad stocks and the multitudes who rode the rails daily. Megalomania is an amazing thing. "Not all the railroads," I decided, "just the Northern Pacific. I want it stopped dead where it is. I want no tracks laid in Lakota Country."

Coyote threw back his head and howled. Lighting struck behind him, turning the prairie wolf into a gray silhouette. Storm winds whirled around me, and I felt my body being lifted up. Coyote, Yellow Legs, and Raven vanished, along with the Medicine Wheel. With nothing around me but night and air, I held tight to the red-striped stick.

Chelton Hills

POP GOES THE WEASEL INDEED. NO ONE IS REQUIRED TO BELIEVE this, but I was flying—sailing through storm clouds and thunder. An alarming sensation, like riding in an open train car across a railroad bridge, then suddenly having the train and trestle disappear. (Some time later, in a dinner conversation with General Custer, he told me what it was like to ride in an army balloon under fire, quite confident that I had never felt the like—the man was prone to such misjudgments.) Fortunately, flying had a kind of dreamy detachment, a feeling of hallucination that kept my first flight from being as scary as it should have been. I had no thought of vast heights or hard landings. Only the stick in my hand seemed solid and real.

Suddenly night and storm vanished, jerked away like a black curtain in a magic act.

No longer soaring, I found myself sitting on a thick carpet in a warm, well-lit room. Lamplight shone off tidy surfaces covered with giltwork and curios. It was a large room in a very Wasichu house, ornate and luxurious, a mansion, really, wonderfully decorated, with paneled walls, tall draped windows, massive furnishings, and grand portraits. For the first time in two years, I sat in civilized surroundings, overwhelmed by light and warmth—as if I had been plucked from the dark peak and whipped straight to Valhalla for a snap interview with the gods. Only this Olympus smelled of lampblack and cigar smoke.

The huge drawing room had a dreamlike familiarity, reminding me somewhat of Sitting Bull's tipi, though the room was big enough to hold a dozen lodges. At the far end sat a group of men, talking and smoking. They too seemed familiar. Not wanting to offend, I sat looking into my lap, watching

103

the men from under my lashes, wondering when women would come with food.

Their conversation revolved around a stubby, round-shouldered little man with a cigar clamped in his teeth. Decent clothes only made him seem overdressed. Like Sitting Bull, he was not much to look at, but I recognized him at once. Every Wasichu in America knew him. He was our most honored living citizen, the savior of the Republic, Commander in Chief of the Union Army, the first full General since Washington, and now President of the United States. I had seen Ulysses Simpson Grant's picture so many times that the man looked like a living, breathing portrait.

Sitting next to Grant was someone nearly as surprising, someone I had met before. (You never expect to renew passing acquaintances in a Medicine vision.) It was Jay Cooke, the railroad and banking magnate. His face was as lean as Grant's was round, with a full curly beard. Deep-set eyes flicked back and forth, keeping watch on the conversation. All at once I knew why the enormous room seemed so familiar. This was where I had first met Mr. Cooke. I was back where I had never expected to be, in the Keystone State of Pennsylvania, sitting cross-legged on the carpet of Jay Cooke's drawing room in Chelton Hills.

When I decided to go off and teach Indians, relatives from the Old Meeting House in the city arranged for me to accompany a delegation of Sheyenna on a tour of Mr. Cooke's mansion. They wanted me to spend time with some real wild Indians before I went west. A sensible suggestion, which proved ludicrously useless—nothing in Philadelphia prepared me for the reality of Lakota Country. Though I knew absolutely no Sheyenna at the time, I was taken on as an interpreter. Stone Calf, the southern old man chief who headed the delegation, thought it natural to have a sturdy young woman along—in case there were gifts to be carried. He had come East hoping to see the good side of civilization, and agreeable young women impressed him far more than street cars and indoor plumbing.

Mr. Cooke had a bug about Indians. He had named his estate "Ogontz," after an old Wyandot chief who used to come to the Cooke farm when he was a boy and sleep in their barn. The farm was on Wyandot land, and Chief Ogontz liked to visit his old home from time to time. Jay Cooke grew up to make millions off the Civil War, but he never lost his bug for Indians. Every chief who came through Philadelphia got a tour of Ogontz.

Stone Calf had stood in this very drawing room, making a polite speech against the railroads, explaining that the Sheyenna had no goods to transport. It seemed obvious to him that the tracks should skirt the Sheyenna hunting grounds so Wasichu could ride in peace, without being bothered by

People and buffalo. Stone Calf had sounded wise and kindly, but Mr. Cooke was busy being nice to me; I doubt he heard half of the speech. He certainly did not run out and sell his millions in railroad stock. Jay Cooke, the friendly millionaire who loved Indians, was also the head of the Northern Pacific Railroad—the man whose name appeared at the bottom of the handbill I had read in Sitting Bull's tipi, promising "humane annihilation" of the Lakotas.

Grant, Cooke, and their comfortable cronies ignored me completely, though I was sitting on their drawing room carpet, making no special at-tempt to be invisible. But by now I was thoroughly used to being ignored while men smoked and talked. Grant's quiet deliberateness reminded me of Sitting Bull. The President and the Hunkpapa chief had much in common. Both were shrewd, daring, but unprofessional soldiers and peacemakers, who had risen to the top through sheer ability—men who shone on horseback but looked shabby in a drawing room.

Every so often, Mr. Cooke gave jovial advice on some point of business, and the President nodded sagely—a sight that made me smile. "Sam" Grant was a military genius and administrative dynamo, who had no more money sense than a mule. Before the war he had been a forty-year-old part-time pin setter in a bowling alley. Like Sitting Bull he was a leader and a fighter, whose idea of finance was to give his friends and family whatever they needed. Whenever he left the government payroll he invariably landed in bankruptcy.

Cooke was too polite to point this out to the President, merely saying, "Sam, I won't lie to you. Since the Credit Mobilier collapsed, you would think railroad shares carried the cholera. We've put up nine million in bonds, with a fifty percent stock bonus, laid more than six hundred miles of track, and opened ten million acres to settlement—but found precious few takers."

Grant grimaced. His administration had been half gutted by the Credit Mobilier scandal. From the vice president down, politicians had fattened off the looting of the Union Pacific. Now the papers were baying for blood.

A dark young man in a smart coat sat at Cooke's elbow. Swirling his brandy glass, he seemed to shift the subject. "Did anyone ever tell about that second night in the Wilderness, during the last year of the War?"

Oh, no, I thought—first the smoking, now the kill talk. Where were the women with food? Did anyone know that I had eaten nothing all day but jerky and greens? Even Cooke looked askance at this new subject—he had financed the War, not fought in it.

But the young fellow insisted on telling his war story, saying how the

Army of the Potomac had crossed the Rapidan and spent two horrible days in a suffocating morass of scrub pines and Confederate trenches. "We pounded the Rebs and the Rebs pounded us, with not an inch of progress to show for thousands of dead and dying. Every two paces there was a tree and every second tree hid a graycoat sniper. The woods themselves caught fire from the constant shooting, burning the wounded where they lay, turning things into a fair imitation of hell." Cigar smoke billowed around him, bringing a bit of those burning woods to Ogontz Estate.

"We lost almost twenty thousand men trying to break out, and ended up not a step closer to Richmond. Whole regiments cracked, cowering in the woods or firing at each other. By that second night I figured we were pretty well licked." The bankers shifted uncomfortably, knowing Grant had been in personal command during the Wilderness fighting. This did not sound like the sort of inspiring war story they were used to. Only the President seemed unperturbed, but he had gone through those two ghastly days, and no doubt seen worse.

Ignoring his audience's horror, the young storyteller plowed on. "When the order came to pack up and pull back, we all assumed we were retreating. I thought, 'Well, well, old Bobby Lee beat us again—back to Washington and warm beds.' In the dead of night we shuffled up to Chancellorsville Tavern. There the road forks. The left fork led north, toward home. The right fork went deeper into that god-awful tangle that had beaten us time and again."

He leaned forward, stabbing his cigar at the seated bankers. "Waiting at that fork was a hobo on horseback in a worn blue coat, sitting on a mare so poor that even the horse artillery would not have her. That dusty man on a dusty horse motioned the regimental guides down that right-hand road, sending us south again, around Bobby Lee's right flank, deeper into that piney morass, to keep on fighting for who knew how long. And as each company made the turn the men began cheering, wave after wave of hurrahs. They cheered so loud and long the Rebs thought it was a night attack, and opened fire into the darkness." The young man settled back in his seat. "Now that stubborn fool on a condemned cavalry nag is president of these United States."

Grant had a half smile on his face—for years now he had heard himself made the hero of a hundred war stories. Tapping Cooke on the knee, he told the banker, "Persistence beats anything. It beats bravery and education. It even beats genius. If bravery, education, and genius could have won the war, Robert E. Lee would be President of the Confederacy right now." Grant had graduated far down on the West Point list, while Lee stood at the top of his class. If Grant ever felt poorly about that comparison, Appomattox had done something to even out the contest. "Persistence saved the Union. Now we'll have to see how much persistence the banks have."

I blinked, unable to stand the sentiment and the cigar smoke. When I opened my eyes the lamps were out and the curtains were pulled back. Morning light streamed in through tall windows looking out on an Italian garden. Only one man remained—Jay Cooke, sitting alone, leafing through a pile of telegrams, giving them a grim look that meant the news was bad. A carriage rattled up on the garden gravel. Mr. Cooke slapped on his hat and stormed out. His carriage spun away from the manse.

Storm winds caught me up again. I was swept outside, to where I could see the carriage crossing the long sweep of lawns, leaving Chelton Hills headed toward Germantown and Philadelphia. I went higher, until the great fifty-room manor dwindled, lost in green shrubbery and sculpted trees. The winds carried me westward, over the dawn-lit fields and waking towns of the Republic. Philadelphia dipped below the horizon, and I could see the whole circle of the world: rivers and woodlands, then prairies pushing up a rumpled mountain blanket. The sun ran backward, coming to rest on the eastern edge of the world.

Suddenly the winds would no longer hold me, and I fell with the morning rain toward dark peaks below. Frightened for the first time, I shut my eyes and screamed.

When I opened my eyes I was sitting between the spokes of the Medicine Wheel. The twin fires were out. Dawn was coming up. Two antelope bones and nine gambling sticks were scattered in front of me. I still held the tenth stick in my rigid right hand, the stick that had carried me from the White Rain Mountains to the outskirts of Philadelphia. I had nothing else to show for for my first Medicine journey.

Wet and numb, I watched Coyote swing his rear toward me and trot off, flicking his tail.

"What happened?"

"We are waiting for you to tell us," Yellow Legs answered. "You sat half the night, not moving since the bone game ended. We thought you were on a spirit journey."

"You yelled out," Raven added, "just as the rain began to fall."

I shuddered. Cold wet drops splashed onto my cheeks. "I suppose I dreamed." I was too tired to give a clear accounting. Tangible evidence faded into memory. Ogontz was gone. So was my talking coyote. No one outside of an asylum or lodge circle would give my story half a hearing.

"Come." Raven stood up, ready to go with barely a rest. "The Crows will be up and moving."

"Can they follow our trail in the rain?" I craved any excuse to sleep.

Yellow Legs was in heartless agreement with her. "They will come this far. Only two pony trails leave this spot: the one we came up, and the one that leads westward."

We set out down the western pony trail. Keeps-the-Fire was still weak from yesterday's climb, and I promised her we would both sleep soon, no matter what the cost.

The sun rose higher, burning away the rain. Yellow Legs stopped to rest the horses at a bend in the trail, where the ground fell away and I could see the whole west slope of the Big Horns, sleeping beneath a thick pine blanket. The air was wonderfully clear, all the way to the Rockies. Wisps from last night's storm trailed off distant peaks rising toward the Backbone of the World.

I thought, This is what eagles see every day. Having spent the night conversing with a coyote and visiting the gods, I felt ready to judge the lives of eagles.

Yellow Legs interrupted my sleepy rapture, pointing with his rifle sight. "There is a big village of Mountain Crows below us."

"Where?" I could see only air and trees.

"There." My husband pulled me closer, having me look along the rifle barrel. Cold metal against my cheek made me concentrate. "See where the air is cloudy with the haze of campfires." I saw it. The air flickered with something opaque.

His hand stayed on my shoulder. "Early morning is the best time to look for smoke. The air is still clear, and a fire smokes most when it is first lit, especially if the wood is wet." From his even tone we might have been discussing bird migration.

"How do you know they are Mountain Crows?" All I saw was a slight smudge above the trees.

"Who else would make so much smoke in these mountains?" His hand tightened. "Here only Wasichu and Crow do not care how much smoke they make. This smoke is not the thick rope of a Wasichu campfire; it spreads, like the cook fires of a Crow village."

"There is more smoke behind us." Raven pointed with her chin. Turning, I saw two broken pillars of smoke rising from the table above the Medicine Wheel, two tall stacks of puffs, as if someone were smothering twin fires with wet blankets, then flipping the blankets back to free the smoke.

Yellow Legs scowled, setting his Medicine rifle across his lap. "Two fires means a returning war party, trying to attract attention in the camp below." Raven agreed, well accustomed to the antics of returning war parties. Rain had streaked her face paint, making her look old and fretful.

With the war party right behind us we had to keep moving, even though the only pony trail led down toward the big village in the valley. Danger ahead did not mean we should wait for death from behind. Yellow Legs had only six shells for his Medicine gun and a like number of loads in his pistol. There were twice that many Crows behind us, and even I could have followed the tracks our tired mounts made in the muddy trail.

The pony trail wound down to a forested meadow, backed by a stream. It seemed terribly absurd for pain and death to be stalking us through sunlit forest, showing the first yellows of autumn. I wanted to tumble off my horse onto the meadow, to sleep away the morning, losing myself in the blue bowl of sky, resting up for a lazy afternoon. What would two dozen Crow warriors do if they found a white woman napping in the bear grass? Hard to tell with Crows, who were tolerably friendly toward Wasichu, except when excited.

On the far bank of the stream we found a mass of pony tracks. Yellow Legs announced that several Crows had watered their horses here around sunrise. "More could come at any moment."

Raven started to swing out of the saddle. "We must abandon the ponies and wade downstream to a spot that won't take tracks. The Crows will be glad enough to get our mounts."

Yellow Legs stopped her with a gesture. "The Crows know all the places to enter and leave these streams. They will fan out on both banks and find our trail. It is better for us to ride straight into the Crow lodge circle, trusting to our Medicine.

She gave him a stern look. "I trust your skill in the woods more than the generosity of Crows." Crow hospitality only extended to Sheyenna who came in peace. Running in ahead of a war party was risky. It would be up to the Crows to judge between us and the claims of those coming behind us, and Crows do not insult your intelligence by pretending to be impartial.

"Either way there is risk." Yellow Legs reminded her.

Raven snorted. "I am not anxious to become the second wife of some Crow." If they went into the Crow camp the worst she could generally expect was captivity, but she was a One-Man Woman, too proud to do anything but share her husband's fate.

Listening to them argue, I knew there was a solution that combined the best of both plans. "There is a surer way," I told them, "one with no risk."

They both seemed surprised to hear such a notion coming from someone so green as me. Raven's eyes narrowed. "Do not suppose you can cheat the Crows as easily as you cheated Coyote."

I looked right at Raven. "It will not be easy for me. You two take to the stream. I will ride into the Crow camp with the ponies. The war party will follow the pony tracks. If I make it into camp, they will not harm a Wasichu." I was giving Raven everything she wanted most. She could have Yellow Legs to herself and a chance to get out of Crow Country alive.

Our husband tried to brush aside my plan. "No, I have my bullet Medicine and my Medicine gun. We beat Coyote; what are a few Crows?" But he was one tired man, far from home and harried by Crows—no match for two determined women. Splitting up was the only plan that promised to save us all. Raven saw that at once. Working together, his two wives wore him down. Under protest he dismounted, standing calf-deep in the swift cold water.

I leaned down and kissed him, not caring what Raven thought of this Wasichu farewell. Warriors are not supposed to be moved by women's feelings, especially before the enemy, but Yellow Legs was too shaken for such stoic nonsense. He returned my kiss, wrapping his arms so tight around me I feared he might never break away. "We will be together," he promised. "Do not try to return alone. I will come for you in the place where we first met. Wait for me there."

Shaking with exhaustion, I nodded. "Where we first met. I will be there."

Raven stood waiting in the chilly water. No goodbyes were needed between us. Still Yellow Legs would not let go. He pressed his Medicine rifle into my hands. "Keep this. It will protect you until I can come for you."

I tried not to take the gun, insisting he would need it. But he stepped quickly away. "I am going." He and Raven turned, heading downstream, leaving me looking helplessly at the backs of their wet buckskins. That was a more usual Sheyenna good-bye.

For a long time I sat crying atop my painted pony, while the stream boiled past—feeling the feathered rifle in my lap, its cold weight a welcome reminder that Yellow Legs would indeed come for me. Eventually I stopped blubbering and herded the ponies up the far bank. If my sacrifice was going to make any sense, I had to get down to the Crow camp, leaving a broad trail for the war party to follow.

Crow Country

For a time the man lived happily with his two wives, but one day the black-haired buffalo wife began to argue with the yellow-haired elk wife. Their disputes grew so bitter that one lodge could no longer hold them both, and the yellow-haired wife left him.

—Cheyenne lodge tale

AS I RODE BETWEEN THE TREES I UNBRAIDED MY HAIR, LETTING it hang limp like wet grain. I could hear a magpie chattering and the far-off drumming of a woodpecker. At the next stream I washed away whatever paint the rain had spared. The splash of frigid water helped wake me. Swaying to my feet, I scrambled up the bank and started stripping off my doeskin dress. It was terrifying to fumble about, half naked and all alone, but I desperately needed to be wearing blue calico.

Still no Crows came. Pulling the sky-blue dress over my head, I kicked off my moccasins and leggings. A couple of the horses had Sheyenna-style headstalls, so I took them off and tossed them into the creek; Crows just loop a lariat around their pony's lower jaw. Keeps-the-Fire had a proper leather bridle, very Wasichu-looking. Now nothing about me was clearly Sheyenna, except for the feathered rifle cradled in my lap with six rimfire cartridges in the magazine—though I doubted the gun would fire for me the way it did for Yellow Legs.

I was absolutely on my own for the foreseeable future. Not alone among others like at Crazy Woman Creek—but utterly dependent on my own resources. And right now my most prized resource was white skin. The most ignorant and upcountry Crow warrior had to know at once that I was totally Wasichu, and any harm done me would bring down the wrath of the Long Knives. On the west slope of the Big Horns, being white was better than bullet Medicine. This was Sweetwater County, Wyoming Territory. Local law and public opinion favored harsh and indiscriminate reprisals for crimes against whites, especially female whites. Wasichu figured they had done well if they punished the right tribe, and even thrashing the wrong tribe was considered a useful object lesson. Such injustice had disgusted me; now I depended on it. Any scruples had been scared out of me.

Despite all these preparations my confidence evaporated when I saw my first Crow coming. He was tall, and would have towered over me if he had not been on foot, walking his horse. His hair was ruffed up in front, like a thick-bristled paintbrush, making him look even taller and more barbaric. Yellow paint covered half his face, zigzagging down across his bare chest. Here was a prime specimen of what newspapers comically called a "peaceful" Indian, six feet plus of touchy painted-up savage, with a razor-sharp hatchet, a horn-backed bow, a pistol in his belt, and a face that could split kindling.

I tried not to pay him the least attention, holding my head high as I rode past, like a Laramie Club Lady seriously lost on an outing. I was leading Keeps-the-Fire and half a dozen ponies, so it was impossible to hear if he fell in behind me. I fought the impulse to look back. When dealing with a strange warrior you must pretend to know what you are doing. Pit your Medicine directly against his. Act weak, and he will think he can do what he wants with you. Act brave, and about the worst you can expect is that a coward will put a hatchet in your back.

Suddenly the man was beside me, mounted up and jabbering away in Crow. Now he did tower over me. Crow is supposed to be easy to pick up; a language somewhat related to Lakota, much as English is related to Russian. He might as well have been speaking Russian, for all I could make of it.

Looking straight ahead, I brought my right hand up to my breast and made the curved belly sign that meant pregnant, then I touched fingers to my nose and mouth and brought them down with a waving motion, imitating the flow of blood from a lung-shot buffalo. That shut him up. Taken together those signs told him he had addressed a strange, menstruating woman, putting his Medicine in serious jeopardy. I had saved him from further error and contamination with women's Medicine. Hopefully he felt somewhat in my debt. Certainly he would not think of touching me.

The brave kicked his pony into the lead and we rode toward camp. Now it was his turn not to look back. As I studied his tall handsome torso, blue breakfast smoke drifted between the pines. Then Crow tipis appeared, spread over a small meadow, the bare tops of their poles rising far above the lodges, forming enormous hourglasses. Everything seems tall in Mountain Crow Country—the land of high pines, big horns, elk, grizzly, and tall tipis.

Crows crowded around. I sat on my pony, holding tight to the rifle in my lap. The brave kept his back to me, riding right into the crowd before turning around. He was a careful fellow, getting credit for bringing me into camp then distancing himself from any complications I created.

The proud brown faces surrounding me looked fully able to express violent hostility if need be. Some of the women were tattooed, with dots and circles on their foreheads and noses, or a thin line from lips to chin. Panther claws hung from the men's necks, and the tipi next to me was fringed with scalp locks. The Crows were not nearly as domesticated as tourist circulars advertised. Wind twirled the coup feathers on the Medicine rifle in my lap while I wondered when the war party would arrive.

A big woman took hold of my bridle. Her sheepskin dress was dyed blue-black, trimmed with ermine and studded with rows of elk teeth, very artful. She said "How" with an easy smile, showing she was used to speaking to whites. I howed her right back, but this happy exchange led nowhere. "Howdy" seemed to be the English word she was most comfortable with.

I signed, "My horses are thirsty." This was not strictly true, but it hinted that the Crows were free to be hospitable, and it established some property rights on the horses. Smiles appeared. I saw I should have signed sooner. Everyone seemed relieved—there being nothing worse than having a dumb Wasichu on your hands, needing to be fed but not knowing how to ask.

The big woman in the sheepskin dress helped me dismount, turning my ponies over to a bunch of boys, who scampered off, happy to be suddenly horse rich. Clearly this was a go-ahead woman who enjoyed taking charge. Signing that her name was Magpie Outside, she led me to her lodge.

At the entrance I saw men's things, so I made the signs for menstruation. Magpie Outside was pleased to find me so polite, signing that her husband had no Medicine that would be harmed by my bleeding. As word of my condition spread through the crowd, men began to drift away. I was fast becoming a woman's problem, which suited me fine.

Magpie Outside set up my little lodge alongside hers, with the aid of a woman named Cherry, who had brown hair and hazel eyes but was otherwise all Crow. The Crows had come up into these mountains to cut new lodgepoles, so there were plenty of old poles lying about. And Crow tipi poles are so tall that one of theirs easily made two of mine.

Right away my Sheyenna training betrayed me when I insisted on using a three-pole base. Cherry signed, "You make your lodge like a Lakota." She was right. Crows, Flatheads, and most "friendly" tribes west of the mountains used four main tipi poles, while Sheyenna, Lakota, and similar "hostiles" used three.

I put on my best idiot Wasichu grin, pretending not to care. A white person was free to ignore anything friendly Indians considered important.

About the time we were done the war party came parading into camp trailing dogs and children. Drums pounded and pipes wailed. Two scouts dressed in wolfskins led the way, their faces blackened with charcoal, followed by the men who had counted coup, waving scalps tied to pine branches. Though they must have seen innumerable returning war parties, the Crows quickly lost interest in me. I was a prime mystery—but the truth is that we Wasichu are always doing things a Crow could hardly comprehend. If a whole Christian women's choir marched into camp, buck naked and singing "Nearer My God to Thee," the Crows would no doubt be impressed; but they would still have to get on with the normal business of hunting buffalo, stealing ponies, and scalping Lakotas.

Happy to slip away in the shuffle, I crawled into my three-pole tipi and fell into a grateful coma—not caring if the Crows turned ugly and set on me in my sleep.

I did not get up until dusk. By then Magpie's husband was on hand, sitting in front of his wife's tipi, toying with a bourbon bottle. I saw at once why Magpie Outside was so friendly and familiar with whites. Her husband was a half-breed, as dark and bowlegged as a Crow brave, but bearded like a Wasichu, wearing a wide-brimmed hat and the plain-type shirt issued to Indians as a treaty annuity. He said his name was Mitch Buoyer, but I had already heard of him. This was Two Bodies, the half-breed the Lakotas called for by name during that second disastrous fight with Custer. Mitch had a ready smile and an easy open manner that won friends even among enemies.

I introduced myself as Sarah Kilory, using my Christian name for the first time in over a year. It sounded strange.

"Is it Miss or Mrs. Kilory?"

"Mrs. Kilory." Why not? I was married, wasn't I?

Mitch took a thoughtful sip from his bottle, then offered me some. Watered whiskey is the national beverage of the western territories—it keeps you warm and happy, without going flat or taking up room in your pack. I took a pull out of politeness, but I did not want the whiskey answering Mitch's questions.

Taking the bottle back, he told me, "Mrs. Kilory, I have seen some strange things come out of the Big Horns, but not a white woman herding painted ponies and carrying a Cheyenne Medicine gun. Not a one. Do you mind if I ask how you got here?"

I was too tired to invent some fanciful story that totally denied my past; nor would the truth go down well. If I started babbling about gambling with Coyote and flying to Chelton Hills, Mitch was going to mark me down as another prairie-crazed white woman in desperate need of incarceration. So I stuck to simple lies, letting Mitch fill out my story with assumptions, saying I was parted from my husband "along the Bozeman north of Phil Kearny."

"I am not surprised." Mitch shook his head. "The Bozeman is more than dangerous. There are Cheyenne camped along Crazy Woman Creek and Oglalas over on the Rosebud. Crazy Horse and Sitting Bull hit an army column on the Yellowstone twice in the last month." I said I had heard the same. He asked to handle my husband's rifle, looking over the coup feathers and the beadwork on the stock. "Mind telling me where you got this gun?"

Living among the Lakota Eaters, I had forgotten what it was like to be questioned about your every action—and I could no longer draw a blanket of silence around me the way a Sheyenna woman would. I told Mitch, "My husband gave it to me for protection. He got it in a fight, before we met."

Mitch grinned broadly. "That must have been a humdinger of a fight. That Henry has got more coup feathers on it than most braves can tote. The Cheyenne who owned it was a heap big Injun." I took that as compliment to Yellow Legs. Mitch gave me back the gun, saying, "Don't know many Kilorys. What is your husband's first name?"

"He's called John." That danced around the truth. All Indian men were commonly called John; people say John Indian, just as they say John Farmer.

"John Kilory. Cannot say I know the man, but I would not mind meeting him. Any man who could get a gun like that must have stories to tell. What were you doing on the Bozeman anyway? It's no spot for a Sunday ride."

"Hunting, mostly—buffalo, antelope, anything but bear."

"Ma'am"—Mitch scratched his head in disbelief—"there are far safer places to hunt than along the Bozeman. Sioux don't like sharing their hunting grounds; can't see why they should make an exception for you." Sioux is what whites call Lakotas; Lakota means "allies," but Sioux means "enemies."

Cherry and Magpie Outside served us meat and beans. Mitch waved a spoon toward my lodge, wanting to know all about how I had learned to pitch a tipi Lakota-style. By this time I had a pat story, more or less the truth. I gave a short lecture on the advantages of a three-pole tipi, telling how it's more stable and less work to put up, then added casually, "I learned to pitch tipis at the Red Cloud agency. I originally came west to teach the Bad Faces the Christian way."

Mitch translated, and my ambition provoked general hilarity. "Do not waste Jesus talk on the Bad Faces," signed Magpie Outside, "everyone knows

Lakotas are neither as friendly nor reliable as Crows." Cherry agreed that all Lakotas were lazy and hopeless—both were making fun of Mitch, who was French-Lakota. He accepted the ribbing with alcoholic good humor, then asked where I was headed and how in hell I hoped to get there.

I told him I aimed to get to the forts along the Missouri and rejoin my husband, making it sound like "Mr. Kilory" was a scout of some sort. This too was true, as far as it went. Yellow Legs said that we should rendezvous at the place where we had first met. But Sheyenna don't have our fixed notion of geography. We had first met in Red Cloud's camp, thirty or so miles below Laramie. Yellow Legs did not want me to return to the particular bit of empty prairie where the Bad Faces had wintered. He wanted me to find the Bad Face camp, wherever it happened to be pitched, and stay with Red Cloud until he came for me. This was not so hard as it sounds. Red Cloud and his Bad Faces were agency Lakotas, who camped where the Wasichu could feed them. Once I got to the Missouri forts the army could direct me. Being old enemies, the Long Knives followed every Bad Face movement. So I told Mitch I needed to get to the Missouri forts by the shortest route—the sort of demand you would expect from a white woman alone in the wilderness: simple, direct, and wildly impractical.

Mitch's helpful curiosity vanished. "Mrs. Kilory, the Missouri is three hundred miles away, through land that is a killing ground for Crows, Lakotas, Blackfeet and a dozen other tribes. Only a lunatic would risk a ride like that." The easiest way to kill a man's interest is to get him arguing. Once he is sure you are wrong, he's honor-bound to stop listening. Mitch told me how they were headed west to the Crow agency. "From there it is a short trip through the pass to Fort Ellis and Bozeman, where a stage can carry you to the Union Pacific railhead in Utah."

A most sensible suggestion, but it meant heading off in the wrong direction, and going more than a thousand miles to get to the Missouri. I was bent on being unreasonable. Lakota Country dragged at my moccasins, but I could not tell Mitch why.

Magpie Outside took her husband's side, saying the Yellowstone country was too wild and dangerous for whites—even the cavalry could not cross it. "Last summer the Long Knives claimed they would ride the Elk River, from Crow Country to the Big Muddy, saying they were the whirlwind and nothing would turn them back. But the whirlwind stopped when it got to Sioux Country." She drew her finger swiftly across her throat, making the universal sign for Lakotas. "Now the Wasichu say the Iron Road is the whirlwind and will not stop. Chief Blackfoot told the Long Knives to whip the Sioux, then come back and make their kill talk. Then the Crows will believe it."

Crows have a sensible fatalism. They were every bit as brave as the Sheyenna—the short list of their enemies included Lakotas, Blue Clouds, Bloods, Piegans, and Sheyenna; nor were they on the best of terms with Flatheads, Bad Lodges, and Snakes. But they knew their limits. They accepted the Wasichu and did not cling to their freedom. The cavalry might whip the Lakotas or the Lakotas might whip the cavalry, but it would make no difference to the Crows. Win or lose, Washington was going to give away Crow land to the railroads. By being friendly and hospitable the Crows lost their right to protest. The army never so much as moved without keeping a keen eye open for hostiles, with flankers coming and going—but a friendly Indian got less notice than a prairie dog hole.

Mitch nodded at his wife's good sense. "The land along the Yellowstone is dark and bloody ground. The Lakotas are the worst, but I don't trust the Bloods or Piegans either. Hell, I don't trust anyone out on the prairie. I was nearly murdered by a wagon train of immigrants I was sent to bring into Fort Ellis. They decided I was some sort of renegade, and made me and Tom Leforge dig our own graves while an old biddy read the Bible over us. I would be getting my scripture from Jesus Hisself if a squad of cavalry had not come over the hill." Having the cavalry rescue you from immigrants sums up the absurdity of life and death on the plains.

At dawn the next day people snuck into the tipis of the successful warriors and pulled their buffalo robes off them, dragging them away from their wives and into the camp circle. The Crows liked to play such games, and a careful warrior always slept in his breechcloth. In the spring the Lumpwood and Fox societies held wife-stealing orgies, but nothing so exciting was planned for the evening—just a respectable scalp dance celebrating their recent win over the Lakotas. The sort of affair tourists could come and photograph.

All morning the wives and sweethearts of the men who had counted coup danced around the camp circle, holding their men's guns and bows, waving the scalps on long sticks. At the feast that night the war party told its story, with a lot of sign-talk, strutting, and pantomime. Two dozen Crows had slipped out of the Big Horns into Lakota Country and crossed the Wolf Mountains that divide the Greasy Grass from the Rosebud. Somewhere on the upper Rosebud they found four No Bows skinning a buffalo. The war party killed three of the hunters running for their horses. The fourth got to the ponies and got away, since the Crows were all afoot. It was common for war parties to set out on foot; moccasins leave hardly any trail and successful braves plan to come back aboard someone else's horse. This No Bow's escape ended the whole business. Knowing Lakotas would now be coming for them, they scalped the three dead men and headed back for the Big Horns.

The Crows found these simple events so exciting they did not mind hearing them again and again from various perspectives. The men who had counted coup or taken weapons enlarged on their exploits, entertaining us with extravagant boasts about their virility—which far exceeded most men's meager capacities. Here Cherry and Magpie Outside translated freely. Women's laughter and comments encouraged the men to even wilder flights of fancy. The Crows knew how to have fun. Crow women did not take their men half so seriously as their Sheyenna sisters. When Cherry's husband visited his sweethearts, she sent gifts of food along, happy to have a man other women wanted.

When the war party was done boasting, others got up to present praise or rough comment. Finds-and-Kills, a transvestite in a pretty mink-lined dress, made a long speech that brought both scowls and laughter. He-she kept pointing at me and at the Crow who brought me into camp. I leaned over and asked Mitch what the man-woman was saying.

"The man who came into camp with you is a River Crow called Goes Ahead. Seems the men in the war party thought they had picked up the trail of three Cheyennes on the way back. They lost that trail in the rain and somehow got onto yours, not realizing their mistake until they had followed you all the way into camp. Now Finds-and-Kills is saying Goes Ahead "captured" their three Cheyennes, despite your dreaded Medicine gun. Just a joke, but some of the war party do not find it so funny."

I found the humor a bit close to home myself.

That night, while the Crows slept off their scalp dance, I folded up my little tipi and slipped out of camp, headed for the far bank of the Yellowstone. I considered asking for a guide, but decided that would only make more trouble with Mitch. Besides, I was not eager to head off into the blue with some brave whose chief self-recommendation was that he was as virile as a herd of rutting bulls. I was not some crazy white woman on a lark, looking to take off with some young buck, then come back in a week or two with our faces flushed and our itches scratched.

A few days later I crossed the Yellowstone at an upstream ford, and found Mitch waiting for me on the far side. I complimented him on his neat job of tracking. Even when middling drunk, Mitch made an excellent scout.

"Weren't nothing." He shrugged, offering me a drink from his green-glass flask. "I knew which way you were headed, and this is the best ford hereabouts. Had faith you'd find it."

I sipped some of his whiskey to set him at ease, knowing he was trying to do right by me. Returning the bottle, I told him I was headed downriver no matter what. I already felt like I was going out of my way. The Bozeman Trail was less than a day away. If I had the daring to go down it alone, I could have gone straight home to Yellow Legs. I just did not have the guts to stake my life on a single draw.

Mitch took a long pull of watered whiskey, getting up the spirit to say something difficult—he took his obligations as seriously as his drinking. "Mind if I ask you a question?"

"Sure," I replied—as long as you're not fussy about the answer.

"What would Mr. Kilory think about you heading off alone?"

"Mr. Kilory knows me well. He will figure I did what I had to do to get back to him."

Mitch eyed the Medicine rifle tucked into my buffalo-robe bedroll. "This John Kilory . . . does he have another name?"

I did not answer.

"Could that other name be Yellow Legs?" Mitch said it in passable Sheyenna.

"Two Bodies"—I used Mitch's Lakota name—"would we still be friends if I said yes?"

He shook his head slowly—not to say no, but to show his amazement. "I heard talk about Yellow Legs having a white wife, but until now I thought it was just talk. Crows like to tell winter stories about him and Crazy Horse; kills the cold and boredom." Half-Lakota and married to a Crow, Mitch was the worst sort of half-breed squawman himself; he had just wanted better for me.

Mitch capped his bottle, giving up trying to plant my moccasins in the proper path. "Look," he told me, "I'm letting you go, but try to stay alive. It is going to make me middling sad to see your hair hanging from a lodgepole."

I told him I would do my best, but even then I had a bad feeling that Mitch's self-sacrifice and sense of responsibility—his desire to do right by others—would end up doing him in. We both tended to show an unhealthy concern for other people's troubles.

The Crow bands were headed west, toward the Crow agency, where they would make their winter camp and give up more land to the railroads. I headed east toward the Big Muddy, so I saw nothing of the River Crow— the "Dung-that-Settles-by-the-River," as their Mountain cousins call them. (To people living in the wide and open, dung does not have such a bad reputation. Buffalo chips are both useful and sacred. Other dung is not so special, unless you plant your moccasin in it, but even the lowliest dropping is a warm reminder of people or animals passing by.) I had the big empty area where the Yellowstone bent northward almost to myself. Or so I supposed.

In the Crow camp, a weather prophet named Pretty Louse had predicted warm days and mild nights. Most days her promise held good, though this was the Moon of Changing Seasons. On the high plains you can see weather coming. Rivers of cloud dragged gray belts of rain behind them. I would ride right through the showers, emerging under double or even triple rainbows, with my wet leather steaming in the sunlight. But past the headwaters of the Porcupine Creeks evenings turned cooler, and winds blew down from the north, ringing the moon with night rainbows. Boreal lights danced above me.

Then in the flats south of Big Dry Creek I did the most silly Wasichu thing of the whole journey, maybe in my whole life.

I came on an old buffalo bull bathing in a dust wallow. Yellow Legs would never give this stringy old bull a second look unless he was almighty hungry; but I had no fresh meat and was determined to try out my Medicine gun. I drew the rifle and swung out of the saddle. I had never shot a buffalo before, but I stupidly supposed that the six rounds in the Henry's magazine made me mistress of life and death.

I walked a few paces forward and the old bull got up out of the wallow, glaring in my direction. Cattle are born and bred to be slaughtered, their eyes always seem wary and sorrowful, but buffalo are different—their eyes are generally angry or aloof. They know we are parasites, not their masters. But this old bull just looked weary. Having no harem, he had wandered away from the herd, waiting for death. And now some spiteful human had come to disrupt his dust bath.

Saying "I am sorry, but I need your meat," I chambered a shell, aiming right where I supposed his heart was. At this range not even I could miss. I pulled slowly on the trigger, just as Yellow Legs and Crazy Horse had taught me. (Annie Oakley says my shooting is "well tutored"—high praise from a girl who started out shooting squirrels through the eye so she could sell their pelts.) There was a big boom, then a dusty whack where the bullet went in. That much was done right.

The bull's knees buckled and he lurched forward, landing just outside the wallow, blood pouring from his mouth. The bullet hit in the lung instead of the heart, but he went down just as dead. The Henry truly was a Medicine gun. But I would soon be appalled that I had ever dared pull the trigger.

Light-headedness swept over me, having never killed anything so big before. Steadying myself, I walked over and leaned my rifle against my victim, getting ready to butcher. Something made me look up, seeing at last what I had done. The land was rolling prairie; gentle rises blocked my line of sight but not the sound of a rifle. One by one, small blobs of color topped the nearest rise in answer to the shot. As they hurtled toward me, I saw they were Lakota riders.

I froze. A few minutes before, I had been the mistress of life and death, firing off my Medicine gun without thinking that the sound would carry.

Now I stood there terrified, the rifle leaning up against the dead buffalo, mocking me, with only five rounds in the magazine. Even if I had the nerve to fire, the finest shooting on earth could not save me now.

The warriors careened closer. Not worried I would escape, they were in a race of honor, to see who would count first coup. The lead horse had a white rump with zebra stripes; its rider wore a hair-trimmed shirt and a fur headdress. Under his paint I guessed he was a Hunkpapa. The next horse was a coyote dun decorated with a line of red hoofprints, showing his rider had stolen many ponies.

The leading Hunkpapa didn't even pause as he slapped my shoulder with a coup stick. My shoulder stung. I had never been struck by a coup stick before, but that novelty was the least of my worries. The next warrior slapped me across the face. Maybe he was mad at having to settle for second. Tears blurred my vision. The third warrior was more gentle, barely tapping me. The fourth man saw I was still holding my skinning knife, something I had completely forgotten. He hit my hand hard with his bow, knocking the knife loose.

Wincing, I watched the first man turn his zebra-striped horse and trot back. As he came up he let his coup stick drop. All the coups Lakotas allowed were counted. My horses were being rounded up by more commercial-minded members of the war party, leaving nothing for the coup counter to do but kill me. His every movement seemed magnified. I watched the coup stick swing on the small thong that tied it to his wrist. His hand went into a fringed scabbard and came out with a sawed-off muzzle loader, the type used for running buffalo. Pointing the business end at my temple, he thumbed the hammer back.

End of the Line

*Often one sees young girls and women undertaking long journeys
alone and without protection, for she finds in every companion a
protector and friend.*

—Nineteenth-century German romantic,
writing about America

TERRIFIED AS I WAS, I KNEW THAT IF I FROZE UP AND DID NOTH-
ing, I would die. This smiling Hunkpapa had me ticketed for the Spirit
World—aiming to give me a deal less consideration than I had given that
old bull. Opening my mouth wide, I yelled "Wait, don't shoot," the first
Lakota phrase that came to mind.

He stopped and stared, shocked to hear a Wasichu woman speaking Lakota, as surprised as if the lung-shot buffalo had sat up and started
talking.

"I am a wife to First Coup. I am a sister to Sitting Bull." That latter was
not strictly true, but I was limited to simple Lakota, and if this man was a
Hunkpapa, the claim would hardly hurt my case. The muzzle at my head did
not waver. The Hunkpapa's finger stayed on the trigger, a tiny pull away
from silencing me completely.

Other Lakotas crowded around, men and horses breathing hard, everyone anxious to see this talking wonder before she was shot. No matter how
much I might want to break down and blubber for mercy, I knew it would
not serve; Lakotas like their women strong. Lakota warriors are born killers,
but seldom take vicious amusement in it—torture is no more common than
it is among Wasichu. And if they stop to talk or rape it usually means they'll
let you live.

Mercifully, I knew some of these men. I recognized He Dog, the Oglala

122

Bad Face, wearing the same white-and-green paint he had worn for the Custer fight. Beside him was Rain-in-the-Face and his overdressed brother Iron Horse. I signed, "Takes-the-Enemy, we were together in Sitting Bull's tipi." I was fairly groveling, using Rain-in-the-Face's grandiose name.

Rain-in-the-Face could never resist the mention of any of his names. He replied in a long stream of Lakota (I had yet to hear the man make a short speech) reciting the whole scene in Sitting Bull's tipi, including the honors that had brought him there. Rain was one rooster who thought the sun came up just to hear him crow—but the Hunkpapa with the buffalo musket seemed to barely listen. Lowering his muzzle loader, he reached down and unbraided my hair, acting as if it were already his.

Too scared to look him in the eye, I gazed past him, telling myself that the man holding my hair did not hate me. Hell, he did not even know me. He was just trying to decide whether he would rather have my hair or have me walking around. Acting as unconcerned as I could, I signed to He Dog, using Yellow Legs's Lakota name, "When you see First Coup, tell him Lakotas killed American Woman."

I pretended to be merely passing a message, but I was also pointing out consequences. Death was a transition. We would all meet again in the Spirit World; maybe as soon as Yellow Legs tracked these Lakotas down. Right now they had the power to kill me, but the next time we met they might be talking with their penises cut off and stuffed in their mouths. Such thoughts make a man consider his actions. And getting a warrior to reconsider was half the contest.

He Dog, nature's diplomat, spoke swiftly and softly. I could barely follow his Lakota, but I could see my show had affected them. The Hunkpapa hesitated. He stopped unbraiding my hair, holding it loose in his hand while he listened. "Look into her eyes," He Dog advised. "You will be sorry if you kill her."

Thanking He Dog with all my being, I turned to look straight at the Hunkpapa who was sizing up my scalp, managing a weak smile. He looked startled, as if seeing me for the first time. Taking a buzzard feather off one of his braids, he tied it in my hair, where it flapped about, brushing my cheek. Then he let my braid slip out of his hand and stepped back, establishing a polite distance, now that we were no longer killer and victim.

He Dog leaned down and tied one of his coup feathers next to the buzzard feather. Rain was next with another feather, followed by the others who had counted coup on me. My head must have looked like a peacock's rear, but it felt good. These feathers were signs of protection; if they were not going to kill me, they had to lay claim me in some other way. Though I still felt I was breathing on probation.

To smooth things over, I invited them to a feast of freshly killed buffalo. With so many sharp knives, the butchering went quickly. Everyone's mood improved. I did my damnedest to impress the Lakotas with my cooking, not easy when you have only an old bull to work with. He was barely fit to be boiled, but I emptied out my Medicine bag to make a stew, and hand-roasted the best parts—liver, tongue, and kidneys—even cooking up blood sausage by rolling rennet packed with blood back and forth through the hot coals until the blood jellied. Settling down around the dissected bull to eat and smoke, these braves on a spree congratulated themselves on having found a woman to cook for them, as pleased as if sparing me had been their idea to begin with. They finished off by breaking up the marrow bones, leaving the buffalo a gutted wreck, nothing but horns, bones, hooves, and hide.

When we mounted up, they loaded me down with weapons. He Dog gave me his lance and my husband's Medicine gun. The Hunkpapa who had almost killed me gave me his sawed-off muzzle loader to carry. He said his name was Swift Bear and that he was a brother of Crow King, the well-known war chief. None of these weapons were for protection; the feathers twirling in my hair were my protection. Lakotas just expected that a woman riding with a war party would help carry their gear. It was strange to be carrying the gun that had nearly blown my head off, but Lakotas have a very practical view of death. Either it happens or it does not. Since I was alive, I ought to be useful.

He Dog was Red Cloud's nephew, so I asked if he knew where his uncle was camped. He Dog said his famous relation was camped on the Smoky Earth River. "The Wasichu have pushed my uncle's agency north, almost to *Paha Sapa,* the Black Hills at the Center of the World." He Dog was clearly unhappy to have Wasichu cutting wood and grazing spotted cattle near the Center of the World, but being naturally polite, he never suggested that this new provocation should concern me. "Many Bad Faces wanted to fight the Wasichu, to keep them away from *Paha Sapa* by force—but my uncle said no." Plainly proud of his far-thinking uncle, he told me, "Red Cloud wants the Wasichu to pay to use our land."

I wanted to know what price could be worth letting a fort and agency sit at the Center of the World.

He Dog looked shocked. "My uncle is does not want gold or green paper; he wants guns and ammunition—ten rifles, ten pistols, ten Winchester repeaters, and ten Prussian needle guns for each Lakota band. With that many guns we could really make a fight over the agency." He Dog never honestly knew from moment to moment whether he was an agency Oglala or a hostile. But he naturally assumed the government ought to arm both sides in the coming conflict. If taxpayers bought needle guns for the Crows and Spring-fields for the Long Knives, they should also arm the Lakotas; anything else would be less than generous.

The next day dawned cold, with ice in the air and sun dogs around the sun. About noon we spotted a fresh buffalo kill, partly skinned and gutted. The Lakotas dismounted, deciding it was the work of Wasichu. Which im-mediately put these braves on edge—worse was to follow.

Looking about, I saw a rag of fur lying under a bush. Strolling over, I dis-covered it was the body of a big she-wolf. She had dragged herself into the brush to die. Farther off lay her mate, a handsome black male with a silver back. Wind rippled the pelts that had cost them their lives.

The Lakotas came over and started cursing. Some enterprising Wasichu had slipped down from the Musselshell River with a rifle, a sack of flour, and a bag of strychnine. He killed the buffalo, then sprinkled the carcass with a half ounce of poison; in a day or so he'd be back to skin the dead wolves. You may imagine what the Hunkpapas thought of someone who snuck into Lakota Country, killing and spoiling one sacred animal in order to poison another one. Swift Bear elected to stay behind and wait for the wolver to come back and check his trap.

The rest of us pushed on across the sandy bottoms toward the big bend in the Yellowstone. Those poisoned wolves were our first sign of civilization; ahead lay the Dead Lands, where the grass was plowed under and the game driven off. I tried hard to keep up a festive atmosphere, babbling away in simple Lakota, commenting on everything we passed: buttes in the distance, birds flying south, colors in the landscape. I hoped they would think me in-sufferably Wasichu and not worth making trouble over. It did manage to amuse them. Rain, Iron Horse, and the others started pointing out sights that had escaped my commentary, playing at being tourists in their own country.

At a ford on the Yellowstone we ran into tourists of another sort—a long string of wagons crawling over the prairie. My first thought was settlers, though even immigrants would hardly be daft enough to wander through country that the army itself only entered in regimental strength. But He Dog told me they were Grease People from Grandmother's Land, Red River Breeds, coming down from Canada to kill Lakota buffalo. Buffalo hides were already popular back east as sleigh blankets and novelties—the plains were being bled to keep New Yorkers' laps warm.

The Grease People circled their wagons and stuck out their long guns, aiming to keep the Lakotas at a distance. Their wagons were stacked with hides, marrow, tongues, and fat. These Mixed Bloods took only the best parts, leaving the rest of the buffalo to rot on the prairie—which is how they got the name Grease People. That alone was enough to make the Lakotas want them dead.

Iron Horse led his Hunkpapas right to the edge of rifle range, whooping and laughing, happy to have made the Mixed Bloods flinch first. After a nervous moment or two a man came out to meet us, a true *bois brûlé* with burned-dark skin and a ready smile, wearing a blue Hudson's Bay cape fastened with brass buttons. Instead of a peace pipe he carried a corn liquor jug.

Telling us to "Get down," he handed the jug to He Dog. The Oglala took a drink, grimaced, then passed the jug to the Hunkpapas. If Iron Horse had been backed by the right number of warriors he would have hacked his host apart, figuring he had done the world a favor. Unable to have their first choice, the Lakotas made themselves sociable, determined to eat as much meat as possible, to stop it from being exported. These Red River Breeds turned out to be a happy lot, generous with other people's meat, loving the Lakotas' wandering life, even as they were destroying it. They brought out their fiddles, entertaining us with jigs and reels. There were women with them, some Mixed Bloods, others full-blooded Crees and Chippewas—all blood enemies of the Lakota—but they enjoyed showing He Dog and the Hunkpapas how to dance Wasichu-style.

Our host in the blue cape sat at my side. I imagine he was mostly Chippewa, but his manners were all French. Mixing French, Lakota, and sign language, he managed to make it understood that I was welcome to stay with them for a night, a moon, or many winters. If it was marriage I wanted, they had a priest and an altar wagon. The nuptials could take place that night. He assured me that my marriage to Yellow Legs meant nothing to the Church. He himself had a pair of Chippewa wives back on the Saskatchewan, but he promised to turn one or both of them out for me—though they were good for chopping wood and making crepes while we lay about in bed.

I merely warned him against giving too much whiskey to the Lakotas; one winter a camp of Hunkpapas had nearly been annihilated by several sleigh loads of whiskey. He laughed. "Do I look like a fool?"

He was wearing white buckskins with foot-long fringes, a blue cloak with big brass buttons, and a floppy fur hat trimmed with wild turkey feathers. For the sake of argument, I said he did not look terribly foolish.

"Only a fool," he assured me, "would serve straight whiskey to a Lakota war party. Sacred Heaven!" He crossed himself with a pair of sloppy strokes. "Not with women around. That would invite the Devil. They are drinking stream water, spiced with cayenne pepper and enough whiskey to make them sociable. A Lakota judges Medicine Water by how terrible it tastes, and the stuff they are drinking tastes vile."

My host spun dozens of stories, all designed to get me to come away to Grandmother's Land with him. Having the good whiskey to himself, he got drunker than anyone, calling for a song in my honor. The song had a haunting melody, and whenever I hear it I think of this Red River Breed:

> Come and sit by my side if you love me,
> Do not hasten to bid me adieu,
> But remember the Red River Valley,
> And the beau who has loved you so true.

Each time I shook my head, my drunken suitor got up and led another verse:

> From this valley they say you are going,
> We will miss your bright eyes and sweet smile,
> For they say you are taking the sunshine,
> That brightened our woods for a while.

I was flattered, but not the least bit tempted to tie myself to a half-drunk, half-French Chippewa. I would take my chances with a war party of Lakotas.

I later met a Snake Medicine woman who cured fevers with cayenne pepper, and that night the cayenne certainly was magic. There was nary a killing; and the next morning the Hunkpapas awoke fit and happy, not at all in the mood for murder. They swore the Mixed Breeds had excellent Medicine water, hard on the tongue but easy on the head.

We crossed the Yellowstone and headed east, toward Standing Rock agency, entering a wide, midgrass prairie. Bluestem and Indian grass rolled in a great waving pelt from one end of the world to the other, constantly changing color: brown, then green, then golden. Even the sun seemed to stand higher, lost in the wide blue bowl above. This had been the Hunkpapa homeland before settlement drove the buffalo from the river. Somewhere past Sentinel Butte, Swift Bear caught up with us, saying the wolver had returned. He had a brand-new Sharps Sporter hanging from his saddle in a flour sack. In typical Lakota fashion, Swift Bear had dumped the flour out, using the sack to carry his new rifle.

Beyond White Butte we picked up the Cannonball River, finding it lined with honking geese. Long skeins of them were headed south for the winter. A day or so north of Standing Rock, Iron Horse called a halt. He Dog and the Hunkpapas settled down to fix their feathers and put on fresh paint. When I asked why, they laughed. Lakotas have reasons for the most unreasonable behavior, so I went and bathed in the Cannonball, changing into fresh clothes.

Once we were looking our best, we rode on. Topping the next rise, I saw a blue-black column of cavalry snaking toward us. The Hunkpapas had seen something I had missed, and my amazement made the joke even funnier. Heaven knows how they knew the cavalry was coming; smoke signals, dust in the air, a reflection in the clouds, or maybe a Medicine dream. None of them would say. Living with Buffalo Indians, you learn to adjust to surprises.

Lakotas love a show, so we cantered straight out to meet the Long Knives. The column halted at a safe distance, and a suspicious young officer rode forward, a sergeant at his side. Rain-in-the-Face greeted him in sign talk, acting as if he were perfectly accustomed to escorting white women about the plains. To see Rain tell it, he was the sort of Lakota who always went out of his way to accommodate Wasichu. He was so proud and worked up he probably believed it; certainly Hunkpapas saw no contradiction between befriending Wasichu at the agencies and fighting them in the wilds. Swift Bear had only recently done what the army would call murder but a Lakota would call tidying up the prairie.

I said my goodbyes to He Dog, then walked out leading Keeps-the-Fire, fully conscious of the show I was making. My hair was down and parted without a trace of paint. I wore a Wasichu dress and a fringed buckskin jacket, and guided a painted pony with a lodge cover on her back and a Medicine gun slung from her saddle—a fairly odd combination to be sure, but you have to be ready for anything on the prairie.

The young officer tipped his hat to me, looking for the trick behind my white skin and strange dress. "Lieutenant George D. Wallace, G Company, 7th cavalry, at your service."

"Sarah Kilory," I replied. "Very pleased to meet you."

His long face lit up. Though not handsome, Lieutenant Wallace had keen eyes and an intelligent look. And he was clearly happy to hear me speak English, glad to be dealing with a real white woman, not a light-skinned Lakota like Given-to-Us. All around me white faces broke into embarrassed smiles. It was overwhelming to be suddenly swallowed by my own kind, after months of being the different one.

Wallace turned to his sergeant, giving an order. It was startling to hear English addressed to someone other than me. The sergeant handed Wallace a big plug of tobacco and a steel knife. The lieutenant passed them on to

Iron Horse and Rain-in-the-Face, who whooped and whipped their horses back and forth, getting dust all over us. The gifts were trivial, but the mere notion of getting something from the Long Knives thrilled the Hunkpapas. We Wasichu have so many things, and the Lakota could not understand why we were so stingy with them.

It occurred to me that right now I could have all my ponies back. At a word from me, this obliging Lieutenant Wallace would arrest any Lakota I cared to name, seizing any property I cared to claim. If he had to shoot a few Hunkpapas to do it, that was all in a day's work. But I could not bear to spoil the afternoon with gunplay, so I let the ponies go, saying a silent goodbye to Carries-the-Lodge.

As He Dog and the Hunkpapas rode off toward Standing Rock, I felt an emptiness I could hardly explain. Logically I should feel less then civil to these particular Lakotas. They had slapped me with coup sticks, threatened to shoot me, then stolen all but one of my horses. Yet they had gotten me almost to the Big Muddy, treating me with what they assumed was respect— and they were my last link with my husband and the free life along the Yellowstone.

Lieutenant Wallace was at my side, bursting to know who I was, where I had come from, where I was going, and what I had to say for myself. I felt defenseless in the face of a thousand Wasichu questions. I must have looked shaken, because the young officer reached over and took my hand. "Do not worry, you are safe. Your hard time is done with. Be at ease."

I relaxed. Wallace invited me to ride with him at the head of the column, where we would not eat the troopers' dust. For a time neither of us said a thing. Then Wallace began to point out sights; he was filling the silence with words, like any Wasichu would. I could see he was enjoying himself, which he freely admitted. "Ma'am, you are about the best thing that has ever come along on the prairie."

"I cannot believe that." I felt very out of place, a burden to everyone.

"It is true," he insisted. "I wish I could ride with such a handsome woman on every patrol."

I blushed and asked if that was what he was doing—"patrolling."

He nodded. "Showing the flag. Our home station is Fort Rice, but right now we are headed for Fort Lincoln, on the west bank of the Missouri, across from Bismarck."

"Bismarck?" I remembered the name from the broadside in Sitting Bull's tipi. "Where the Northern Pacific railhead is?"

Lieutenant Wallace nodded. "Where it is, and where it is likely to stay. Bismarck's the end of the line."

"Won't the railroad be crossing the river soon?" The weather was getting colder, snow would halt construction, but surely work would go on in the spring.

"Nope," Wallace replied, "the rails will rust right there. The Northern Pacific is busted. Jay Cooke and Company went belly-up bankrupt."

I said nothing, thinking of Jay Cooke's big parlor and his kill talk and smoker with President Grant.

"Fact is," Wallace went on, "everybody's going bust. The New York Stock Exchange closed its doors. The Credit Mobilier is paying fifteen cents on the dollar. Banks are failing all over the country. I'd say half the businesses in Bismarck are shutting down. No one has seen the like of it. I am glad to have my pay and commission, otherwise I would be on the bum. Maybe a quarter of the troopers behind us are men the Northern Pacific let go." As he spoke he looked about, turning in the saddle to check on his railway recruits.

Up ahead, a lone coyote eyed the column. Wallace settled back down, saying, "It's been in all the newspapers, but I guess you have not seen a newspaper in a while." A judge would call that a leading question; I merely nodded. Hearing that the railroad had stopped dead was awesome. "Already they say the panic is spreading overseas. It all came on like a breaking storm in the middle of last month."

I smiled. "I am afraid I do not know when the middle of last month was. I have not seen a recent newspaper, a calendar, nor a working pocketwatch in a long time. You'll have to tell me what month this is."

"This is October." Wallace returned my smile. "Last month was September. The panic came right around the time that the weather broke here, when the hot spell ended and we got that big line of thunderstorms. You remember all that thunder and lightning a few weeks back?" I said yes, I remembered the lightning.

The coyote gave a triumphant yip and flicked his tail at me, disappearing into the grass and thistle. A score of overeager troopers banged away at him, missing by a country mile. Old Man Coyote carried all the bullet Medicine he needed.

The Winter the Buffalo Went Away

1874

Most of the money Sitting Bull made in the Wild West Show went into the pockets of small, ragged boys; he could never understand how wealth could go brushing past poverty.

—Annie Oakley

*　　*　　*

The white man knows how to make things, but does not know how to give them away.

—Sitting Bull

Fort Lincoln

So Coyote could do miracles. I sat on my borrowed cavalry mount, astounded and amazed by the wreck of the Northern Pacific. The banks were busted; the railroad lay dead in its tracks—not the way I would have wanted, but without so much as a crosstie being laid along the Yellowstone. The world overflowed with possibilities. All I needed to do now was get to Red Cloud's camp, where Yellow Legs could come for me.

I knew better than to mention my newfound happiness to the nice cavalry officer at my elbow. Even on short acquaintance I could tell that young Mr. Wallace was not the person to babble to about Medicine journeys, gambling with Coyote, or a misplaced Indian husband. What I had seen in Lakota Country had opened a yawning gulf between my world and the "Yes, ma'am—no, ma'am" terra firma Lieutenant Wallace inhabited.

A Sheyenna camp may be a model of decorum amid chaos, but troop G of the 7th cavalry marched and camped to bugle calls. The sun could not so much as rise or set on Mr. Wallace's war party without a musical fuss being made. That first evening I sat admiring the twilight routine. At stable call the men marched to their horses, pulled the picket-pins, and paraded to the watering place, then lined up to have nose bags filled with forage. While their horses ate, men went to work with brushes and currying combs. Afterward came mess call, and the men lined up again, this time for hardtack, beef, and coffee. Retreat sounded a little after sunset and the troopers stood to be counted—though I doubt the army would very much miss any man witless enough to go over the hill in Hunkpapa territory.

When Indians are in a mood to be entertained they will watch such shows for hours. Their silent observation might make a thoughtful Wasichu nervous, but they are usually just enjoying the act, and too polite to applaud.

I must admit to enjoying myself. A cavalry troop was more rigidly male than a Sheyenna war party, which made me even more of a marvel to the troopers. Every man smiled and tipped his hat. The more ambitious spent spare hours inventing things to do for me, since Lieutenant Wallace made it plain that I could have any reasonable thing I wanted, and quite a few unreasonable things as well.

Natural wariness warned me not to become obligated to this ardent young officer—but I helped myself to his mess furnishings: a sheet-iron cookstove, a Dutch oven, an iron kettle, plus stewing, frying, and baking pans; more cooking equipment than Black Shawl could imagine, and all of it mine between bugle calls. Not a lick of loading, unloading, or washing went with it—men did that for me. Whenever I deigned to make a meal, Wallace was as pleased and complimentary as if I had taken him to dinner at Delmonico's. Though he was no more handsome than a horse trough, the man had that attentive knack for making you feel special.

After dinner I would lie beside his fire, sheltered by a tent fly, reading, or talking in quiet tones about New York, Philadelphia, or some civilized place, or listening to the low notes of the bugle and the click of currying combs in the autumn twilight. No wonder Spring Grass loved campaigning with Custer. Even a wild Sheyenna could see the sense in being served and waited on. If ever you feel a lack of male attention, flag down the nearest cavalry troop and let them take you wherever they are going.

One morning we topped a bluff, and there was the Big Muddy—not the mile-wide river you see south of Cairo, but still an immense sheet of water splitting the prairie. Wallace "helped" me dismount, and we stood on the bluff above the bank, arms still linked. "The Father of Waters," declared Wallace, "as big as the Nile and Ganges together, with the Rhine thrown in to make up the difference."

He had the benefit of a West Point education; all I could do was mumble a Crow phrase Magpie Outside had taught me: "Our bodies are water."

Wallace cocked an eyebrow. "Was that Lakota?"

"No, Crow—though the languages are related."

"What does it mean?"

"Our bodies are water—it is their invitation to drink." Crows measure water in skin bags or by eyeing rain clouds, and know nothing about the Nile or the Ganges. As far as they are concerned, there was only one great river in the world—the one rolling below us, cutting the continent in half.

His long face lit up. "You speak Crow and Lakota! Is there nothing you can't do?"

"Oh, I hardly know any Crow, and my Lakota is spotty." This was the moment when a respectable woman finds a way to mention her husband—

but I had to be wary about bringing Yellow Legs into casual conversation. We fallen women must watch what we say.

"But it is so rare to find a woman who understands anything about the West, and especially Indians." I could not tell if Wallace was complimenting me or stating a general principle. "Women are usually mortally terrified of savages or full of ridiculous romantic notions."

I admitted to coming west with some very romantic notions. "But almost every idea I brought with me turned out to be impractical or irrelevant."

"What sort of ideas?" He found my personal history uncomfortably fascinating and made no attempt to move away or let go of my arm. I could see I was going to pay for those pleasant evenings by his fire. It depressed me to know that if I was even half honest with this overfriendly officer he would start to loathe me.

"My family is Quaker," I told him. "I came out west intending to teach the Lakotas the Christian way."

Wallace found this ambition nearly as amusing as Cherry and Magpie Outside had. "Ma'am, I imagine you've seen the error in that. There are plenty of Indians that you can only Christianize with a carbine." Having spent a summer campaigning on the Yellowstone, Wallace considered himself a complete authority on wild Indians. "I respect your religious feelings— but next to the Sioux, Quakers are the most determined enemies the army has out here. So I suppose you do not think much of soldiers."

With Wallace still hanging on to my arm, I had no defense except to say, "My husband is a soldier of sorts, or at least a fighting man."

Wallace straightened up, letting go at last—there was still some Medicine in claiming to be married. "I'd like to meet your husband," he mumbled. Having been on the Yellowstone this summer, Mr. Wallace had most likely met my husband, or at least seen him at work.

The first big blow of winter caught us coming into Fort Lincoln. Rain, then freezing sleet flew straight in our faces. By the time we passed the fort's outbuildings a full blizzard tugged at my blanket. Snow swirled off the lee eaves, and huge banks were piling up to windward.

Troopers trudged out to take our horses. Accustomed by now to this luxury, I felt no pang of separation from Keeps-the-Fire. I had other worries. Wallace brought me wet and shaking into his commander's office. The slab-sided iron stove threw out waves of heat, and I stood shivering in a puddle of melted snow, my hair wringing wet. A woman would have offered a dry blanket, but not Major Marcus A. Reno. From the way he looked me over, I might have been wearing black garters and a peacock fan.

I later discovered that there was nothing special about my appearance; Reno treated any young woman that way. After Sheyenna propriety—and

Wallace's ardent courtesy—Reno's ogling was a shock. No Sheyenna would follow a war chief who acted the fool in front of women, but cavalry troopers cannot pick their leaders—the army did that for them, and Reno had risen all the way to brevet brigadier general during the War. But he was a mere major now; the real commander of the 7th cavalry was a colonel named Sturgis off in Missouri somewhere. Whatever his rank, Reno had no way with women. I never developed the full loathing of Reno that infected Ella Sturgis and Libby Custer, though his alcoholic gallantries did have me wishing I was back out in the blizzard.

† Since I positively would not change clothes in his office, Major Reno found me a small room off the kitchen in the rambling and unfinished commanding officer's residence. The room was tiny, with wind blowing in the cracks, but it beat pitching my tipi in a snowstorm. I hauled in a copper kitchen tub and boiled water for a bath. There was no lock on my door— Major Reno had learned something in the War about tactical advantage. So when the tub was full I pushed it against the latch, then slid naked into the warm soapy water, while a Dakota blizzard beat against the walls and blew through the cracks. It was all very unreal, after bathing in streams, summer and winter, and living under nothing more substantial than a smoke hole.

After my bath, I dressed and answered a knock at the door, fearing it would be Reno. I was relieved to greet a Mrs. Carlin, who had come almost a mile through the storm to take tea with me. Her husband was in the infantry garrison—he too had been a general in the War.

I told her she need not have bothered, but she said a blizzard was no bother. "Besides, there might be something you would want to say to a woman." Indeed there was. I had been alone among men for weeks. We talked about food, family, and new fashions in the States, but despite our common gender the conversation stayed awkward. I felt like I was taking tea with Given-to-Us, who was more Mrs. Carlin's age and disposition. My hands fidgeted, wanting to make signs.

Her hands were busy too, moving teacups and arranging saucers, observing that "Lieutenant Wallace is not much to look at, but he is a smart young man." I agreed, right smart. "But he is a man," Mrs. Carlin reminded me. Very much a man, no argument there. She started to fidget again. "I was wondering of you might want to tell me something. If anything happened . . ."

"Oh, quite a lot happened. It is hard to know where to start "—especially when you do not want to tell too much.

She forced her hands into her lap and held them there. "Women alone with Indians are very often—well, mistreated. Forced to do things . . ."

Like chop wood? Carry water? Eat raw liver? You betcha, as Sitting Bull would say. But I guessed Mrs. Carlin did not mean forcing down bizarre meals or doing miscellaneous domestic chores; I knew which bush we were beating around. "Do you mean raped?"

Mrs. Carlin nodded, her teacup stopped rock-steady halfway to her lips. You could hear the timbers creak in the wind.

"No, I was not raped by those Lakotas. The worst they did was steal my ponies and threaten to shoot me."

"I am so glad to hear that." Mrs. Carlin sighed and took a sip of tea. I can well believe she was glad. Who would want to hear some awful story, then have to repeat it to her husband and the lecherous Major Reno?

After that, our tea went down much easier. I rambled on about Crow scalp dances, the best ways to cook buffalo, the three-pole tipi, and the like. Mrs. Carlin must have soon deduced that I was more than a bit mad—another addled white woman won back from the Lakotas. But like any well-behaved lunatic, I kept the real story to myself. Mrs. Carlin must have gone away convinced my insanity had saved me. Many Wasichu firmly believe that no brave would rape a crazy woman, or spare a woman with her senses about her. Both halves of this notion were absurdly far from true. Like most nuggets of misinformation, this one was nearly backward. Lakotas thought all whores had to be crazy, and any woman who wants to avoid being staked out on the prairie had damn well better have all her wits about her. Otherwise she could end up being the proverbial "good time that was had by all."

The storm blew past. Standing on the commanding officer's porch, I got a first good look at Fort Lincoln: a flat white parade field surrounded by barracks, storehouses, log huts, stables, a guardhouse, and little lines of tents poking up through the snow. Beyond the buildings I could see a flood plain backed by a long chain of bluffs. There were no ramparts or stockade. Like Sparta, or a Sheyenna camp, the walls of Fort Lincoln's were the arms of her fighting men. Our safety depended on Major Reno and six companies of the 7th cavalry—thank God I was only staying until Keeps-the-Fire could recover.

My first thought that morning was for my mare. Slogging through the snow toward the stables, I passed troopers shuffling about like sleepy bears, wearing heavy gloves, fur caps and buffalo coats. Inside the horse barn, shafts of morning sun filled the thick air of the stall with bars of light and shade. Keeps-the-Fire was lying in the dark. I bent and touched her. Her body was already stiff and cold, no longer the living thing that I had loved.

Tears welled up. My most constant companion was dead. So many times during the last moon I had imagined her dying, but always with her big black-and-white muzzle in my lap. I never expected she would go without any warning—there in the evening, gone in the morning. Had she been dragging herself along, seeing me safely to the Big Muddy? Yellow Legs would say she was finally free to leave for the Spirit World. But I did not believe in the Spirit World. I just felt miserable and guilty, leaving her to die among strangers.

Outside of the gloomy stable, tears froze on my jacket. Suddenly feeling hollow and frail, I fell into a hopeless funk, keeping to myself, avoiding helpful officers and housekeepers, hoarding my sorrow and loneliness. At nights I dreamed of riding my black-and-white mare alongside Yellow Legs at the Center of the World. But during the day I despaired of ever getting to Red Cloud's camp—stranded with no pony, no money, hundreds of miles from the Center of the World. Even Wallace's ready gallantry could not stir me. And soon he too was leaving, taking G troop back to Fort Rice. I lay about, losing a whole week to this lethargy.

Before he left, Wallace tried one last time to shake me out of my sorry state. He and Reno were the only ones bold enough to try to intrude on my misery. Taken in by Wallace's sympathy, I made the mistake of telling Wallace right out what I wanted—to go to Red Cloud's camp.

All my honesty got was an irritated rebuff. "The army goes to great expense and risk to win women back from the Sioux. We do not outfit lone female expeditions into hostile country. You were lucky to come out once. Heaven knows what got into those warriors who delivered you—the hand of God, I suppose."

My story about stumbling upon a helpful Hunkpapa war party sounded terribly hollow, even to me. I protested that Red Cloud was lodged on reservation land, just like Fort Lincoln. Couldn't they merely call it a move from one piece of federal property to another?

That got a loud long laugh from the lieutenant. "Red Cloud claims to be a good agency Indian, but that does not make a spit of difference. Sioux are Sioux. On the Yellowstone we saw coffee grounds, tin cans, and government flour sacks left behind by the hostiles. The only difference between your good agency Indian and a wild hostile is his mood toward whites at the moment."

It was damned difficult to argue with the truth—Lakotas did as they pleased, not bothering to define themselves by their attitudes toward white authority.

Wallace left for his post, assuring me that Reno had dispatched messages to the Red Cloud agency, telling my husband where to find me. I knew the Red Cloud agent well, a fine Episcopal churchman named Daniels. Agent Daniels would be delighted to learn that I was married, since he had always considered me too much of a temptation, working alone among the Lakotas; but Yellow Legs was not going to be getting any letters or telegrams addressed to John Kilory. He could be feasting right now in Red Cloud's lodge, but word would never reach him.

If the army would not give me a horse and provisions, then I needed a job. I could not see myself competing with the company laundresses—sturdy professionals who guarded their claims with heavy laundry bats—but I had talents the army would pay for. I could speak Sheyenne and some Lakota, even a little Crow, and the army hired female interpreters. Spring Grass had been one without knowing English—she had known what Long Hair wanted.

I took that suggestion to Major Reno and got a good pawing for my pains, escaping from the job interview with honor intact, if not dignity. The major made it plain that Spring Grass's job was open—not the interpreting part, but the position as post commander's concubine. Reno would not have cared if I could only speak Chinese.

Giving up on the army, I caught a wagon headed for Bismarck. Almost at once I saw a prime chance for female employment. The east bank of the Big Muddy, just off the reservation, harbored the canvas dramshops and gambling dens that serviced the troops, places like My Lady's Bower or the Dew Drop Inn. A few nights work as a "white squaw" and I could have ridden to Red Cloud's camp in style. But some things are out of reach even when they are right at hand.

Bismarck was a tiny clapboard metropolis on the prairie. I slogged through its muddy streets talking to merchants, and a town commissioner who told me, "Thank you, ma'am, we sure can't use you." Main Street was lined with boarded-up shops, and with the railroad gone bust there would be precious few children to teach; no one was planning for the next generation in what was likely to become a desert. Coyote had not skimped on the misery, making sure nearly everyone was short of cash money. People called the latest coinage act a crime—but the Republicans would neither print greenbacks nor coin silver. Only gold would do.

Returning from Bismarck I saw the whorehouses and gambling hells rise up out of the frozen plain. Brothels and saloons were staying open to sponge up the fort payroll with whiskey and women. It was find a job here or winter at Fort Lincoln. Now we would see just how much I wanted to share a tipi with Yellow Legs.

Whoring made my skin crawl. I had only known two men: one I loved and the other I still respected. Young Dr. Warren had given me grim lectures about the dangers that came with degrading yourself—not wanting his young Irish concubine bringing home syphilis or gonorrhea. The thought of prostitution made even fish-eyed Major Reno appealing. Bad as he was, the major was only one man. But gambling was another matter. I asked some troopers boarding the ferry if they knew of a place needing a dealer. Playing cards was work that I could live with.

They shuffled, scratched their heads, and finally admitted that My Lady's Bower was short a faro dealer. "C Company caught him using a spring-loaded box an' force-fed him a full deck of cards, including the bug." (Daddy always told me, "Real poker needs no joker." If this faro shark had heeded that advice, he would have had one less card to eat.) I could have kissed those embarrassed boys. There is no harm in faro; you can't find a more fair and even game.

My Lady's Bower was worse than I imagined. Stale smoky air held in by a rotting canvas roof reeked of bad whiskey, smelling so strongly you could have bottled it and sold it to the Pawnees. Wads of chewing tobacco spotted the floor, with a single clean spittoon standing as a monument to poor marksmanship or gross indifference. A drunk, sprawled face up atop a table, peed contentedly into his pants, while whores sat waiting for customers. The younger ones were Rees or maybe Mandans, wearing trade blanket dresses and dull sullen faces. The older women were white and rouged like circus clowns.

One look had me ready to run. I am not naturally prudish and regularly shocked the Sheyenna. I liked cards and drinking, and was overly fond of making love. But here pleasure had been stripped of its humanity. The drink was despicable, gaming was just a way of taking a soldier's pay for nothing, and behind canvas curtains people swapped diseases in a parody of love-making, where one partner's pockets were emptied while the other got no pleasure. Purgatory could not have been worse, or more boring.

To top off the horror, My Lady's Bower was actually run by a woman— a big solid creature, looking about fifty, with oily hair and black-currant eyes peering out from under puffy lids. She sat tilted back on a stool, rolling a tobacco cigarette on her beefy thigh. Propped against the bar beside her was a tall black man wearing a silk shirt and sugarloaf sombrero. He had a .44 Remington tucked into his belt and a huge Bowie knife on his hip.

Pulling the string on the Bull Durham bag with her teeth, My Lady gave me a broad smile, nudging the dark dude with her knee. The man behind her struck a match on his belt buckle, leaned down, and lit her cigarette. She took a soft drag, saying, "Honey, have a seat—we'll get ya a beer."

I thanked her but did not sit, saying I came to work, not to drink. I said I heard she was short a faro dealer, assuring her I could deal a fair hand and handle the table on my own, keeping the count in my head.

My Lady thanked me with a wink, saying, "Sure, honey, I bet you do. And I got a dealer down with indigestion right now. But I got to tell you straight out, there is no money in a fair game. Can you stack a deck with pairs, or deal seconds out of a crooked shoe?"

I admitted I could, but doubted that I would.

My Lady's companion laughed and spit on the floor. She took a long pull on the cigarette, leaned back, reached between her legs, and scratched. "You are pretty, but I do not pay my dealers thirty a week to look pretty. Dollars are scarce. I cannot afford to hire choirgirls just to dress up the place. I am not asking you to do anything demeaning—no shortchanging customers, no palming chips—just the honest shaving everyone expects. I am not even expecting you to hook on the side. Though if you did, I'd want a cut."

I blushed and tried to back off, but My Lady went on. "When I was young and pert, I thought I was too good to cheat or earn a dollar on my back. Time taught me different. Come back when you are really hungry— and not so young and pretty." Her speech was all the more chilling because she never lost her smile nor showed a hint of malice. When the barkeep arrived with a beer, My Lady took the glass, offering it to me. "Before you go, have that beer. I do not wish you to think bad of me. When you are ready to hook and hustle, I hope you do it here."

I trudged back to Fort Lincoln, thinking this is what comes of living too long with the Sheyenna—civilization confused and frightened me. The army was at least glad to feed me. Fort Lincoln suffered from the same shortage of single young white women that afflicted My Lady's Bower. My absent "husband" did not count for much. Fort Lincoln was full of absent husbands, most of whom were faithful only by force of circumstances.

The next time Wallace came up from Fort Rice for a visit, he brought word that the last train of the year was leaving Bismarck. The bankrupt railroad had neither the money nor the inclination to run trains in winter. As soon as I heard, I was bent on being on that train. I had no plan beyond that; no notion of how to change to a Union Pacific train, nor how to travel the many miles between the rail line and the Center of the World. I just wanted to get away and look for Yellow Legs, to winter in a warm lodge circle where selling your body was considered a form of insanity.

Making excuses, I slipped into the stables and borrowed a mount, Sheyenna fashion, taking clothes, a bedroll, some hardtack, and the Henry rifle. I figured if I let the horse go outside of Bismarck he had brains enough to find his way back to his feed bin.

Wallace caught up with me just short of the station, steamed enough to swear. "I knew I shouldn't have mentioned that damned last train. I suppose you mean to be on it."

I gave him a defiant nod, saying I did not want to be trapped in Fort Lincoln when my husband was waiting for me. Wallace shook his head. "Women always come back from the Lakotas acting crazy, but you seem worse off than most. I could arrest you for horse theft, but instead I am going to escort you right to the station and show you just how loco you are."

When we got to the train, a town mob was shoving men and women into the cars, shouting and cursing at the ones already aboard. Fights were breaking out. I sat on my stolen horse and stared.

Wallace leaned forward in his saddle, saying with slow sarcasm, "There you are. Hop aboard. No one is going to check for a ticket. The town dumps all its undesirables on the last winter train."

Men waved guns from the doors and windows of the carriages, yelling insults at the good citizens staying behind. I sat horrified, realizing that without money I was bound to end up at some man's mercy, and the selection did not look good. As the train pulled off, passengers leaned out the windows, snapping pistols at the people seeing them off. Anyone waving goodbye to Granny had to keep his head low.

Wallace took my reins and turned me back toward Fort Lincoln. "Will you admit that you cannot just ride where you please and do what you will?" I admitted nothing—making it a frosty ride back to the fort.

Tired and defeated, I reached the parade ground to find the commanding officer's quarters lit up like Christmas time. Smoke poured from the chimneys and a thin thread of music hung in the night air. As I drew closer I realized the regimental band was playing and men were singing. The last strains of "Home Sweet Home" faded into the starlight, then the band struck up a faster tune. The words came hurtling from hundreds of deep strong chests:

> Let Bacchus' sons be not dismayed
> But join with me each jovial blade;
> Come booze and sing, and lend your aid
> To help me with the chorus.

Happy as a schoolboy, Wallace leaned over and slapped my saddle. "This will cheer you up. Custer's back."

Moon of Grass Coming Up

Precious Darling,

    *Well we are at last at the far-famed and far distant Yellowstone.
How I have longed for you in what seems a new world—a
Wonderland. Our march has been a delight, each step a
kaleidoscopic shifting of views, sublime beyond description. I wear a
red shirt to show how happy I feel. . . . General S. is acting badly,
drinking, and I anticipate trouble from him.*
                 —Custer to Libby, on the Yellowstone
                   Expedition, Montana Territory, 1873

*   *   *

*The country adjoining the Yellowstone is repulsive in its rugged,
barren ugliness. Custer is a cold-blooded, unprincipled man;
universally despised by his officers excepting his relatives and one or
two sycophants. He brings an old Negro woman and a cast iron
cook-stove into the field. . . . I will try not to have trouble with him.*
                 —General Stanley, Commanding the Yellowstone Expedition,
                   Montana Territory, 1873

THE JUBILANT OFFICER SWUNG ME OFF MY STOLEN HORSE AND
pulled me through the throng, shoving soldiers aside, making me feel like
one of the outcasts of Bismarck being hustled onto the train. Light spilled
out of the commanding officer's quarters onto the snow. In the doorway
stood the soldier in red, encircled by women, as relaxed as when I had first
seen him on the Yellowstone. Taller than Crazy Horse, though not so tall as
Yellow Legs, he was just as Spring Grass described; deep-set blue eyes, a

143

long straight nose, and a tawny mustache. He wore his strawberry curls shorter than a Sheyenna would, but from the tilt of his head I could tell he was just as proud of his hair. Wallace's introduction rang like steel: "General George Armstrong Custer."

Long Hair's manner was shy, as if my sudden appearance made him unsure, even in the midst of his regiment. He stuttered as he introduced his women; Elizabeth, his wife; Margaret, his sister; and Agnes Bates, a young friend from Ohio. There were others, but these were the ones standing closest to him: Libby proud and pleased, Margaret weary, Agnes hollow-eyed and thin.

Turning to Wallace, his stutter vanished—words came easier from a commander joking with a junior officer. "Found her on the prairie, Mr. Wallace? I marked you as a promising officer; now you perform miracles. We moved heaven and earth to bring Agnes from Ohio, and you pluck pretty women out of the wilderness."

I started to back off, feeling already included in Long Hair's lodge. My tiny retreat only made the General bolder; he lunged, taking hold of my arm, telling me, "You must join us at dinner." I tried to say I was wet and filthy from my ride to Bismarck, but Libby took my other arm, smoothing over her husband's brash gesture. "Dear girl, this is the army. If we ate when we were fresh and rested, that would make two meals a month."

Inside, the huge residence blazed with candles. Fires roared in the hearths. Mary, the Custers' black cook, had spread out a formal military supper. Tall glasses stood picketed around the table. Wallace was gone. The meal was for family and ranking officers: General Carlin, the infantry commander; General Dandy, the quartermaster; even Reno, the demoted fort commander. Long Hair sat at the head, with his women and his brothers. The Custers were a huge clan; there were nearly a dozen of them, from two marriages—like a Lakota, Long Hair constantly forgot which siblings came from which mother.

They chattered on about how fine the meal was and how ghastly the food had been on the trip, Agnes saying she had lived on soggy loaves and burned potatoes. Libby wanted to know who I was and where I had come from, a more dangerous subject than soggy rolls. I told my usual story, about coming west and meeting Mr. Kilory, plainsman, Pawnee fighter, and buffalo hunter, omitting only the most important detail. I hesitated when I came to my husband's supposed military career.

Libby smiled. "Is Mr. Kilory a southerner?"

"He was born in Texas." More truthful misdirection; Yellow Legs had been born out on the Staked Plains, part of the Texas Panhandle inhabited by Snakes, Kiowas, and *comancheros*.

"And you are no southerner," Libby observed.

"I was born and raised in Adams County, Pennsylvania."

"Anywhere near Gettysburg?" The General had heard me from his place at the head of the table. I looked down into my plate, saying my mother's farm is just out of town on the Chambersburg Pike, west of Herr Ridge.

"Did you hear that, Tom?" Custer cocked his head the way a warrior would who wanted to make a point at a kill talk; Tom Custer wore the Congressional Medal of Honor on his dress blues, but I guessed he had missed Gettysburg. The General's eyes gleamed. "I rode right down that pike with Gregg's Brigade, chasing Lee back into Maryland." He winked at me. "If you were watching, you'd have seen me ride by."

I kept studying my place setting, unused to warriors being so bold. "It rained in sheets that day, washing out the rail fence we used to sit on." By then our house and barns were filled with wounded. I did not need to run out in the rain to see soldiers.

Long Hair's excitement faded. "How could I have forgotten that horrible rain? Nothing dampens a battle like a downpour." He had so many Civil War battles to remember—I had only one.

Mary brought in meat pies. "Look," exclaimed Boston, the youngest brother, "beef potpie."

"Do you know where to get the best potpie?" asked James Calhoun, Margaret's husband.

"At Mother's," Calhoun and the three Custer brothers chorused.

Libby leaned over, touching my arm. "No one thinks it ill if your husband fought for his home state during the War. General Rosser and my husband fought each other on several occasions—now they're the best of friends." Rosser was an engineer for the Northern Pacific, but he too had been a general in the war. I looked at the head of the table. Custer, Carlin, Reno, Dandy; they had all been generals—sitting at Long Hair's table you got the feeling that the War Between the States was fought solely by general officers.

Libby continued to console me over Yellow Legs's supposed Confederate sympathies. "We just finished doing duty in the South, and Armstrong found chasing after the Klu Klux Klan very distasteful."

Long Hair leaned our way again. "I fought to free the Negro, not to make him our equal. We want the nation to bind its wounds."

This was too smug and comfy, even for me. Black hands had made our meal: Mary had been a slave; now she was a servant. I spoke up, letting my voice carry over the scrape of silverware and the chime of crystal. "My mother was a Quaker, who taught me to forgive my enemies. I came west to make my peace with the Lakotas."

You could have spooned the silence onto your plate. Agnes's eyes went wide. I do not know if she had seen a wild Indian, but she was outside the States, on land reserved for Rees and Lakotas, so she should get ready. General Custer gave me a cool look, stepping into the breach without a stutter. "When I was at West Point I took a romantic view of the noble Redman. Out here, such sentiment is suicide. I have seen the Indian as he really is."

"And as *she* is?" I kept thinking of Spring Grass, trying to imagine her with this man. Her son's hair was light and curly, but that did not make him Custer's. Yellow Bird's father might have been some Swede sergeant, but that was not a question to raise when Spring Grass had her skinning knife handy—or at the Custer dinner table either.

"Indian women are often the worst, the most ignorant and vindictive," added Libby. The fork in her hand shook.

Only Major Reno found my remarks funny. "Your doe-eyed, dusky maiden is a rare find." He raised his glass to the Custers. "But well worth the hunt." No wonder they hated him. The Custers ignored the toast, either because it hit too close or because it came from Reno.

Custer observed dryly, "I never hit a camp that did not have white scalps, branded horses, or kidnapped women."

I looked straight at him. "Before coming west, I worked as a maidservant in New York City. Never a week went by without the papers reporting murders, robberies, or women abducted. Not once did the army come marching up Broadway, looting, burning, and shooting bystanders to teach the city a lesson." This time the generals all laughed, taking it as a joke. Tom said he had seen neighborhoods on Manhattan begging for a visit from the cavalry.

Custer patted his wife's hand. "This subject distresses Libby. She has a dread of Indians."

"I am not a soldier," Libby explained, "and not required to be brave. I wince whenever the regiment marches away, and not just for the men in my family. It is no pleasure being left behind. Women who fall into Indian hands have suffered unspeakably. In Indian Territory Armstrong rescued two women from the Cheyenne. One went mad. The other wanted to go back."

That shut me up. What right had a renegade horse thief to argue with her betters? To say more would only confirm their prejudices and incriminate me. To them marrying an Indian *was* unspeakable degradation—worse than rape.

Custer held tight to Libby's hand, as sure as any Sheyenna brave that women were no judge of war. "You need not worry—the Seventh can whip all the Indians on the plains."

Brother officers smiled, but neither Libby nor I believed him; like Black

Shawl, she feared the enemy would kill her man. That stubborn disbelief formed a bond between us. I had seen a powerful lot of savages out on the plains, and Libby had seen hardly any. From opposite poles we were drawn to the same conclusion: that despite the 7th's hundreds of men and horses, despite its battery of Gatling guns, and its thousands of carbines and pistols—the man was dangerously wrong.

After dinner the General retired to his room. I admired the way Libby soldiered on over brandy and coffee. She had come hundreds of miles by train, ferry, and wagon, and still she was seeing to her guests—until a stiff young orderly came down to say her husband wanted company. Then she packed us off to bed.

In a curious way Wallace was right: The Custers made me feel happier. Libby was not a woman who let you mope around. By breakfast she had found things for me to do. The men were exceedingly proud of the new commanding officer's quarters, but of course they left it half finished—for the next three months we painted, carpeted, and curtained.

Captain Benteen, senior Custer hater in the regiment, called Libby heartless and cold-blooded—mainly for putting up with the General's infidelities. (Benteen was always glad to blackguard the Custers—especially when drunk—and one of the few officers who would talk about Spring Grass. He boasted that after the attack on the Lodgepole there had been a general "squaw roundup" and that Spring Grass had done "blanket duty" for both the General and brother Tom.) But if Libby was cold, it was an icy fire that burned inside her. Like Spring Grass told me, the Wasichu Mrs. Custer meant to have the world the way she wanted it. Working under Libby was a tonic that never gave me time for staring out over the snow, thinking of Yellow Legs lying in Raven's lodge.

Both Custers prided themselves on Libby's supposed ignorance of military matters, and Long Hair liked to tease his women by reading the army regulation giving him "complete control over female camp followers." But any veteran camp follower knows regulations are not written for the real world. I often heard the General snap off an order to an aide, too quick to be understood—surely a distressing habit in battle. Each time, Libby explained the order quietly and clearly to the perplexed aide. In reality Libby was about as unmilitary as a siege mortar, and beat Napoleon at the indirect approach. Armstrong refused to let his wife in the kitchen, so she made me her liaison to the pantry—the sort of task Irish serving girls were made for.

It turned out to be a soft billet, with little work attached. The kitchen was a separate command run by Mary, who needed my advice every other month. Having been born a slave and having campaigned with Custer,

Mary did not care much for the opinions of footloose whites or freeborn blacks who had never known military discipline or worked to the beat of a whip.

I spent many hours in the Custer kitchen. It was the warmest room in the drafty building, and one of the few places where you could hear Lakota spoken freely. Isaiah Dorman, an interpreter from Fort Rice, would stop there after bringing dispatches upriver. He was very tall and very black, and his long legs covered the distance between the two forts in less than a day. He had a Santee wife, and his Lakota name was "Teat," a typical Lakota pun. Isaiah sounds like Lakota for "nipple," and his face was black and wrinkled like a buffalo teat. To be named after any part of the buffalo was big Medicine—most colored troopers were proud to be called Buffalo Soldiers—so the Lakotas must have liked him. I certainly did. Isaiah was strong and thoughtful, and loved the country.

We would lounge about the kitchen sipping coffee and swapping Sitting Bull stories. Not much that was said in the kitchen ever made it into the main rooms; it was their loss. If Long Hair had sat down at his kitchen table he could have listened to at least two people who had been in the lodge of his most influential enemy. But Long Hair did not even let his wife into the kitchen.

Snow and cold slowed even Libby, making time for tale-telling and dancing. We put on stage plays and Indian pageants, with the General as heap big chief; I played pretty squaw. But best of all were the Christmas balls. Barracks messes were decorated with stacked arms and battle flags, and a grizzled first sergeant would lead out the opening dance in dress blues, with years of service braid on his sleeve and Libby at his elbow. Trim young officers in tight-fitting uniforms waited patiently for a turn twirling Agnes or me about, while the caller sang, "Oh, swing those girls, those pretty little girls, those girls you left behind you."

My dance card was always full. The best dances were those I danced with Wallace; the worst was one with Reno. With Wallace, Myles Keogh, or any of the Custers, you had the excitement of a strong arm pressing at your waist, while soldiers' voices rang against flag-draped rafters:

> If ever I should see the day,
> When Mars will have resigned me,
> Forever more I'll gladly stay,
> With the girl I left behind me.

But when I saw President Grant's familiar gaze staring through paper laurel leaves, or when they played "Garryowen," I would remember coyotes howl-

ing around a lodge circle and the world of night drums and winter dances I
had left behind.

> My mind or form shall still retain,
> In sleeping or in waking,
> Until I see my love again,
> For whom my heart is breaking.

Libby let me see that what I missed in the white world was family. Railway towns, army forts, and gambling hells are almost monastic communities.
Make money, subdue the West, and move on. Whoring was meant to take
the place of home life. The most squalid Santee village was closer to my girlhood in Adams County.

Fort Lincoln had its version of family, mostly for officers and their
women. In the evenings we had romps, frolics, and pillow fights. Former
generals and Medal of Honor winners would chase us up and down the
stairs. But it was never fully a family—Libby had no children, and the little ones learning their letters on Armstrong's lap belonged to servants. If we
were up past curfew, a stern orderly would rap at the door, delivering two
white nightdresses "compliments of the commanding officer," Custer's way
of saying it was past Libby's and Agnes's bedtimes. Happily, I was never a full
member of the official family; there was no nightdress for me. I felt free to
sleep past reveille, or as late as Mary would let me.

Early in the new year work on the quarters was complete as it ever got—
we never did get it snug. The green boards shrank, letting in the Dakota
winter, making the place draftier than a tattered tipi. The world outside froze
solid. Soldiers had to saw through five feet of ice just to draw water from the
river. I watched coyotes trot dry-shod across the Big Muddy, invading the
east-bank farmlands in their eternal quest for an easy meal.

One clear frigid night I awoke to a frightful bang, followed by a roaring
overhead, then drumming feet, yells, and carbine shots. Throwing on a buffalo robe, I ran barefoot onto the snow. Someone screamed out, "Lakota attack!"

But Lakotas had better ways to spend the Snowblind Moon than paying
social calls on the cavalry. Sparks and burning plaster cascaded off the roof.
One look and I started throwing everything I valued out onto the snowy parade ground.

Custer strode about in vest and nightdress, giving orders that could
hardly be heard, and didn't matter. Men cried for water as though wounded
and dying of thirst, but we were in a frozen waste, with not enough wet water
to fill a trough. Howling red flames swarmed higher. Gas from petroleum

paper beneath the plaster began exploding, blowing great holes in the walls, tearing off the roof. My little room, Mary's kitchen, the banisters we slid down, the parlors we played in, were all burned to charred timbers. The yip and yell of a coyote came out of the cold and dark, and a voice laughed inside my head, *"It will all go to ashes."*

The court of inquiry found a chimney had exploded, clearing Custer of any fault in the disaster. But the burning broke Libby's spell. I got a shared room, in separate quarters, lodging with an old Mexican laundress called Nash after a former husband who had deserted her but left his name behind. She was a tall awkward woman who had been abandoned by a string of men, but kept remarrying. We got on tolerably well, though she was one of those decency fanatics—refusing to bathe in front of me or undress when the lamp as lit. I wondered how she had ever put up with a husband, much less several.

Without a house and work to hold us together, I saw less of Libby and the General—and more of Wallace instead. He escorted me to dances and invited me on sleigh ride. Any excuse sufficed. I could feel him slipping under my guard: the hand on my thigh as we mounted the sleigh, the close way he held me as we danced.

He even asked me to an Arikaree dance. I went, though until then I had kept away from the Ree scouts. I have nothing against Rees, but they knew the Sheyenna far better than the Long Knives did. I did not want some Ree remembering me from a chance meeting or lodge talk. Still they were friendlies, paid and armed by the government, but otherwise ignored. How much danger could they be?

The Rees were quartered in dirt-floored log barracks that sank into the snowy ground. Unlike Custer's burned down mansion, the Rees' longhouses were warm and airtight. When the thick wooden door closed behind me, I waded into a stifling sea of woodsmoke, cooking smells, sweat, excrement, and kinnikinnick tobacco—a Sheyenna winter camp is positively clean compared to a Corn Indian long lodge.

A bonfire in a big hearth threw deep shadows down the length of the plank ceiling. I was startled to see Lakotas—mostly Hunkpapas and Yanktons—sitting side by side with the Rees. I asked Wallace what blood enemies were doing coming armed to an Arikaree dance. He shrugged. "The Sioux wanted a peace talk. Maybe they just got lonely and hankered to trade war stories." I preferred to hope these Hunkpapas really wanted peace—the lion should lie down with the lamb, even when the lamb carries a Spencer carbine.

I was nearly as shocked to see Libby sitting on a bench by the fire. Custer was there too, talking to Myles Keogh. Libby got up, greeting me with a nervous smile. "Armstrong wants me to get over my dread of Indians. We have never been stationed near a peaceful tribe before—I am actually excited by the spectacle."

I had heard the Rees called imaginative names—Corn Huskers, Dirt Dwellers, Walking Wolves, Rotten Pricks—but "peaceful" was a new one. Men were stripping down to dance, armed with guns and scalp knives, their clay-whitened bodies speckled with painted-on bullet pocks. The evening's spectacle was already looking more exciting than I had fancied—but Libby saw what she wanted to, especially around Indians.

With Wallace as our escort, we strolled to the back of the longhouse, where the women sat. It was dark and dirty, smelling of death. Libby wrinkled her nose, saying she had missed the really big Indian show. "The one Buffalo Bill gave for the Grand Duke Alexis. Armstrong went. Flirting shamelessly with Chief Spotted Tail's daughter, from what I hear." Spotted Tail was Crazy Horse's uncle.

This led naturally to Libby's flirtations with the Grand Duke. "Russian men are wonderfully polite, and able to drink without becoming silly. We got to be very Russian in our habits, having rolls and coffee in the continental fashion, then eggs and toast at noon."

I could not keep my mind on continental breakfasts. From what I was seeing, the whole Ree nation could have used several servings of eggs on toast, or even a roll and sugared coffee. These were the most bony Indians I had ever seen—worse than Utes. Some had huge unhealed sores. The destruction of the Corn Indians was a tragedy that kept on happening, and I had avoided the Rees partly for fear of what I would see.

Proud mothers sitting on unpainted bunks held up their babies for the Long Knife chief's wife to inspect. Libby looked perplexed. "Such enthusiasm over a few skinny babies. You'd think that those were the first children born in the world."

"Or the last." I thought how Bloody Knife's mother had left the Hunkpapas to bring her sons back to her people. "Any woman who raises a Ree right now has a right to be proud."

Libby stiffened. "It is their own fault—if they would just learn farming they could feed themselves. I have seen plows and farm equipment rusting in reservation sheds."

I gave Wallace an exasperated glance. Tipping his hat, he took my part. "Mrs. Custer has not yet had the difficult pleasure of trying to farm this land. In Bismarck a cabbage sells for as much as a new cloth coat—when you can find a cabbage." So much for the Northern Pacific's "fertile crescent." I vowed to kiss Wallace for standing by me. Men say the obvious with so much authority.

"Starvation is killing the Rees." I repeated Dr. Warren's professional evaluation of government rations: "Lean beef, flour paste, and corn mush will kill you as sure as strychnine, only slower and with a deal more agony. The Hunkpapas who brought me here told how the Big Muddy used to be black with buffalo coming down to drink—we saw only a few head of hungry cattle."

I asked Wallace's opinion of Lakotas in the wilds.

"Did they look puny to you?"

He smiled. "Hard to say. When they come screaming at you in paint and feathers, they all look ten feet tall. But I would say the Prairie Sioux are some of the finest physical specimens on the planet."

"Has there been much decline in their numbers?" We all knew the fall of the Rees had been appalling; barely one in five had survived reservation life.

"There are more hostile Sioux than I would care to call on."

I nodded toward a kettle of corn mush and trash scrapings, noting that food like that had brought my father to America. Wallace lifted an eyebrow. "Your father had eccentric tastes."

"No, he was Irish. During the Starvation the British tried to feed all Ireland on corn mush. One taste and he left for America. If corn alone could keep you alive, the Rees would be well off. Ree women are famous corn growers." I demonstrated the cornhusking motion that means "Arikaree."

Women laughed to see a female Wasichu making signs. One of the older warriors turned, staring right at me. He had a hawk face, hunter's eyes, and an attractive touch of gray in his braids. Most of the men were stripped to leggings and breechcloths, but this Ree warrior wore cavalry pants and an army jacket, with a private's single chevron on the sleeve. His face seemed distant but familiar, like a reflection in a dusty mirror.

Wallace waved the man over. "Mrs. Kilory, I would like you to meet Bloody Knife."

At that moment I was surrounded by Medicine Bear's curse. Long Hair was standing a short way off, and I could have touched Bloody Knife if I dared. Wallace went cheerfully on, winking a challenge to the scout, "Bloody Knife is the best shot in the outfit—next the General."

"I shoot straighter than ten generals," signed the Ree.

The dance began, and Wallace asked the scout to call the turns. Bloody Knife signed that most of the dancers were Strong Hearts, warriors in their prime who had purchased their places with gifts to the existing members. I knew some Strong Hearts myself: Sitting Bull, Gall, and Crow King all belonged to the Hunkpapa branch of the lodge.

"Purchased how?" Wallace asked. "With horses?"

"Horses, yes and . . ." Bloody Knife made the quick finger thrust between spread fingers, meaning wives had prostituted themselves to get their men into the Strong Hearts. Such casual relations gave the Rees a bad name. But Bloody Knife clearly did not worry about Wasichu opinion.

I pointed out one dancer who must have been all of four years old, his small body twirling about between the legs of the men. "What did he buy his way in with?"

"He is only an honorary member," signed the scout. "His mother helped him stab a wounded Sioux." Declaring the child was nothing special, he directed our attention to the dancers with turkey feathers tied to their rumps. Their limbs were painted green and blue, and they bobbed and weaved around a bubbling cauldron, imitating the movements of crows around a corpse. One by one they plunged their arms into the boiling pot. I winced, but their white-ringed eyes did not even blink.

Wallace mumbled something about bear grease and purple coneflower root keeping them from being scalded—but that sounded frightfully weak. It would take more grease than you could get off a grizzly to make me stick my arm in searing water.

Bloody Knife scoffed, "Whites do not like to see us making Medicine they cannot make." Wallace told Bloody Knife the Rees could keep their ghastly customs, for all this officer cared.

"Do not worry," Bloody Knife assured him. "I am a good Arikaree. I sing hymns and shoot Sioux; that is the Jesus way." Indians took Christianity the way they found it, which often had exasperated me when I was bent on Christianizing them.

The hot dancers were just a curtain-raiser. Warriors began to count coups, holding up bedsheets with their exploits painted on them. The bravest and most generous would toss painted sticks into the crowd, promising, "This is a pony." I wished one had tossed a stick or two my way, but I suppose they thought all Wasichu were horse rich. One old matron, carried away by such valor and generosity, threw her blanket and moccasins to the warriors. Leaping into the Medicine circle, she kicked off her leggings and was working on her breechcloth when they hustled her off stage—there were Wasichu present.

During intermissions, Lakotas would get up and comment, filling in their side of the fight. Any Ree tempted to stretch his exploits risked being exposed by the Lakotas. Not all contributions were taken in good grace. After one old Lakota's speech a young Ree jumped up, shouting and signing, "Be silent, old man, I shot your son dead. Fight me now, if you are brave enough." The old Lakota did not look at him, but stared into the smoky distance—the Peace of the Camp stood between this man and his son's killer.

Libby looked fairly disgusted, but I suppose this was her first kill talk. I could have told her that things were done with more decorum in Sitting Bull's tipi. Rain-in-the-Face's bragging had been positively restrained.

James Calhoun tried to comfort his sister-in-law, saying we would see hives of industry replacing dirty wigwams, and seminaries of learning driving out heathen lore. Calhoun was either stone blind or a romantic idiot. Maybe both. We had all seen the stretch of civilization between Bismarck and Fort Lincoln—there was not a single seminary to be had, and whorehouses had replaced the wigwams.

We left the dance and kill talk plenty shaken. Wallace questioned Bloody Knife about the prospects for peace with the Lakotas. Bloody Knife laughed long and hard. "There is Hunkpapa blood in me. I swear by that blood that when grass comes up and the ponies are fat, we will be fighting again."

"This summer will be different," suggested Wallace. "We have a fort here and a regiment of cavalry. With allies like these, the Arikarees will be too strong for the Sioux."

"You are young," signed the scout, looking Wallace full in the face. "And much of your life was wasted in the Land Where the Sun Comes From. Arikarees do not need allies. Our grandfathers drove the Lakotas out onto the prairie. Our grandmothers had the Medicine to call the buffalo down to the river."

"Everyone knows the Arikarees are great," signed Wallace. This was a ritual lie that Wasichu repeat when Rees are around. No one cared a pressed grape for the great days of the Corn Indians, least of all cavalry officers.

Curling his lip, Bloody Knife gave Wallace the look the old Lakota had given the taunting Ree. "How can a Long Knife know the Medicine of the Arikarees? When my father was young, Long Knives came to burn our villages. Fearing our power, they brought a thousand Lakotas—Hunkpapas, Yanktons, and Two Kettles—to fight for them. If the Long Knives wanted to test our Medicine, they should have come alone. Arikarees have no allies, only enemies."

I could not subscribe to Bloody Knife's philosophy. Every man is not my enemy—it only seems that way sometimes. But life for the Rees was a losing struggle, and having an ally who always wins can just encourage cynicism.

Wallace winked at me, as if to say, See what a good scout he is? If he was not the best, Custer would not put up with him. Happy with Wallace for the way he had stood up to Libby, I deluded myself into thinking that we felt the same. Sitting beside him in the sleigh, I asked, "Do you hate what is being done to the Rees?"

He shook his head. "I dislike it. But it is not a soldier's duty to hate government policy—no matter how shortsighted."

"So you save your hate for the Lakotas?"

"Yes. But any Indian who stands up and fights gets a soldier's respect." I knew if we kept talking Indians, things would get complicated fast; it was easier just to let Wallace have his kiss and walk me back to my lodgings, where Nash nervously awaited my return.

Fired by the hot dance and kill talk, the Ree women put on their own show a few days later, shuffling around the parade ground, waving their husbands' weapons until Long Hair gave them a beef to take home. They had lost the power to call buffalo down to the Big Muddy, but still had the Medicine to bring meat into their lodges.

The new moon was the Moon of Grass Coming up, and I caught Libby trodding on the first green shoots of spring, grinding them into the ground like a wanton boy taking revenge on life. She looked ashamed and confessed she too thought there would be fighting as soon as the grass was up. When it came to Lakotas, Libby was closer to Bloody Knife's views than to her husband's.

Later I found the General looking off over the new shoots as well. Two hawks circled overhead, calling to each other with talons thrust out. They were redtails, courting each other on the wing. Seeing me, Custer smiled and took off his hat, running fingers through his thinning hair; like Crazy Horse, he had been called Curly as a boy, another coincidence pulling the Medicine circle tighter. Yellow Legs always laughed at my notion of coincidence, calling it a neat way to keep the Medicine hidden.

I asked the General if there was really bound to be fighting when the grass was up.

"A soldier lives to fight." He exuded the shy confidence of a warrior speaking to a woman, once again being the bashful boy-general—the Army of the Potomac's *beau sabreur*. Custer lacked Crazy Horse's compact sureness and singleness of purpose, but he was brave to a fault. Aloft in a balloon or leading a charge, he had that dauntless courage than makes females melt and brings on disaster.

I protested that there was nothing more to fight about—no need to survey up the Yellowstone for a busted railroad.

The General hardly seemed to hear me. I had once asked him about smoking the peace pipe with Medicine Arrows; he just laughed, saying, had the Sheyenna had known what he was thinking they would never have offered him a puff. No wonder Brave Bear knocked the ashes on his boot.

Plucking a grass shoot, Custer twirled it between his fingers; it was wheatgrass, which sends out the first runners of spring. He spoke softly. "You love this country don't you?"

I nodded. "In spring, when the buffalo stand knee-deep in the bluestem and the meadowlarks sing, there is nowhere on earth like Lakota Country."

"I could tell." He tossed the stalk aside. "It's not easy for me to imagine living without bison to hunt and Sioux to fight. I will miss them dearly. And I suppose if I were Sioux I would want to go down fighting." Custer did not drink and hardly needed to buy women—he was probably as appalled as I was by what starvation, whiskey, and whoring had done to the Corn Indians. But I could not fathom how a man could claim to love the West, while working to destroy it. Libby shared his ambivalence, if not his keen soldierly confidence. I had once asked her about the attack on the Lodgepole that destroyed Yellow Legs's village and killed Spring Grass's father. She had told me, "I do believe Armstrong did right. But can the Indians be entirely wrong? All these broad prairies did belong to them."

Custer stared off toward the Center of the World, as if it held some special secret. "This summer Sheridan is giving me complete freedom to exercise my command. I will take the Seventh where I see fit. No one, not Grant nor Sitting Bull, can stop me. Big things will happen, but it all must wait until the grass is up."

She Wore a Yellow Ribbon

HAWKS MATING ON THE WING MEANT SPRING WAS HERE. I HAD to get to Yellow Legs or burst from loneliness. The Iron Horse did not wait for the grass to come up, and the Northern Pacific began running as soon as the weather relented. Bankrupt and laying no track, the line still ran trains to pay off creditors. So when Wallace next came to call, I sat the young officer down, telling him there would be no more outings, sleigh rides, picnics, day trips, balls, or Strong Heart dances. Wallace looked suitably aghast, but I told him the only invitation I wanted was to a poker game.

He stared as though I were speaking in tongues, saying regimental card games were not fit for respectable females.

"Nonsense," I retorted. "Everyone is trying to teach Libby cards."

"Mrs. Custer is learning bridge—not poker."

"And a good thing too. She promises to be easy money." Libby could not tell a trump from a turnip. Like a lot of shrewd women, Libby was stubbornly ignorant when she needed to be. Gambling was one of Armstrong's weaknesses, and Libby did not aim to encourage his reckless disregard for odds. I don't much like gambling myself, which is why I planned to play poker.

Ignoring Wallace's astounded scowl, I laid out my winter earnings—thirty-eight dollars, seventeen and a half cents, mostly in American money. Libby was not rich, but she paid better than teaching Indians did. Wallace rolled his eyes at the pile of coins and crumpled bank notes. "You are starting to act crazy again."

"Trains are running, and I am going to meet my husband. If you won't get me into a game, I know a woman at My Lady's Bower who will."

Wallace recoiled. "You have no idea what goes on in a place like that."

157

"I know in some detail, which is why I would rather play on the post. But I will take whatever game I can get."

Seeing himself outflanked, he promised to sneak me into the next suitable game, but then took so long about it that I feared he was being clever. Finally he came for me on a frigid spring evening. Halfway across the parade ground he offered me his blue coat and yellow cavalry bandanna. As he knotted the bandanna our breath misted together in the moonlight. It occurred to me that we Wasichu have our own bans and taboos, and I was breaking down every barrier decent behavior put between us. Once you cross an invisible line, it can be awfully tricky stepping back. Nash, my much-married roommate, already considered me far too forward and trusting, claiming I did not know men like she did.

The game was in a Sibley tent, shaped like a little tipi and lit by a single oil lamp. The tiny tent was warmed by two lieutenants, a civilian, and a bottle of sipping whiskey. The lieutenants were Calhoun and Godfrey—and the bottle was bourbon.

"A new recruit," Calhoun declared, grinning at my blue jacket and officer's bars. "And as handsome a lieutenant as I have ever seen commissioned." He winked at Wallace. "But you, Mister Wallace, are out of uniform." James Calhoun was a Custer only by marriage to Maggie, but he had the family mustache, haircut, and cutting tongue. Seeing the bandanna, he and Godfrey broke into song:

> *'Round her neck, she wore a yellow ribbon,*
> *She wore it in the springtime, in the merry month of May,*
> *And when I asked, why the yellow ribbon?*
> *She said it's for her lover who is in the cavalry.*

It was plain the bottle had been around more than once. Bourbon slurred the chorus:

> *Cavalry, cavalry,*
> *She wore it for her lover in the U.S. cavalry!*

The civilian passing the bottle was an angular Missourian in shabby homespun, whose current alias was Independence Jake—a man more likely to have ridden with Quantrill than with the cavalry. During the War, the only thing three Yankee officers would have shared with Jake was a stout limb and a short rope. He confessed to being a Clay County James—"but we got so many Jameses in that part of Missouri, I took the name Independence." Clay County Jameses were notorious bank examiners and railway inspectors; last summer they and their cousins the Youngers loosened a rail on the Rock Island line between Adair and Council Bluffs, riding off with the train's express box and a collection from the passengers.

Just by the way Jake held his cards I knew these horse soldiers were going to pay for their drinks and then some. Jake had the mechanic's grip: deck face down in his palm, fingers all around the cards. Hold the deck like that and you can make the cards stand up and whistle "Dixie" if you have a mind to. Since a lady sits where she likes, I took the place on Jake's right. Nothing could tempt me to let him cut to my deal.

They were playing Jackpot Draw, five cards down and jacks or better to open—I would have preferred Stud, a more scientific game. Riding out the first hands, I was quick to fold on Jake's deal. You cannot see a skilled mechanic deal seconds, but I could hear the soft swish of a card sliding out of the pack instead of being flicked off the top. Jake dealt seconds so often the top card got dusty waiting to be played. And from the first cut I knew he was using a crimp, folding the cards so the natural cut was where he needed it. I was careful to cut right to the crimp. I wanted Jake to rely on my cut, to think he could pass me a stacked-up deck and get the cards back the way he wanted them.

I felt bad for the lieutenants, but West Point should teach its officers to play poker. A keen knowledge of cards would be more use out west than the campaigns of Hannibal or the Elements of Moral Philosophy. At the very least the Point should teach them not to play poker with likable gents having no last name and a city or state for a first one.

Independence Jake was generous with his skill. Only taking a pot from time to time, he let the money and whiskey circulate, keeping the wheel of fortune spinning by lubricating the losers. The big winner on Jake's deals was Lieutenant Calhoun—which was something new. One reason the game was in a small cold tent was that Maggie, Libby, and the General were out to curb Calhoun's gambling. That only shows their ignorance. Properly played, poker is a game of skill—not luck. Every hand has a fixed chance of coming up, so a good player knows when to fold, check, or bet. Lieutenant Calhoun was not a good player, yet his style of play was not exactly gambling either—being closer to giving money away.

But a one-eyed monkey could play the cards Jake tossed Calhoun—so with Calhoun winning for once, and everyone drinking, the game galloped along. My cautious play was not winning the money I needed, so I decided to shake the game up, suggesting we raise the ante.

Wallace looked shocked. Godfrey said the stakes were high enough. I had marked Godfrey down as a careful officer and watchful card player.

Calhoun was neither; taunting his brother officers, he claimed they were afraid he might get back some of the money lost in games gone by.

Jake took his time, trying to see how I fit into his plan. I guessed he was using Calhoun as a cover, to catch people's attention and sweeten the pot. He looked me up and down, then decided, "Sure, let's have a dollar ante and play Progressive Jackpots. *La partie continue.*"

Showing some of the Custer command, Calhoun dragged Wallace and Godfrey with him—against their better judgment. Jake dealt. No one had jacks or better, so the deal went to Godfrey, with queens for openers. Another round of checks and another ante, then it was Calhoun and kings. When it came to Wallace we needed aces. More checks, more antes, and the cards came to me.

I was looking at twenty-five dollars in an unopened pot. I hefted the deck—it felt light, and the high pairs had vanished. I said nothing, dealing straight to see what happened. No one had openers. The deal went to Jake. He used a long overhand riverboat shuffle, perfect for stacking a deck. Blowing smoke from a dying cigar, he claimed maybe now we would see some cards: "For a little fun I think I will deal this hand Shotgun."

No one objected, so he gave me the cards to cut. The deck came crimped as usual. I started to sweat. This had to be the hand. The high cards Jake was holding would now reappear. Cutting to the crimp, I took a quick peek at the top card—if you are careful, you can always check the top card as you cut. An ace peeked back at me. Godfrey's ace. This was the end of Calhoun's lucky run. Jake had his chickens set for plucking.

I cut one card below the crimp, burying the ace at the bottom of the deck, changing the order of the hands. Now Jake would get the hand he had stacked for Godfrey. Godfrey would get Calhoun's. Calhoun would get Wallace's. Wallace would get my hand. And I would get the hand Jake had planned to play.

I did it almost without thinking, then sat back, watching the cards flick across the tabletop. Jake dealt off the top, sure of his crimp and my cut, giving us each three cards, then setting the deck down.

Putting some of Libby's sweet ignorance into my voice, I asked where the other two cards were. The men all laughed, explaining that in Shotgun Draw you bet before seeing your last two cards. I smiled. "Can we can at least have them on the table?"

Wallace thought that sounded fair. Jake hastened to agree: "Anything for the lady." His smile looked a quarter inch shorter as he dealt each of us two cards face down on the folding camp table. I knew all about Shotgun deals. I just wanted all five cards on the table before Jake saw his hand.

We looked at our first three cards. A silent ripple ran around the table, like the tingle of a galvanic circuit closing. Bleary eyes narrowed or went wide; lieutenants held their cards closer to their blue blouses. Jake had to have stacked their hands with aces and face cards; after seeing so many fives and sevens, the high cards hit like a Northern Pacific freight. But Independence Jake must have felt he'd been kicked up the butt by a Missouri mule— staring at the cards he had meant for Godfrey, only they were shy an ace.

I tipped up the corners of my cards. A pair of threes peeked at me. Not a promising sight. In fact, a sucker hand. I had thrown in three better ones looking for openers. Was I wrong? If Jake had been feeding another pot to Calhoun, why the ace for Godfrey?

Godfrey bet and Calhoun raised. Wallace raised. The bet was eight dollars to me. A pair of threes, when the betting opens at queens, is a fine hand to fold. Nothing short of aces or three of a kind justified a bet. It took a heroic act of will to push ten dollars into the pot, raising the bet to Jake.

The Missourian stared from me to my ten dollars. He knew from the way he loaded the deck that I was holding two threes. To push a low pair against three hands holding queens or better made me a phenomenal fool. Or a lady who knew more than she should.

Calhoun started whistling "Marching Through Georgia," adding to the Missourian's misery. Jake grimaced, then ground his cigar stub into Uncle Sam's table, throwing his three cards on top of the pair lying face down. The hand he had meant for Godfrey was not nearly good enough for him.

The lieutenants and I each took a card. I got the three of spades, a real black widow of a card—making my hand better, but nothing to bet the farm on. Godfrey liked what he got, betting again. Everyone raised. Jake bit on another cigar, not bothering to light it. I watched him chew on the cold stogie. If this bushwhacker had not stacked the deck to win, mental arithmetic told me I would be flat busted. The chances of getting a full house with the fifth card were fourteen to one against me. A fourth three was forty to one away.

Last cards; we all reached and looked.

Mine was the card that would beat them all. A trio of blood-red splotches—the trey of hearts. I was holding four threes, a thousand-to-one hand. We were not playing straight flushes, so only four higher cards could beat it. And Jake must have spread the court cards around among his victims. Each of them would be holding a couple of high pairs, aiming for a full house; they would not even be thinking four of a kind. The money on the camp table was mine, if I could just stay in the game.

But Calhoun sat whistling Sherman's march, happily driving up the bet—it cost me everything I had just to stay in for the draw. Calhoun and Godfrey each took a card. Wallace stood pat. I stood pat too—hoping to scare them off. Nothing could improve my hand, but even a dollar bet now and I would be raised out.

Cautious Godfrey checked. Then Calhoun bet five bucks, and I wanted to cry. Wallace raised him five, making it ten dollars to me. All my capital had gone into the pot. There was close to two hundred dollars within reach, but I needed ten dollars more to seal it.

Embarrassed silence hung over the table. Everyone could see I was broke. What did I have that was worth ten dollars? Only one thing. The Medicine rifle. Yellow Legs swore it would protect me—now was the chance to prove it. Shooting it off had only gotten me in trouble. I set my cards face down. "All I have is that Cheyenne Medicine gun. Will one of you lend me something on it? It belonged to a brave who got it at the Fetterman fight."

Fetterman was a red flag—like giving three cheers for Crazy Horse at a Crow kill talk. The Fetterman massacre was the worst defeat Lakotas and Sheyenna had ever handed the cavalry.

Wallace reached into his pocket and pulled out a twenty-dollar gold piece, tossing it over to me—that was better than a week's pay, and more than the gun would bring. "That gun's just gonna get you into trouble. You'll be better off without it."

I pushed the coin into the pot, trading it for ten bucks in silver. Calhoun started pounding on the table with the butt of the bottle:

> 'Round her leg she wore a yellow garter,
> She wore it to bedtime in a very merry way.
> And when I asked, "Why the yellow garter?"
> She said it's for her lover who is in the cavalry . . .

They slapped out the chorus, then Wallace added a verse of his own:

> Behind the door, her husband keeps a shotgun.
> It's loaded with a double dose
> Of buckshot so they say.
> And when I asked, "Why the double buckshot?"
> He said it's for her lover who is in the cavalry.

Calhoun kept beating time on the table until singing shook the tent.

> Cavalry! Cavalry!

Just a happy trio of horse soldiers, their hands full of high cards.

Calhoun called the bet. Godfrey folded. Calhoun put down two pair, jacks and tens. He should never have pushed jacks up against two pat hands, but who said Calhoun could play cards? Wallace turned over a full house, kings over queens. Half the high cards in the deck were showing by the time I laid my threes on the table.

You could hear the wind moaning in the tent stays. These soldiers never expected all those court cards would fall to a handful of threes. Only Independence Jake saw it coming, but what could he say? That the hand had been meant for him? No tarnished southern gentleman was going to accuse a lady of cheating—not on his deal, and not in front of three drunk and disappointed Yankee officers with army Colts in their holsters.

Feeling sorry for one lieutenant, who deserved to be a little less broke, I took the twenty-dollar piece out of the pot, passing it back to Wallace. Then I raked in the rest, pleased as a parson at collection. All this army pay was mine—none of them knew enough about cards to get it back. I took a comforting sip from the bottle.

When the deal came back to Jake he passed the deck to me without a crimp—no longer trusting me to cut like a lady. The card shark had been bitten. Without a dishonest chance of separating me from that army pay, he left, taking Godfrey with him.

I should have gone too. But victory is as intoxicating as whiskey. And victory and whiskey together are well nigh overpowering. Accustomed to losing, Calhoun kept at it until he was flat, then begged Wallace for a stake. Lieutenant Wallace had loaned money already that evening, and gotten a poorer return on his investment than the Northern Pacific had payed. Calhoun staggered off to face Maggie, busted again. By now I was beginning to see the bottom of the bottle.

The more I drank, the more I felt I owed Wallace. It had been mean to take advantage of him. With intoxicated precision I divided my winnings into two neat piles—pushing one toward the lieutenant, telling him, "Money takes half. I would not have won if you had not staked me."

He said he did not want my money.

Lurching to my feet I tried to unhook the kerosine lantern. "Take it," I insisted, full of drunken desire to do right by Wallace, to give to him in return. Swaying like a train conductor I twisted at the lantern thumbscrew, meaning to get a little more light. A hand closed over mine, forcing the screw the other way. A moment later Wallace was holding me in the dark.

I thought, My God, he is going to kiss me. I opened my mouth to say something, and he did kiss me, long and hard like a man who knows how. My first kiss from Yellow Legs had been infinitely more tentative.

Wallace's hair was short as well and did not fall in my face. When I hooked my hands behind his head it felt like the pelt of an animal. We swayed together in the darkness as his tongue perused my mouth. Then I heard the creak of an army cot. The bans between us were totally broken. Waves of triumph and pleasure swept over me, rolling off into the black Dakota night. I heard myself murmur again and again that I was going home.

I awoke to hard morning light, my head aching, back in my room, with no idea how I had gotten there—a sure sign I had been having a better time than the law allows. Nash was splashing about at the washstand with her back to me.

In bits and snatches the whole night came back. I was shocked, appalled, then terrified. The call of blood was stronger than I had thought. Wallace was not just a man; he was a world, a way of life. I never knew how easily I could slide into it. If I so much as *saw* Wallace again, his strong familiar world threatened to engulf me—and I would never get back to Yellow Legs. I pictured myself as a cavalry wife. No longer riding free. Spending my summers on a porch in some dreary post waiting for my man. Libby was not allowed to ride out of sight of Fort Lincoln—not even as far as Bismarck.

The money. For a frantic moment I thought I'd lost it. Then I felt it, tucked under my pillow. I leaped up, determined to blot out the night before with movement, nearly knocking over Nash, who gave a great gasp.

She dropped a razor into the washbowl. She had been shaving! And not her armpits either. Nash went white with fear, seeing "her" secret was out. But I was not as surprised as I should have been. I suppose living with the Sheyenna had prepared me. Things just came together: Nash's big bony body and gravelly voice, her terror of nudity, and her series of disappointed "husbands". No wonder Nash figured she knew men so well.—Fort Lincoln had more need of female labor than any Lakota camp, and this man-woman had been willing to meet that need.

Getting my things together, I announced I was leaving—not just the room, but the fort and territory as well. Nash nearly shook with relief. Sharing a lodge with me must have been an awful strain.

I redivided the money, wrapping half in a piece of writing paper, penciling Wallace's name on the outside. Tying the packet together with string, I gave it to the surprised paymaster. Wallace would be the first officer at the fort to be handsomely paid for a night of fun.

At the ferry dock I got a seat on a sutler's wagon returning empty to Bismarck. We went with an escort of troopers, so Wallace would know by nightfall where I had gone. Sitting up beside the driver, feeling the cold clean air blowing through the weave of my dress, I remembered I had not said goodbye to Libby. Well, she was a soldier's wife. She could never be sure that even Armstrong would give her a proper goodbye.

I had enough money to go first class, riding a Central Pacific Silver Palace car all the way to the Golden Gate. Instead I bought an immigrant ticket, riding in cars crowded with travel-stained women, as worn and faded as the kerchiefs in their hair. Few of them had wanted to come west. Most were poor and displaced, driven by the money panic, seeking land, jobs, or husbands. They found the West dirty and uncomfortable, and complained that the shortgrass prairie all looked the same, as though the train were standing still in immense emptiness. Their eyes were accustomed to seeing no farther than across the street. To me the prairie is never empty. Out the train windows was the world's greatest stage show: hawks circling beneath high clouds, antelope racing ahead of the Iron Horse. As we approached the green curving line of the Platte, I could feel the roaring locomotive carrying me closer to Yellow Legs and the Center of the World. Iron wheels sang to the rails; *Paha Sapa, Paha Sapa, Paha Sapa.*

Coyote's banking crisis had become international. Beside the cold platforms I saw Cornish miners and Spanish shepherds, stripped to the waist, splashing themselves with pump water or bathing out of buckets. Only the children seemed to share a sense of adventure, scampering over piles of luggage, hanging off the platforms, playing on the tracks. At Grand Island on the Platte, I shared a dollar breakfast with Lea, a ten-year-old orphan going to live with relatives in Ogden. Her mother was dead and her dad had gone off. Her aunt had sent her west—being brought up a Latter-Day Saint in some Mormon harem was better than starving on the sidewalks of New York. Lea took to our dollar breakfast like a tapeworm, downing beefsteak, antelope chops, fried eggs, Indian corn, sweet potatoes, and pancakes, with syrup over everything. It came with a soup that Lea called chicken, but I recognized as plump, greasy prairie dog. You could still eat well in the States— if you had a dollar.

I got off at Ogallala, Nebraska, a board-and-canvas cow town where the Western Cattle Trail crosses the Union Pacific tracks. The big wide streets had grass growing in them. Idle cowhands told me the Texas herds would be late and lean this year, and the only beef going north was a government herd bound for the Spotted Tail agency. I looked up the trail boss for this northbound herd, a sturdy grizzled Texan named Mr. Blass who had lost an arm at Chickamauga—like young lieutenants, trail bosses are all called mister. I told him my story about being a teacher trying to find my husband, asking if I could ride the chuckwagon as far as Spotted Tail's camp.

Mr. Blass gave me a queer look, even for a Texan. "Mrs. Kilory, you are welcome to ride north with us—if you give the cook a hand. Forgive my plain talkin', but I do not let my boys drink, swear, nor whore around. I will expect the same from you." I told him I would resist the temptation.

Before setting out, Mr. Blass made a short speech about me. The men looked down at their hats the whole time—they were tough bandy-legged hands, more confident with maverick cattle than stray females. Mr. Blass sidelined as a Methodist preacher and ran the most godly cattle drive I ever saw, reading from the Bible every Sunday and singing hymns to the herd. Just like Lakotas, cowhands have a taste for intestines cooked with the cud inside, but in Mr. Blass's camp we called it "sweet tripe soup," not "sono-fabitch stew."

I served beef and beans all the way to the Niobrara, and for the price of a little conversation, bone-weary hands would help me gather wood, tend fire, or grind the next morning's coffee. When supper was done and I'd thrown the dirty dishwater under the wagon, we sat on tarps and blankets, talking, or listening to the night watch singing lullabies to the cattle:

> Yippie tie eye oh, sleep along little doggies,
> It's your misfortune and none of my own,
> You'll be stew beef for Uncle Sam's Injuns;
> Heap, heap, beef I hear them all cry.

> Yippie tie eye oh, sleep along little doggie,
> Them injuns will eat you all by and by.

None of them liked herding government beef, which was weak and skittish—"nothin' but hide, horns, and holler."

When Mr. Blass had delivered his herd, I asked if I could buy a couple of ponies from the remuda. Texas cow ponies were perfect for the trail, tough hardy geldings, able to live on alkali water and jimson weed. And no matter how bad things get, a Texas horse has seen worse.

Mr. Blass scratched his pinned-up sleeve—the arm that used to fill it was buried in Georgia, taken off by a ball from a cavalry carbine. "Of course you can have the ponies. Got no use for them now. The way money is, I'm not half likely to get another herd. But I sure do hate to see you going off alone."

"Oh, I won't be alone. I'll be with the Lakotas."

"That is what I mean." Blass looked me in the eye. "I like Injuns. If it were not for Injuns, I would not have worked this spring." Mr. Blass had been tickled by the way the Interior Department did business, paying the same price, no matter how sick or skinny a steer was; selling to Uncle Sam was like being the only sober player in a poker game. Otherwise he had little love for a Republican government that shot his arm off, but could not coin enough money to keep the cattle business going. "We could use a heap more Injuns," he declared.

I noted that not many people held that opinion.

He laughed. "Look at Jesse Chisholm—half Cherokee. But his trail is choked off by settlement. I wish the Sioux and Cheyenne would drive every nester and homesteader back to Ohio; I surely do. And an Indian war would mean more army contracts too—so I got nothing against the Sioux. But I do worry about you. You are a walking temptation. Last winter a white man was killed right here on the Niobrara. Those bucks will rape and scalp you as soon as you are out of the sight."

But he gave me my pick of the remuda for free. Mr. Blass was a man who spoke plain and expected folks to do as they pleased. I thought enough of his opinion to buy a box of fifty rimfire cartridges for the Henry.

Spotted Tail's people were camped on open bluegrass prairie beneath a line of buttes. The Burnt Thighs feasted me just as though I were Grand Duke Alexis or Buffalo Bill, and I met Crazy Horse's cousin, the one Custer danced and flirted with. Several families of Burnt Thighs were headed over the divide toward Red Cloud's camp, to visit Bad Face cousins. Moving and camping with them eased me back into the rhythms of the camp circle. My Lakota was still spotty, and the long silences let me adjust my manners and feelings, and savor this last loneliness. I gave rock sugar to the children and tinned vegetables to their elders, to show I was not the sort of Wasichu who expected to be taken care of for free. Lakotas have a good opinion of any-one who feeds them, and these Burnt Thighs were plain tickled by canned tomatoes, assuming they were like corn—vegetables that grew in their own container. I took some of the miracle away by telling them my people put the tomatoes in the cans.

Riding into the Bad Face camp I felt fit as a ferret, ready to greet Yellow Legs, anxious to put Wallace and my stay with the 7th cavalry behind me. He Dog was there, back from Standing Rock, telling me to get down. Every-one was polite, in the reserved way of Lakotas dealing with a familiar Wa-sichu. But my husband had not been seen there all winter. He Dog had heard he was up on the Powder as usual, camping with Crazy Horse—he for sure had not come for me.

The Center of the World

Wherever you are, that is the Center of the World.
                                —Black Elk, Oglala Lakota

I SAT WRAPPED IN MY BLANKET, STUDYING A MONTH-OLD COPY of the *Bismarck Tribune*, when a voice asked, "Light-Between-the-Legs, are you going to the Center of the World?" I did not look up. From the tone and manner I knew it must be Woman's Dress. Woman's Dress was not a man-woman in the usual sense—at least I never saw him tanning hides or pounding pine nuts—but he wore a pretty beaded dress with elaborately fringed half-sleeves.

"Yes, I am going to the Center of the World." I pulled my blanket tighter, doing my best imitation of the modest Sheyenna wife. Woman's Dress impressed many people, including the Wasichu at the agency, but he never much pleased me—except when he introduced me to Yellow Legs. Even that introduction had the air of an elaborate joke. How could Woman's Dress know that Yellow Legs and I would get on so famously?

"Tell me, Light-Between-the-Legs, why are you Wasichu so curious about the Center of the World?" Men-women are allowed to bestow obscene names, and Woman's Dress's name for me played on a common curiosity about blond pubic hair.

"I heard there would be an *inipi*, and I would like to make myself clean." With that I rose and walked away. I knew better than to expect courtesy from Woman's Dress, but I did not have to stand for straight-out questions. My Medicine was my concern.

If I had wanted to puncture this prettified Bad Face's composure, I would have read a paragraph or two from the *Bismarck Tribune*—a paper whose business-first philosophy was so heartless and philistine it would have rooted for Goliath to bash David (JEW SHEEPHERDER BEGS FOR STOMP-

ING!). The *Tribune* made its feelings for Lakotas and Lakota Country fairly plain:

> Humanitarians may weep for the Indian, and tell about the wrongs poor Lo has suffered, but he is passing away. Their prayers, their entreaties, cannot change the law of nature; cannot arrest the causes which are carrying them to their ultimate destiny—extinction. The American people need the country Lo occupies; many of our people are out of employment; the masses need new excitement. The War is over, and the era of railroad building has been brought to an end by the greed of capitalists and the folly of grangers. Depression prevails on every hand. An Indian war would do no harm, for it must come sooner or later."

Three moons among the Bad Faces had sharpened up my Lakota, but I was still not fluent enough to express the full feeling behind those words.

You did not have to be Lakota to find the news dismal—the *Bismarck Tribune* showed why Yellow Legs considered illiteracy a blessing. Money was so short that the Secretary of the Treasury had been tossed out of office, and Congress was forced to take a pay cut—times don't get any worse than that. But the Republicans still refused to mint silver, preaching the gold standard and "sound money" while the economy bellied up. The Grant administration was dead. Nothing but a monetary miracle or a rigged vote would keep the Democrats out of the White House. And heaven alone could save us if that happened.

I arrived among the Bad Faces in the Moon of Grass Coming Up, expecting to find Yellow Legs waiting. I waited through the Moon When Ponies Shed and the Moon of Making Fat, thinking he could come at any time. Now the grass was long up and the cherries were red. Braves riding down from the Powder said Yellow Legs showed no inclination to come to the agency. What was keeping him away no one would say. There was no normal reason why he could not be here, but there might be medicine reasons. Sometimes Yellow Legs read my mind as easily as Coyote—he might well know about Wallace. It gnawed at me that my Medicine might be what was keeping him away.

The Bad Faces were camped on the Smoky Earth River, a day's ride from the agency, where they could draw rations without being reminded that Long Knives camped almost at the Center of the World. Seeing Long Knives every day would make even *aguiapi, paezhuta sapa,* and *chahumpi ska* taste sour. That is: brown-all-over, black Medicine, and white sap—bread, coffee, and sugar. I now knew enough Lakota to order a continental breakfast.

I went with the Bad Faces on ration day, to buy my own beef. Even when rations were short, there was always a steer to sell for silver to a Wasichu. The Lakota cattle were parceled out one by one. As each puny steer came out the chute, young bucks on horseback would chase down the bawling animal in a pale imitation of a buffalo run. Then women would close in with carving knives. I brought my own beef live into camp, where I could repay Bad Face hospitality with fresh meat when ration day was only a memory.

My tipi was pitched back from the camp circle, near No Water's: a big Bad Face related to Red Cloud by marriage. No Water, a man with two wives and his own tipi to entertain in, insisted that I share his camp—No Water was big enough to be generous even to Wasichus. Camp urchins gathered at my lodge to learn English and play counting games, while I improved my Lakota. Some attended my open-air school out of novelty, others came because I gave out rock candy prizes. For the young, the camp circle is an educational smorgasbord—horse tamers, arrow makers, tipi cutters, and schoolteachers all practice their art in the open, attracting whoever was interested. My original Lakota name was Talks-to-Children.

Class was out for today, and my sometime students were playing Cowboys and Lakotas. Girls set up play tipis, while boys picked to be Wasichu strutted about, wearing annuity shirts, black hats, and buffalo-hair beards, pretending to drive a flatbed wagon parked among the lodges. Black Buffalo, one of No Water's wives, threw gambling bones with her smallest daughter, a quick learner with wavy hair and light features—the sort of child Yellow Legs had said he wanted to have with me. Black Buffalo was He Dog's cousin and shared much of his open generosity. As my money dwindled, I was increasingly dependent on the generosity of Lakotas.

Sitting down beside her, I started sewing on a moccasin, showing I had traveling on my mind. Noting the moccasin, Black Buffalo told me, "People are setting out for the Center of the World. Stabbed's band has already left to cut lodgepoles."

"People are going," I agreed. Some Medicine telegraph had alerted everyone that I was headed for *Paha Sapa*—as surely as if a Caller had gone around camp.

"Few Wasichu have seen the Center of the World," she noted.

I told her I had wintered with the Minniconjous on the slopes of *Paha Sapa*—now I needed to see it again. My Medicine felt flat. At the Center of the World I could only be stronger.

Lakotas are seldom openly curious about a stranger's problems, but I found myself telling Black Buffalo my whole story, about losing Yellow Legs in Crow Country and him not coming for me. I told her I meant to look for him, and the Center of the World seemed a good place to start from. I would stay in *Paha Sapa* until found a band headed for the Powder River country. With my Medicine rifle I could at least feed myself. Game was sparse here along the Smoky Earth River, but there were deer and turkey at the Center of the World and buffalo along the Powder.

Black Buffalo thought over my troubles. "You could have thrown yourself off a cliff," she decided. Lakotas consider suicide a useful way of proving a point, and Black Buffalo was not going to stoop to cheering me up. "But that would have been much—especially over an old Sheyenna married to someone else. I am not a One-Man Woman either, but that does not make me any less a Bad Face." Though I had not mentioned Wallace, Black Buffalo naturally assumed there was another man muddying up my Medicine.

She pointed her chin toward the lodge circle. "My husband is only a tipi away, but you do not hear me calling for him. I am happy he spends his nights in the lodge of a second wife." I had noted the distance between No Water and Black Buffalo, but I had never dared ask about it.

"I left No Water for another warrior, going off with my new man on a war party. No Water borrowed a revolver from Bad Heart Bull and tracked us to a timbered creek that runs into the Powder. When No Water burst into the lodge, my warrior would have fought, but Little-Big-Man grabbed his knife hand. No Water shot my man in the face."

"Did he die?" Her story sounded horrible.

"No, my warrior lived. Bad Heart Bull and He Dog made a peace settlement, since Bad Heart Bull's pistol had done the shooting and He Dog always smooths things over. No Water gave horses, including his best roan and a big American bay. I came back to him, for the sake of peace between the bands—No Water, Woman's Dress, and Red Cloud insisted on it. Now my warrior has married another. He has a daughter and I hear he is happy."

"If he lives in the Powder River camps, perhaps I know him?"

Black Buffalo lifted her chin. "Everyone knows my man. When we were children we called him Curly. Now he is Crazy Horse. You can tell him by the star-shaped scar on his cheek where No Water's bullet went in."

I did know her warrior, though "happy" was not a word I'd use to describe Crazy Horse. I did not need to ask how long ago this had happened—her daughter was colored like Crazy Horse. Black Buffalo had a living reminder, growing taller with every winter, like a pine seedling planted to mark the year. I wondered which was worse: to live in doubt, or to know exactly why you could not have the man you wanted.

When I was done with my moccasins, Black Buffalo asked to see them, turning my work over in her hands, feeling the soles. "The hide is thick and the stitches are tight—they will take you a long way. Chips is leading his people into *Paha Sapa*, to call on the Great Mystery and Grandmother Earth. You should go with him. Chips has the power."

"No one told me Chips was going." My first thought was that they would not want me to come and were keeping the *inipi* secret because I was Wasichu.

"Of course no one told you. No Water thinks Chips gave Crazy Horse the love Medicine that made me run off. No Water's people all mock Chip's Medicine. It is foolishness. Crazy Horse did not need a little stone to steal my heart."

I had overrated myself again—the Lakotas had their own problems, too weighty to include even friendly Wasichu. I said I had seen the stone. "It keeps him safe from bullets."

Black Buffalo folded up her blanket, to show she was leaving. "It did not stop No Water's bullet." One more wound inflicted by a woman.

I came up from White Clay Creek with some Loafer Lakotas, dragging our lodges, trailing dogs and prairie dust. A sweet green breeze blew into my upturned face. Ahead I saw the hills, black with pines, rising straight out of the plain.

Pa-ha sa-pa. Say it slowly and even the name has power. Eons before we emerged from Grandmother Earth, a great sea of grass rolled unbroken below Devil's Tower and Bear Butte, from the Big Muddy to the Backbone of the World. Colossal beasts wandered the prairie, whose mammoth bones still remain, pressed into bedrock and shale. In the center of this flat expanse Grandmother Earth gave birth—the ground swelled up and a gigantic volcanic bubble a hundred miles long rose more than a mile into the sky. The rock bubble burst, showering gray granite boulders onto the plain. The broken remains of this bubble form the Black Hills of the Dakotas.

The prairie is a wild dry ocean, roamed by the buffalo herds that are bread and butter to Lakota and Sheyenna. The Center of the World is rich in another way. *Paha Sapa* has everything that the prairie lacks: water, timber, shade and shelter, high places spread with alpine blossoms, elk and wild turkey that will not come out onto the plains. Seeing the hills, feeling the wind, I remembered the lines I had seen parodied in the *Bismarck Tribune*, the first epistle in Pope's "Essay on Man":

> Lo, the poor Indian! whose untutored mind
> Sees God in clouds, or hears him on the wind . . .

Pope does not sound half so funny on the magic slopes of *Paha Sapa*.

We entered through Buffalo Gap, where Magpie won his race with the buffalo cow called Slim Walking Woman. By betting on Magpie, men won the right to hunt and kill the buffalo. But for all I know the race was fixed. Coyote was the judge, and I considered him about half as honest as Independence Jake. Buffalo Gap is still used by the animals for their midsummer councils, so summer hunts are taboo in this part of the hills. Beasts seem to know this. Buffalo from the plains mixed with deer and bighorn sheep from the high meadows, while coyotes sat watching. No one paid much attention to a band of Loafers or my Medicine gun.

Later the sun would burn the hills brown, but right now green slopes were covered with flowers and berries, turning *Paha Sapa* into a feast for eyes and body, a second Eden in America. I bathed and did my washing in a creek south of Vision Peak. Loafer women are accustomed to white skin—many had Long Knife Lovers of Wasichu fathers—so I worked nearly naked in the sunshine, scrubbing my clothes by the stream bed, admiring the way my finished work sparkled. Laying out the wet leather, I scraped at the most stubborn stains with my thumbnail.

Some of the sparkle came off on my thumb. I stared down at my nail, stubbed and broken from constant use, now flecked with gold—flecks no bigger than a pinhead, but real. Looking beyond my thumbnail, I watched the creek cut a shining path through grass and pines. Children splashed in the shallows. Reaching down, I sifted through the wet sand; there was gold in the creek—so much gold that tiny grains stuck to your fingers.

Letting the sand slide back into the stream, I rubbed all trace of the metal off my hands. Women around me scratched at the banks for tubers, ignoring a stream full of gold. With a pan and shovel I could have made more money in a day than I had earned all winter at Fort Lincoln—but I was headed for a place where gold did not matter.

North of Vision Peak, we followed Rapid Creek almost to the edge of the prairie before we found Chips's people. I pitched my tipi beside the lodge of a woman named White Cow, married to an old lame Medicine man, a cousin of Crazy Horse. White Cow and I had shared food and work before, and she had relatives at Fort Robinson, so she was wise to our ways. In my overcurious fashion, I asked White Cow if there was much of the yellow metal in *Paha Sapa*.

She said nothing. Thinking maybe she could not follow my Lakota, I made the coin circle with my fingers. Instead of answering my question, White Cow began a longish tale about an Oglala eagle hunter who shot a badger at the Center of the World. He wasn't particularly hungry for badger, but he wanted to see his fortune in the animal's blood—Lakotas believe that the face you see reflected in a badger's blood is the face you will die with. Pulling the dead varmint out of his hole, the Oglala noticed gold nuggets in the badger's mound—he promptly forgot the badger, figuring he had found his fortune. Filling his skin bag with gold, the Oglala headed off for Fort Laramie to buy a big American horse. On the way he showed some Burnt Thighs his find. The Burnt Thighs got excited, beat the Oglala, took his clothes, scattered his gold, and shot his pony. He walked cut and bleeding into the Bad Face camp, begging his fellow Oglalas to punish those Burnt Thighs. But he got no pity. Bad Faces told him it was better if the yellow metal stayed in the ground.

"They did this out of concern for the Wasichu," White Cow explained. She twirled her finger beside her head. "The yellow metal drives them crazy." White Cow was telling me, in polite, round about Lakota fashion: Shut the fuck up about finding gold at the Center of the World. First-rate advice. I did not fancy losing my horses and having to walk bruised and naked back to Fort Robinson.

That evening lightning flashed over the foothills, and I sensed the same electric foreboding that I felt in the bluffs above the Greasy Grass. Black thunderclouds rolled out of the sunset, driving thousands of split-tailed swallows ahead of them, darkening the sky. Enterprising boys began to peg rocks. Young warriors-to-be were supposed to maim small animals when they got the chance—but it made me angry. The place seemed special.

Young Black Elk, White Cow's son, a slender sensitive boy of about eleven, picked up a stone, started to throw, then stopped—letting the stone fall from his hand. Another boy asked why he did not throw.

"We will never hit them," Young Black Elk answered. "They are *wakan*, flying straight from the Great Mystery." Summer is the Medicine season, when children hold their own dances and *inipi* in imitation of their elders. But these were strong words even for a Medicine-man-in-the-making like Young Black Elk. "I saw them in a vision," Black Elk warned, "when we were camped near the Greasy Grass. The air was full of frightened wings, like swallows fleeing before a storm."

Wind and cold made me shiver, and I folded my arms into my buckskin half-sleeves. This movement caught the two boys' attention. They stared, then walked away. I think until they looked, they had forgotten that I was Wasichu.

No storm broke that night. Next morning, people prepared for Chips's *inipi*, setting up a sweat lodge "square with the world" and facing the sunrise. A straight path connected the sweat lodge to the sun fire and a mound standing for Grandmother Earth—the Pipe-woman would carry the sacred pipe along this Medicine path. All other movement had to be in sunwise circles, retracing the path of the sun through the sky. When the red-hot rocks from the sun fire were rolled into the lodge and doused with water, all the elements would become one; and the Medicine lodge would fill up with earth, air, water, and fire.

No one invited me into Chips's mixing of elements. I was not excluded for being a Wasichu, but for being a woman—Lakotas think sex is more primary than skin color. A woman's *inipi* could have included me, but I did not think I would find the peace I wanted sweating in a breechcloth. I wanted to have an open-air *inipi* among the wildflowers in the summer meadows.

So I set out alone up Rapid Creek—without food or weapons, for I meant it to be a Medicine journey. There were bears in the hills, grizzlies, and cinnamons as big as a horse, but I sang as I walked to warn them. In summer the Center of the World is one great camp circle, and I felt no more fear than in front of my tipi. The sounds of Chips's *inipi* faded beneath the murmur of Rapid Creek.

Finding a flowered meadow that reminded me of the dresses Spring Grass wore along the Yellowstone, I sat down, trying to compose my thoughts. But it was hard to concentrate amid such stunning beauty. Reaching out, I gathered a handful of blossoms: mountain violets, dandelions, pink mallows, and cornflowers. Farther up the meadow I could see columbines. Was I really ready to test my Medicine? I decided to dedicate this first day of my *inipi* to making peace with myself—I would put off calling Yellow Legs until tomorrow.

Letting the sun saunter overhead, I lay back, closing my eyes. I dreamed of Wallace, riding along in full uniform with flowers in his hatband and a bouquet in his hands.

I awoke with a guilty jerk. Swift brown feet pattered across the meadow. A flock of Lakota boys ran past clutching small bows in their fists. Dead squirrels dangled from their breechcloths. I felt my peace had been violated, until I saw that they were not whooping or playing, but running scared. Young Black Elk was with them. He stopped when he saw me, shouting, "Go back. Go back to camp."

Standing, I felt a blast of chill air. "Why?"

He hesitated, then answered, "I heard a voice say: 'Go home, go home.' It sounded like a grandfather." He looked so upset I had to obey, or deny the power of his vision.

Back at camp I found the whole band in motion. Women were striking tipis and loading travois; men and boys were bringing in the ponies. The sweat lodge stood half-stripped and empty, like a gaping skull. White Cow told me Chips had heard the warning too, sitting in his steam bath—a voice that told him to leave at once, something bad was coming.

I stood stock-still in the midst of the frantic action, unwilling to return to the agency. What I wanted had not happened yet. I was only beginning to feel clean—and I had not yet called on Yellow Legs. Besides, the warning had come to Chips and Young Black Elk, not to me. The boy sat on his mother's travois looking tired and exhausted. I thanked him for his concern, but told him I had to look for Stabbed's people, who were camped deeper in the hills. I would take his warning to them.

Young Black Elk gave me that weary look that says, Why waste Medicine on a Wasichu? White Cow lashed the pony into a trot and the travois bounced away.

Alone in encroaching darkness, I packed my cow ponies and headed back up Rapid Creek, relying on *Paha Sapa* and my Medicine gun to protect me. The sun sank into long midsummer twilight, and the Moon of Red Cherries rose full and bright. I made good time, guided by white rushing water and the dim halo of a comet near the Big Dipper—not stopping to sleep till after midnight.

Birdsong woke me to a day bursting with of power. Feeling sunlight on my face, I could hear my hobbled ponies cropping at the dewy grass. When I opened my eyes, sky, earth, and pines all appeared at once, vibrating with color. The air felt buoyant. Each breath brought in more Medicine. A tremendous eagle soared overhead; staring up at her, I knew my *inipi* was truly here. I set off again. With my Medicine rifle I felt safer than I had been the day before, sleeping unarmed among the flowers—not even bears scared me. If I moved no faster than I pleased, I could still be in Stabbed's camp before nightfall.

As I walked I shuffled through my memories. Did I have the power I wanted? Of course I did. I had beaten both Coyote and the Northern Pacific. Then why did I need Yellow Legs? Because I loved him. Because he cared for me, and tried to coax this power out of me. He would not say what I felt was female giddiness or heathen superstition.

Birds and animals appeared. I saw a great white crane with wings longer than Touch-the-Clouds was tall. Fat passenger pigeons—hunted to extinction outside of Lakota Country—pecked at the earth in peace. A family of elk stopped to watch me go singing past. Seeing them made me sorry that I had ever eaten elk meat, and been glad for the change from buffalo steak. Rows of elk teeth decorated my dress—but life comes from death, and it was better to wear elk teeth on your dress than to deny where your food comes from. Still, I resolved to eat no meat today, only berries and stream water.

As I walked—gathering sweetgrass, sage, and wild cherries—I came up on a white buffalo skull stripped by the birds, bleached by sun and rain. Kneeling down, I turned the skull square with the world, facing the sunrise and rebirth. Mixing up some of my paint, I drew a blue line down the center of the skull, connecting heaven and earth. Then I burned the sage and sweetgrass, offering water and cherries to the skull, singing the words of a woman's *inipi*.

> *I move in a Medicine way,*
>   *My walk is a Medicine walk,*
> *Bringing the power to make things new.*

I considered adding a prayer to my mother's God—to bring Yellow Legs back, I needed all the Medicine I could call on. But I decided not to. Praying to Jesus in *Paha Sapa* over a painted buffalo skull made as much sense as doing a hot dance at Sunday Meeting. Every Medicine has its time and place. Remounting, I rode on, calling out for Yellow Legs to come. My voice carried clear across the valleys, echoing off green hills and high cliffs. I was ready for him. How could he stay away? I wanted to make things new.

Afternoon shadows were creeping over the meadows by the time I got to the narrow canyon where Stabbed's band was camped. Tired and hungry, I walked my horses. At the mouth of the pass I stopped in a small stand of pines to braid my hair and paint my face, so my white skin would not startle Stabbed's people. Coming into a strange camp it paid to look part Lakota.

I heard men's singing, and the *trit-trot* of ponies riding past my stand of pines. Pushing aside the boughs I spotted three riders headed my way, with flowing hair, vermilion faces, and calico shirts. All my carefully made Medicine vanished. I dropped like a scared doe. They were Rees—Rees at the Center of the World, carrying carbines and freshly honed scalp knives. You could bet the farm they were not alone. One Arikaree might be crazy enough to ride alone into Lakota Country, but not three—more armed men were bound to follow.

Crouched down, I listened with every ounce of my being. All I heard was my heartbeat and the undulating monotone of a Ree death song—not especially terrifying, unless you knew what a death song was. Then came the heavy clump of ironshod American horses, at least a troop of cavalry, maybe more. Hunching up in my pine thicket, arms hugging my legs, head resting on my knees, I gave the Rees and soldiers plenty of time to get away. Then I slipped the rawhide hobbles off my horses and headed in the opposite direction. There was going to be trouble, shooting trouble, and I wanted to be far and away when the first shots were fired. At the edge of the pines I peeked out of the thicket.

"Holy Jesus," I whispered to my ponies, motioning them back. A huge column of cavalry was standing at ease, stretching way back up the valley. I could see white wagon tops, dark masses of horses and mules, and close to a thousand troopers sitting about, resting their mounts. With them were infantry, civilians, Indian scouts, teamsters, and a whole brass band. The band started playing—giving me a guilty start—trumpets and tubas pumped as loud and proud as if it were Fourth of July in the States. Familiar words rang in my head:

> Instead of water we'll drink ale,
> And pay the reck'ning on the nail;
> No man for debt shall go to jail,
> While he can Garryowen hail.

Long-Hair Custer had come to the Center of the World. Worse still, he seemed to have followed me. After nearly a thousand miles by boat, wagon, railroad, and pony, I was a slim hundred yards from what I had left back at Fort Lincoln. This was the full regiment for sure: the Custer boys, Wallace, Reno, Godfrey, Keogh, and Benteen, maybe even Libby. My Medicine never looked more ludicrous—coming around to give me a swift, resounding clout alongside the head. I spent all day calling for one single Sheyenna, and the whole 7th cavalry came instead.

Calamity

Moments like this show the Great Medicine truly has a sense of humor. I turned my horses around and slunk back into the timbers, feeling like a guilty vagabond caught camping on a railroad right-of-way. I never even considered showing myself. This far into Lakota Country my presence—painted and dressed in buckskins—would provoke difficult questions, for which I was totally out of answers. At best I would come off as a serious lunatic and be dragged back to Fort Lincoln.

I sat listening to Custer's band beat away, growing hungrier by the hour, berating myself for being so pure and having nothing in my belly but berries and stream water. Between concerts I could hear Custer's troopers play baseball. With Rees cheering on the sideline. From the sound of it, Custer's men were not the Cincinnati Red Sox—which actually made the game more exciting. Professional pitching and alert fielding can easily make the national pastime as boring as cricket.

At dusk, bugles sounded stable call, then retreat, and finally taps. Aside from sentries and pickets, the whole command was officially asleep. Covering myself with a dark blanket, I smeared paint on my face, then led my horses out of the timbers.

Watch fires flickered up and down the valley. I found my escape blocked by horselines, dark wagons, and a ghostly battery of Gatling guns. Nor was the camp anywhere near asleep. Soldiers were sitting by the fires, talking, singing, drinking, and staggering up to piss it away. But all this blundering about lulled the sentries. If I had been half the horse thief Yellow Legs was I could have come away with a string of cavalry mounts and a score of sturdy mules.

Edging past an especially noisy fire, I heard a shout of alarm. Followed by a big revolver going off, banging to wake the dead.

My ponies bolted. I flung myself full-out on the dirt, my head hitting hard. Seeing bright lights, I thought, God, this is what it's like to be shot.

Cringing in the dirt, numb with fright, I waited for a second bullet to crash into me. Only the elk teeth on my dress kept me from getting any lower. Nothing happened. Feeling gingerly about, I decided I had not been hit. Not yet anyway.

I waited some more. No one came out of the night to prod me with a pistol. My next notion was that Lakotas had gotten in among the horselines. But there were no more shots. No sound of fleeing hooves.

Listening to loud voices around the nearest fire, I discovered the soldiers were not firing at me or even at Lakotas—but at each other. A man was yelling that his watch had been stolen, addressing the others with the alcoholic authority of a senior officer. From the angry replies, I gathered he was a colonel named Grant—whose Christian name was Fred—and he was waving a revolver at several nervous companions. The only Colonel Fred Grant I knew of was the President's son—Libby had been particularly proud to entertain him.

Wanting no further part in the evening's entertainment, I inched through the dark grass, leaving the army to sort out its problems. I do not know if Colonel Grant ever got his watch back—he was still drunkenly demanding it when I left, swearing he'd shoot the thieving whoreson who had it. But the lost timepiece had cost me my horses and kit. Ponies, lodge cover, robes, and Medicine rifle had all run off into the night.

There was a certain heavy irony in this. Most of what I had lost was purchased with payroll dollars taken from similarly fuddled officers. My Medicine had doubled back on me, and I could hear Coyote laughing inside my head.

I felt more like crying. I was cold, hungry, scared, and afoot (actually on hands and knees), with no hope of finding my horses. Finding my way was hard enough. Light from the campfires faded. Scrambling to my feet, I plunged into a tangle of brush, crashing along and making a horrible amount of noise.

A large shaggy bulk reared up before me. I thought, Oh, my God, a bear. That made my Medicine complete, to fetch into a grizzly just as I was getting free of the army. The grizzly must have been as surprised to see me, because she whirled about on her hind legs, saying, "Stop right there, you red bastard, or I will blow your head off."

"Don't shoot," I shouted. "I am white." It seemed as good a reason as any to spare me.

"Shut your lying mouth and come over where I can see you."

Stepping forward, I saw that what I thought was a bear was actually a tall, robust woman who had been hunched over a small Indian-style fire. She kicked the ashes, stirring up sparks so we could get better looks at each other. She had on man's trousers and an army jacket with no markings. Her hands were big, like a man's, but what really took my attention was the huge horse pistol she held in one fist—aimed at me. A whiskey bottle sat at her feet, but her aim was rock steady.

"Sit down, Indian. An' stop lookin' so scared."

I sat. She seemed vaguely Indian herself, with long dark hair, high cheekbones, and wide-set eyes; but her skin was whiter than mine. Her mouth was a thin line, curving up at the corners when she smiled. "You do not look much like a Sioux."

I told her that was because I was white.

She cocked the pistol, casually leaning down to snag her bottle. "Don't give me any more crap. Maybe you are Mandan. A muleskinner swore he saw Mandan trailing the column."

Her cocked pistol made me change my tack. "Yep, you guessed it, I'm a Mandan. Couldn't hope to fool you."

"Prove it," she demanded. "Say somethin' in Mandan."

I said "You're a big drunken fool" in Lakota, which seemed to satisfy her—even a sober Wasichu can seldom tell Mandan from Lakota, the two tongues being very much alike.

"Smile." She held out her bottle, leaving open a clean line of fire. I smiled. She laughed, pushing the bottle closer. "Don't you Indians understand 'smile'? It means have a drink."

"Not thirsty," I replied.

"Bull." She shoved the bottle between my fingers. "I never seen an Indian turn down a drink. Lo, the poor Mandan, must have her problems. Drown your sorrows, or at least take 'em for a swim." I took a sip. The bottle contained genuinely horrible rye whiskey—fit to take the sting out of a half-ounce pistol ball. It bit my tongue and burned my throat, but did make the night seem more friendly.

"That's the ticket. Now tell me your name."

"Sarah Kilory." My second drink of rye hit even harder than the first.

"That don't sound like Mandan to me."

"It's not." I meant to add that I was not Mandan, but bit it back. I did not want to sour our relationship, not when we were getting down to drinks and introductions.

"Well, I want your goddamned Indian name."

American Woman would clearly not do, so I admitted the Bad Faces called me Light-Between-the Legs, saying the name in Lakota. Looking pleased, she brushed hair out of her eyes with her pistol, reaching across the fire to take back the bottle. "But what does it mean? Every Indian name has got to mean something. You know, like Buffalo Prick or Pissin' Bare."

Here was the moment when an agile person might have leaped over the fire, kicked the gun out of her grip, and beat her unconscious with the bottle. But I was far from agile, and the bottle was doing a decent job of knocking both of us unconscious. Instead, I told her what my Bad Face name meant in English.

Putting the pistol in her lap, she rocked with laughter. "I like you, Indian. You are gonna be great fun." She passed the whiskey back. "Here, drink some more, an' I promise I won't shoot you." I drank some more, asking what her name was.

"Didn't I say? My name is Martha Jane Cannary. That won't mean much to an Indian, but a canary is a small yellow bird. My friends all call me Calamity, which means an affliction or misfortune. Guess my Indian name would be 'Bad-Luck-Yellow-Bird,' or someways like that."

I tried explaining to Calamity that I was not an Indian, but she was so tickled to be drinking and joking with a Mandan squaw that she refused to discuss anything different. "Listen," she shushed me, "do you like liquor?"

I admitted I was beginning to ripen to rye in a bottle.

"Of course you do." She waved a meaty finger at me. "Well, liquor is just one of the many great things white folks invented. Fact is, I can understand your wanting to be white." Calamity rattled off the short list of great white inventions, the one that includes "spirituous liquors, readin' and writin', numbers, railroads, electricity, Jesus Christ, chewin' tobacco, and dime cigars." When she lost interest in vain boasting, Calamity sat down to teach me the obscene verses to "Sweet Betsy from Pike:

> *Out on the prairie one bright starry night*
> *They broke out the whiskey and Betsy got tight,*
> *She sang and she shouted and danced o'er the plain,*
> *And showed her bare ass to the whole wagon train.*

Fortunately I knew the song, since Calamity could not have carried the tune with a wagon and a ten-mule team. When we got to the verses about Betsy shooting Indians, Jane suggested I should not sing along if it hurt my feelings, but after all that rotgut rye, I hardly had any feeling left to hurt.

I won't say that every Wasichu in the Black Hills was booze-blind that night—from the President's son to Calamity Jane—but I sure was. As high as a flag on the Fourth of July. One hell of a way to infiltrate Indian Country. Of course, Custer did not drink, so the man looking over the whole operation was stone sober—a comforting thought when you are stretched out on the cold ground, drunk as a bug in a beer bucket, surrounded by liquored-up Wasichu and soon-to-be-angry Lakotas. It did trouble me that falling asleep drunk was becoming a habit.

Harsh sunlight hammered at my dry head. I found myself staring up at a morning sky colored like a lizard's belly. Somewhere nearby I heard a band playing and men singing—just as if the party were still going on. I tried to stand, bracing myself against Jane's warm bulk, which had rolled on top of me during the night. Standing proved impossible. *Paha Sapa* spun about whenever I moved. And I had a tough rawhide halter around my neck— Calamity must not have wanted her pet Indian to run.

I wasted some time trying to free myself from an impossible muleskinner's knot. The long end of the lariat was wrapped several times around Jane, leaving me no slack to work with, and the rawhide knot had shrunk up in the night—I might as well have tried to untie a twisted steel rail. It was a miracle that I had not strangled in my sleep.

Giving up, I propped myself against Jane's broad back, saying good morning to the Center of the World. Birds chirped maniacally back, and last night's liquor pressed on my bladder. The day was already testing me. I ached in new and unusual places, and was disappointed to discover that Calamity Jane had lice. During the night the little vermin had immigrated into my dress and leggings. I wished desperately to be far away—free to piss, bathe, and burn my clothes.

Searching Jane's big body for a knife, I merely succeeded in waking her. Calamity rolled herself over a couple of times, unwinding the rope as she went. Stopping at the brink of the burned embers, she worked herself up on one elbow, looking at the morning like it was a snake about to strike. Feeling around, she found last night's bottle lying open and on its side. Tipping it straight up in the air, she swallowed the last of the rye, then reached into her pocket, producing a filthy fat-streaked piece of bacon. Sticking it in her mouth, Calamity started to chew. The thought of rye dregs for breakfast, with or without raw bacon, made me want to vomit, but I had nothing much to toss up.

Shaking more bacon out of her pants, she offered me some. "By dawn's early light you make a damned sorry Indian." I admitted I made a pretty poor Indian at any time of day. My paint was badly smeared, and my hair was pretty dirty—but clearly blond.

The band broke out a new tune, and Calamity sang along:

> She jumped in bed and covered up her head
> And said I could not find her.
> I knew damned well that she lied like hell,
> So I jumped right in behind her.

She started pulling on her boots. "Time to march. 'Girl I Left Behind Me' is Custer's going-away song. The General is a looker; I suppose he left few dozen girls behind in his day." She stopped to frown into the bottle, making sure it was completely empty.

I was also torn. But not between drinking and getting my boots on. I dreaded seeing Wallace again, or trying to explain my present condition to Libby; but I had no ambition to sit in *Paha Sapa* picking lice. I had no food, no horses, no tipi, and no Medicine gun. It was a long walk back to the Bad Face camp—and as news of this new invasion spread, Lakotas were bound to take a sterner view of Wasichu mooning about at the Center of the World. My Medicine was down about as far as it could fall—then the bottom dropped out. I heard the soft clip-clop of pony hooves. Calamity stopped, her foot in the air, one boot half on, staring at me.

Four legs at a time, painted ponies passed between us. Six armed warriors entered our little camp, all painted up and ready to raise hell. I nearly pissed right through to the dirt beneath me. Calamity groped for her gun, saying, "Who the Devil are you?"

If the Devil himself had ridden into camp I could not have been more frightened. "Don't touch that pistol," I told her in a friendly, urgent tone. "A shot now is sure to get someone killed."

Her hand froze a few inches from the gun butt. Five of the riders were stripped down to breechcloths, their bodies daubed with yellow paint; raven feathers nodded in their hair, and bone whistles dangled from their bridles. Spencer carbines and buffalo muskets rested on their knees, pointed negligently at the sky.

The lead rider made the others look almost harmless. A fresh scalp hung in his belt, and he carried a German needle gun, but it was his face paint that I'll never forget. He was painted black around the mouth, and red all the way up to the scalp lock, and his eyes were pure blue and unblinking. The effect was fairly terrifying; like seeing the sky through the sockets of a burned and bloody skull.

Fool Dogs

"SO WHO THE HELL ARE THEY?" CALAMITY SOUNDED AS NERvous as I felt.

I studied my moccasin stitching. "These are *real* Mandans. The yellowskinned ones are young Fool Dogs—grown boys crazy to be warriors. The older one is a Black Mouth; they act as police and sort of keep the younger ones in line." I had not seen many Mandans, but Teat had described the paint to me and Rees wore similar colors.

The Black Mouth kicked his leg up and swung off his pony, landing so lightly I barely heard the pat of his moccasins. He strolled between us, soft as a shadow, stooping to pick up Calamity's pistol, paying no attention to her half-extended arm. Turning the pistol over in his hand, he felt its weight, then thrust it through his breechcloth strap next to the scalp. There was dried blood on his bare leg where the scalp had bled.

"Hey, fellow," croaked Calamity. "That's my gun."

The Fool Dogs greeted her declaration with barks of wild laughter. If the Black Mouth knew any American, he did not show it.

"Try not to rile him," I pleaded, pointing out he was the reasonable one. "Those Fool Dogs walk on burning coals in bare feet and stick their hands in boiling water, just because they haven't enough scalps to dress up a serious kill talk."

The Black Mouth lifted the rye bottle, sniffed it, then thrust the empty bottle into his breechcloth between the scalp and revolver. Spitting on his thumb, he pinched my cheek, rubbing off some of the dried paint. Then he ran his fingers through my hair, making a remark in Mandan the Fool Dogs found funny. He smiled as he did it, and I tried to paint a cheerful picture

185

for Calamity's sake. "Don't let the guns and frowns fool you. Most Mandans are tolerably friendly—toward whites."

I did not add that much had happened to the Mandan's that might make the reflective warrior less friendly. People say the Rees were once great, but many believed it about the Mandans. They had been the proudest of the Corn Indians, with the farthest to fall. The Indian extinction that the *Bismarck Tribune* looked forward to was nearly complete as far as Mandans went—smallpox and starvation had carried off nine out of ten—but the pittance that remained were proud enough for a hundred times their number.

The Fool Dogs dismounted. I saw they were leading my cow ponies; the stock of my Medicine rifle was still sticking out of its scabbard, but my lodge cover and rawhide cases were gone, probably dumped where they found the horses. Mandans were too polite to raid Custer's horselines, but loose ponies in Lakota Country belonged to anyone who threw a rope over them. I said nothing about my prior ownership, not wanting to do anything that might make my presence awkward. In a war party you never want to make a play you cannot back.

While the Fool Dogs arranged themselves in a circle, the Black Mouth got out a fancy flat-stemmed red-and-black pipe, trimmed with horse tails. He made his offerings to earth, sky, and the four directions, then passed it around the circle the way the sun goes overhead. Calamity crawled closer to me. "Talk to 'em. Tell 'em General Custer is leaving and I have to go with him."

"They know General Custer is leaving," I whispered. "Every Indian in the Dakotas heard that band playing. If you really want to go, get up and go."

"But what will they do?"

"The way to find out is to stand up and start walking."

Calamity looked at me like I was crazy. "Without a goodbye or nothing."

"Sure—none of them said hello. Personally, I plan to sit here until that pipe has gone around. That is one powerful pipe. The red and black represent day and night, good will and bad will, all the Medicine there is. If they plan on taking us to the General, they aren't about to lose him, not as long as Custer packs a brass band and a regiment of cavalry. If they are not taking us to Custer, spoiling their smoke won't change their minds, or make them a whit more manageable." The Black Mouth was admirable in a scary sort of way; sitting down for a smoke at the Center of the World was his way of showing everyone the Mandans still had the Medicine.

While the Mandans puffed away, a lone rider came easy as you please into the clearing. He had dark skin, graying braids, and a big American horse. The Fool Dogs howled like they had never seen an army scout before, but the Black Mouth ignored their antics. As the new arrival swung slowly out of his saddle, Calamity exclaimed, "Hot damn, it's Custer's scout."

This time she knew her Indian. Bloody Knife was wearing the same private's jacket he had worn at the Strong Heart dance. I felt the Medicine circle tightening—none of these men was going to just give me my horses and let me go my way. I had to start thinking how I was going to put my case to Custer.

Of course, Bloody Knife's coming meant there had to be another pipe passed around. Calamity leaned closer to me. "What are they saying?"

I took a guess. "The Black Mouth is probably telling Bloody Knife what a great war party he's had. He has got two horses to boast about, a rifle and pistol, a scalp, and of course us."

"Us?" I could tell Calamity was just not used to being listed in war party plunder.

"Sure. The two of us are worth a handsome gift from Custer." Thank goodness.

Then the Black Mouth brought out his prize. Propping Calamity's empty rye bottle between his legs, he pulled out a weaselskin pouch, pouring a golden stream into the bottle. Calamity gasped as the Black Mouth held the bottle up to the light. "My bottle's got gold in it." She sounding just as proud as if the bottle were still hers and not the property of a mean-looking Mandan.

It was gold, all right, but the bottle might as well have been full of blood or gunpowder. If it got to Custer and he came out of the Black Hills saying there was gold at the Center of the World, it would be war for sure—war to the knife between Lakotas and Wasichu. I could imagine what the *Bismarck Tribune* would say: DRIVE THE SIOUX OUT! START THE EXTERMINATION NOW! Eastern papers would be almost as restrained. From Philadelphia bankers to Free Silver grangers, everyone agreed that the country had too little gold. Well, here it was, gleaming in the sun, ready to be coined—money for business, work for the jobless, a cause to fight for.

After a fair amount of friendly negotiating, Bloody Knife got up and went over to where Calamity was sitting. He signed, "You are coming with me. The three-stripe soldier chief in charge of the wagons misses you."

Calamity understood and was all for it, thanking Bloody Knife just as if he were white. She had a quick, active imagination—the kind that took to sign talk. The scout seemed moderately pleased to find a Wasichu who could recognize a favor.

Next he strode over to me, rifle in hand. Kneeling, he spit on his palm and used it to wipe more paint off my face. Grabbing his hand, I told him I could wash myself. I might be a mess, but it was not my ambition to bathe in Arikaree spit.

Bloody Knife twisted his wrist out of my grip. Tapping me lightly on the breast with his gun barrel, he signed, "You are the white woman who speaks with signs, the one who came to the Strong Heart dance. You ran off to join the Sioux. A very crazy thing to do."

Right then I was hard put to argue. Grinning at the paint on his fingers, he signed again, "You are lucky to be white. If you were Sioux or even Arikaree, you would be in a bad way. But whites always act crazy. I offered the Black Mouth big presents for you—but he is Mandan and does not know me. He must *see* the presents. He also thinks you might make a good Mandan woman. I told him you were crazy, but he will not listen. Mandans must see everything for themselves."

Bloody Knife stood up, his gestures becoming brisk. "Sit here and do what they say. I will be back." I stared up at him. Despite what his Hunkpapa relations had to say, Bloody Knife was not a bad sort. He just had a clear, hard view of the world, a kind of cynical fatalism. But if Bloody Knife had commanded the 7th cavalry, quite a few men might be happily fornicating, or boring their grandkids with tall tales, instead of lying in their burial tipis or beneath the yellow Montana grass.

The Black Mouth went over to the ponies, took the Medicine rifle out of its scabbard, and tossed it to the youngest Fool Dog. Then he handed that same lad the leash that Calamity had made for me. Everyone but me and the boy mounted up and rode off with Bloody Knife. The last I saw of Calamity, she was riding one of my cow ponies, looking like she had seen more than enough Indians to fill up her morning.

I was left sitting in the dirt with a rope around my neck and a crazy-to-die Fool Dog at the other end. Fortunately the boy looked level enough, for a yellow-painted savage whose idea of fun was walking on fire. Right now he was more excited by the Medicine rifle than by me. Boys do love their toys.

My main concern was that my need for a morning pee had become close to intolerable. As far as I know there are no decent signs for "Excuse me, I must pass water in private." It is the sort of thing a Buffalo Indian gets up and does, without making much of a speech about it. But I did not expect that this young Fool Dog would just let me slip off behind a bush. I was too valuable to be trusted. So I found a spot as far away as my leash would allow and squatted down with my blanket about me.

The Fool Dog gave me a suspicious glance, then grinned as my blanket began to bump about—I had to get out of my underwear and lace down my leggings. He stopped fondling the Medicine rifle and sat back to watch the show. Presently the clearing filled with the soft patter of passing water. Letting out a loud indelicate chuckle, the Fool Dog rested the rifle suggestively on his hip, barrel erect. When the thin trickle of dusty urine emerged from under my blanket, he threw back his head yipping and laughing. I felt fairly mortified.

Seldom have I seen a joke go sour so fast. Just as the Fool Dog was getting off a really good guffaw, a lariat snaked out of the brush behind him. The line dropped around the barrel of the Medicine rifle, snaring the gun in a noose, then jerking tight. With a bark of dismay, the Fool Dog leaped to his feet, yelling in Mandan, dropping the rifle as if it were a rattler.

A tall warrior stepped out of the brush, reeling in the rifle, while aiming a big Colt revolver with his free hand.

Hot shock swept over me. The tall warrior was Yellow Legs. After months of waiting, and yesterday's calling, here he was, big as a vision and easy as you please. He had hardly changed a stitch since I had left him in the Big Horns, wearing the same fringed Medicine shirt and wrinkled smile.

I forgot everything, even the rawhide rope around my neck and the leggings around my ankles. Starting to scramble up, I tripped, tottered, and nearly landed in the damp dirt. Then I remembered this loving husband had kept me waiting just a few moons short of a year. If he wanted an ecstatic Wasichu greeting, he had to do something more than just appear. Clutching my blanket, I started furiously pulling up my underwear and lacing my leggings, trying to maintain a proper Sheyenna calm.

The poor Fool Dog looked as flustered as I was, shifting from foot to foot, not sure if he should grab at the retreating Medicine rifle or make a dive for his own cap-and-ball buffalo musket. Either move would be crazy, even for a Fool Dog. The Colt in my husband's hand was no Medicine pistol, but Yellow Legs stood close enough to put holes in the Mandan faster than I could drive a needle through muslin.

My husband smiled broadly, gesturing with his pistol hand, palm out, fingers extended—one finger thrust through the trigger guard. Twice he brought his gun hand slowly down and forward. The first movement meant "Stop," the second meant "Keep quiet and still."

The Fool Dog stared back, looking like he was trying to decide if Yellow Legs would be better served boiled or flayed. Mandan and Sheyenna did not mix much. The two tribes had once been best of friends, back when the Sheyenna were Corn Indians by the Big Muddy. Then guns and disease drove the Sheyenna out onto the plains and their closeness disappeared. At times they fought, and at times they were friends, but the Mandans had shrunk so much that the two tribes were neither neighbors nor enemies.

Yellow Legs picked up the Medicine rifle, tapping it to his chest to sign that it was his. Moving slowly, so as not to excite the Mandan, he came over to me. Thrusting his pistol through his breechcloth, he handed me his knife. I cut the rawhide loop that ran around my neck and kicked my leash aside. The Fool Dog was still holding the other end of the line, looking rather silly.

I tapped myself and Yellow Legs, then made the married sign, laying index fingers side by side, smiling in matrimonial fashion. My marriage may not have mattered a moldy corn kernel to the Mandan—in fact this whole loving reunion was more likely a source of serious aggravation. All I wanted was to leave, without seeing him blown across the clearing.

Logically the Fool Dog should have shared my concern. Yellow Legs had a Colt pistol in his belt and a Henry repeater in his hand. The Mandan's single-shot muzzle-loader was on the ground, two risky steps away. But I do not think like a Fool Dog—thank God. He may have been priming himself to leap at a fully armed Sheyenna, ensuring a brass band reception in the Spirit World. Luckily he was alone. Two Fool Dogs are ten times as danger-ous as one, since neither wants to back down in front of the other. A lone warrior is more thoughtful. What is the good of dying in style if there is no one to tell your story?

Yellow Legs strolled over, knocked the priming cap off the musket, then tossed the buffalo gun into the brush while grinding the cap into the dirt with his moccasin. Then we backed out of the clearing. The Fool Dog gave a bark of disgust, but made no attempt to follow.

I felt born again. An absurd reaction. The Mandans had taken my horses, dumping my lodge, utensils, dresses, and notebooks somewhere on the trail; plucked again would better describe my condition. All I had was my blan-ket, my filthy outfit, and Calamity's lice. But I felt like I had my whole life back. I had Yellow Legs. I no longer needed to account to Wallace, or Libby, or anyone, no longer needed money or employment. This was the Center of the World, with food to be found, picked, dug up, or brought down—on my empty stomach that was reason enough to be light-headed. Love can make you as silly as a Fool Dog.

Yellow Legs led me to where his horses were hobbled, swinging me onto a big American bay with a saddle and bridle, smiling up at me in the same old way. But before I could bend down and kiss him, he was mounted and heading off into the brush. I wanted to catch him, to ask a flood of questions. How had he found me? Where had he come from? Where were we going? Communication proved impossible. Riding a strange horse through broken country, it took all my effort just to stay mounted. Yellow Legs was adept at letting actions speak for him.

He set a war party pace, but I did not complain. Fighting might break out at any second, and Yellow Legs was riding like lightning away from the action. Sheyenna warriors fought or fled at whim, and I wanted to encourage his uncommon good sense. Swept up in the thrill of success, I supposed this running was temporary. I was sure I would soon have things just the way I wanted. Watching Yellow Legs riding ahead of me, his body flowing with the beat of the hooves the way a fine rider's does, I thought how I had brought him here in the flesh too—not in some nonsense Medicine dream. I had called Yellow Legs to the Center of the World, and this big warrior had come running like a camp dog looking for a handout. No doubt about it, I was one Medicine-filled woman. I put out of my mind the moments of acute embarrassment brought on by the 7th cavalry and a Mandan war party.

My Medicine drained as the day wore on. By afternoon we reached Rapid Creek with barely a stop to breathe our horses, covering in a single gallop half the distance I had walked the day before. Yellow Legs started to ford the stream, but I swung off my mount, sitting right down in the creek. Cool numbing water felt wonderful on legs and rear, sore from miles in the saddle. Yellow Legs turned his horse in midcurrent and trotted back, obedient once again. I lay back, soaking my sweaty body.

It was the hottest part of the day, and the sun beat down through a yellow lacework of leaves and boughs. My husband dismounted, taking some dried meat and fry bread out of his parfleche saddlebag and producing his small black pipe, trying to look wise and aloof, doing his best to give the afternoon a serious tone.

Sitting up, I struggled out of my lice ridden dress, equally determined to enjoy myself. After some tugging and splashing, I left my dress floating in the current, pinned in place with a heavy stone. I called to him, asking if he had a spare buffalo robe. He brought it down to the bank, a light spring robe, freshly tanned with the hair off—black triangles were painted on the white surface. Raven's work.

Pulling the robe around me, I sat down next to him. We talked, ate, and admired the Center of the World. This was one of our finest times together—a small plateau of happiness, bridging two great chasms of grief. He acted warm and wise, while I sat almost naked beside him, ravenous for food and affection. Dried meat and cold fry bread tasted sublime. And I knew that no matter how aloof he pretended to be, we would soon make love. Postponing that pleasure made it all the more delicious.

My big bay had the double-bar brand of the Swan Land and Cattle Company on his hip. I asked where the horse had come from. He assured me that he had not stolen it from the Wasichu, but from Bad Lodges. "I do not like to steal from Bad Lodges. They cannot be trusted to have anything worth taking. But I had little choice. It was good to find the Bad Lodges were horse rich." The bay was a fine horse, strong and friendly, but the brand made me nervous—if I was caught on a Swan Company horse without a bill of sale, it would be useless to blame it on the Bad Lodges.

"How did you find me?" I wanted to known everything at once. His sudden advent seemed totally miraculous. By comparison, beating Coyote at the bone game by the Great Medicine Wheel was a trivial amazement. Instead of replying he got up and pulled a fringed saddlebag from his mount. Opening a flap, he showed me my books and notebooks, along with my skinning knife, my awl, my beadwork, and my needles—all the small but vital things that made up my life. I fingered the tools with tears in my eyes, thinking they had been gone forever.

"It was time for me to come," he explained. "A vision warned me bad things were happening in *Paha Sapa;* and you would need me. I found your things, then I followed the Mandans to you."

I was terribly excited to have my books, tools, and beadwork, but he was as much a man as the Mandans. He had left my lodge cover and possible-sacks behind, filling his saddlebag and leaving the rest. Warriors complain about a woman's love of possessions, forgetting that *we* must produce those possessions. Months of work had gone into my clothes and lodge cover. Annoyance eclipsed my happiness. I asked why he had not come for me sooner.

He reached into his Medicine bag and produced a white buffalo chip. Placing it on the ground, he set the pipe on top of it and looked up at the sun. "By sunset you will see why I did not come sooner. Let us have this day. There will be many days afterward of knowing, but never another day like this."

I sat wrapped in another woman's buffalo robe, looking him over, Wasichu fashion. His gaze stayed fixed on the black pipe and white chip. He looked older. The wrinkles around his eyes were deeper. Time was moving across his face. This day *would* come only once. I felt the deep-rootedness and self-possession that had first attracted me, and that I always respected. Tomorrow might be better or worse, but it would never be today. Something told me this was my special moment, more precious than knowing everything. Trickles of water, or maybe lice, moved between my thighs. I remembered Wallace. I was not ready to spill out all my secrets. I could wait to hear his.

Without speaking, I opened the robe, passing my arm under his, pulling him toward me. By surrendering my questions I said I was ready. We copulated right by the waters of Rapid Creek with the sun overhead and the creek rushing past my toes. It was not inventive and measured lovemaking, but straight and compelling Sheyenna coupling. Saying a swift prayer, he plunged into me, driving my heels and buttocks into the cool river mud. I told him about the lice, but he only laughed. If it was not a bear, he did not fear it.

When we were done, I noticed that his pipe was still resting on the buffalo chip. He had been careful not to kick it. Even in the midst of animal abandon he had his mind on his Medicine.

Washing the mud off, I watched him fetch another saddlebag. Inside he had a buckskin shirt, old leather leggings, and a length of cloth. He laid these out on the bank, saying, "We must be going. It is not safe to lie about here."

He had hardly given my thighs the rest they needed, but I dressed anyway. The old leather shirt felt soft against my nipples. I folded the piece of fabric into a fair imitation of a breechcloth, but I refused the men's leggings. My wet dress and leggings went across the bay's broad rump. They would dry in the wind and sun, and help hide the Swan Company brand.

We rode side by side, buoyed by a sense of being and belonging, talking only about the day and how good it was to be together. The power of *Paha Sapa* spun time into an endless strung-out afternoon, threaded through high stands of spruce and pine, bordered by grassy valleys. We crossed dusty elk trails and thick summer bluestem, cropped and trampled by deer. Beavers had dammed the streams into chains of flat glistening ponds. This bit of magic had to last me a long time, because my life was about to be wrenched around again.

At dusk we came to a wide flowered meadow finer than any I had seen, dappled with yellow, crimson, and purple blossoms. A lone tipi sat beneath a twist of white smoke, and a woman knelt beside it fleshing a green hide. Even at a distance I recognized Raven's broad hips and thick badger-tail braids. She too seemed to have grown, not older but larger. Meadow grass softened our hoofbeats; we were almost on her before she heard us.

Men say that when women are startled they grab for what is dearest to them. What Raven reached for was a bundle wrapped in rabbit fur, bound tight to a cradleboard. She clutched the bundle to her big breasts, saying, "Get down, husband. Get down, American Woman."

I sat stock-still, as openmouthed as any Wasichu fresh out on the prairie, staring down into the red wrinkled face of the baby Raven held—knowing full well why Yellow Legs had waited nearly a year before coming for me.

The Big Dry Time

THE BABY WAS A TINY GIRL NAMED NOTHING. JUST A BUNDLE lashed to a cradleboard; but from the first Nothing meant a lot to me. She showed me right off what a year Yellow Legs had had for himself. While I had been mooning about, missing him, he had been busy grunting over Raven, getting her in a family way. What else should a Sheyenna husband be doing? Sweaty pleasure did not bother me nearly as much as the closeness that had to follow; watching her belly swell, feeling the baby move, then, after the birth, lying down at night with the new baby between them—all things that I had wanted, but now bitterly resented.

Her cradleboard told it all. Someone had lavished time and skill on it, nailing brass tacks along one side, hanging coup feathers and charms from the cradle bow. Nothing heard the soft rattle of deer hooves whenever the wind blew. It was not Raven's work—coup feathers and brass tacks were hardly her style. Yellow Legs had never made anything half so artful for me.

And he had not even dared tell me straight out. This was another fait accompli—like when he brought me back from the agency simply figuring Raven and I would make the best of it. When I got to Crazy Horse's camp, Raven was there waiting, ready to unsaddle our horses. Now at the Center of the World, Nothing was waiting for me.

I swung off my mount and stalked into the meadow, mad at Yellow Legs, mad at Raven, mad at the flowers under my feet, feeling my anger grow and ripen. Raven began rubbing down the horses with sweetgrass, as cool as the day we met, though I bet she got more satisfaction out of this rubdown.

I stood fuming, my back to the tipi. Yellow Legs's moccasins made no noise on the meadow grass, but I heard the rustle as he sat and opened his medicine bundle, taking out his black antelope-bone pipe. Good move,

Medicine man, but it was going to take more than a peace pipe to get me off the warpath. Sick of Sheyenna dodges and courtesies, I snorted, "So this is why you did not come for me?"

"I did come for you."

"Why you did not come *sooner.*"

Slowly packing his pipe, he made his excuses front to back, Sheyenna fashion. "We found Crazy Horse camped on the Rosebud. As soon as Raven was safe in Black Shawl's lodge I borrowed a horse and headed back for Crow Country, searching for you. I could not find you. When I returned to Crazy Horse's camp, Raven told me a baby was coming—we had no horses, no pounded meat for winter. Crazy Horse is openhanded, but he is not a big chief with a lodge full of women, and herds of horses to give away. I spent the winter stalking game in the snow and teaching the Bad Lodges to mind their ponies."

"You could have come for me when the grass was up." Grass tops were turning blond in the summer sun.

"Lakotas coming up from the Bad Face camp brought no news of you until the baby was nearly here. I left camp, searching for a vision. After four days without eating or sleeping, a helper came to me, in the form of a female hawk, calling to me from the wing. She told me to come for you in the Moon of Red Cherries, at the Center of the World."

Thanks for the flim-flam, Medicine man. All his hallucinations and missed meals meant was that he had come for me at the last possible moment. By sundown I would have been with Long Hair or headed for a Mandan lodge. I was second to Raven in his heart and second to Nothing in Raven's lodge. And it was indeed Raven's lodge. By leaving my clothes and tipi cover where the Mandans had tossed them, Yellow Legs had sprung another neat little ambush. I had no home to run to, no robes to keep me warm, only his cast-off clothes to wear. I had to accept Raven's hospitality or ride alone into Lakota Country on a stolen horse.

Yellow Legs sat there, not speaking, the perfect image of a stoic Sheyenna warrior berated by his woman. But I could play Indian too. I strode back to camp, mounted my stolen horse, and prepared to depart for parts unknown. Ready to throw myself away.

Riding off without food or weapons on a worn horse was a hopeless gesture; fortunately the Sheyenna are in love with foolish pride. Yellow Legs met me at the edge of the meadow. (Heaven knows what I would have done if he hadn't.) Standing with arms spread, he looked like a romantic's statue in fringed buckskins. He asked, "What must I do to have you stay?"

Shadows filled the spaces between the pines. An owl hooted in the twilight. Here stood a proud defiant infidel, who dreaded neither God nor the

Devil, but did fear losing me. Knowing I was not going to get my way by being pissy, I tried to think what I really wanted. Right now I was just running away, not going *to* anywhere. What he had done was no worse than what I did with Wallace, just a sight more productive. And I had long ago given in to sharing him. Raven and Nothing would be obnoxiously tolerable if everything else could be set right. "I want things different—not just different, but better."

"It is hard to have things any way but what they are."

"Not true," I retorted. "We Wasichu are always redoing the world."

"Then tell me how the world must change."

I got down, still holding the drag rope. "For openers, we must get rid of war—I want you off the warpath, now and forever." This was an old argument, but at times like this, all the old arguments come back. "It may seem small to you, but I hate wondering if you are sprawled on the prairie with a bullet in your chest or a lance in your gut—I was not raised to feel good with that."

He folded his arms. "I did not make the warpath. You were raised in the Jesus way—I respect that. Jesus would have made a fine man-woman, healing the sick and working in wood. But Jesus never had to worry about the Long Knives burning his camp or stealing his women and horses."

I was beyond arguing Bible stories. "I want to live in a place where there is no war, where we can be at peace with our neighbors—and with each other."

"Is there such a place this side of the Spirit World?"

"Yes, in Indian Territory. You could enroll at your proper agency, with the Southern Sheyenna."

"What would I do there?" He was having trouble imagining a world without war.

"You could hunt." The warm southern plains were the great wintering ground for migrating animals, home to the huge Southern Buffalo Herd. "We could ranch or farm as well."

"I know nothing about caring for Wasichu cattle."

"I know how to farm. Raven could learn. You know horses. We could raise horses. And not stolen horses either. I mean raising them from foals and colts."

"We could do that." It was a flat statement of fact, not yet a promise. "If the Long Knives let us."

"Soldiers will have nothing to say. The agency is administered by my people, by Quakers. They will let us live as man and wife—no one will question it." Indian Territory was one of the few places where white squaws were accepted.

He smiled. "A land with only Sheyenna and Jesus people, it is worth going south to see that. I will take my moccasins off the warpath and will raise horses. What else must I do?"

"Nothing more—for the moment." I also wanted a baby, but I was too mad to let him touch me. If there were a less personal way of getting pregnant, I would have mentioned it. He held out the black pipe—by touching it I accepted that the argument was over.

Raven was still to be heard from. She had a dozen good reasons why we should stay right here. The winds were warm, and the cherries were ripening, and good white prairie potatoes could still be found. "Fall is when we should go south, when the plums are ripe. That is what the buffalo do." Every year the huge Southern Herd drifted north to escape the heat and flies, going south again in the fall. This was the great pulse of the prairie, a migration that brought more meat north than all the cattle drives out of Texas. Raven had a Sheyenna view of the trail—not a path between two points, but an endless chain of seasonal campsites. She said going south in the fall would make sense. "It is going to be a hard winter."

"Yes," our husband agreed. "It will be a hard winter." He looked at me, clearly wishing he were in the hills, with nothing to fear but cinnamons and grizzlies.

I was not to be brooked. The winter could be hot as July in hell for all I cared—but we were leaving *now* for Indian Territory. "There will be nothing but fighting up here."

He turned blank-faced back to Raven, trying to sound like the masterly Sheyenna husband. "We will go south."

Raven snorted. "So American Woman can have her way, we will give up living with my people. We will all become farmers on some southern agency, herding horses and spotted cattle. And you will no longer be a warrior. That much is good—you are a father now, too old for the warpath." She stared past him to me, not even pretending to be polite. "Your white skin and yellow hair are like the sun on a frosty day. I do not hate such winter days—I just sit warm in my lodge, waiting for them to pass away." A dozen moons and a new baby had not improved relations between me and my sister-wife.

We headed south, leaving the hills below Buffalo Gap, riding through a booming prairie dog town, filled with plump dogs, plus all the shifty characters that hang around a well-to-do dog town—weasels, red-tails, and black-footed ferrets. Prairie dogs actively farm the land, rooting up sage, letting parts lie fallow while grazing on others—making for a very productive patch of prairie.

A trio of little ground owls dived into an old dog hole as we passed, clicking out an exact imitation of a rattlesnake's rattle. Old Man Coyote and

Mr. Badger weren't fooled. Badger started to dig while Coyote watched the bolt hole. Quick-thinking, fast-acting Coyote and slow but powerful Badger, with his keen senses and digging claws, were longtime partners. They could snag more meals together than each could cadge on his own.

I broke up their joint hunt, shooing the moochers off, shaming them for hunting nestlings. The coyote trotted a dozen yards, then turned with a sly look, yip-barking back at me. I looked to Yellow Legs for the translation.

He laughed over his shoulder. "Coyote called you a meddling yellow-haired bitch. But that is a compliment. Bold light-haired females breed good pups."

In two sleeps we reached the Platte at Scotts Bluff, a giant gnarled mesa frowning down on the floodplain. At a distance, the stiff layers of marly clay looked like an abandoned city—parapets, verandas, temples, and amphitheaters towered over a great bowl-shaped basin floored with short grass and yucca. Heat and haze spread shimmering moats around the monuments, and a humming telegraph wire snaked along the river, marking the line of the old Oregon Trail.

Any greenhorn who gets as far as Laramie hears some horrible version of the Hiram Scott story. Scott was a clerk for General Ashley's fur brigades—no Jedediah Smith or Jim Bridger, just an honest accountant, eager to do the company's bidding. On the way downriver from a fur rendezvous he took sick and was abandoned by hardier companions. Stories differ as to what happened. Some say the sick and crazed clerk walked and crawled for sixty miles. Some say he swam the Platte. Everyone agrees that when his companions returned for next year's rendezvous they found his bones, and named the nearby bluff for him—it being the least they could do.

I awoke next morning to find a delicious mess bubbling in the cooking pot. The jerky we had been chewing on was now part of a vegetable stew. Raven shuffled about with Nothing on her back, doing a gruff imitation of a grizzly with cub. "This is really good," I admitted, finding it easier to compliment her cooking than her cussedness.

"Yes." She took my statement as fact, not a compliment.

I recognized currants, rose hips, prickly pear, and fleshy green cactus buds, cooked soft, with the spines burned off. Raven's raw energy could be frightening. With her at his side Hiram Scott would have lived to see stagecoaches, the Pony Express, and telegraph lines pass his rock. Indian women were a wonder of nature. Any Wasichu who made a mark on the wilderness bigger than Scott's Bluff nearly always had a Pocahontas or Sacajawea to help him out. Bold Cortez, Lewis and Clark, Kit Carson, and General G. A. Custer all found brown-skinned women indispensable, or at least worth fighting over. People like Libby who come along later, pitying a squaw's poverty and ignorance, never tried to do her day's work. Try living on the prairie with a few homemade tools and a cooking pot. You'd never match Raven's level of comfort—and would be doing tolerably well to survive a single winter.

And Raven did all this with Nothing always on her back or propped in the shade, watching, sleeping, waking to nurse. When the baby fussed, Raven swooped down like a mother hawk, smothering her cries with a tit. Sheyenna children are introduced early to the cycle of feast and famine. As long as there was milk in her breast Raven would feed her baby, or any baby—but when food ran short and milk dried up, children were the first to die.

I complimented my sister-wife on her sturdy offspring, asking why she was named Nothing—more work had gone into the cradleboard than into the baby's name.

"A special baby needs a special name," Raven replied.

I asked what was so special about "Nothing."

"Nothing is special about Nothing. I am waiting for the special name to come." Pure Sheyenna—the child was too special to have a name.

Scotts Bluff had an archaic, deserted air. The rock I picked up to pound seeds with was full of petrified shells. Deep wagon ruts marked the old line of the Oregon Trail. Alongside lay the remains of carved oak bureaus and teak tables—hauled halfway across the continent, then thrown overboard at the base of the bluff to lighten the family wagon. I found a black felt bull-whacker's hat that even the fleas had abandoned. The trail and stage line had given way to the railroads, and Fort Mitchell was dropped from the army rolls when Red Cloud made peace and moved closer to the Center of the World. Now the bones of buffalo and bighorn whitened in a forest of pine stumps. Civilization had come to Scotts Bluff, cut down the trees, killed off the game, then moved on, leaving the land to jackrabbits and prickly pear.

Leaving Lakota Country made me worry about my Swan and Company horse, with the big double-bar brand on his hip. Yellow Legs tried to be re-assuring, telling me, "These Two-Bar Wasichu must have many more horses than they need."

I reminded him that he was off the warpath. "Even horse-rich Wasichu do not lend spare mounts to footsore Sheyenna."

He protested that stealing horses was not war. "A thief who must fight a man for his horse is doing very poorly."

Raven sided with him. "American Woman, all our horses are stolen. If we give your big bay back to the Wasichu, must we give our ponies back to the Bad Lodges? Do we walk to Indian Territory?" It is almost impossible to do a Sheyenna a favor. An Indian on a branded horse is assumed to be guilty of theft, if not murder, and the fit subject for a necktie social. But they readily agreed to cover the bay's rump with yellow paint—Buffalo Indians prefer horses that brighten up the landscape.

I named my big bay Stolen Swan, and we saddled up and rode south, swinging past the tall spire of Chimney Rock, trusting Yellow Legs to get us through to Indian Territory. He was convinced we could move invisibly over the landscape. The country south of Court House Rock, between the forks of the Platte, was old and familiar territory, and he had that aboriginal ability to read and memorize ground as effortlessly as a seasoned actor learned Shakespeare. Yellow Legs kept up a running commentary—not on what we were seeing, but on what lay just over the flat horizon. What the country would be like. Where we would find water. Another of his Medicine tricks.

He pointed out hidden creek beds, and the remains of an army camp where he and Crazy Horse had gotten many American horses with the Long Knife mark on their hips—he traced a "U.S." in the air with his finger. Anything out of place got instant attention. A smudge of dust or smoke. A peculiar animal movement. Several times he saw the bones of dead buffalo that had not been there before. Each time he dismounted and piously turned the eyeless skulls to face the sunrise and rebirth, doing his bit to assure the yearly return of the buffalo.

He timed our march to cross the Platte Road at night. Not just a single road, this included the Union Pacific tracks, the South Platte rail spur, as well as the wagon road and the South Platte River below Julesburg. A very populated corner of Colorado. Riding under the waning moon, Raven sang softly to Nothing, holding the restless baby's nose to keep her from crying. I considered that was a cruel thing, but Raven dismissed my concern. "Spring Grass says it was a crying baby that led Long Hair to our camp on the Lodgepole—that was the cruel thing." Two moons old, and Nothing was already learning about life on the run.

This was the Big Dry Time, and the Platte had sunk to a trickle in its mile-wide bed, a thin boggy film hiding sinkholes and quicksand. Of course we could not use the recognized crossings—but Yellow Legs saw that our horses barely wet their fetlocks.

By dawn we were on the divide between the South Platte and the Republican River. Tall skeletal yuccas stood out against the cool blue sunrise. By stages the land grew greener, shaded by stands of juniper and cedar, becoming a hidden paradise. I never knew a place so wild and pretty lay this close to the busy Platte road. "We call this Wasichu Water Creek," Yellow

Legs explained. I thanked him for naming such a pure sweet stream after my people.

"We did not name it for your people. An old Wasichu lived here, who took beaver pelts in trade for the Wasichu Water that makes you silly. We rode down this creek singing our thanks"—so much for the romance of a name. Drunk or sober, the place was pretty.

In the valley of the Pawnee, we camped with a band of Cut-Off Lakotas, who already knew all about Long Knives coming to the Center of the World, saying that the Corn Indians with Custer had killed Stabbed and scattered his band. How this bad news had come south so fast was a mystery—we had ridden almost straight from *Paha Sapa* to the Pawnee—but Lakotas have private ways of communicating, faster in some cases than a telegraph.

Last summer Oglalas and Burnt Thighs had ambushed a Pawnee hunting party near Prairie Dog Creek, and the government indignantly declared that Lakotas could no longer hunt south of the Platte. But here we were, deep in the "Cornhusker" state of Nebraska, sitting in a wild Lakota lodge. The war party that massacred the poor Pawnee's numbered a thousand braves, and there were hardly a hundred Wasichu in this stretch of Nebraska; not one of that hundred was fool enough to enforce the order from Washington.

The next day we came on the remains of a Corn Indian village, almost certainly Pawnee. Double rings of post holes surrounded small mounds of ash and fire-reddened earth. In the rear of each lodge was an earth altar supporting bird bones or a bleached buffalo skull. As with all Corn Indians, the story of the Pawnees is intensely tragic. Wasichu call the Pawnee the Republican River; not after the party of Lincoln but for the Pawnee Republic, which elected its chiefs when we were still ruled by kings. The Pawnees were no angels. Like the Roman Republic and the Tribes of Israel, they practiced human sacrifice. But the Pawnees gave up their bloody customs, made peace, farmed the land, and scouted for the Long Knives, doing just about everything the Wasichu claimed to want. In return they suffered worse than the most stubborn Lakota. Washington drove the Platte Road through the heart of Pawnee Country, taking the best land and settling Delawares, Wyandots, and Iowas on the meaner portions. All that remained to the Pawnees was a postage stamp reservation north of the Platte. Now they dared not come home to the valley of the Pawnee, even to hunt.

Heading south we found the valley of the Pawnee badly picked over. Rotting buffalo lay in heaps, pecked at by clouds of vultures, looking like a panorama from some apocalyptic gospel. You could tell it was the work of commercial hide hunters: skinning stopped at the hip. Heat and stench were overpowering. We passed on without bothering to turn any skulls toward sunrise or otherwise pay our respects.

On the Arikaree Fork, Yellow Legs spotted a pair of riders. Two Black Wasichu riding a bald-faced blue and a coyote dun. He decided it was safe to let them see us. They were armed with an old single-shot Enfield, and being several shades darker than Yellow Legs they were unlikely to be incensed at seeing him with a white woman. Closer up, you could see they were cowhands, wearing dusty chaps, loose flannel shirts, and broad-brimmed hats with rope sweatbands. Their horses had 21 brands on their hips.

Al and Douglas were their names. We all "got down" and Al fished into his pocket, producing a Bull Durham bag and starting to roll. If he found it funny to see me traveling with a family of Sheyenna, he was too polite to say so. Instead, Al talked about how the whole valley was pretty well done in. With the buffalo gone, the sod farmers downriver were living on boiled flour. Last month they had sat down to dinner, their fall harvest in the field, when they heard a roar and a rush overhead. A silver cloud of grasshoppers dropped out of the sky.

"Like snow in July," added Douglas, Al's poetic nephew.

Al shook his head, handing the smoke around. The locusts ate everything. "But more families keep comin'. Pourin' in from the East. No money. No food. No train ticket home." He showed me a handful of Omaha fliers advertising free farmland—the ads were so common people used them for toilet paper. "Course the land is free. No crops. No water. No buffalo. Nothin' on it but what the grasshoppers had left."

These same grasshoppers had descended on the Lakotas, landing on lodges and ponies, eating every leaf and shoot. I told the two cowhands how the Bad Faces had leaped up, herding the locusts into pit fires. Dinner was roast grasshopper, which is not as horrible as it sounds, especially when you're hungry—a lot like a flying crawdad. We ate them as quick as they came down. Douglas thought it was a great story, very biblical.

Hearing we were headed south, they owned up to having been longtime cowhands in Texas—first as slaves and then free. We talked for a time about the Lone Star State, touching on the unpleasant weather and the barbarity of the natives. The railroad panic had hit Texas hard, and even big cattle-men like Charlie Goodnight were going under. But it was Democrats that drove Al and Douglas north. The Republican experiment in multiracial government was over. The Democrats were back in, saying there had been too much talk about "rights" under the Republicans.

Al insisted I take a pouch of tobacco and a can of coffee. I tried to refuse, but he claimed they could get all they wanted, with the buffalo gone and the settlements starved for beef. They were a friendly sociable pair—but pretty typical Texas cowhands, with all the usual prejudices, promising to pass on the grasshopper story to the next hungry homesteader. They headed off, toward the Colorado line where the 21 Outfit was running cattle, singing a tune that was well on its way to being the state song:

> Hurrah for Nebraska! The land of the free,
> The land of the bedbug, grasshopper, and flea;
> I'll sing of its praises, I'll tell of its fame,
> While starving to death on my government claim.

We went up the Arikaree fork. Timber thinned out into clumps of cottonwood and willow separated by stretches of open prairie. In a couple of sleeps we came on a plum-tangle island sitting in the dry channel. Yellow Legs mounted the low eroded bank, striking out over rolling shortgrass prairie, saying the next stretch of river was very bad.

I looked back at the sandy bed. "Quicksand?"

"No, that is the spot where Roman Nose was shot."

It was the worst of the Big Dry Time. The Kansas-Colorado line is never wet, but now it seemed burned over. Furnace winds split my lips. Buffalo wallows that usually hold the rankest sort of water were caked and dry. But each evening Yellow Legs would show us where to dig, leading us from one dirt well to the next, finding the headwaters of streams that became big rivers farther east. This was the Great American Desert, almost treeless and utterly unsettled—too dry for farming, and well to the west of the cattle trails. It had become the broad sage and cactus highway of the Sheyenna, connecting Indian Territory with the Center of the World.

We crossed the lonely tracks of the Kansas Pacific, relieved to put that last rail line behind us. From there on we sat higher in our saddles, looking for signs of buffalo. Ahead lay the great shortgrass pasture of southern Kansas, where buffalo came together to carpet the earth. When Coronado crossed Kansas the herds were so huge that his army could not push its way through them and had to march around. The Southern Herd had shrunk since then, but was still awesome, the largest accumulation of meat on the hoof in the Americas. And south of the Flint it all belonged to the southern tribes.

Just reaching the Flint River would be a relief. The Medicine Lodge Peace Treaty reserved the hunting grounds south of the Flint for Sheyenna, Snakes, Kiowas, and Apaches, and I wanted my husband on the right side of every treaty ever written. Finding the Southern Herd and fresh meat would be a treat, but I would have eaten raw prickly pear if it got us closer to the Sheyenna agency.

In shimmering noontime we saw the Flint cutting across the plain. But between us and the river was something not in my husband's mental universe—a fresh line of rails. Dark eyes narrowed, and laugh wrinkles disappeared. "There was never an Iron Road here."

"It has to be the Atchison, Topeka and Santa Fe," I told him. Last I had heard the line was stalled somewhere in East Kansas; I never expected to find it flung across my path, headed into Colorado—connecting Topeka to nowhere. The ground around the twin steel threads was dotted with alabaster mounds. Yellow Legs recognized the white objects first. His lips tightened, and I knew we were riding into trouble. Piled along the tracks were the bones of thousands of buffalo.

We crossed the tracks and reached the Flint, watering our horses in a vast boneyard. The buffalo had been cut down as they came to drink. Wagon tracks and boot marks showed who had done the killing. When Coronado crossed Kansas his men had never been out of sight of buffalo, not for a single day. We had seen nothing but empty wallows—now we knew why. The railroad and buffalo hunters had turned the Flint River into a line of death, killing the Southern Herd as it came north.

The Staked Plains

Not a stone, not a bit of rising ground, not a tree, not a shrub, nor anything to go by.

—Coronado's Report to the King of Spain on *El Llano Estacado*

I WAS ROUNDLY SHOCKED. YELLOW LEGS HAD SENSED DISASTER as soon as he saw the Iron Road. But I had no innate fear of railroads to warn me—now I wished I had told Coyote to rip them all up. What puzzled my husband was why the Wasichu would kill all "their" buffalo in a single season, "leaving nothing for winters to come?" Not a paltry question. Knowing my people better than he, I doubted the killing would stop at the treaty line—but hunters feeding the railway gangs could only haul meat so far. Spoilage would limit the swath cut by the Atchison-Topeka.

Putting the boneyard behind us, we pressed on, crossing the old Cimarron Trail, then the forks of the Cimarron itself, finally entering Indian Territory. It made no difference. Dead buffalo where everywhere. Only here they were killed for hides alone, leaving the meat to rot. On the North Fork of the Canadian we found fire pits and felled trees. Hunters had wintered in Indian Territory, leaving only when there was nothing left to kill.

I took this moment to remind Yellow Legs he had sworn off the warpath. "Then we best not meet these buffalo killers," he replied. "My scalp shirt is trimmed with the hair of men who did me far less harm."

No longer surprised—just monumentally sad—I did my damnedest to hurry them down the North Canadian and onto the Sheyenna agency, hoping it still might mean something to be on the right side of the treaty lines.

We were almost to Wolf Creek when Yellow Legs smelled smoke. He signed, "A small fire of Buffalo chips, with bacon and coffee cooking. Maybe

205

wolves for the Long Knives." By that he meant army scouts. It had to be an Indian fire, because I could neither see nor smell the smoke.

Leaving Raven and the baby behind, Yellow Legs and I wriggled forward, resting his brings-'em-close-glasses on a bit of rising ground. He peered through—then motioned for me to look. "Two wolves, probably Delawares. A Wasichu is with them." Through his field glasses I saw two Indians in army coats. Lord only knows how he figured them for Delawares. The Wasichu with them was younger, wearing a natty silk shirt, red bandanna, and black bowler hat. Despite being young and out of uniform, he was bound to be in charge. The youngest, greenest Wasichu generally outranked any Indians.

Setting the glasses down, I signed that I should talk to them. "No," Yellow Legs signed back, "too dangerous."

I insisted. We had to know why they were camped so close to the agency, and I could ride down and ask without causing trouble. Grudgingly he saw the logic in that; there was no telling how two Delawares and a Wasichu would react to a lone Sheyenna. We were outside the States, on land promised to the Southern Tribes, but that might not mean a lot. Those two blue-coated Delawares were a sure sign the army was following in the boot tracks of the buffalo hunters.

Sliding back down the rise, I dusted off and went to the gully where we had hobbled the horses. Not that I needed a horse for so short a distance, but it would stop fool questions about how I had gotten here. I led out Yellow Legs's pony, not wanting to have to explain the Swan Company brand on my big bay. Indian ponies were free goods, able to be roped, traded, or stolen without exciting comment.

I still caused a fair stir coming in. Both scouts grabbed carbines. The boy had a .50 Sharps, made to drop a buffalo at a quarter mile, also a handy man killer—crack shots in the army were called "sharpshooters."

"Howdy." I waved, feeling like William Penn preaching to the mouths of cannon. "No need for the artillery—just a friendly morning call."

Seeing nothing more dangerous than me, the boy put down his Sharps and doffed his bowler. He had dark eyes and a cocky teenage smile. "Why, ma'am, you look nearly white."

"Was when I woke up." My blond hair was covered in dust and my face was smeared with paint to cut the sun, which was fairly relentless so late in the Big Dry Time. Dress and leggings were pure Sheyenna.

"I only knew of one white woman in these parts, an' she left in a hurry." He meant that as a joke, but no one found it funny. Not me. And not the edgy Delawares, who neither took off their hats nor put down their rifles. That I was white and a woman did not make them a whit less suspicious.

He signed for them to lower their carbines. Reluctantly they obeyed. It takes more than a pretty face to fool a Delaware. "My name is Masterson— William Barclay Masterson. My brothers call me Bat."

I told him my name was Kilory, and he could call me Sarah. Between the Fool Dogs, Boston Custer, and young Mr. Masterson, there were entirely too many teenage boys roaming the plains this summer, all spruced up and looking for someone to shoot.

"More than pleased to meet you, ma'am." Scratching his head with his hathand, Bat tried to imagine what to make of me. "How can I help?" Any lone white woman was by definition in some form of distress.

"You could start by offering me coffee." I nodded toward his fire, acting anxiously natural. He poured black coffee into a tin cup. Real Wasichu coffee—strong enough to float nails—not the brown watery brew the Sheyenna make do with. One sip brightened the whole morning.

I told him I was a Quaker, coming down to teach Indians at the Cheyenne and Arapaho agency. The old agent, a dear man named Darlington, had died a couple of summers back—whoever had replaced him would speak for me. Any Quaker would.

Bat chuckled at that ambition, pouring himself a cup, saying I'd find damn few Indians to teach. "The Cheyenne and Comanches have jumped their reservations. I'm scouting for General Miles and can take you down to Camp Supply. The general can see you sent safely back to Kansas."

Not aiming to go back to Kansas—safely or otherwise—I asked if Bat had actually seen hostile Cheyenne. More people had told of Indian fights than had ever been in them.

"Seen hostiles? Hell, I fought them for three days."

"Where was that?"

He pointed his bowler upriver. "Out on the Panhandle—Cheyenne, Comanches, Kiowas, maybe some Arapahos. They had us cornered at Adobe Walls. Killed three whites."

"They just went berserk and tore into the army?"

"No, ma'am, no army. Just a couple of dozen scared white folks. I joined up afterward. Figured if I was going to shoot Indians I should get paid for it."

"What were you doing on the Panhandle?" I had a fair idea, but I wanted to hear it from him.

"Hunting buffalo," he answered happily, "at least until that war party showed." I asked what he had expected, shooting buffalo in Snake Territory. Southern Snakes—called Comanches by the Spanish—were true-blue Texans, homicidally wary of foreigners and death to trifle with.

Bat gave a wan smile. "I see now it weren't so smart. At the start we thought it was a lark—joking about, playing Indian to scare the greenhorns. But hell, buffalo are getting rare. You have to hunt them where you find them." He swore how Kansas was picked clean, but there were still "buff" out in Texas. Lots of them. Hunters shot until their guns got red-hot. Then they poured canteen water down the gun, or pissed on the barrel, and shot some more. It would not stop until the buffalo were gone.

Furious, I told him the whole prairie from here to Nebraska was starving. "Homesteaders along the Pawnee are living on flour paste and belt leather, and you're feeding buffalo meat to the buzzards like some crazed bird lover."

Bat looked at me like I was too long in the heat. "Hides are what the railroad pays for. Can't help it about the meat." No wonder Snakes and Sheyenna tried to lift this boy's hair. They are poor businessmen—tell them buffalo meat is worthless and they will brain you out of plain frustration.

"What are Indians going to eat when the buffalo are gone?"

Bat shrugged. "I guess the government will feed 'em. This is Uncle Sam's coffee we're drinking, and government bacon on the fire. They pay me to shoot Indians. Someone else has to feed 'em." Seeing he was having trouble getting through, Bat allowed how times were hard. "And not all of us are turned out to teach school. The buffalo are going. If you want to see them, you better look fast. If you want to get a buck out of them, better do it now."

Such monumental extermination made the baby-faced killer reflective. "Don't know what I'll do when the buff are gone. Word's come to Camp Supply that Custer found gold in the Black Hills. Maybe I'll head north."

Right—go north and rob the Lakotas. Crazy Horse will love this boy. Disgusted, I got up to go.

Setting down his coffee, Bat stepped closer, aiming to stop me. "See here, I am truly sorry if I upset you, but it would be nuts for you to just ride off." He was a boy used to having his way by force.

Bat had about as much chance of getting me to go with him as he had of proposing marriage to the Pope—but I hoped to get away without a fight. I handed him my coffee, to keep his hands busy—young Mister Masterson looked to be the type who practiced his draw. Maybe Bat was not as mean as he made out; but he was a little nervous and a whole lot green. All set to kill Indians, he stood with an uneasy grin on his face and Yellow Legs's never-miss Medicine rifle pointed at his head. His pistol was on his hip, his Sharp lay against a log. All Bat had in his hands was a bowler hat and a coffee cup—and the brave drawing a bead on him already thought that buffalo hunters belonged in the Happy Hunting Ground. His two Delawares had read me better.

I took a step sideways, clearing the line of fire, assuring him I was fully grown and could find my way without an army escort. If Bat got his head blown off it would not be my doing. It was the Delawares that had me worried.

He hovered for a moment, without touching me—held back by the Medicine of a Wasichu woman on the plains. This was one time women's Medicine saved a life. Bat shook his head. "Since you're set on suicide, you hardly need advice, but don't try heading down to the Darlington agency on your own." He painted a cheery picture of how the Sheyenna had finished off a pair of buffalo hunters, staking them down "with their heads propped up so they could *see* what was being done to 'em."

Bat gave me a last dubious glance, then looked down at the coffee growing cold in his grip. I must have seemed passing strange, but Bat was not a boy who pondered deeply on other people's problems. I walked the pony back to where my husband waited. We had come hundreds of dry miles to avoid a fight, and found a full-out war.

Nothing could provoke Yellow Legs into riding farther down the Canadian. I scolded and ranted, reminding him of his promises to enroll at the Sheyenna agency. He listened with arms folded and a wooden look on his face, refusing to budge as long as Bear Coat Miles and his Long Knives were between us and the agency, paying Delaware and the buffalo hunters to shoot Sheyenna. "Since you have taken me off the warpath, I may not even shoot back."

Nor was Raven any help. "Let American Woman go alone," she advised. "They will not shoot a Wasichu."

I told her to go mind her baby, asking our husband where the hell he intended to winter. Yellow Legs pointed his stubborn chin southward. "We will winter on the Staked Plains. There are places there known only to the Snakes and Kiowas."

With good reason—I had heard grim things about the Staked Plains. Few parts of Texas can be called habitable, but that section of the Panhandle put savagery to shame.

We turned about and trudged back up the Canadian, crossing over to the south fork, where the river wound through pokeweed meadows shaded by hackberry trees. Farther on I saw the stands of stumps that mark a settlement, then a few sod buildings and a square corral. Here was the abandoned post at Adobe Walls, where Masterson and the other buffalo hunters had made their stand.

An air of fresh calamity hung about the place. Doors and windows stared blankly back at me, and a dozen severed heads stood watch on the corral posts. Some had ears cut off and eyes gouged out; all were scalped. Beneath each exposed skull was the mummified face of a Snake or Sheyenna brave. One was so black he might have been a Negro. Yellow Legs wanted to stop and dig lead out of the bullet-pocked buildings, but Raven and I insisted we ride on, agreeing for once that this was no place to linger. Littered with buffalo bones, broken whiskey bottles, and dead sun-blackened ponies gutted by vultures, the place thoroughly lacked a woman's touch. No wonder the only other Wasichu woman around had taken off.

Farther up the Canadian we turned straight south, leaving the cool gallery forest and entering canyon country, where the creeks were all alkali and powder dry. Climbing past the line of cap rock, we struck out across the griddle-hot plains at the heart of the Texas Panhandle, raw unyielding unvarnished prairie. No hills. No trees. No buttes or mesas. Not a hint of rising ground, though I knew we were high in the air, higher than the hills in Adams County. The cap rock atop the buttes along the Canadian formed the bedrock of these high plains.

Phil "The Only Good Indian Is a Dead One" Sheridan once said, "If I owned both Hell and Texas, I'd rent out Texas and live in Hell." Scorched grass stretched from one end of the world to the other, making progress impossible to measure. Perspective vanished. A moving speck might be a cloud shadow, a herd of pronghorn, or a rider ahead. The first Wasichu to see this tableland were Coronado's conquistadores. Fearing they'd be lost in such immense emptiness, the Spaniards marked their trail with tall upright stakes, which stood long after Coronado had passed on, giving the vast expanse its name—*el Llano Estacado*, the Staked Plains.

There were few trails. Stiff wiry shortgrass sprang back as soon as it was trodden on, but Yellow Legs went about the business of searching for Stone Calf's Sheyenna, finding dust prints and poking through horseshit. Snake ponies ate only buffalo grass. Barley seeds in the dung meant Long Knives. Corn kernels meant *comancheros*.

We wandered about, camping for a time with the Kiowas in the Place of Chinaberry Trees until Bad Hand Mackenzie's cavalry came and routed us out. The Big Dry Time finally broke. Thunderclouds gathered and lightning arced in all directions. We were caught in a genuine Baptist downpour, the first of series of gullywashers that turned the gray-white earth into gummy muck, dragging at our travois poles and ruining our moccasins. Sometimes wind-whipped rain would combine with blown dust until it was actually raining mud, big dirty drops that splattered over everything.

We ate little and slept less. Hunger and fever compounded my hopelessness. Too sick to walk or ride, I ended up flat on my back, being dragged about on a travois, seeing where we had been instead of where we were headed. Not that it made a thin bit of difference.

One day at dusk, Yellow Legs went hunting rabbits while Raven collected buffalo chips to cook them on. (The treeless landscape had reduced us to burning turds.) Lying on my travois, sick and miserable, slipping in and out of sleep, I dreamed Coyote came trotting up. Stopping to sniff, he sat back on his haunches, giving me a smug slantindicular look, as though deciding if I was dead enough to eat.

"Go away," I told him.

"*Why?*" he replied.

Too stupefied to answer, I sat up, looking about, not sure if I was asleep or awake. Yellow Legs was still off rabbit hunting. Raven and Nothing were nowhere in sight. Coyote scratched himself, turned about, and trotted off at an angle into the twilight—looking back over his shoulder, totally confident I would follow.

Which I did. Staggering to my feet, I stumbled after him in dreamy fashion, feet barely touching the ground. The prairie wolf led me to the base of gray rounded bluffs, strung along a stream like a row of burial mounds. Which proved this was a dream—there were no such elevations on the Staked Plains. Without being told, I knew the bluffs contained the Camp of the Dead. My father had given me bleary lectures about the Land under the Hill—inhabited by faeries and the dear departed. By one of those eerie coincidences, Buffalo Indians also thought the Spirit World could be found inside some high place.

A creek ran along the base of the bluffs. I realized it was the Greasy Grass, the far-off stream at the sunset edge of Lakota Country. A circle of men sat by the water, waiting to cross over and join the dead. Crazy Horse was there, playing cutthroat poker for pony stakes with the Custer brothers—the General, Tom, Boston, and James Calhoun. With them was Bloody Knife, Custer's scout, and Colonel Myles Keogh. Crazy Horse had won all the ponies—and the 7th cavalry officers were having to throw in their clothes as well. Crazy Horse had a royal flush, and the best they could come up with was aces and eights.

Men looked up from their cards. The General stammered a greeting. Brother Tom took off his tunic, tossing it to Crazy Horse—I saw the big American eagle tattooed on his chest. Colonel Keogh got up, giving a courtly bow—a lovely Irish gesture, except that he was dressed in just his socks and the medal from the Pope he wore around his neck. He nodded at the shallow ford where Medicine Tail Coulee climbed the Little Big Horn Bluffs, saying, "Ladies first."

Shaking with fever, I started across the ford, though I knew that death lay up the coulee. I heard my dead Mother calling to me, the way she used to call us home. I opened my mouth to answer.

Bluffs and water vanished. Suddenly I was back on the Staked Plains, standing beside my travois. Coyote and the whole ghostly company were gone. By the time Yellow Legs returned I had firmly convinced myself it was all a fever dream—nothing as monumental as that night next to the Medicine Wheel. Of course my husband would have none of that, blandly assuring me it had been a full-blown Medicine vision.

Shivering, I shut up. Vision or not, the dream's meaning was frightfully clear. Crazy Horse, Bloody Knife, Myles Keogh, and the Custers were all ticketed for the Spirit World. But I was going to go before them.

Late the next afternoon we spotted figures on the plain, emerging gently out of the landscape, showing first as dots, then as three tall men on horseback, skinny men on scrawny ponies. I did not need a Medicine dream or horse droppings to know that these were Snakes. At about rifle range, they vanished. We kept going, assuming they would reappear. Which they did, sitting patiently in a dusty buffalo wallow, as though we were of no concern—which meant they had looked us over carefully and judged us harmless. Their ponies were hobbled lying down, bony flanks heaving quietly.

The three braves greeted Yellow Legs, then came over to look at me. Sick and bedraggled, lying on a travois, I was still an object of interest. Staring down at me, these Snakes looked as tall as Crows, wearing grimy untrimmed shirts and leggings. I won't say I looked much better, lying on my back, smelling like a dead moose. My last bath had been in a gravel pool on the South Canadian.

After several fitful sleeps I awoke in a Snake camp, brown dingy lodges with big ear flaps strung along a shallow arroyo. Raven proceeded to pitch her tipi. Snakes are as casual as Kiowas are formal. Your best introduction is to go about your business, watching to see no one borrows your horses. I helped Raven with her tipi, so as not to look like an utter invalid. Snakes have no pity for weaklings. Once the lodge was up I collapsed inside, wrapped in a blanket, feeding twigs and dry grass into the fire. Raven took Nothing to find water.

My privacy only lasted as long as it took Yellow Legs to corral someone to smoke with. He sauntered into the tipi accompanied by a tall, well-built warrior with grim blue-gray eyes and the wild confident air of a war chief. Clearly a person of consequence, though the Snake political system never pretends to be anything but anarchy—Snakes follow whomever they please for as long as it pleases, exasperating both friends and enemies.

I pulled my blanket tighter, and we pretended to ignore each other. A war chief does not waste Medicine eyeing other men's wives. And a proper Sheyenna wife does not stare at a visiting Snake as if he planned to pinch the silverware. Heaven knows there was no excuse to leap up and play hostess.

Yellow Legs insisted on making introductions. "This Snake's name is Quanah, which means Smells Sweet." For the first time since setting out on the Staked Plains I had to stifle a laugh. Snakes aren't prized for their aroma, and despite his blue eyes, Smells Sweet was all Snake.

Seeing I was sick, he signed that he would call for a Medicine woman. I did not much want anyone burning sweetgrass over me, but it was useless to protest—to a Snake, impulse and action are one and the same.

While we waited for the Medicine woman, Yellow Legs and Smells Sweet smoked and swapped stories. Smells Sweet told his own version of what had happened at Adobe Walls, most of which concerned a Medicine man named Coyote Dung. Coyote Dung was one of those living wonders of the plains who could stop the rain with a smile and vomit up wagons full of ammunition, as well as being adept at all the lesser parlor tricks like turning back bullets and raising the dead. Smells Sweet claimed we had been feeling Coyote Dung's power all the way down from Nebraska, because it was Coyote Dung who had decreed the Big Dry Time—and now he too promised a cold hard winter. But I was never much impressed with Medicine men who could make it hot in July and snowy in January.

After a trip to the Spirit World and a chat with the Great Medicine, Coyote Dung had tackled a problem bigger than death or the weather—getting all the Snakes together for a Sundance. In this he succeeded, and at this first-ever Snake Sundance, Smells Sweet passed the war pipe against the Wasichu who made war on the buffalo.

"So we rode north," he explained. "Many of my people. Many Sheyenna. Some Kiowas. White Bear brought a Buffalo Soldier who played music on White Bear's bugle." That explained the head of a black man stuck on the corral fence at Adobe Walls—it was not the first time that an army deserter fought alongside Buffalo Indians, but I had never before heard of Kiowas and Snakes attacking to bugle calls.

"All the way to the Canadian, Coyote Dung talked big, saying we would kill many Wasichu, promising that when the Wasichu fired their guns, the bullets would dribble out the barrels or bounce off us. Then we would kill them all, like old women caught digging turnips." All Medicine is big before it is tested.

"As usual, the Wasichu did not know how to fight," Smells Sweet complained. "They hid in their lodge, only sticking out their gun barrels to shoot. I rode right up to their lodge entrance and beat on it, but they would not come out." The thought of this big warrior pounding on a door asking to come in was fairly comical.

What followed was not so funny. "Coyote Dung's Medicine began to look very weak. Many men were shot. My own horse was shot dead under me. A bullet bounced off me, as Coyote Dung promised. But it hurt, knocking me down. I lay behind a dead buffalo, unable to use my arm, thinking there is not much to Coyote Dung's Medicine. We could have been shot just as easily without his protection."

When the fight was finished everyone blamed the defeat on Coyote Dung. "The Sheyenna had lost a chief's son and wanted to pony-whip him. Coyote Dung claimed a Sheyenna had broken his Medicine by killing a skunk on the way to the fight. The Sheyenna said he certainly had skunk Medicine—but we still would not let them beat on him."

Yellow Legs asked which chief's son was killed, and Smell's Sweet said it was the son of Stone Calf—the peace chief we had hoped to lodge with. An awful sign. If it weren't for bad luck, we'd have had no luck at all.

The Medicine woman arrived. Smells Sweet introduced her as Curandera, Spanish for "Healer." I could not tell if this was a name or title—probably it was both. As much Spanish as she was Snake, Healer was round-armed and dark-eyed, with an abrupt air, showing small deference to the men. There was an outright tension between her and Smells Sweet. Snake women can be very free and forward, slipping into another woman's tipi at night, if she has a man worth getting at.

Healer went right to work, poking me unmercifully, asked with signs and simple Spanish how I felt. *Dolor? Nauseas? Fiebre?* When I did not understand, Healer acted out the symptoms. She did not burn grass, paint me up, or put her clothes on backward, but she did demand a full description of my dreams. Naturally my latest Coyote dream impressed her the most. I tried to pass it off as a bout of fever, but that was hopeless. You cannot even discuss dreams with Buffalo Indians without laying claim to all kinds of vision power. The sign for "dreamer" is the same as the sign for "Medicine man," and a dream is "night-seeing" or "sleep-work." Arguing them out of their superstitions is hard enough when you're in the best of health; an invalid hasn't a shot at it. No one but me doubted that I had conjured up a serious Medicine vision.

Healer signed her diagnosis: "She is Wasichu." Pointing at me with her chin, she drew her hand across her brow. The men puffed and passed the pipe, as though this observation were fairly profound. "I too am part Wasichu," she added. "There is much Medicine in the blood of Wasichu women. We do not sicken the way People do. A Wasichu can walk about when the whole camp is dying, then crumple up when the work is hard or the weather turns rainy."

The men signed that they too had seen this, Smells Sweet adding that his mother had been white. On his mother's side Smells Sweet was a Parker, related to some of the best white folks in Texas, which explained his blue eyes and boastful smile.

"She is also a *bruja*." Healer said it evenly in Spanish, making the sign for Medicine woman. A nice way of saying I was a witch. When I objected, Healer added, "She is a *bruja* who does not know she is one. Power whips around her like an unruly wind." Her hands swirled and she puffed her cheeks, blowing and making the signs for wind and Medicine. She promised I could look forward to whole new forms of dementia.

Fed up with arguing, I merely protested that there was no use to Medicine you could not control.

Healer chuckled. "To a Wasichu, everything must have a use." The men laughed, saying that was certainly so. "Take care and cultivate this Medicine: it will grow." Healer's hands shot up like a corn plant in the sun. "Deny it, and it will whirl out of control, carrying you off."

She rummaged through her Medicine bag, producing powders and herbs. "I will give you a broth to drink now for your fever, and stronger Medicine to help you on your journey."

I signed that she had done plenty and that I felt wagonloads better, but Healer ignored my protests; perhaps she was merely completing her own Medicine.

"These are your helpers." Healer held out four small wrinkled cactus buds. "Keep them with you. The winter ahead will be a hard one. When you need them, scrape the hair off and eat one—even though they are bitter." She combined the eating sign with a comical grimace.

I mumbled a *muchas gracias*, putting the buttons in my Medicine bag, alongside my herb teas, patent pills, and the gambling peg that had carried me to Pennsylvania and back. By now our luck was so thoroughly bad a few cactus buttons weren't about to turn it around. Since the day I had seen soldiers on the Yellowstone and Medicine Bear was shot, nothing had worked for me. Every success brought greater calamity. I had beaten Coyote and the Northern Pacific, but the railroad panic had unleashed hordes of jobless onto the plains. I had gotten Yellow Legs back, only to be burdened with Raven and Nothing.

Healer brewed up a broth that was mostly cayenne pepper, claiming it would clean my spirit and get me on my feet. Which it did—scorching my sinuses and blistering my gullet going down, then getting me on my feet and out of the tipi at a run. I did not stop until I was out of camp squatting among the ponies. It even burned coming out.

When I recovered from her cure, we set off again, traveling between storms. Freezing rain turned to snow by the time we found an abandoned campsite in the buttes and canyons of New Mexico Territory. From a pair of moccasin prints and a turkey feather, Yellow Legs deduced the camp was Sheyenna.

We followed their trail until one snowy morning we came upon a hundred-odd lodges pitched beside a cottonwood creek. The air was so cold the limbs on the cottonwoods cracked like pistols going off. Yellow Legs signed, "Get down." Tipi markings told him this was Stone Calf's band of the Southern Sheyenna. Our winter home. Last fall I had been close enough to Canada to hear French spoken freely: now I was on the far side of the prairie, in what once was Mexico. From Montana to Texas I had seen the plains torn by war and bled by the steady slaughter of the buffalo. With a hard winter coming on, things would only get worse.

Catherine

By the Moon of Frost in the Tipis, the hard winter Healer, Raven, and Coyote Dung had promised was here. We were all crowded into Raven's lodge trying to stay warm. Nothing cried constantly, her tiny ragged breaths misting in the icy air. Raven was weak with fever, so I had to care for the baby—like Healer said, I was Wasichu, likely to be up and about when People lay sick in their lodges.

Nothing had diarrhea. Her rabbit-fur bundling was always dirty, but there was no way to wash or dry the fur in freezing weather. I just replaced the sage padding, apologizing to her for the dirty fur. At least Nothing got to have her black and watery bowl movements indoors. I had to do my business on the frigid iron-hard ground outside.

When I was finished, Raven opened her buffalo robe, taking the baby to her hot breast. It scared me to see Raven so helpless. The woman who could do the work of ten Wasichu was weaker than me. I was now Yellow Legs's working wife. You could tell by the makeshift look of the tipi: Our robes were ragged, the fire was feeble.

Bad as things were, our tipi was paradise compared to most of Stone Calf's camp. No one had died in our lodge. Whole bands had come into camp worse off than we were—trudging in, their feet wrapped in rawhide, having lost everything, right down to their frostbitten toes. No horses. No lodges. No warm robes. No meat for the winter. Long Knives were attacking the camps, burning lodges and winter stores. Bad Hand MacKenzie had taken a whole herd of captured ponies to Tule Canyon, shooting them with firing squads. A thousand horses lay in frozen heaps.

Nothing stopped crying and started to suck, a good sign. Raven still had milk. Young Dr. Warren often lectured on a nursing mother's need for cal-

217

cium—so I was making bone soup, but that needed more firewood. Tucking a small ax under my blanket, I crawled out the entrance flap into the searing cold.

Lodges stretched up and down the glacial creek, a chain of tiny snowsided volcanoes, blackened at the tops where the smoke trickled out. The stunted cottonwoods along the creek bed were dying, stripped of their bark for as high up as a women could reach or a pony could chew. Spots of blood showed where horses had gnawed on the frozen trunks. Smaller branches were mostly gone, and the bigger limbs were cased in ice. Hanging among the crystal limbs were grisly little bundles dripping with icicles: the frosted bodies of children wrapped in swaddling skins.

Swinging the ax as high as I could reach, I chopped at skeletal branches, swearing that next time I would get Yellow Legs to do this. He was off seeing to the horses. The man could be a mountain of energy where horses were concerned. Every morning he dug under the snow to cut grassroots for our ponies.

I let my blanket slip, to get a good swing with the ax, not seeing the young Sheyenna until he was next to me, grabbing my hand. I could barely believe I was being manhandled in camp, and thought he was making some fool attempt to help me—a Sheyenna version of courting behavior, though this was hardly the moment for some random brave to get romantic.

Then he twisted my wrist, hard, making me to drop the ax. So much for courtship. The grinning bastard yanked my blanket off—going straight for a roll in the snow. I gave up the blanket, grabbing my skinning knife lefthanded, screaming "Let me go" and slashing his wrist.

His grin faded and he let go, staring at his bleeding wrist. "You cut me."

I scooped up the fallen ax. "Yes, and I will chop you too. Give me my blanket."

He let the blanket drop. Wind howled between us. There was a knife in his belt, but he seemed to have forgotten it, saying, "I thought you were the crazy Wasichu."

I waved the ax in his face. "You are the crazy one. Attacking a woman in camp. Assaulting a guest of Stone Calf." I wanted this dumb brave to know he was the one in the wrong, the one who had broken the Peace of the Camp.

He looked hurt and stubborn. "I thought you were the crazy Wasichu who gathers wood for Long Back."

I had never heard of Long Back. Snatching up my blanket, I told him, "I know your face. Bother me again and I will tell my husband. I will tell Stone Calf. You will be driven out on the prairie." He could stick his impatient prick in a frozen gopher hole. I did not know if I really could get this buck thrown out of camp, but it sounded good. Nothing confuses a warrior more than threats that he cannot meet—especially from wild-eyed women. Now he had to worry about his standing. There were no coups to be won wrestling with another man's wife in the middle of camp.

I backed into our tipi, thoroughly shaken. This was the first time I had ever been flat-out menaced by a strange brave in camp. I had been threatened with mayhem and forced marriage out on the prairie, but the most miserable camp circle was meant to be a woman's haven.

When Yellow Legs returned from his precious ponies, I told him he would have to gather the wood. "A man grabbed me. It is too damned cold to cut wood with someone going through your clothes." He looked properly aghast, grabbing his Medicine gun, asking who this man was.

"No one I know personally." My husband's show of concern made me feel better. I took away his gun and handed him the ax. "Here, cut some wood. I think it was some mistake." No reason to ticket my attacker for the Spirit World. Then I added, "Does anyone know of another Wasichu woman in camp?"

Ax in hand, he considered the question. "Someone might, but not me." He vanished through the tipi flap.

I sat in the back of the lodge, cold and frightened. This oversexed brave had not acted snowblind or stir crazy. He was convinced that there was a Wasichu crazy woman in camp—ready to meet any man's demands—which chilled me as much as the wind outside. I had to find Long Back's lodge, to see for myself what the man had been talking about. Raven was sick and asleep; no sense in waking her. Pulling my blanket tight around me, I went looking for this Crazy Wasichu. Fearing what I would find.

People passed like ghosts between the lodges. Stiff bodies of ponies and mules lay sheeted in ice, half eaten by hungry Sheyenna. Dogs slunk about, looking for food while aiming not to become a meal.

Halfway down the creek an especially thin wraith emerged from a lodge. Wrapped in a threadbare blanket, she darted over to the bushes by the stream bed, tugged wildly at the brush, breaking off frozen branches with raw hands. Her feet were mud-spattered and blue with cold, but her ankles were white. I walked slowly over.

She started like a frightened bird, then went back to work. The glimpse I got of her was harrowing. She looked crazy. Her eyes were hollow and sunken, half hidden by unkept hair—and she was definitely white. Not a white Indian like Given-to-Us, but a girl born and raised Wasichu. Like me. Calmly as I could, I asked, "What is your name?"

She stiffened. With my face painted against the cold, I doubted she could tell I was white. Her soft child's mouth moved hesitantly. "My name is Catherine."

Shivering, she went back to ripping at the brush, frantic to tear off a few twigs of firewood. I bent down to help her, drawing my heavy knife, chopping at the branches. "How did you get here?" A dumb question, but I had to ask.

She gaped at me. "I was captured."

"Where?"

"Far away. Up north. In Kansas."

We sure as hell weren't in Kansas anymore. She looked around, then bent down and bundled up her sticks, scrambling back toward the tipi she had come from. Turning, I saw two men coming, not fast, but with easy confidence. One was the warrior who had grabbed me.

I kept between Catherine and the men. They did not try to pass. Seeing the girl disappear into the tipi, they sat down a couple of paces off. When I stared, they turned their heads politely away. Going to get Yellow Legs, I kept looking over my shoulder. The men sat on the ice-hard ground, like Old Man Coyote and Mr. Badger covering the exits to a prairie dog hole, waiting for the poor creature to come out.

Yellow Legs was back in the lodge, sitting proudly beside an immense pile of twigs. I told the whole terrible story, begging him to go to Long Back's lodge and get Catherine out. He could have my horse and anything else Long Back might want in trade. Yellow Legs took his pipe and left.

Raven was awake. After a long silence she spoke up. "It would be good to have another woman in the lodge, now that I am so weak. But we need your horse too."

I snorted. It was not as if we were riding anywhere. "I want that girl out of Long Back's lodge because she is being horribly mistreated. Men in camp are raping her."

"Some men will do that," Raven acknowledged. "It is a part of men's Medicine I never understood."

"No," I snapped, "it is not men's Medicine. It would be men's Medicine if they were raping each other. You would not accept it if she were Sheyenna."

"If she were not Wasichu, you would not be so worried."

Sweating and shaking beneath her buffalo robe, with her pitiful thin baby at her breast, my sister-wife was still full of fight. I thought of the men I had seen so set to kill: Bat Masterson, with his blind certainty; Crazy Horse and Custer, with their smug warrior ethic. None of them were out here on the Staked Plains, gathering wood barefoot, being raped while they worked.

Both sides boasted how they fought to protect their women, yet hardly a brave or soldier had died in this buffalo war. The few small-bore battles did not compare to a minute or two at Gettysburg. War parties fought when they felt inclined, while the army blundered about, raiding villages and peace camps—pushing women and children into the front lines.

I told Raven, "Every camp makes its own Medicine, and the Medicine in this camp is terrible. Raping girls will not make it one whit better. No wonder children are dying." If you believed in bad Medicine, it was no surprise that this was a death camp.

Yellow Legs entered, striding to the back of the lodge and sitting down. Dim flames lit his dark features. "I smoked with Long Back. He is happy with his new woman, who fetches wood well enough, though she is weak and cries at night. He says he does not need horses, though I offered him my warhorse and my best buffalo ponies; there is nowhere to ride and no buffalo to hunt. Long Back would of course prefer a proper woman, perhaps a Ute or even a Mexican, but no one is offering any. He told me to come back when there are buffalo to hunt, or when the grass is up. Then he might need more horses and fewer women."

Yellow Legs stared straight into the fire, then went on. "Long Back wondered why I wanted such a weak and clumsy woman. He claimed some men in camp were curious about how it felt to copulate with a Wasichu. He himself was not curious, being very happy with the wives he has. But to show he was generous, Long Back said I could take her out and copulate with her. I told him I was not curious."

There it was. A girl with sad scared eyes was being tortured in camp, and there was nothing to do about it. I wanted to scream.

Raven groaned and got to her feet, handed Nothing to our husband, then turned to me. "Help me go outside." I stared dumbly. "Help me go outside," she insisted. "I will talk with the women."

I helped her out of the lodge. Her flesh felt loose and flabby, but the frame beneath was still strong. She went first to a hollow in the creek bank, squatting in the snow with her dress pulled up. A hellish wind sang down the creek bed. From the color of the snow in the hollow, the whole camp had diarrhea. Only the cold kept us from stinking clear to California.

When she was done we hobbled along the line of tipis, stopping at a big smoke-darkened lodge. Raven scratched at the entrance flap. We were ushered in by a wrinkled old scarecrow named Yellow Hair, the mother of a war chief called Medicine Water. With her were two sisters, Two She-Wolves and Stands Apart. Throughout camp, families were doubled and tripled up.

We traded news. The sisters told how Gray Beard's camp had been raided by soldiers riding in wagons. Few were killed, but everyone lost food and lodges. Two She-Wolves and Stands Apart had brought their daughters to Stone Calf's camp hoping to find things were better. By now they knew things here were almost as bad. Yellow Hair had trudged all the way to the agency, but what she saw there sent her scurrying back to the Staked Plains. "Long Knives are taking away guns and ponies, locking people in corrals with only trash to eat."

More women came in, and half the stories had to be retold. The newcomers included Yellow Hair's daughter-in-law, Medicine Water's wife, a giantess with angry eyes called Buffalo Calf. She must have grown some since her parents named her. Buffalo Cow would have been closer to the mark.

The only good news was that Medicine Arrows, the Arrow Keeper, had slipped past the Long Knives headed for Lakota Country, taking the Sacred Arrows with him. These old flint arrows were the Crown Jewels and the True Cross of the Southern Sheyenna, as precious as the Buffalo Hat belonging to their northern cousins. I cannot say it lifted my spirits a lot—the fate of Medicine relics seemed trivial when the tribe itself was dying.

Sitting near the lodge door, saying nothing, I kept my blanket pulled up, waiting to see what Raven had planned. My sister-wife sat beside me, breathing softly, summoning her strength. Finally she spoke. "I heard there is a Wasichu in Long Back's lodge."

This nonquestion was directed at no one, but Buffalo Calf spoke up, saying that in the Big Dry Time she went with her husband to get revenge for the buffalo. They crossed the Flint, going as far as the Fat River, ticketing about a dozen Wasichu off to the Spirit World. Buffalo Calf only discussed those killings she had a hand in, but when she did her eyes lit up like hellfire, and she went into unnecessarily grisly detail, mimicking the sound an ax makes when it splits a woman's skull.

At no time during this amiable romp was Medicine Water's war party in the least inconvenienced by Bear Coat Miles's cavalry or the army garrisons in southern Kansas. They had gone north as easily as Yellow Legs brought us south. The way war parties moved invisibly over the prairie helped make war on the plains so terrible. Baffled by the braves' invisibility, the army would attack the villages—as often as not getting the wrong village or even the wrong tribe, turning the whole brutal show into an innocent-killing contest.

Eventually Buffalo Calf got around to telling how Catherine's family was massacred—an easy stroll from the nearest army camp. Catherine and three younger sisters had been brought south, along with the guns and horses that signified a successful killing spree. Two She-Wolves and Stands Apart added to the story, telling how the two youngest sisters were left behind when Gray Beard's village was attacked. The little girls were given to a Sheyenna boy, who left them sitting on a buffalo robe for the Long Knives to find. Neither sister knew the boy's name, but I thanked God for him. He could as easily have killed the children—even wars of atrocity and annihilation have their heroes.

Raven spoke up again. "The one that is with us should go back with her sisters. She is bad for the camp Medicine. Men have been forcing her to copulate. Such things can happen among Utes and Crows, but we are People."

"She is not a Ute or Crow," replied Buffalo Calf. "She is a Wasichu, a crazy woman who does not say no." Several others agreed, as if that explained it all.

Raven refused to be put off. "If she is crazy, she does the camp no good."

Buffalo Calf glared, running a righteous eye over us from her place in the back of the dark tipi, making my face paint feel pretty thin. "You are northerners and may not know how we have suffered. In the Winter When White Antelope Was Killed, we made a peace camp in the Big South Bend, near to the Long Knives' fort. The Long Knives came anyway, raping and killing."

This was Chivington's Sand Creek Massacre. We had passed Sand Creek on our way south, but Yellow Legs would not go near it—"Too many ghosts." Buffalo Calf had hid in the snow, watching Chivington's troopers drag women and children from her tipi: "I saw three aunts and five sisters taken by the Long Knives. They copulated with the older ones, then killed and scalped them. A Long Knife chief took out his pistol and shot the little ones one by one, while they screamed for him to stop. My whole family was murdered—but even that did not make me crazy."

Maybe not crazy, but awful darn close. One look into Buffalo Calf's eyes told the whole tale. She was never going to forgive Catherine's people, not while they were still busily destroying her tribe.

Two She-Wolves and Stands Apart said they too had fled the Sand Creek camp with their daughters, hearing screams and shots, but not daring to look back. "We would have died in the cold and snow, but a coyote took pity on us. He caught hares for us to eat, and guided us to Gray Beard." Cynical as he was, even Old Man Coyote found winter war tough to stomach.

"Yes." Raven shivered. "But that was many winters ago, and even a coyote can have pity."

"A coyote can have pity," Buffalo Calf agreed, "but the Wasichu do not. If we have pity on this girl, will they have pity on us?"

I wanted to speak up, to shout, "Yes, of course we would." But I knew the answer was most likely no.

"It would be better for People everywhere if this crazy girl never leaves the Staked Plains," reasoned Buffalo Calf. "If she lives they will use her words against us. And if she dies they will treat us no worse."

Buffalo Calf was actively hateful, but most of the others just had more immediate problems. Two She-Wolves and Stands Apart had their own daughters to protect—there being no promise that the Long Knives would not rape them. They *knew* what had happened at Sand Creek. And Yellow Hair's son was dead sure to be jailed or hung, even if Catherine were handed over healthy, unhurt, and made into an honorary tribal princess.

But bless her stubborn heart, Raven would not give in. "I too have a daughter," she told them, "and I do not want her to die on the Staked Plains. We are not Snakes to live on what coyotes leave—the young and weak must go back to the agency. And they must have this girl, to trade for food and blankets."

My sister-wife was coldly clever, driving a wedge between Medicine Water's family and the rest of the women. Yellow Hair herself admitted that Medicine Water was likely to be hung no matter what. Raven held out the thin chance that by bringing in Catherine the others might get better treatment—slim odds to be sure, but Stone Calf's band was hard up for hope.

"Medicine Water is a warrior," she reminded them, "sworn to protect the camp. No one hounded him to into going north, saying he must kill this girl's family. He chose the bow; for that we feed and honor him. But we do not shield him behind the bodies of defenseless ones."

One by one women agreed to ask Stone Calf to lead them back to the agency—with the captives. Medicine Water would fight on all the better with only warriors to feed.

We returned to our tipi. Tiny rivers of ice ran down the sides of the lodge from frost melting around the smoke hole. Nothing was crying. I pulled back the entrance flap, waiting for Raven to worm her way in. The walk and talk had weakened her—but she had shown me the proper line to take with the Sheyenna. I owed her for that.

Yellow Legs looked godawful relieved. Swiftly handing the baby to Raven, he resumed his seat of honor at the back of the tipi. Stoic courage and a Medicine gun cannot stand up to a sick child. I settled into the wife's place nearest him. This terrible winter had put new lines in his face, but I was going to have to add to my man's burdens. I told him we had to take Catherine's case to Stone Calf.

"Cath-er-ine." Raven drew out the Wasichu name, which meant nothing in Sheyenna. "If she were a Ute or Pawnee, you would not be so concerned."

I was tempted to say the Christian thing, to swear I would be just as concerned. But winter on the Staked Plains stripped you of pretense, leaving little in the way of hope or hypocrisy. Raven deserved the truth. A Ute or Pawnee girl in Catherine's place would provoke compassion, but not the same urgency. Catherine was white like me and never meant to be here. Only snakes shed their skins.

"She is Wasichu," I admitted. "That is why Long Knives and Buffalo Soldiers will come for her with wagon guns and many-firing rifles. Do the Utes have wagon guns? Do you want to see your people broken like the Pawnees?"

Yellow Legs sighed, picking up his Medicine bundle. "We will speak to Stone Calf." He could never stand to have his wives fighting. Polygamy is not all frolicking under the buffalo robes—just ask a Mormon.

In the peace chief's tipi I sat on the women's side, and Yellow Legs went to sit with the men. Stone Calf's wife, a woman with wide-set intelligent eyes and a proud pointed chin, served us token bits of dried mule, showing her husband was still a chief, even among beggars. Stone Calf looked as if he had aged twenty years since I had seen him at Ogontz Estate on the outskirts of Philadelphia. Dog Soldiers and war chiefs had tried to hound him from the tribe for talking peace, threatening to shoot his ponies. His son had thrown his life away at Adobe Walls. Still he sounded the same. In a dirty frozen tipi or in front of Ogontz's French windows, Stone Calf spoke out for peace and reason, just as he had at Harvard College and at the Sundance councils.

He had sent runners to ask the agents and the army for peace terms. The army's answer was no terms. An unconditional surrender. No protection for the buffalo. No punishment for the hunters who had robbed the Sheyenna. Just reprisals against anyone who had left the agency.

I studied the worn edges of my long winter moccasins. The Long Knives were plainly determined to crush the southern tribes. Sheyenna, Snakes, and Kiowas were going to be pinned to the agencies, while buffalo hunters destroyed what remained of the Southern Herd. The great pulsing heart of the southern plains would be stopped forever. Not everyone was as resigned as I was. Cloud Chief had come back from raiding into Texas, bringing guns and horses. More ponies were on their way from Mexico. Howling Wolf wanted to raid the Wichitas for guns. There was still talk of war when the grass was up.

Stone Calf doubted many would live to see grass in the spring. "Tall Bull has already taken his family in; when a Dog Soldier goes in, it must be near the end. It is fear of what will happen at the agencies that holds us back."

At Anadarko, Long Knives and Buffalo Soldiers had opened fire on the Snakes and Kiowas who had come in to give up their guns and be counted.

This was my moment. Only I could pretend to speak for the Wasichu. I felt miserable, knowing the unvarnished truth would do no one any good. Not Stone Calf. And certainly not Catherine. But Raven had shown me the lie that would work.

"Go in," I told Stone Calf. "And take Catherine with you. Bring her in alive and they will give you food. Enough to keep you from starving." Hell, I could have promised them hump ribs, heated lodges, and repeating rifles—it wasn't conscience that held me back, but respect for their natural cunning. By now they knew us rather well.

"Do you really think this?" Stone Calf looked at me.

"Certainly," I lied, "they are bound to treat you better if you bring her back, and treat you worse if she dies. We Wasichu care about our children too."

Silently I cursed myself—one more well-meaning Wasichu making promises we would not keep. We would not stop killing off the buffalo, or whittling down the reservations, or cutting back on rations—not out of thanksgiving for the return of one poor white girl. Catherine's story would only confirm white opinion. Buffalo Calf had realized that much, without being particularly sensitive to the Wasichu way of thinking. For all I knew, Stone Calf's people would be shot down as soon as they turned over their weapons. The country was primed for another massacre—it could happen anytime.

But my brand of humbug was what this old chief wanted to hear. Stone Calf stood up, saying, "I will go to Long Back. Those who want peace can come to the agency with me. Those who want war can stay on the Staked Plains." Someone had to say no to the fighting: *The war stops here*, come what may. If my lies gave Stone Calf the ammunition needed to end the shooting, so be it. I would take whatever punishment providence dished out.

I do not know what he told Long Back and the others, but he returned with Catherine and her sister Sophie, who had been with Gray Beard's band. He put them up in a lodge next to his. In that lodge I learned enough of Catherine's story to know I did not want to hear all of it—it being about as bad as I had imagined. Her sister Sophie was a few years younger and had been treated rather better, but what she had been through was suitably horrible.

Stone Calf led the trek toward the agency, heading into the sunrise. Almost everyone followed. Even Buffalo Calf's tipi came down; Medicine Water was coming in. All the talk of waiting until the grass came up was just talk. Even the worst Wasichu haters were sick of grass stew and pony steaks. We looked like the children of Moses coming in after forty years in the wilderness.

At the edge of the Staked Plains we met some Blue Clouds coming the other way, climbing past the cap rock. Stone Calf invited Yellow Legs and me into his lodge to hear what they had to say.

The Blue Clouds had stayed resolutely out of the war with the buffalo hunters. "Everyone loves the Blue Clouds," was their boast. To the Corn Indians they were the "Trading People." Lakotas called them "Wanders-Under-the-Cloudless-Blue-Sky." Somewhere or other they had picked up the name Arapaho. Squawmen liked them because their women never seemed to say no—a tribe so good-hearted, one sign for them is to touch the left breast.

Sage, or Wise One, told their story. Long Knives had come to Darlington carrying a paper with names on it. Everyone whose name was written on it was taken away. Hearing there were Blue Clouds on the list, Sage and his friends lit out for the Staked Plains—without even finding out if the braves on the list would be hung or merely locked in stone lodges. For people used to wandering under the blue sky, being buried alive or buried dead was a thin difference.

Naturally the Sheyenna wanted to know if there were any Sheyenna names on the paper. Sage signed, "The Long Knives would not let us look at the paper, nor can we read their writing." He neatly mimicked the act of writing to make his meaning clear. "But they spoke of one Sheyenna, a chief they especially wanted." Sage made the sign for rock hard, then for buffalo and birth—together they meant "Stone Calf."

We were aghast. Sage hesitated, then signed, "They claim he copulated with two female captives." Blue Clouds copulate pretty freely, and Sage seemed puzzled that the Wasichu would take this seriously. Several Sheyenna braves looked uneasy. I wondered if they had satisfied their curiosity on Catherine, and now regretted being inquisitive.

Stone Calf was unshaken. He was taking Catherine and Sophie to the agency—a chief must be ready to sacrifice everything for the good of the camp. I myself was sick at seeing how seriously I had misled the friendly old peace chief.

That night in our tipi I explained the gruesome sense of it to Yellow Legs. "Stone Calf sent runners in saying he took the girls into his lodge. We Wasichu think that no chief would keep a young white woman except to copulate with her." By offering protection, Stone Calf had singled himself out for punishment. I promised to speak for Stone Calf. And Catherine would tell how he saved her. Remembering my interview with Mrs. Carlin at Fort

Lincoln, I pictured Catherine telling her story to some officer's wife—that was one tea party I did not look forward to.

Yellow Legs stared straight ahead, hardly showing he had heard me. "It is good you will talk for Stone Calf, because I will not be there."

"Why not?"

"I am staying here on the Staked Plains."

In times past I would have torn into him, reminding him of his promises. Now I could summon neither the energy nor the conviction. My pleasant little dream of a horse ranch in Indian Territory was as dead as the buffalo. Everyone who had been to Darlington agreed the agency offered only idleness and short rations. I merely pointed out that Raven and Nothing were too weak to winter on the Staked Plains.

"That is why you must take them into Indian Territory."

It showed how bad things were that I did not shriek at the notion of going off with Nothing and my big difficult sister-wife. I merely went "Whoa?" in surprised Wasichu.

"I was a warrior." Yellow Legs spoke gravely, as if this were somehow news to me. "I have not touched the pen since Medicine Lodge. My name may be on the paper that the Long Knives are carrying around." Not an impossible thought. He was a well-known warrior off his proper reservation— and the army was clearly using this buffalo war to round out old scores. "But my family must go safely into Indian Territory. If you ride in the lead the Long Knives would let you through."

I had never thought of Raven, Nothing, and I as a family, but I suppose the idea came naturally to him. It was neatly laid out. I could go straight to the Quakers, taking Raven and Nothing with me. They were Northern Sheyenna—no relation to Stone Calf's renegades. With a white woman to speak for them they should be utterly safe. No matter how I turned it about, Raven, Nothing, and I needed to go. He needed to stay.

Taking my shoulders in his hands, he kissed me, saying, "Now you know how I felt in Crow Country." In a perverse Sheyenna way, the Medicine was balancing out.

We had figured in everything except my sister-wife. The woman whose health we were so concerned about listened dutifully to her husband—then refused. Raven was not leaving him. Not this side of the Spirit World. She graciously thanked us for thinking of her, but she was not going to waltz off to Indian Territory with me for company. Starved, sick, and exhausted, facing the death of her child, the woman was twelve times more stubborn than I could ever aspire to be. I was too sad to laugh and too amazed to cry.

So what could I do but stay? I had no desire to go on alone into Indian Territory, to take part in what was sure to be the final calamity of the Southern Sheyenna. I did not need a Medicine dream to picture the downward spiral they faced: disarmed, dismounted, subjected to disease and starvation on a steadily shrinking reservation. No, ma'am, life is precious, but not to be bought at that price.

We sat in front of Raven's tipi wrapped in whatever would keep us warm, barely speaking, watching Stone Calf's people march off in a straggling line over the snow. With hardly any horses and pitifully few possessions, the Southern Sheyenna were disintegrating even as they crawled in to surrender.

Catherine and Sophie walked with Stone Calf's women, behind the peace chief. It is impossible to imagine two more different people than Catherine and Stone Calf; one was a man, a hunter, a warrior and statesman, old and respected, a lecturer at Harvard, his life nearly completed; the other was an orphaned girl in her teens, despised, abused, and generally considered crazy. Yet each held the other's fate. Stone Calf had made himself Catherine's protector, and Catherine had become his alibi. If there was no new war when the grass came up, white families from Texas to Kansas had Stone Calf to thank. But all the Wasichu would care about was Catherine's story. She alone could save Stone Calf from prison or hanging. Somehow, I trusted them both.

The last of Stone Calf's People disappeared into the damp morning, descending past the cap rock toward the plain below. The war to save the buffalo was over.

The Southern Herd

WE WERE LEFT BEHIND IN STONE CALF'S LAST MISERABLE LITTLE campsite on the lip of the Staked Plains, surrounded by blackened fire pits and the frosty stone rings where tipis had stood. Returning to Lakota Country would mean heading north into the teeth of one of the worst winters in memory—something too ghastly to contemplate, with Nebraska starving and southern Kansas a graveyard littered with the bones of the buffalo. Instead we headed west, into the direction of death and sunset, searching for Smells Sweet's Snakes.

And found nothing. No sign of game. No sign of Snakes. Nothing but empty rutted trails radiated out from the buffalo wallows. Veering southeast, we searched the heads of the canyons that split the plateau. Between freezes the ground became a bog, turning to gray gummy clay that balled up so badly on pony hooves and travois poles, it had to be hacked away.

I fell ill again. Not with fever or diarrhea, but with the sick lassitude that signals starvation. My stomach shrank. I made soup for Raven and Nothing by boiling grass, rawhide, and crushed bone. They ate it, but the soggy mess did not tempt me.

As I weakened, more work fell on Yellow Legs. Despite having two wives, he was the one who took down the lodge and made up the travois each morning. With one person doing most of the work—and a man, at that—our little camp lurched across the bleak expanse, making less progress each day. But then, we did not seem to be going anywhere special.

One dark silvery dawn the sun cut a new notch on the black horizon, but Yellow Legs did not leave the tipi, no longer having the strength to strike camp. Here it ends, I thought. We had eight horses left, and we had to choose one to kill and eat. That would leave seven starving ponies to carry the lodge, packs, and four people. You can get only so far feeding on your-selves.

Breaking the ice scum on a small arroyo, I drew breakfast water. Grass stalks were slippery with frost, and a dark mist hung on the northern hori-zon. More snow was coming. I could smell the damp smoky odor of a blue norther on the way. Beneath it was another smell, earthy and familiar, but harder to place. Back by the tipi I started a fire, searching through my Med-icine bundle, looking for something that might give strength and flavor to the stew. All I found were the four cactus buttons Healer had given me.

Turning Healer's gift over in my hands, I thought how her most dire pre-dictions had all come true. Now was the time to find out if she had given me a helper, or merely hexed me.

Scraping the fuzz off one with my thumbnail, I tested it in my mouth. The bud was bitter, with a sharp green undertaste. Chewing it puckered my mouth. Swallowing was like trying to put away the whole cactus, thorns and all. I washed it down with dirty ice water.

Nothing happened. The bitter little button neither filled me up nor tempted me to take another. So much for Healer's helper.

The cold cast-iron wind howled about me. Dead grass bowed back and forth, rippling like a cyclone was coming—though this was hardly cyclone weather. Flecks of whistling sleet sizzled in the fire. Taking the horses around to the lee side of the tipi to protect them from the storm, I heard Nothing crying inside. My big, stolen American horse looked as poor and bony as any Snake pony. The others were in worse shape.

Flakes of snow hit my face. I ducked into the lodge to see to the baby. Raven was asleep, and Yellow Legs was having a hapless time trying to calm his daughter. Smiling, I took the baby from him, holding her inside my blanket, against my milkless breast. Though Yellow Legs was a doting father, his daughter already treated me as her second mother.

As soon as I stepped back outside, she quieted. Babies often react that way to light and air. By now snow was pouring out of the sky, smothering my fire. Time to go back into the tipi. But the bright snowfall had lulled the baby. And the air was actually warming, the way it often does when snow starts to fall.

By now I was resigned to never having the child I wanted, so I sat by the tipi hugging weak little Nothing—my poor replacement. This was life, a contagious, incurable, and ultimately fatal condition. And now I was headed for the Hereafter. Ahead of Crazy Horse, Bloody Knife, Myles Keogh, and the Custer brothers. My Medicine dream had told me as much. Having no choice, I had to accept it. Starving and freezing were no worse than sleep.

And at least I was dying clean. By lying to Stone Calf, I had saved

Catherine, Sophie, and heaven knows how many Sheyenna children who would have died on the Staked Plains. There was a rough justice in being left behind, to face the fate my lies had saved them from. My Medicine felt lighter. I had a *reason* for being here; I was ready to face the consequences.

Searching through my stock of Medicine songs, I found only one that fit this desperate situation. I began to sing it softly to the storm:

> *Amazing Grace, how sweet the sound*
> *That saved a wretch like me.*
> *I once was lost, but now I'm found,*
> *Was blind, but now I see.*

The song welled inside me, and I felt a prickly anticipation, as though the cactus bud were spreading through my veins. The storm broke into a million colors. Rainbow flames shot up to meet the snow, like a Fourth of July on the plains. Amazed and delighted, I sang louder, my voice carried upward by the colors:

> *T'was Grace that taught my heart to feel*
> *And Grace my fears relieved.*
> *How precious did that Grace appear,*
> *The hour I first believed.*

The storm seemed to slacken. The rainbow flames sank down, smoldering at my feet. I heard a stirring inside the tipi, as though someone were fumbling with the entrance flap. Dark patches of smoke condensed in the mist, growing bigger and more solid, parting the shimmering curtain of snow. Holding tight to Nothing, I sang to the dark patches in the storm:

> *Through many dangers, toils and snares,*
> *We have already passed.*
> *T'was Grace that brought us safe thus far,*
> *And Grace that keeps us all.*

The nearest shadow thickened into the image of a great buffalo bull forging through the wall of snow, striding toward me in absolute silence. I did not think to flinch, knowing this midwinter mirage would dissolve in another moment. Instead I marveled at the minute detail of my latest Medicine vision. Frost clung to his curly broad shoulders. There were black tips on his curving horns.

Then I felt his steaming breath puffing from flaring nostrils. My imaginary bull was about to trample me. I scrambled out of his way as he brushed past, giving me a wary look from under long brown lashes. Another bull followed, then another.

Amazing Grace, how sweet the sound
That saved a wretch like me.
I once was lost, but now I'm found,
Was blind, but now I see.

Shadow after shadow loomed larger, each one becoming a buffalo. Falling snow turned to steaming mist, melted by the heat of shaggy bodies. Standing up, I could see brown backs stretching off on all sides, their living mass blocking out the storm. I pulled back my blanket so Nothing could see. The child was awake and squirming in my grip, dark eyes scanning the huge beasts, brown fingers clinging tight to my dress.

Yellow Legs stood up in the lodge entrance, hands quivering at his side, croaking in ecstatic Sheyenna, "It is the Southern Herd."

They plodded purposefully along, in no particular hurry, parting as they passed our lodge, each buffalo giving us no more than a brief glance before being replaced by another. Yellow Legs stepped out to join me. Raven sat up, propped in the entrance. Now we were among the cows and calves, strong young animals like we had hardly seen all summer. After so much hardship and horror, the great herd was finally here; the lifeblood of the southern plains flowed past us, smelling warm, earthy, and intoxicating. I could feel the deep rumble as millions of hooves mashed through the snow, shaking the Staked Plains clear down to the cap rock.

Morning melted into afternoon, and still they kept coming: uncurious, unafraid, unending. We sat huddled against the lodge alongside our horses, humbled by the sheer mass of the herd, lulled by the steady beat of its hooves. I napped, and awoke to the same scene: the buffalo passing, Yellow Legs sitting and smoking, Raven nursing Nothing; our hunger, our worries, our weakness, overwhelmed by this outpouring of life. I could barely remember how bleak and barren the Staked Plains had been.

Not until it was nearly dark, and the herd began to thin, did Yellow Legs dare bring down a cow with his bow. As her kin continued to pass, he said a short prayer for the spirit of this cow, and of every buffalo, then ripped open the belly with a two-handed pull of his knife.

While I made a fire, Raven laid Nothing beside the steaming body cavity. The little girl giggled and moved about, licking blood from her fingers. I spread out a deer hide and Yellow Legs heaped meat on it: fatty back ribs, thick steaks, and the intestines, liver, and kidneys. We roasted the meat on sticks, stuffing it half-cooked into our mouths, cracking the bones to get at the marrow.

Night came. Wolves and coyotes padded past, a couple stopping to sit at the edge of our firelight, looking for an easy meal. Later, lying in the tipi next to Yellow Legs, I heard them snarling over scraps and bones.

Morning dawned bright and empty. Seeing the Staked Plains stretching from horizon to horizon, I might have thought the day before was a dream, but for as far as I could see the snow was churned into frozen slush, dirty with buffalo dung. Yellow Legs collected the fat from our kill, boiling it in Raven's pot along with herbs and melted snow to make a Medicine soup. Such a breakfast sounds revolting, but we soaked it up, swallowing it in great gulps. I felt a thousand times better. Lassitude and starvation fell away.

Yellow Legs and I broke camp, eager to be off. There was no question about direction. The Southern Herd was heading down off the Staked Plains toward Indian Territory. Descending past the line of the cap rock, we saw knots of buffalo grazing in the canyons. Two days before we would have greeted them with shouts of thanksgiving, unable to believe our luck. Today we just noted how beautiful their bodies were, how sleek and majestic, and went on. Nothing would satisfy us except to see the whole of the herd.

Our tired horses could not catch up until late afternoon. Coming out of the canyons I saw the herd again, this time from a distance under clear skies, a broad brown river flowing east toward the Big Muddy. The buffalo seemed to be following the Kiowas and Sheyenna, headed for the agencies. I could not imagine a greater irony than a million buffalo arriving in mass, just as the southern tribes were being penned up to starve on stringy government beef.

Soon we were looking as fit and sleek as the buffalo, though still horribly tattered. The herd was moving so fast we had no time to properly tan hides or do much mending. Though Raven was hardly idle. She gloried in her returning strength. Late in the evenings, rolled in my buffalo robe, I could hear the soft thunk, thunk of a scraper at work outside the lodge. Winter robes are the warmest, and it is easiest to scrape off excess flesh when the hide is stiff and frozen.

Crossing the Red River, we said a grateful goodbye to the great state of Texas, entering Indian Territory. Lines on the map did not matter to the buffalo. The herd flowed straight for where the Wichita Mountains stood up on the horizon. Seeing the Wichitas, I knew we were deep within the reservation shared by the Kiowas, Kiowa-Apaches, and Honey-Eating Snakes. But we saw no one, not so much as a pony herd. It was no winter for wandering about.

Rising straight out of the plain, the Wichitas form a granite gateway. Be-

yond them lay Fort Sill and the Chisholm Trail, where Custer and Spring
Grass camped together. I remembered a Kiowa tale about how the buffalo
fought the soldiers, going right onto the grounds of Fort Sill, trampling the
fences and gardens, trying to drive the Long Knives away. I had thought this
was wishful exaggeration, but now I was not so sure. Were the buffalo going
to throw their bulk against the fort? No army regiment carried enough bullets to kill them all.

We camped at the northern edge of the Wichitas, on a night filled with
nervous expectation. There was nothing dreamlike about this latest miracle.
The Southern Herd was solid and real. If anything, the world seemed too
real, too rich, balanced on the brink of some all-consuming event.

Yellow Legs and Raven wanted to know, "What will the Wasichu do
when they see the buffalo? Will the Long Knives fight the buffalo? Will
they let the Kiowas and Sheyenna hunt?"

I was their resident sage when it came to the customs and folkways of
Wasichu, but I did not have a ready answer. The herd was certain to attract
Kiowas, Snakes, and eventually soldiers. But even hard-bitten cavalry troopers had to be awed by the herd. The buffalo promised to bring peace and
plenty to the starving agencies.

Suddenly Yellow Legs gestured for silence. "The herd is moving." We
scrambled up, stepping out of the tipi. Standing under frosty stars I could feel
the beat of hooves, moving off, fading away. It was unusual for a herd to
move at night, unless they were spooked or stampeded.

Despite our weariness, we broke camp at once, wanting to stay as close
as possible to the moving miracle. Walking our horses through the darkness,
we followed the broad trail left by the herd. Normally night tracking is incredibly frustrating, but tonight it was ludicrously easy. We did not have to
see or even feel the million hoofprints that broke up the ground, trampling
down obstacles. The odor of buffalo, the howling of wolves, the rumble of
the herd, the stink of dung all marked the way. By the time it was light
enough to ride, I was supremely exhausted, swaying in the saddle. Coyotes
loped alongside us in the predawn light, their tongues hanging out, tired and
unafraid, wanting only to keep up with the buffalo.

The Wichitas have little in the way of foothills, rearing directly out of
the flats. Morning light reflected off the peaks like giant granite prisms,
turning the slopes purple, yellow and crimson. A thin patch of breakfast
smoke hovered over a fold in the northern slopes, marking a Snake or Kiowa
camp. The buffalo seemed undeterred by the mountain barrier, though they
were prairie beasts and I had never heard of them climbing much of anything. The herd surged straight into the mountains.

As the ground rose up, I reined in, seeing a miracle more awesome than anything in my dreams—easily the most amazing thing anyone ever saw sober.

The largest and nearest peak in the Wichitas split at the base. The rent opened in dead silence, widening as it went upward. There was no earthquake, no lava, no volcanic action; the mountain just peeled back, like a tipi splitting along a seam. No molten rock poured out. Instead of pumice and magma, I saw a world within the mountain, a world without snow or winter, a world filled with sunlight, where plums hung heavy on the trees. A breeze blew out of the mountain as sweet and warm as fresh milk.

This was the Spirit World. No question about it. Not a little glimpse like in a fever dream, but the broad land itself opening up before me. The bards' undiscovered country that we are all headed for.

Sitting there on my big American horse, I stared about in stupid amazement as the Southern Herd thundered into the gap in the mountain's flanks. I moved my mouth to speak, wanting to say something to Yellow Legs, to get human confirmation. But he and Raven were already headed into the gap, not questioning what they saw any more than the buffalo did.

Nothing had prepared me for this. Not my dreams and Medicine visions, nor my conversations with Coyote. Turning in the saddle, I looked back at the real world behind me. It was bleak and stark, locked in winter. Nearby was the morning smoke of a camp that might or might not be friendly. I could go back, alone, into a hungry world torn by war and hatred. Or I could go on into a world that vibrated with towering clouds, green leaves, and ripe plums.

The plums decided it. My mouth ached to taste fresh fruit, to ease the bleeding sores beneath my tongue. Kicking my big American horse, I followed the Southern Herd out of the cold gray morning, into a world where the summer sun stood directly overhead.

THE WINTER IN THE SPIRIT WORLD

1875

HAPPY HUNTING-GROUND—No general sign, except to denote a country beyond death and living; i.e., DIE, point to ground BEYOND, and INHABIT . . .

It is impossible to learn at this late day what the Indians believed prior to our advent, but I think they have always pictured a hereafter of clear waters, white tipis, and good hunting. Our missionaries have earnestly sought to convince them that there is a hell of eternal torture as surely as there is a heaven of endless bliss. Though Indians freely admit that whites can and probably will go to hell, I have yet to see an Indian who in his heart of hearts believes any Indians will go there.

—Captain W. P. Clark, *Indian Sign Language*

Light-Haired Woman

When the yellow-haired woman came to camp, people spread a
buffalo robe and sat her on it, carrying her into the lodge circle. That
night there were animal noises. Next morning the Caller cried,
"Buffalo are here." The herd came right into the camp circle.
Buffalo rubbed against the tipi where the yellow-haired woman slept.
She sat up and laughed.

—Cheyenne Lodge Tale

IT IS ALWAYS SUMMER IN THE SPIRIT WORLD. AT LEAST IT WAS
summer in those parts that I saw; when I saw snow and ice it was not the sort
that comes with long winter nights. The world within the mountain was a
bright mirror image of the earth we left behind. We had entered headed
south; and we emerged from the cleft riding north with the Wichitas behind
us. Only these Spirit World Wichitas had no sprinkling of snow on the
foothills, no camp smoke coming from Medicine Creek.

The mist that entered with me shredded and vanished as the mountain
closed. Snowflakes melted on the grass tops. This was no fever dream or
nightmare, no vision on a stormy peak. In cold bright morning I had ridden
through a crack in a mountain, right into summer. The most charitable explanation was that I had gone stark mad.

Ahead of me, the Southern Herd spilled onto lush green prairie, breaking into groups to graze, stopping their long flight. Here was the world they
were headed for—no wonder the herd had moved with such solid purpose,
quickening their pace at the end. I swung off my horse and sat down in the
grass, spreading my hands out to touch the earth. Was I dead? Could my
frozen body be lying in a cold gully beside the "real" Wichitas? Probably. But
my flesh felt as solid as the ground beneath me. I was hungry, thirsty, tired,

and a night of riding had given me a very mortal pain in the rear—clearly I had not left the cares of the body behind.

Getting back onto my wobbly legs, I led my horse down the slope to where Yellow Legs and Raven were sitting on their ponies. "Where are we?"

They looked down and laughed, like I was a bumpkin fresh off the turnip cart, gaping at the plains for the first time. Nothing hit the deer hooves hanging from her cradle bow, happily making them rattle. Yellow Legs nodded at the golden-green prairie, dotted with brown buffalo. "This is the Spirit World."

"Where is the world we left?"

"Behind us." He cocked his chin toward the Wichitas. "You were there only moments ago."

"How is that possible?"

He gave me his sweetest Medicine man smile. Explaining the Spirit World to a Wasichu was as hopeless as me trying to teach a Snake trigonometry, or explaining to the Burnt Thighs how stewed tomatoes got in the cans.

"Are we the only ones here?" The place looked godawful empty, horribly cut off from everyone and everything I knew.

"Look, American Woman, see the buffalo." Raven sounded as if she were talking to an impossible greenhorn. "The whole Southern Herd is with us."

"Right, the buffalo." What if this was some buffalo heaven, picked by the Southern Herd because there were no humans to hunt them? "I mean, are we dead? May we go back?"

"Do you feel dead?" Yellow Legs looked solicitous.

"No, but I feel very cut off."

Raven laughed. "We have been cut-offs ever since we left the Lakota Eaters. If we must live outside the camp circle, would you rather be on the Staked Plains, or at some starving agency?" Winter in Indian Territory held no attraction for my sister-wife.

I tired of asking questions with no reasonable answers. We were in the Spirit World. Somehow the buffalo had brought us across the great gap that separates day-to-day life from the land of ancestors. Healer, Ice, and Coyote Dung insisted they could step easily from this world to the next—even Yellow Legs talked like he had done it all before—though for the rest of us the gulf is pretty damned awesome. But I was learning to live in the "here and now." Our place in the living world had been tenuous at best, freezing in a pathetic camp on the cap rock; I could not complain if we had missed the messy complication of dying.

The Southern Herd drifted north and west. We had nothing to do but follow, letting the Wichitas slip under the southern horizon. It was eerie to see no people, no dwellings, not so much as a wagon track. No sign of the Indian agencies or the Western Cattle Trail. We kept heading north, fording the Lodgepole near Antelope Hills, and Yellow Legs pointed out the big horseshoe bend where Long Hair had attacked his village and killed his old man chief, a spot burned into his mental map of the universe. Here he had counted coup and taken scalps, while Spring Grass was "marrying" Custer. I saw no sign that a huge camp had been there. No circle of fire pits. No tipi rings. No spent cartridges or iron arrowheads. Only a coldness, as if the endless summer of the Spirit World were chilled by the shades of so many who had died in the same place far away.

Beyond the Lodgepole the wind at our back was scorching hot. It was nearing midsummer. At night Raven's big tipi felt like a sweat lodge. I would lie amid buzzing mosquitoes, wondering if Yellow Legs was feeling amorous. Some time back I had given up being Miss Granite Drawers, no longer holding Nothing against him. By silent agreement the next baby would be mine. But my sole enjoyment of Yellow Legs was tempered by living in the same tipi, and knowing that Raven was nursing—not all that interested. I was Yellow Leg's second helping.

Day brought black clouds of buffalo flies, driving the herd northward like tiny wolves. I rode with my mouth shut tight, to keep from swallowing them. Only starlings kept the hungry insects in check, descending in flocks onto the buffalo's backs, pecking up the miserable bugs. When violent fly attacks threatened to stampede the horses, we took to riding at night, staying ahead of the herd and away from water holes. Yellow Legs would lead, singing to the summer night, ending each serenade with a quavering howl. Old Man Coyote would answer with his fast-yipping falsetto that sounds so much like laughing.

The herd followed Wolf Creek to the North Fork of the Canadian. There we saw no Camp Supply. No Long Knife tracks. No Adobe Walls. At the Flint there was no railroad north of the river. No buffalo bones littering the banks. Farther north, the Kansas Pacific had likewise vanished, leaving no trace of rails or roadbed. We reached the divide between the Pawnee and the Platte, with its steep-sided canyons and flat grassy floors—a favorite hunting ground of the Burnt Thighs. But there were no Burnt Thighs.

Animals were our sole companions. Past the Pawnee, we came upon antelope in incredible numbers, mixing with the buffalo, weaving tawny-white threads into the brown tapestry. Some of these Spirit World antelope were tiny, less than two feet high. I thought they were infants, until I saw a whole herd of midget pronghorn. Spirit World bison were a bigger surprise. Yellow Legs brought one down in a sheltered draw, a young bull, over seven feet tall at the shoulder with a mountainous hump, and splayed horns sticking straight out of a yard-wide skull. His insides were the same, only huge.

Coyotes loped over to investigate, gathering in a circle around the kill, sure there was a meal for them in this, if they could figure out how to get at it. Coyotes will dine on nearly anything: old harness leather, dirty moccasins, snails and scorpions, hot peppers and corncobs, as well as more normal fare like bullfrog and skunk. I never sank to eating skunk myself, but then I never had it served up when I was really famished.

Hearing four paws padding up behind me, I set down my skinning knife and reached for a rock. A big coyote parted the grass, looking old enough to know not to disturb a woman at work. Seeing me heft the rock, he sat back on his haunches and spoke. "*American Woman, you have much meat. Surely old friends can share.*"

This was more like what I had expected from the Spirit World. I kept hold of the rock, still angry at the way he had paid off his gambling debt. "What makes us friends?"

"*You wanted the Northern Pacific stopped, and I stopped it.*" The mangy beast carefully eyed the rock; if he read my mind, he knew how close I was to throwing.

Yellow Legs had been carving arrows, slim tapered shafts, measured against the distance from armpit to fingertip. He set them aside and strolled over to his pony, drawing the Medicine gun from its scabbard. He worked the lever and checked the action, chambering a rimfire cartridge. "I have wondered if this Medicine gun would work in the Spirit World. Naturally we will not find powder or lead to reload the shells, but I have promised myself I would test it if I found some suitable target."

Coyote sat with his head cocked, wearing the false grin all hungry dogs have. "*You need not be so rude.*"

Raven scooped up Nothing. "No, neither do we need to be polite."

Coyote scratched lazily. "*I had hoped you would be good for a chew and a smoke. Alone and so far from home, it would profit you to be generous. I know this place far better than you.*"

Yellow Legs looked over at me.

"Let him eat," I decided. The bull had way more meat than we needed. "But no more double-edged promises."

"*I make no promises, except to speak the truth.*" A formidable promise, most especially from this prairie wolf. I missed many people from the world we had left behind. My older sisters. Spring Grass. Sitting Bull. Black Shawl and Crazy Horse. Mitch and Magpie Outside. Coyote was not my first choice as a visitor. Nor even my fiftieth. Still, he was someone.

Yellow Legs set down his rifle and unwrapped his Medicine bundle.

Raven went back to butchering. Nothing began to crawl over toward the big dog's tail—our baby being both brave and curious.

Lighting his pipe, Yellow Legs puffed smoke at our guest. Coyote basked in the smoke, smiling at Nothing, letting her tug at his tail, indulging his well-known fancy for young females. "*Last time we haggled I told you there was a wholeness to the world. You cannot push against the hoop without feeling it all around the circle. You wanted the Northern Pacific stopped, without asking what it would take.*"

Some Spirit World magic—a banking collapse.

"*It takes more than a red flag to stop a railroad.*" Coyote went right on reading my thoughts. "*You whites are like a flood, pouring over the plains, killing buffalo, digging for gold at the Center of the World. Dammed in one place, you overflow in another. I have learned to swim with the tide, not struggle against it.*"

He pointed his snout toward the buffalo grazing in the sun. "*Like the buffalo, I strive for balance. Whites drove the Southern Herd into the Spirit World, so they brought a white woman with them.*"

As if called down by Coyote, more buffalo spilled into the draw. Only a small overflow from the main herd, but I marveled at the slab-sided mountains of flesh and muscle. Why me? I wondered. By bringing me, the buffalo seemed only to have added to their enemies.

Coyote yawned. "*You are not a terrible choice. Headstrong and opinionated, to be sure—but what female is not? And you have sought balance, which pleases the buffalo. But I will warn you. Not everyone is as accepting as I am—or so easily swayed by a pretty pale face. Do not try to contaminate the Spirit World with silly Wasichu sentiment. If you ever say 'Oh, that poor beast,' neither I nor the buffalo can protect you.*"

"Protect me from what?" I always thought of Coyote as a nuisance—not a protector. And what could be wrong with feeling pity for animals?

"*Beware.*" Real anger shone in his yellow eyes. "*Such false sentiment drips contempt. Whites pretend to feel sorry for wild animals, while destroying our homes, killing us for sport, and locking the survivors in cages—so they can come and cry over the 'poor little animals' inside.*" I thought of the zoo being built in Philadelphia. I suppose when it was done it would hold buffalo—should any somehow survive.

"*The truth is your people cannot stand to see anything wild and free. You must tame the land, cut down the trees, and pave over the prairies. You care only for the pets you have enslaved.*" Prairie wolves have utter contempt for domestication, happily eating housecats and lapdogs whenever they have the chance. But I still could not see what I was doing for the buffalo.

"*Whites look at the wild and see only savagery. Buffalo know better. They would rather be free and hunted than caged and cried over. The hunted needs the hunter; otherwise the grass eaters would strip the prairie and starve. We coyotes gave the jackrabbits their strong legs, long ears, and timid cunning; without us they would be fat stupid breeders, like the rabbits farmers raise in cages—to coo over, then strangle and put in the stew."*

He gobbled the last bit of meat and got up to go. *"Respect us and you may stay. Dare to call us 'poor beasts,' and neither I nor the buffalo can save you."*

"Save me from what?"

Coyote loped off, clearly tired of wasting his wisdom on such an impossible greenhorn.

Four days after that Medicine visit we topped a rise and saw our first Spirit Worlders, an almost frightening shock. The landscape had been so empty, so long. We reined in, watching them approach. The men in the lead wore giant wolfskins, with the wolf's head forming a hood and the paws dangling, making them look like wolf-headed spiders. Behind these upright wolves walked a small band of people wearing unsewn hides—rectangular pieces tied at the shoulders and sides with leather thongs. Dresses, shirts, leggings were all knotted, without a stitch of sewing.

They had no horses. Dogs the size of timber wolves dragged their travois; each woman seemed to command a half dozen of them. Some wore dog-sized packsaddles and saddle pads. Those carrying meat were muzzled. One bitch, whose load was slipping, stopped and sat on her haunches, howling for her mistress to come and retie her saddle girth. Dogs can be as smart and cooperative as ponies, especially when the dumb and ornery end up in the stew.

Yellow Legs looked impressed. "These are very old-time people."

The men in wolfskins came forward. They spoke a few respectful words in what might as well have been Mongolian, then made the eating sign, using their fingers to shovel imaginary food into empty mouths—just as a Sheyenna might sign "Let us smoke" to a stranger.

We dismounted. That simple act caused some excitement, as though they had thought we might be centaurs. Instead of passing a pipe we passed a parfleche bag of buffalo jerky, as tasty and nourishing as old shoe leather, but much appreciated by our guests. In return they gave us parched corn. The women carried woven baskets, and children clutched corncob dolls; clearly they were Corn Indians on the march. They had put their seed in the ground somewhere, then set out onto the prairie, living off what they could find while the corn ripened. Some were as thin as Rees.

An awkward pause followed the meal. Women and wide-eyed children crowded closer. The meat had made us popular, so Yellow Legs held his hands up like horns on his head to indicate buffalo. He pointed to windward where the herd had spread out ahead of us, then made a drawing motion as if firing a bow. Did they want to see a hunt on horseback?

Grinning, they imitated his buffalo sign: "You betcha."

Seeing Yellow Legs remount sent another wave of excitement through the Spirit Worlders. I could not tell if they had seen horses before; certainly they had never seen a rider. Faced with such a receptive audience, Yellow Legs could not resist giving his own version of a Wild West Medicine Show, lashing his pony back and forth before the crowd. The man could positively strut on horseback. He fired arrows straight up from the saddle, riding out from under them, letting them fall point first into the earth. Then he turned and galloped back, hanging by his legs, plucking the shafts out of the ground. Spirit Worlders cheered and hooted, impressed by tricks from the land of the living.

When we caught up with the buffalo he gave the full-dress performance, painting his face and donning his eagle-feather bonnet. The Spirit Worlders had been prepared to hunt in the old style, dropping down in their wolfskins and crawling upwind toward the herd—or by using calfskin decoys, imitating the cry of a lost calf to call the cows. Stalking buffalo on all fours is as difficult and dangerous as you might imagine. A disguise that works at a distance may not stand close inspection. Buffalo have undependable eyesight—if you look like a wolf but smell like a person, a buffalo will go with its nose. And scared or wounded animals can gore or trample a hunter on foot—just ask the Lakota Eater they call Buffalo-Did-Not-Kill-Him.

Well mounted and supremely confident, Yellow Legs still planned his approach methodically, riding forward on his warhorse, keeping his best buffalo pony fresh. We all crowded after him to get view of the chase. Using one of the smaller draws, he got within a hundred yards of the herd, then he burst from cover, whipping his pony with his bow. The buffalo nearest to him broke and ran. The commotion spread, becoming a stampede. These same buffalo had paraded past us on the Staked Plains without so much as a nod, but they were smart enough to know when a man and horse turned dangerous.

Spirit Worlders were awestruck by the spectacle. A good hunter and a trained buffalo pony are a wonder to watch, and my husband was a gifted hunter, almost as good at running buffalo as he was at stealing horses or spinning stories. He would pick his victim, then drop the reins and raise his bow. Without any other signal his pony would position him just behind the right shoulder, following the chosen buffalo through twists and turns over broken ground, despite billowing dust and flying clods—letting Yellow Legs place an arrow as exactly as Raven might place a stitch.

The herd, our husband, and his pony were soon far from sight, leaving only settling dust and dying buffalo. Hungry Spirit Worlders swarmed forward to finish the work. Watching them butcher, I wondered where the souls of these dead buffalo went, since we were already in the Spirit World. After dropping a dozen victims, Yellow Legs came trotting back to receive hoots and applause. His Medicine shoot and pony show had brought down the house.

I won't say the Spirit Worlders worshiped our moccasin prints, but from then on they stuck to us like ticks. They were there when we awoke in the morning, and when we went to bed at night. In between they cheerfully attempted to anticipate our every need. Two young women immediately attached themselves to me—signing that they were chiefs' daughters—ready to take up any task: skinning, cooking, tanning, and even bedding Yellow Legs, should that become a burden.

As long as Yellow Legs hunted, there was always fresh meat on the fire. Nor was there any need to put aside pounded meat for winter, since it was always summer. The Spirit Worlders hunted some, to keep their pride, but the whole band hunting together could not bring down as much meat as my man and his pony.

Women were ecstatic with so many skins to work, happy to have their husbands at home, helping with the chores, instead of out crawling after game with wolfskins over their heads. They found countless ways to pay us back, cutting wood, drawing water, doing our fleshing, supplying rabbit-fur gowns for Nothing. In turn we taught them the many uses of the buffalo: making awls and scrapers from the bones; bags from the guts; glue from the hoofs; ladles, spoons, and cups from the horns; and fly swatters from the tails—all those little handy items that make a buffalo herd into a moving meat locker and general store. Men spent their newfound free time smoking with Yellow Legs, learning the basics of his buffalo religion. Our kill sites were all marked by lines and circles of painted skulls, their hollow sockets staring toward the dawn and rebirth.

Without intending it, I came to symbolize the newness of it all. I looked and dressed most different—the golden-haired horse goddess. And I was the one making a new tipi, something Spirit Worlders had never seen done. I had the pick of the hides, laying them out and lining them up in the rough shape of a lodge cover. Then I started at the top, with the smoke flaps, cutting each piece to fit. Raven watched and advised, but I wanted this to be my work, my tipi.

Staking out personal property proved impossible. Spirit Worlder women were too eager to help. They had only simple skin tents like the Bad Lodges make; real tipi making was incredibly new and exciting. Soon they were sewing along behind me, learning to make tight waterproof Sheyenna stitches. I found myself again teaching Indians, but instead of simple mathematics and Christian Gospel, I gave lessons in tipi making and the uses of the buffalo.

When we reached the green curving line of the Platte, where the Union Pacific used to run, we cut lodgepoles and set up my new tipi, with all the usual feasting and celebration. The Spirit Worlders signed that this was as far north as they dared venture. None of them had ever crossed that great swath of prairie between the Platte and the Center of the World. And back on the Pawnee the corn would be ripe.

But the buffalo had other notions, fording the Platte in a huge brown wave that completely engulfed the river. With the right kind of Medicine you could have crossed dry-shod on their backs. As long as it was summer they would keep going north; nothing seemed likely to stop them short of Canada.

Here the Spirit Worlders split, the young and adventurous wanting to go on with us. Families divided. Grown children left their parents. Sweethearts took this moment to marry. You could tell by smiles and frowns which matches had been looked forward to and which came as unsettling surprises. Several couples eloped, slipping over the Platte to wait for us out on the prairie.

On the far shore we made a rough thirty-skin lodge for the Spirit Worlders to live in. This communal tipi was crude and overcrowded, but the Spirit Worlders were used to sharing a dirt roundhouse. Their only privacy was out on the prairie. They had always looked to the rolling sea of grass for lovemaking and adventure, or just the uneasy thrill of being alone under the sky.

We crossed the headwaters of the Niobrara, skirting the southern edge of the badlands. The buffalo swung around the Center of the World, headed for the Belle Fourche and the Powder River country—being plains animals, they never went that deep into *Paha Sapa*.

Here for the first time we saw wild horses, big as Arabians, but stockier, with slender dainty hooves. Our new band of Buffalo Indians was terribly horse poor, so Yellow Legs set about lassoing mares who had colts or foals, bent on showing the Spirit Worlders how a horse could be more than a meal on the hoof. We camped in the foothills with our newly captured remuda, gathering berries and pounding acorns. Yellow Legs gave up hunting to train horses and teach Spirit Worlders to ride.

Sitting before my new tipi, shaded by pines, I could see slowly moving buffalo, filling the great grass basin west of the hills. Closer in grazed our growing horse herd. It seemed that no one could want for anything—but I did. I missed the outside world. Living in the Spirit World was uncomfortably like being dead. I would never know what was happening with my sisters and friends, never get a letter or see a newspaper. Never again have a civilized conversation, or hear a banjo playing.

I felt pulled to repeat my *inipi,* to go off alone into the hills, measuring what had happened since my last visit to the Center of the World.

Walking alone, I counted my disasters, disappointments, and triumphs. Yellow Legs was with me now, closer in some ways than ever before. I shared him with Raven and Nothing, but not with his war Medicine, and not with the whole Sheyenna nation. Living with the Spirit Worlders had put us all on the same plane. To them I was never an unwelcome intruder. I was Light-Haired Woman, who had come with the horse and the buffalo. I was still an oddity, but as an individual, not held responsible for everything from Medicine Water to the Iron Horse.

Sunlight streamed through the straight tall pines; birds called and bees hummed in the heat. *Paha Sapa* whispered to me, "Is this so bad? This is peace. This is life. Treasure it now, before it is no more."

Would I grow old and die here? Spirit Worlders did. When a woman was too old or lame to walk, they left her in a lean-to with corn and water and enough wood for a small fire. That was the last they saw of her. Spirit Worlders knew no more about the Great Mystery than we did—they had taken to Yellow Legs's buffalo religion like sinners to a tent revival.

Suddenly there was a doe next to me. I started. She froze for an instant, then bounded off. I cursed my carelessness. Instead of blending with the Center of the World, I was blundering through the woods, with my head full of worries. I sat down in a small meadow dotted with blue flax and a yellow wallflowers, letting the animals come to me.

By now I had seen the full cycle of summer in the Spirit World. Flowers marked the subtle shifts that took the place of seasons. Summer began wet and mild, with wild tulips, yellow bells, and prairie stars, followed by Indian blankets and primroses. In the full heat of summer we had goldenrod, zinnias, and sunflowers. As the weather edged toward autumn, cool rains came and the cycle began again. I was enough of a practical naturalist to know that this was wildly unnatural. Prairie and pine forests need winter; but I could no more explain why the Spirit World stayed the way it was than I could explain why a primrose blooms.

"*American Woman, why can't you just enjoy?*" I started again. Coyote squatted at the edge of the clearing.

I wrinkled my nose at him. "I was moderately happy, until just now."

He gave a little yip and chuckle. "*Nonsense. Wasichu are never happy with the world as it is. You must cut and clear, dam and scrape. Do you know what your people are doing to Paha Sapa?*"

Disliking his smug superiority, I said I did not care to know.

"Very wise." The prairie wolf laughed. *"Wasichu have come by the thousands. Cutting down trees. Killing off game. Digging up the land and burying the creeks."* I could picture the mining camps, crowded with tents, swamped in mud, swarming with men and mules. *"They are crazy for the yellow metal. Men shoot their best friends for it. Women spread their legs for it, letting disease into their wombs."*

I glared at him. "You cannot judge them. They need money to live. Coyotes eat rats for the same reason."

"What is wrong with a fat tasty rat?"

"Go off and find one." I wanted to peg a rock at him, but he was not worth breaking my *inipi.* "This is my world now."

"Is it really?" He gave me a sly sideways look.

"Yes." I felt conviction rising in me. "Here I am free. Here everyone but you treats me with respect."

Coyote sat there, wearing his most idiotic grin. *"Perhaps. But do not claim this land too soon. And do not say 'poor animal.' "* He threw back his head and howled.

I was about to add that I did not need advice from a dung-eating dog—but I stopped. A pony trotted into the clearing. Not a wild Spirit World horse, but a mare with crescent moons painted on her black-and-white flanks. It was Keeps-the-Fire, no longer dead and frozen. I leaped up, throwing my arms around her neck, not caring if Coyote saw me cry.

My pony nuzzled me back. She was real and solid, as full of life and power as the day she beat Calf Road's pinto. Seizing her mane, I swung onto her back, remembering the dream I had at Fort Lincoln—the one where I rode her at the Center of the World. Nightmares are not the only dreams that come true. I was so happy I actually turned and called to Coyote, truly meaning to thank him.

But he was gone, his yipping laughter fading in my head. There was no doubt where I wanted to be, and who I wanted to be. I was Light-Haired Woman, the Bringer of the Buffalo. There could be no trading summer for winter, plenty for want, or life for war.

Poor Beast

Coyote said to the yellow-haired wife, "I am sending you to these
people for a special purpose. These people have only fish and birds to
eat. As long as you are with them they will have plenty of game,
plenty of buffalo, but as long as you are with them, never pity any
suffering animal. Never say, 'My poor beast.' "

—Cheyenne Lodge Tale

THE BEST WAY TO MARK TIME IN THE SPIRIT WORLD WAS TO
watch our girl grow. Nothing shot up like a grass shoot in the warm sun,
lengthening out, no longer a baby, but a little woman. Now that we had
food, she ate furiously, smearing cornbread and berries all over her face,
holding rib bones in her little fists. Once I saw her sitting with a trio of Spirit
World children industriously eating ants off an anthill. She would lean forward looking serious, pinching at the tiny creatures with two fingers. Ten got
away for every two she ate.

She was talking now—not just babbling to the birds on her cradle
bow—mixing English, Sheyenna, and the language of the Spirit Worlders.
She still held extended conversations with ground squirrels and prairie dogs,
and Yellow Legs encouraged these fancies, afraid she would lose the ability
to talk to animals as she learned human tongues. She was walking as well,
and riding too. On lazy Spirit World afternoons, I sat her in front of me on
Keeps-the-Fire. My mare loved it. I loved it. And Nothing squealed with
pleasure. Yellow Legs and I were working hard on another baby—my
baby—but for right now Nothing was not a bad replacement.

Without winter to hold them back, the Southern Herd kept up its slow,
capricious drift northward. The great mass would fragment, then reform, like
a huge brown wave, breaking, gathering, then flowing on. This suited my

family just fine. Sheyenna find it easier to move than to stay in one place. Yellow Legs was always ready to see what lay over the next hill, and Raven never had to sweep out her lodge, as long as there were fresh places to pitch a tipi.

North of *Paha Sapa* the nights felt frosty, and the land got more arid. Bluestem and wheatgrass gave way to shortgrass prairie—mostly needle-and-thread and buffalo grass—worn thin in places by the constant cropping and trampling, like a ratty old robe left out in the sun. Bulls would wallow in the bald spots, while cows and calves kept pushing north into greener pasture.

North is called Where the Cold Wind Comes From. In the Spirit World this is literally true. As we neared the Yellowstone, a cool breeze blew out of the north, so constant you could use it as a compass. Sometimes the breeze was tiny and mischievous, rippling the grass tops; other times it blew strong and hard, bringing those strange sudden snowfalls that can blanket the plains in early summer, only to melt in the noontime sun.

When we reached the Yellowstone the land itself began changing. Northern feeder streams were bigger and more numerous than I remembered; the river was wider, swollen almost to flood stage. With no winter snowpack, I could hardly guess where all the water came from. The north wind was so dry it took my breath away, but signs of water were everywhere, in small meandering streams and innumerable boggy spots under the grass. I could feel a cloud forest beneath my feet. Even the soil seemed different, overlaid with a light yellow grit blown south by the constant wind. It was eerie enough to see all signs of civilization vanish, but having the landscape twist and alter filled me with a feeling of impending doom or discovery.

This weird new world had strange inhabitants. I saw humpless camels in among the horses, and giant ground-dwelling sloths, like the type Cuvier described. Reading Cuvier's description of their bones in no way prepared me for the beast itself, which was as tall as an elephant, with a massive chest and great crushing forelimbs. I thought nothing could top an animal like that—until I saw one of these huge sloths pulled down and eaten by a pack of bobtailed lions with terrible curving canines. They used their saberlike teeth to stab the giant sloth to death, then settled in to feed, tearing off reeking hunks of flesh and bolting them down. Life in the Spirit World was not for the squeamish.

One day a slim line of gray clouds appeared on the northern horizon, as if a real blue norther was brewing—but the clouds did not come closer. Next morning they were still sitting on the horizon, getting taller as we advanced, turning into a high thin mist stretched across our path. Sunset became a glowing spectacle, full of purples, greens, and yellows.

When the herd reached the line of mist the buffalo recoiled abruptly, abandoning their long northward march. Up until now nothing had stopped the herd—not swollen rivers, nor a twisted landscape, nor vicious packs of sabertoothed cats. It was an unsettling omen.

I could hear strange noises coming out of the mist, a distant popping and crashing. The buffalo saw no reason to investigate, but of course Yellow Legs had to see what lay ahead. Rather than letting him gallop off alone, I mounted up and rode with him. Buffalo parted to let us pass, but did not scatter or stampede; whatever had stopped them had not spooked them. As we picked our way through white cloud swirls, I saw the ground plowed as if by some drunk Paul Bunyan. Grooved and broken boulders lay where they had fallen. The tortured groans ahead grew louder.

A great shadowy mass emerged from the clammy fog, blocking our path, a mountain of dirty crystal so high I could not see its top. Veins of blue-white ice showed between the layers of windblown grit. It was a grimy iceberg— sitting tall and proud on the summer prairie, half a continent from the nearest ocean. Yellow Legs had never seen the like, and I had to explain what an iceberg was.

Farther on we saw others, a frozen flotilla beached on the shortgrass. Beyond them the landscape bent upward. We came face-to-face with a steep-bouldered moraine, gouged out by the mother of all ice mountains. A sheer topless wall of white crystal rose up, and up, and up. There was no going around it—the ice stretched east and west, disappearing into misty distance, a groaning mass that must have been a mile high and a continent wide. Most of Montana and all of Canada had to be buried beneath the glacier. We had come to the world's end.

Yellow Legs and I rode along the glacier's murky edge. The cool north wind flowed directly off that ice, creating a permanent bank of fog. I saw nearly vertical canyons carved by melting streams, and dark caverns cut deep into the interior. Out of these cave mouths came the crash of icefalls and the rush of stream water. The glacier was a living, moving mass, melting along its edge as the weight of falling snow pushed it forward; advance and retreat had scoured the landscape, shoving boulders before it, strewing icebergs over the prairie. Gleaming shards lay all about, broken off the ice face.

The misty tumble of ice and stone held something even more amazing. We came on a frigid stream running the length of a small valley, its grassy banks grazed by giant humped beasts, huge slab-sided monsters larger than anything I had seen so far. Their bodies were covered with long, dense hair, and their heads were shaped like elephants' heads, only hairy. Great curving tusks grew out of their upper jaws on either side of a sinuous hairy trunk.

This northern end of the Spirit World seemed scaled to inhuman proportions. The giant long-haired elephants waded through the buffalo like shaggy mountains in a furry brown sea.

One look and we were headed for trouble. Yellow Legs was absolutely frantic to try his hand at bringing down the behemoths. Riding back to camp he would talk of nothing else. I kept silent. The man was a dedicated nimrod, but it disturbed me that he could not see a new and wondrous animal without wanting to kill it. I had no good argument against it—there was enough meat on one of these hairy elephants to feed camp for a week. Killing one of them was no worse than slaughtering its weight in buffalo. But still . . .

He told our story to the Spirit Worlders, with a lot of hand waving and expansive gestures. It was a big story, but everything about this part of the Spirit World was big. The Spirit Worlders swallowed it whole—one more wonder in the string that started with the horse, the gun, and the Southern Herd. If Yellow Legs told them we were going to hop to the moon, they would have tightened the laces on their moccasins and gotten ready to jump. Men sang their chants and splashed on their paint. There was no warpath in the Spirit World, so the hunt and the dance were the only things men got painted up for.

Yellow Legs headed the march, aboard his favorite buffalo pony, lance in one hand, reins and bow in the other. I went along with the throng, thinking, This is madness. The gray mist and heavy landscape gave off the same sinister warnings I sometimes got in my dreams. At the lip of the shallow valley Yellow Legs signaled for the Spirit Worlders to spread out behind the ridge crest, where they would not alarm the animals. Then he circled downwind to drive a tusker toward us.

I flattened out beside Raven and Nothing, my heart hammering so hard I could barely hold the binoculars steady. Yellow Legs came cantering up from the south, smoothly confident, his Medicine gun holstered behind him in its saddle scabbard. The constant north wind blew directly at him, and I doubt the big beasts knew he was coming.

At the edge of the herd he halted, his mount taking a step or two sideways; man and horse looked reflective. I thanked God, thinking he had seen reason. But Yellow Legs merely swung one leg up and slipped off his horse. He led the Appaloosa away from the herd and hobbled him. His horse had balked. The same breeze that blew their odor away from the herd had blown the elephant odor up the Appaloosa's nostrils. Showing more sense than his master, the buffalo pony was having nothing more to do with this unnatural hunt.

Setting aside his bow and puny-looking arrows, Yellow Legs walked toward the herd, lance in hand. I cursed him for leaving his Medicine gun, but I suppose he wanted to kill this beast with weapons he had made. The buffalo parted swiftly for him, sensing a madman on the loose. The Spirit World giants paid no attention, not having learned to fear the wolf that walks two-legged. Selecting a healthy-sized tusker pointed in the right direction, Yellow Legs edged up from behind, going the last few yards on all fours. Then he leaped up and thrust his lance into the tenderest part of the elephant's rump.

When a bull elephant is stuck up the rear with a ten-foot lance, I am here to say the squeal is deafening. The beast bounded straight for us, bawling like a herd of bull elk, trailing the lance from his rear. Animals went wild. Buffalo scattered. Elephants lifted their trunks and trumpeted, thundering off whatever way they happened to be facing.

These hairy elephants had probably never been hunted by humans and did not know what to make of the attack. The same cannot be said of our buffalo. A big mean-eyed bull spun about, instantly spotting Yellow Legs as the source of the trouble. Seeing his tormentor was afoot and helpless, he lowering his head and charged.

Yellow Legs had no lance, no bow, and no hope of outrunning an enraged buffalo. Nothing but first-rate Wasichu Medicine could save him from being knocked down and stomped to bloody bone meal. Dropping to one knee, he drew his pistol from his belt, aiming it with both hands. I said a prayer of thanks to the Colt Arms Company, and the Department of the Interior for giving him the gun.

Maybe the first shot went wide. It certainly had no effect. Nor did the second. The third was fired from too close to miss. Through the brings-'em-close-glasses I saw a half-inch pistol ball slap into the charging bull's face. The fourth shot must have scorched the beast's eyelashes.

Then the buffalo was on top of him, hooking its head to gore, half blinded by the last shot. Yellow Legs threw himself sideways, banged off the speeding beast's flank, and spun about. His revolver flew from his hand. The maddened bull ran straight forward for a score of yards, then began circling toward his blind side. My husband found his gun, picked it up, and fired another shot, hitting the beast in the neck. The buffalo flopped down dead.

We had no time to cheer. The wounded elephant was upon us, coming upslope like a runaway freight. A line of Spirit Worlders rose up out of the steppe grass, making wolf howls and flinging their spears. Against such a target who could miss? Flying shafts whacked into front and flank. The stricken beast reared up, lifted his trunk, and trumpeted at the sky, blood streaming down his face and flanks—a terrible, unforgettable sight. He came down, turned, and crashed off downslope toward Yellow Legs.

Seeing my husband unhorsed and in the path of the rampaging beast, I yelled for Keeps-the-Fire. She is a mare you do not have to hobble. As she galloped up I grabbed her drag rope and a handful of mane, pulling myself onto her back. Without breaking stride, she bore me right over the rise.

Ten tons of wounded tusker went bellowing straight at Yellow Legs. His pistol still had a shot in the cylinder, but he might as well make faces at the beast for all the damage the gun would do. Spirit Worlders were brandishing their spears, sprinting after the monster, but their lunatic yelling had the frantic animal running faster. Lamed by the buffalo, Yellow Legs limped for his horse, trying to get to the Medicine gun. The terrified Appaloosa hobbled away from him, starting an absurd race between a limping man and a hobbled horse. Neither had a snail's chance of outrunning the elephant.

Holding hard to Keeps-the-Fire's mane, I screamed for her to run. My pony stretched her neck and sprinted, her muscles extending beneath me, her hooves pounding downslope. In heartbeats we were neck and neck with the charging elephant, careening toward Yellow Legs like a pair of mismatched jockeys fighting for the inside pole. Smart money had to be on the elephant. I could smell the beast's bleeding flanks and steaming breath. An angry little eye glared wildly at me.

Bit by bit Keeps-the-Fire pulled ahead. The elephant slowed when we hit the flat valley bottom, drained by its wounds, no longer aided by the slope. Seeing us surge past, he hooked sideways with his massive tusks, trying to gore.

I squealed in fright. But Keeps-the-Fire kept her head, turning nimbly to avoid the tusks. The elephant turned too, swinging around to get us. Keeps-the-Fire flew over the turf, dodging boulders, with the elephant thundering behind us. Yellow Legs flashed past, forgotten in the scramble.

When I dared look back, the gap was widening. The elephant lagged, losing interest, no longer running after us, but just running, hurt and afraid. I turned my mare, circling around to where my husband waited. He had finally caught his hobbled pony. A huge bruised scrape ran down his right side, from hip to shoulder—the first time I had seen him hurt in war or hunt.

Leaping down, I threw my arms about him, saying, "God, you stupid savage. Don't ever again do anything this silly."

He brushed windblown hair out of my face, shaking his head. "This is what I get for marrying a woman who rides like a Snake and speaks like a Wasichu."

We had no trouble tracking the speared elephant. His wounds left great gouts of blood staining the grass, getting larger and closer together. I dreaded what would come next. The beast had been so magnificent, so strong and vital; but he was dying bit by bit. The whole hunt had been a dangerous and pointless attempt to show our superiority over any animal, no matter how majestic. Was hairy elephant even edible? I wanted to lash out at Yellow Legs, but I was too thankful he had not been pounded like a pine nut.

The dying giant lay on his side, half filling a small depression in the prairie. He had stumbled into the bog hollow and collapsed, too weak to climb out. Blood flowed from his mouth and rear, and from a dozen wounds in between. One eye stared wildly upward, its anger dulled by shock and suffering.

Spirit Worlders swarmed into the hollow to finish him. Trying heroically to fight back, he swung his tusks as painted hunters plunged spears into his hairy stomach. His trunk rose and swayed, its tip turned up, a fleshy little finger on the end waving at the sky, making the sign for "life."

I shook my dazed head. "You poor, poor beast."

My words hung in the icy air, raising hairs at the nape of my neck. Off over the tundra, coyotes howled. Yellow Legs turned in his saddle, facing the cold north wind, saying wolves must have gotten to the buffalo carcass.

Spirit Worlders set to work, stripping off the elephant's hairy hide, cutting great steaks out of the steaming flesh with flint knives and hand axes. By nightfall, enormous fatty back ribs sizzled on a bonfire. I insisted on feeling Yellow Legs's ribs one by one, to see none were broken. He complained, but I said he ought to hurt, to remind him not to be so stupid. There was no checking my tongue. Coyotes and wolves collected in a baying circle just beyond the firelight.

By morning a bear had joined the ring of scavengers—a cinnamon, as tall as a man but bulkier. For all its age and size, the bear behaved stupidly, shambling past the wolves, invading the campsite. Men seized their spears, meeting the bear at the edge of the hollow. A pair of thrown spears pierced his coat, but still he kept coming, acting determined, strangely energetic for a cinnamon, who are the laziest of the bear tribe. Despite a mob of men sticking at him and brandishing torches, the bear did not turn until it was bleeding from a dozen places.

By then it was too late. As the cinnamon staggered back, scavengers closed in. We were treated to a terrible snarling spectacle at the edge of the campsite, watching as Spirit World wolves tore the wounded bear apart. One wolf had its back broken, but the rest settled in to feed, fighting with coyotes for the scraps.

Yellow Legs sat smoking his pipe, staring purposefully away from the fight. I wondered why bears were so special to him. Many Indians think bears have human spirits, since they walk upright, enjoy music and games, and shed tears for their loved ones. This cinnamon was no genius, but grizzlies are smart and humanlike, more so than even dogs or horses. With a small measure of kindness cubs can be taught to answer to their names and eat at the table. I talked to a Two Kettle Lakota who raised a grizzly from a cub, nursing him at her own breast and teaching him to carry her packs. And I once saw a grizzly emerge from its winter den and sit entranced, watching the northern lights flicker overhead.

But I never asked Yellow Legs how he felt about "that animal." His Medicine kept him from even acknowledging the subject.

Next day we headed east and south, following a fresh buffalo trail. The herd seemed to be fanning out as it recoiled from the glacier. There was no hurry, and certainly no reason to hunt. I was glad just to put the kill site behind us, with its great bloody elephant bones and scattered remains of bear.

Early in the afternoon there was a commotion at the head of the march. People shouted. Dogs howled. I saw Yellow Legs go sauntering off, showing the uproar was no concern of his.

Behind him, Spirit Worlders were falling back, pressed by a massive male grizzly, half again as large as the cinnamon they had driven off the day before. Dogs were on him, some still dragging their travois poles. It was an incredible chaos of flying spears, snarling dogs, and frightened ponies, with the grizzly rearing upright in the midst of it all, coolly fending off both man and beast. The Spirit Worlders had no hope of bringing it down.

Since my husband could take no part, I ran to get the Medicine gun. Chambering a cartridge, I turned back toward the slaughter.

Seeing me coming, the grizzly surged forward, dragging dogs and scattering Spirit Worlders. He had several spears in him already, but kept coming on, growling like a wounded warrior does who wants to show he is still full of fight. Feeling like I should be bolting in terror, I raised the rifle, praying for a clear shot—it was only the second time I had taken aim at a large animal, and this was nothing like shooting that stolid old bull on the Yellowstone.

Bears can move blindingly fast—fast enough to bring down buffalo on the hoof—but this one lumbered deliberately, as though he had all the time in Creation to get at me.

Finally he shook free of the dogs. I breathed deep and pulled the trigger. The rifle roared and bucked every time I fired and levered in another round. I took time to think between each shot, the way Yellow Legs and Crazy Horse had taught me, aiming for the animal's huge chest, trying to find the heart. By now the bear was so close I could see my bullets slam into him, not well grouped, but every one a hit. He was a ghastly big target and I had a Medicine gun.

The grizzly slowed, staggered, lurched sideways, then came at me again. His eyes weren't angry, just puzzled, as though rifle slugs were something new. At the fourth shot he fell forward, spear shafts splintering under his weight. I stood shaking as Spirit Worlders stabbed and hacked at him, making sure he was dead.

That night we had fresh bear meat and a big party. The Spirit Worlders skinned the grizzly and danced with the head and pelt. Two of them played the bear, while the others reenacted the kill. Yellow Legs took no part in the feast—but I was the guest of honor. I was not particularly proud, but I did not want to disappoint the Spirit Worlders. There was fear in their dance, as well as bravado.

In the morning I found my husband's Medicine gun and scabbard tied to Keeps-the-Fire's drag rope. I could not tell if that was a tribute to me or a sign that he expected more bear trouble.

The next bear was even bigger. We were in open country, and I was riding a little to the right of the line of march, so I saw him coming a long way off. He begin as a black dot that might have been a lone buffalo. I rode slowly forward. Yesterday's bear had been a good-sized grizzly. This one was half again as large. You hear tales of Pacific Coast grizzlies that big, but you hope never to see one.

Some grizzlies will follow the buffalo herds, feeding on stragglers and carrion, but even the boldest steer clear of human hunters. I turned Keeps-the-Fire around and trotted away, fairly horrified by what was happening. The bear kept coming. Already I suspected it would do little good to shoot him. Circling wide, I watched the bear match my movements, hungry for more than elephant meat. Very bad Medicine lay behind this. I felt a chill go down my spine, freezing the soles of my moccasins.

By now I knew the bear was after me alone. And Yellow Legs could not help me. No one could. Feeling naked and vulnerable, I searched for a point of safety, a tree or rock pile, but there was none. The prairie here was vacant, buffalo grass bending and waving in the north wind.

Terror knotted in my gut. Kicking Keeps-the-Fire into motion, I made for a low ridge well south of our route. Every time I looked back, the bear kept getting closer. Reaching the ridge, I climbed a steep coulee on the northwest face, leading Keeps-the-Fire, hoping that the slope would slow the grizzly. At the crest I fumbled through my Medicine bag, finding I had three cactus buttons left. This was obviously some weird Medicine battle. I did not know what good the buttons would do, but they could hardly hurt. Mumbling a prayer, I scraped the skin off one and popped it in my mouth. The button tasted so dry and bitter I could barely get it down. Healer help me, I thought. Jesus help me. Coyote. Anyone. I did not much care.

Lying flat out, I rested the gun on a small hummock, trying to relax, readying myself for the kick of the rifle. My hands shook. Tears blurred the sights. I could not believe that a few days before I had been sobbing over a stupid elephant hunt. Now I truly had something to cry over. The bear hit the coulee bottom at a run, scrambling over the rocks, eager to chew me up.

Cheek against the stock, I struggled to steady the rifle. When I could see into his little black eyes, I fired. The first shots did not slow him. He just got bigger, galloping at me, growing in my sights. Muscles bulged beneath his fur. My third shot staggered him. He stumbled and started up again.

I put a fourth bullet into him and he collapsed at the lip of the coulee. For several heartbeats I lay staring at the body. Then I stood up, meaning to get my pony and go.

Never turn your back on bad Medicine. The moment I looked away, the bear burst into life and came roaring up at me. He took a swipe with his claws that would have disemboweled me if I had been a step closer. Then he lunged with jaws agape, trying to snap off my head. Levering the rifle, I banged off a shot, hitting him full in the face. His head snapped back. He staggered, slipped, then tumbled back into the coulee. I kept pumping the Henry, firing until I was sure he was dead.

Then I sat down at the head of the coulee, stunned and scared, knowing for sure there would be an even bigger bear tomorrow. The bright warm Spirit World had turned as murderously vicious as the Staked Plains.

Keeps-the-Fire came over and nuzzled me, like I was a lost foal. As I sat there sobbing, being comforted by my horse, the landscape began to glow with rainbow fire—I recognized the effect of Healer's cactus Medicine. The air rippled with a thousand shafts of colored light: radiant greens, reds, and purples, wavering like water. The shafts shot upward, filling the sky, calming me with dancing color. I still had power. I still had hope. Though I was fast running out of ammunition.

Bear Lodge

THERE WAS NO BEAR DANCE THAT NIGHT, NO VICTORY FEAST. We dined on cold elephant steaks, which were chewy and had lost considerable flavor in the last few days. The wind off the glacier howled like a hungry wolf. Yellow Legs looked totally done in, ashamed that he could not defend his wife. I was in no better shape. Another bear was bound to come tomorrow—unless it was always the same bear, growing bigger every time we killed it—and tomorrow was the fourth day, the Medicine day.

"What's happening?" I demanded. None of this was the least bit natural. Bears are touchy and sensitive, and prone to take offense, but they don't generally hunt down humans. It is about as normal for them to eat people as it is for people to eat people.

Raven said nothing. Yellow Legs gave me a weary look. "It is the curse."

"Which curse?" A logical-physical explanation had been too much to hope for. We were in the Spirit World, after all.

Raven piped up, "Medicine Bear's curse." Having no bear taboos, she felt free to be blunt. Here we were, back to General Custer, a long-dead brave, and that miserable day on the Yellowstone.

Once I would have scolded Raven, calling this superstitious slander. Now I merely asked our husband, "Do you believe this too?"

He looked at me. "Does Light-Haired Woman want to hear the truth, or only what will make her feel better?"

"The truth, damn you."

"Yes. This man means to drive us out of here. To see the circle completed."

My husband was being tactful; it was *me* that Medicine Bear was after. No matter how blameless I felt, Medicine Bear clearly considered me responsible for getting him gutshot—by allowing Custer and Bloody Knife to break his Medicine. And despite being stone dead, he held a monumental grudge. "What can I do?"

"We cannot outrun our Medicine," Raven declared cheerfully.

But could we outrun this bear? The morning would tell. That night in my tipi, Yellow Legs comforted me the only way he could. We made love, so passionately and violently that I seemed certain to conceive. I sat up afterward, wound too tight to sleep, waiting for dawn in a buffalo robe. My single interlude of peace and security since leaving Lakota Country was over, shattered by Medicine at a distance.

There was a scratching at my lodge entrance. I got up to see who it was, half terrified it would be the bear. Holding tight to the Medicine gun, I undid the laces. The flap fell back. Two wicked animal eyes gleamed in the darkness—I nearly jumped out the smoke hole.

"*You called for me?*" Coyote came padding in, sitting down beside the remains of my fire, looking sleek and happy. His coat was thick and silvery, and there was a glint of general satisfaction in his yellow eyes. Life in the Spirit World clearly agreed with him. I pulled the buffalo robe tight—my body still smelled of sex and sweat. You may not believe a coyote can leer, but this one's look made mating dogs seem decent.

Tongue hanging out, he grinned at the Medicine gun in my hand. "*Your husband is big and brave, so long as it is not a bear.*"

I said nothing, needing to hear what Coyote had to say.

"*I warned you not to say 'poor animal.'* " He cocked his head sideways, snout upward, tilting the black tear lines behind his eyes into an imitation of sorrow, without losing his openmouthed grin. "*I warned you against insulting us. But Wasichu will always do as they please. Luckily, I am here to save you from your folly.*"

I wondered aloud at his show of concern.

"*Coyote cares for all foolish young women with tender thighs.*" He licked his grin, making me feel like a meat entrée.

"How can you help me? What must I do?" By now I knew every word had to be scrutinized.

"*You might start by offering me some elephant. That would be decent.*" He looked wistfully up at my meat case hanging from a lodgepole. I got up, opened the parfleche, and tossed meat to him. He gnawed hungrily. "*I can take you to a place of safety.*"

"Where is that?"

"*The bear cannot get there. What more must you know?*"

"A lot more."

But the dirty dog read my bluff; dawn was coming, and I was terribly afraid of what the day would bring. It was go with him or face the bear alone. *"Bring your husband and family, if you must. Better yet, leave them for the bear. We could enjoy an evening together in some snug spot."*

Bestiality "dog-style" with Coyote held small attraction; I'd take my chances with a grizzly. I struggled to dress without dropping the buffalo robe, trying hard to maintain some dignity. It was scary to know Coyote held all the high cards this time. I did not for a moment imagine I could escape this bear on my own. Even normal grizzlies have supersensitive smell and hearing, and know all the tricks of hiding a trail. In the wilds they are as clever as humans, with keener senses and immense strength. Only guns and horses give us the edge.

At first light I woke Yellow Legs, who was not the least disconcerted to find Coyote breakfasting in my tipi. The Spirit Worlders were devastated by our leaving, hacking at their hair and dirtying their faces. To them this was a calamity of unimaginable proportions. But they had sewing, horses, and the Southern Herd to remember us by.

Dawn was a blood-red smear in the east when we set out, abandoning our travois and lodgepoles. Nothing sat on the front of Raven's saddle. Yellow Legs rode his best trail pony. Coyote led, padding along at an ambling trot, glancing back every so often. Unless Old Man Coyote is running for life or lunch, he never works up a sweat—but when he goes full out, most dogs would have a better chance of running down a bullet.

At first we had nothing but the cold, dry wind at our backs. It was well into the afternoon before we saw the bear. He was some distance off, but there was no mistaking him: bigger than a buffalo, bigger than any bear had a right to be. He reared onto his hind legs to fix us, then put his head down and charged. I cut loose my precious lodge cover—months of tanning and endless stitching, abandoned on the prairie. Raven did the same.

Whipping our horses, we found we could keep ahead of him by changing mounts every so often. By evening the bear had fallen back out of sight, but Coyote still set a brisk pace across the darkening landscape, leaving the north wind behind. For the first time in weeks I felt a warm southern breeze in my face. We were leaving the grip of the glacier; and I hoped to God that would weaken the evil Medicine from that elephant kill. Perhaps our luck would be better at the Center of the World.

When Coyote called a halt, I collapsed next to Yellow Legs, instantly asleep. But I could not escape the bear. I kept waking, thinking he was bursting out of the darkness, all jaws and claws, roaring to get at me. Each time I discovered it was only nightmare—not that my dreams could ever be safely ignored.

By noon the next day he reappeared. Even at a distance I could tell he had grown during the night, reaching monstrous proportions. I had hoped that by not shooting him, by not adding to his Medicine, he might at least not grow. But the bear grew on its own, becoming an ever bigger menace. Though we changed mounts continually, we could not shake him.

Days blended together. We were always either moving or sleeping. For sheer hopeless misery this march beat even the Staked Plains. The bear kept getting bigger. By the time we reached the Yellowstone he was big enough to ford the swollen stream standing up—no longer a flesh-and-blood bear, but a nightmare image, bigger than the hairy elephants, tall as a pine when he stood on his hind legs. When he lowered his head and lumbered after us, his broad back rose above the folds in the prairie.

We could not keep running forever. But Coyote would not tell us where we were going. The closer we got to the Center of the World, the less I expected to find safety there. Hope is easier to sustain at a distance. I was not feeling heroic, and it was hard to keep faith in Coyote, trotting happily along, laughing at our fate.

We entered the foothills of *Paha Sapa* at the headwaters of the Little Mississippi. Coyote led us around the worst of the hills, onto the rolling country along the banks of the Belle Fourche. Crossing Blacktail Creek, I began to entertain wild hopes that Coyote did know what he was doing. All day I had seen nothing worse than a bobcat. The sun dipped into the hills and a gold haze settled over the Spirit World. Coyote stopped, resting on his haunches. When we caught up, he pointed with his snout. *"There it is."*

South of the sunset glow a stubby mass rose above the folds of the Belle Fourche floodplain. I recognized the black outline of Bear Lodge backlit by summer twilight. "You are mad."

Coyote laughed over his shoulder. *"The Bear won't climb it."*

"Of course not. Neither can we." Bear Lodge is a great stump-shaped pillar of gray volcanic columns rising almost a quarter mile into the air. Tall pines cling like shrubs to its base. The first third of the rock is ringed with rubble, but the last two-thirds are nearly vertical, aimed straight at heaven. Wasichu call it Devil's Tower.

Coyote chuckled, pointing his snout down the valley. *"Wait if you want. I am going."* Behind us was the bear, striding up the valley, his feet straddling the Belle Fourche.

We raced after the prairie wolf, making for the darkening tower in a mad steeplechase, crossing a prairie dog town and dodging between the pines. A big sloping field of boulders appeared among the trees. Coyote bounded up them. At the base of the black tower, our horses could go no farther. There was nothing to do but dismount, tearing saddles, packs, and blankets off our horses, undoing their drag ropes.

I hugged Keeps-the-Fire's sweating neck, basking in her hot familiar breath. It was sickening to leave her, but if I kept running I would only ride her into the ground. I would not kill her a second time. Then I said a swift goodbye to Stolen Swan.

With the drag rope coiled around my arm and saddlebags slung over my shoulder, I climbed after Coyote. Raven was carrying Nothing on her back. My husband had his rifle, Medicine bundle, and buffalo robes. The rest of our possessions lay strewn where the rocks met the trees. Our horses stayed clumped together, looking up at us, nickering and whinnying. Stolen Swan's big pale form and the white patches on Keeps-the-Fire stood out against the darkening wood. Then there was a tremendous crash as the bear hit the timbers. I watched the horses bolt, streaming away into the trees.

Ahead of us, the vertical half of Bear Lodge reared dark and solid against the gloom. Boulders and loose scree ran flush into closely packed columns of volcanic stone. Behind us I could see pine tops swaying as the spirit bear barged through the timbers. Coyote scampered right up to the rock face, leaping at it with all fours. His paws struck the stone.

I expected to see him bounce and fall back. Instead Coyote clung there, defying gravity, as though his four paws were fixed in cement.

"*Come on.*" He grinned down at us from his impossible position, completely pleased with his inexplicable trick.

"How?" Yellow Legs looked as surprised as I was. Slinging rifle and buffalo robes onto his back, he clambered over to where Coyote stood four-legged on the cliff face. Raven and I followed.

Coyote took several steps up the cliff, then called out, "*Use the rope.*"

Scrambling closer, I could see a white rope, thick as a cable, adhering to the cliff face. This pale strand snaked upward, vanishing into the twilight. I could not imagine how Coyote was holding on, without fingers or toes.

Yellow Legs reached out and touched the rope. "It sticks."

I touched it too. The rope was milky white and sticky, like a stupendous spider's thread. Coyote was going up into the inky darkness, paw over paw. "*Wait there, if you want. The bear will be along soon.*"

The bear broke through the treeline. Rising onto his hind legs he towered over the pine tops, fixing us in his gaze. Then he bent down and galloped upward, leaping from boulder to boulder.

Raven went up first, propelled by a mother's urgency, with Nothing lashed to her back. Yellow Legs motioned for me to follow. I stepped smartly up, glad to have my husband between me and the bear, taking a warrior's place at the rear of a retreat. Now that there was no question of *fighting* the bear, he seemed much less afraid; turning and running was a time-honored Sheyenna tactic that he felt absolutely comfortable with.

I seized the rope with both hands, and they stuck. So did my moccasined feet. For a moment I hung there, suspended by four limbs, feeling scared and silly. The rocks in front of my face stank. Coyote had pissed right where my nose would be—just the type of vulgar trick he could never resist.

Yellow Legs gave my butt an insistent boost. I tried shifting my right hand higher. As soon as I pulled away, my hand broke contact, while my other limbs stayed firmly attached to the sticky white cord. It was impossible to fall without an act of will. I reached my bare hand overhead to pull myself up.

The bear roared. I scrambled hand over hand up the rope. Claws clattered on the boulders behind me. Looking back, I saw Yellow Legs's face flush with my rear. Behind him was the great bulk of the bear, hairs bristling, mouth agape, eyes glittering like black moons.

I redoubled my efforts. Rock fragments fell from farther up, striking me or the cliff face, bounding off into the night. I had to feel for the tacky rope with my moccasins. If I took an instant too long, Yellow Legs gave my foot a guiding shove. I could hear the bear's forepaws raking the rocks, furrowing the stone, the way a tall grizzly marks a tree.

Twice I thought I had reached the top. Each time it was a false summit where the rock columns tapered inward, only to turn vertical again.

Suddenly the stone face before me disappeared. I scampered across a wide flat area, flagged by the tops of columns. The rope crossed the bouldered tops, then rose at a gentler angle toward the center of the tower. I had pictured the top of Bear Lodge as naked rock, but the summit is a small hill covered with buffalo grass and sagebrush—birds must bring the seeds. I glanced back to see Yellow Legs scrambling over the lip of the cliff, his Medicine gun and buffalo-skin bedroll dangling at a crazy angle, banging at his legs.

Behind him the bear's huge claws sank into the cliff top, flexing with effort. He looked certain to heave himself up behind us, then the cliff face gave way. Boulders tumbled backward. I could hear the claws sliding down the cliff, digging trenches into the stone, sending shivers up my spine.

Yellow Legs appeared beside me, pushing me forward. I swarmed up the last part of the rope in a crouch, never completely letting go. When the ground beneath me was flat I turned again. The bear was not following. His huge size defeated him. The white rope was too thin for him to grasp.

I lay down in the buffalo grass, laughing, shaking, staring up at the starry heavens turning about us, dizzy from the frantic climb, but delighted to be at a spot the bear could not get to—not caring that it was a vacant peak, thrust into the sky, without food, water or shelter.

Voices brought me back to the Spirit World. Raven was sitting a few paces from me, whispering to Nothing, getting her to nurse. Yellow Legs had unrolled the buffalo robes and gotten out his Medicine bag, figuring it was a fine time for a smoke. Upwind I could smell Coyote.

I sat up, seeing someone who had not come with us. At the end of the spider rope was a strange gaunt man dressed in black, sitting on a white buffalo skull. His tall torso was a single diameter from his hips to his shoulders, and his limbs were long and sticklike, folded at awkward angles. He had a craggy ageless face, topped by a wild mop of white hair tied with a black headband. His shirt and leggings were so dark that it was hard to tell if he had a waist. Coyote sat beside him, scratching.

"Welcome to Bear Lodge." The strange man spoke flawless Sheyenna. "I am Wihio, the Spider, Daddy Long Legs on the Mountain Top, the one the Lakota call Iktome. You have been climbing my web." He reached down between his legs and plucked the thick white rope, making it sing like a taut bowstring.

"We are all grateful for your web." Absurd as the situation was, I struggled to be polite. Quakers aim to be friends.

"I know you, Light-Haired One, Sarah Kilory, the American Woman that Talks-to-Children." He said Sarah in perfect English, and added a touch of brogue to Kilory. It was nice that he left off my more vulgar names.

Coyote yawned. *"Wihio knows too much. Which makes talking to him so boring."*

Laughing, the Spider Man cuffed Coyote behind the ears, knocking him off his haunches. "Howl at the Moon, dog, if you want empty talk."

Yellow Legs struck a match and lit his pipe. Without rising he offered the stubby pipe to the heavens, four directions, and the rock beneath us. Then he puffed and passed the pipe to Wihio. As the pipe moved I could hear the bear brushing against the cliffs. I doubted he would just go away.

"It is you who must go away." Coyote chuckled as Wihio blew smoke for him.

The Spider Man nodded toward the bear below. "The spirit of Medicine Bear is stubborn and one-sided, wanting nothing but revenge." He returned the pipe to Yellow Legs, who handed it to me.

"Must we smoke with a woman?" Coyote cocked his head and lolled his tongue at me.

"You need not smoke with anyone," Yellow Legs replied.

I touched the pipe to my lips, to be included in the Medicine. "Revenge for what?" All I had done was cart the burdensome brave back to camp.

"Oh, no." Wihio laughed. "He does not want revenge on you. He wants revenge on the men who killed him—Bloody Knife the Ree, and the Wasichu called Long Hair. You thwarted this revenge by coming here, breaking his curse just like you broke his bullet Medicine." By now I half believed it; none of this was fair or reasonable, but evading and denying had done me no good.

Coyote let loose a high yip. *"We would have protected you. You were welcome among us as long as you did not insult us."*

"I did not insult anyone. I merely spoke my mind." The unfairness of it still irked me.

"Speak your mind," Coyote replied. *"Shout anything you want from this mountaintop. Enjoy your free speech."*

"Don't let the unfairness worry you," Wihio advised. "Winters ago I came to the Sheyenna. I told them there is a new man coming who would scare off all the game and pen the Sheyenna up on little plots with dust to eat. What do think the Sheyenna said?"

Yellow Legs answered for the People. "We said we did not want that."

The Spider Man smiled. "See, they too thought it was unfair." I could see Wihio was enjoying this, telling a Wasichu how things must be. "They did not want a neighbor who would dig up the earth, cut down the trees, steal the hides from the buffalo, muddy the streams, and starve out creatures great and small. But that is the way it must be."

"What if I refuse?" There was no sense groveling, so I might as well be obstinate.

"We will do nothing." Wihio grinned. "I will roll up my web and go. You may have this whole big bluff top to be your reservation, as long as the rivers flow and the grass grows.

"And up here you will not be tempted to eat some 'poor animal,' " Coyote added. They had me, of course. Through no fault of my own I had made a perfectly outstanding enemy in Medicine Bear, who was determined to drive me out of the Spirit World.

Yellow Legs got up and walked over to sit beside me. "I have been happy here in the Spirit World, as happy as a man may be, but I will go where my wife goes."

Raven had nursed Nothing to sleep. She came over and sat on the other side of Yellow Legs. "I will be with them, with my family." Very stoic, very Sheyenna. Raven never said she wanted me around, but I was the price for being with Yellow Legs. She had no curse on her, except to be saddled with me.

I studied Wihio and Coyote, wondering at their motives. This improbable pair had not brought the bear into being—that was Medicine Bear's doing. Yet they were pushing events toward a climax, acting as if it were all a grand joke. Whatever their reasons were, I told them I accepted. I would leave the Spirit World and face my fate.

Wihio stood up and clapped his hands. The clap reverberated like thunder, rolling outward from the Bear Lodge over the valley of the Belle Fourche. The spreading shock wave brought winter with it, radiating out from the tower, turning the landscape white. The ground froze beneath our moccasins. The wind turned bitter. The sun dimmed, becoming a dull coin far away in the winter sky. The Spirit World was gone. We were on the other Bear Lodge, the lonely tower in Lakota Country.

Wihio clapped again. There was another peal of thunder. A long strand of thick spider silk dropped down from the gray winter sky. Wihio rolled up into a ball, becoming a real spider, losing his human face, standing on eight legs. Without a word the spider swarmed up the white rope. Nothing was left but his silk line dangling above the buffalo skull. Then that too disappeared.

I walked over to the brink of the cliff, bracing myself against the hard frigid wind. There was no giant bear down there, just bleak winter landscape. I saw the Belle Fourche slick with ice, twisting between gray and leafless cottonwoods. We could only go back the way we had come, a long, cold descent. When we reached the bottom the spider rope retreated up the cliff. Our last tangible link with the Spirit World vanished. All we had to show for our year-long stay was the scruffy insolent Coyote who had come down from Bear Lodge with us.

THE WINTER THEY KILLED LONG HAIR

1876

As I was out ridin' one morning in May
As I was out ridin' one mornin' 'fore day.
Spied General Custer and Buffalo Bill,
And they claimed they found gold in them dreary Black Hills.

Oh, don't go away, stay at home if you can.
Stay away from that city, they call it Cheyenne.
I'd rather be home layin' sick in my bed,
Then a target for some of ol' Sitting' Bull's lead.

—Dick Brown

Snowblind Moon

BEAR LODGE TOWERED BEHIND US, FROSTED WITH SNOW. WE
returned from the Spirit World the same way we had entered it, stepping
straight between high summer and the Snowblind Moon. But this time we
went from summer to winter, with no horses, no tipis, and only the food in
our bellies. For our first "real world" breakfast, Yellow Legs brought down a
porcupine trying to hide in a bare tree. The poor beast screamed like a small
child and lay whimpering in the snow until Yellow Legs finished him off—
I could now say "poor beast" as much as I pleased. Our homecoming feast of
partly cooked porcupine tasted every bit as noxious as it sounds.

Coyote's nose for garbage led us to an abandoned campsite. Amid rings
of tipi stones and blackened fire pits we found some tattered beadwork,
worn winter moccasins, and dented cooking tins. While Coyote licked the
tins and gnawed on the moccasins, Yellow Legs and Raven studied the beadwork. Their verdict was that the band had been Northern Oglalas, probably Crazy Horse's people, who camped here before heading off toward the
Little Powder.

We set out, freezing and afoot, following the pony trail west, crossing
Prairie Creek and the big grass basin separating the Little Missouri from
the Little Powder. My sister-wife was her usual mountain of energy, taking
trash from the campsite and fixing up a small sled with buffalo-rib runners,
so we could drag Nothing along. Given time Raven would have had us riding in an open sleigh drawn by snowshoe rabbits, and dining on badger pie.

She even tried making a travois for Coyote, who absolutely refused to
drag it, indignant at being treated like a dog. He preferred to lope ahead,
coming back at night to our makeshift wickiup and smoky fire, boasting
about a delightful day spent chasing prairie mice and grass voles. Twice he

brought white-tailed jacks for the pot, so it was not all talk—but sharing a skinny rabbit with three Sheyenna and a coyote is a comedown when you are accustomed to dining on elephants.

Before we reached the Little Powder, snow came down in big flat flakes, blotting out the trail. We could do nothing but lie in our wickiup, waiting for the storm to pass. Coyote did not come back that night, and I actively missed him. Not that he cared one whit about me, except in a carnal way, but his blunt self-confidence and arrant cupidity were a tonic, a welcome change from formal Sheyenna courtesy.

When the storm lifted we had no trail to follow. But before noon a tall rider appeared, leading a knot of ponies. It was Touch-the-Clouds, the Minniconjou, son of Lone Horn. Yellow Legs told him to "get down," and they sat on the frigid prairie having a talk and a smoke.

Listening to Touch-the-Clouds I realized a whole year had passed while we were living in timeless summer—and much had happened, most of it bad. Armed bands of gold miners, gamblers, and gun hands had invaded *Paha Sapa*, setting up stockades and tent towns on Lakota land, using the "Thieves Road" Custer had blazed. A gold rush has its own laws and logic. Prospectors were laying down lot lines and staking claims—jostling, arguing, even shooting each other over land that none of them owned.

While we had been basking in the Spirit World, the Lakotas had been having hard winters. The Southern Herd had not come north—no news there—and with the valley of the Pawnee played out, the only buffalo left were in those smaller herds that wintered in the north. Many bands had gone begging to the agencies. Even the Lakota Eaters had gone south to camp with Red Cloud and eat Wasichu cattle. I thought of Calf Road living on cracked corn and army beans in a canvas tipi, hoping she remembered how free and easy things had been on Crazy Woman Creek when I was the only Wasichu she had to deal with.

Touch-the-Clouds himself had gone south to sample agency life; now he was back. His father, Old Lone Horn, had traveled east with Red Cloud, asking the Great Chiefs in Washington to enforce the treaties and drive the fortune hunters from the Center of the World. As usual the Washington Chiefs would not listen, and only wanted to know how much beef, how many blankets did Lone Horn want for the Center of the World—talking as if the land were already gone. When Old Lone Horn protested, they showed him a treaty paper that said even the Powder River country was only a "hunting ground," and Lakotas would no longer be allowed to live there.

Yellow Legs asked how the Lakota could hunt along the Powder without living there. To a Buffalo Indian hunting was living. Touch-the-Clouds merely said that he could not read, but that the writing on the treaty papers was always changing, like wind blowing over the buffalo grass.

When Touch-the-Clouds's father returned to the camp circle, the old man said he would eat no more Wasichu beef, and lay down on his blanket to die. His family pleaded with him to live, but the old peace chief said words were useless—what the band needed now was a fighting chief. He would seek the uncertainty of the Spirit World rather than wait to see what the Wasichu would do next. Now Touch-the-Clouds led his father's band, and was getting ready to fight when the grass was up.

What about Crazy Horse and Sitting Bull? Yellow Legs asked if they were camping at an agency.

Touch-the-Clouds laughed. No. It would take more than government beef and words on paper to bring them in. "Sitting Bull is camped on Beaver Creek in the Blue Mountains." He pointed his chin at the string of ponies he was leading. "I brought these horses to take you to him."

My husband said they were indeed a fine string of ponies, but how did he know we would be wandering the prairie, lost and horseless, happy to get to Sitting Bull's camp?

Touch-the-Clouds cracked a mysterious Minniconjou smile. "A coyote told me."

I rode a high-spirited sorrel to the Hunkpapa camp on Beaver Creek, where we got a Sitting Bull welcome. "Come, friends, feast with us. We have flatbread. We have meat." The Hunkpapas had found buffalo trapped in the snow, so there was plenty to eat. We drank coffee sweetened in the pot and told Spirit World tales.

The news from the here and now was not so good. Loafers had come up from Fort Robinson, promising Crazy Horse a big feast if he would trade away the Center of the World. Crazy Horse's people were so angry the Loafers were lucky to leave camp alive. So they scurried over to see Sitting Bull. The Hunkpapa told them he was not interested in trading away land, "not even this much"; Sitting Bull held up a pinch of dust to show the quantity indicated. He had not lost his sense of humor.

"They must not have heard my answer," Sitting Bull concluded. "They sent a second invitation, saying we must come in before the snow was off the ground or there would be trouble."

The Hunkpapas treated the second "invitation" as an absurdity—since there were buffalo on the Powder and everyone knew the agencies were starving. Why invite in more Indians when you could not feed the ones you had?

But to me it had the ring of an ultimatum. I told them a Wasichu winter tale—one my father never tired of telling—the story of the Glencoe Massacre. At King William's order the Earl of Stair demanded that the Scots highland tribes submit to royal authority by January 1. Delayed by wretched roads and a highland blizzard, the chief of the Glencoe MacDonalds could not make submission until six days into the new year. Seizing on the week's delay, London ordered the Glencoe men massacred, an order that Clan Campbell of Glenlyon happily carried out. Two companies of Campbells came as guests to Glencoe, then turned on their hosts, slaughtering the men and driving women and children into the snow. Winter war against recalcitrant tribesmen did not begin when the Wasichu reached the plains.

Sitting Bull promised to remember Glencoe and not turn his back on uninvited guests. We, of course, had a standing invitation.

But we could not live completely on Hunkpapa generosity. Sitting Bull's big lodge was full to bursting, with more on the way. Four Robes was hugely pregnant, and twins ran in the family. So Raven and I set to work, sewing a new tipi out of tanned hides and an old cut-down lodge cover.

Sitting Bull's women helped, as did Rattles Track and Holy Lodge, the wives of his nephew White Bull. White Bull collected women without paying much mind to keeping peace in the tipi, and his two wives detested each other. Whenever he showed attention to one wife the other would complain. When Holy Lodge had her first son, Rattles Track retaliated by throwing away White Bull's war Medicine. Being well beyond that sort of thing, Raven and I listened and smiled.

Yellow Legs set off almost at once on a borrowed horse, aiming to earn his keep, coming back half a moon later leading a string of big American horses laden with elk meat. His new mounts all had U.S. stamped on their hips, but we avoided our usual spat over whether horse stealing was making war. Hunkpapas were already admiring the meat and horses, and only a hopeless shrew would berate such a hardworking husband.

He claimed to have been a model of restraint, saying, "I took no scalps and counted no coups. I did not so much as shoot a Long Knife. If the Great Chiefs in Washington want everyone to live at their expense, then it is better to steal steal honestly than to go begging to the agencies."

Even I had to admire his stealth. He had snuck into an army bivouac on the Powder, cutting the hobbles on the best-looking horses. Feeding the bell mare some rock sugar, he slipped a Crow bridle around her jaw, leading her silently away from camp—and the unhobbled horses all followed the lead mare. He passed so close to the soldiers that he could hear them talking. One boasted they had burned Crazy Horse's camp.

Visiting Oglalas laughed, saying they had just come from Crazy Horse's camp, which was not far off, on a creek east of the Powder—very much intact. But Sitting Bull was quick to point out that if Crazy Horse's lodges had not been burned, someone's must have been. It was too much to hope that the Long Knives had raided Snakes or Bad Lodges by mistake.

Before Sitting Bull could send out runners to see who had been hit, Crazy Horse himself arrived. With him were some bedraggled but familiar faces—I recognized Two Moons, Old Bear, Ice, and Last Bull, coming in at the head of a band covered with snow, some without robes or blankets. The band the Long Knives attacked had been the Lakota Eaters.

It was strange to suddenly see them again. During more than two years of exile so much had happened that I could hardly hate them. At times I had imagined meeting them again, but never like this. The whole band looked more destitute than I had been that day at Crazy Woman Creek when they threw me away. Half naked, without lodges or winter meat, and having slept several nights in the snow, they were the sorriest-looking Indians I had seen since leaving the Staked Plains.

The-Bull-Seated-Among-Us met them at the edge of the camp circle, happy to show off the wealth and generosity of the Hunkpapas, making good on his promise to feed people as freely as the buffalo. This was Sitting Bull's winter for taking people in out of the cold. Two huge council lodges were set up to shelter the stricken Sheyenna. Women came two by two carrying kettles of boiled meat, offering whole tipis, or the hides to make lodge covers. Men brought tobacco and horses. Small girls brought buffalo robes. Medicine men gave up their pipes.

People called out, "Who needs a blanket?"

"Who needs a soup pot?"

"Here is pounded meat."

Crazy Horse dismounted, embracing Yellow Legs in a rare burst of public affection. As men, they had much in common. They had ridden together for half their adult lives: hunting, horse stealing, and on the warpath. They shared the bullet Medicine, and neither needed to boost his self-esteem with continual boasting. Each set his own standards and let the camp circle think what it liked.

Young Two Moons told his version of what had happened. The agent at Red Cloud had cut the Lakota Eaters' rations because they refused to leave for Indian Territory. Having *been* to Indian Territory, I could understand their stubbornness. Old Bear and a few lodges of Lakota Eaters had been camped in the hunting grounds all summer; others joined them, including He Dog and some Oglalas. It seemed safe enough. After all, they were there to hunt. What else were hunting grounds for? The Lakota Eaters were trying tolerably hard to obey a treaty whose changing terms might as well have been written in Hebrew. Last Bull thought the Long Knives would attack, but he brought his family anyway—either too hungry to care or looking forward to a fight.

As usual the Long Knives did not know how to fight, riding in on a snowy night, when the most bloodthirsty warrior was warming himself with a woman. Bullets sang through the snow, but the Sheyenna outran them, climbing the cut banks, firing down at the Long Knives, who found themselves trapped in the burning camp. They fled, leaving their dead to be stripped and cut up. A young Lakota Eater named Wooden Leg came in wearing a soldier's coat, happy to have something, since he lost his clothes, robes, rifle, pipe, and eagle-bone flute when the camp burned. Braves tracked the Long Knives through the storm, getting most of their ponies back. Loafers up from Fort Fetterman later told us that the cavalry came home frozen and demoralized, sick of horse meat and the Snowblind Moon.

The Hunkpapas approved, seeing it as a smart little affair: coups counted, scalps taken, Wasichu killed, and no Lakota dead to mourn. Only a single Sheyenna was killed, and some ponies were lost—along with all the Lakota Eaters' lodges and possessions.

Crazy Horse had little else to cheer about. His daughter, They-Fear-Her, had died of cholera—making me terribly sad. The little girl had been so lively and brave. Her mother's health was hardly better. Black Shawl had a coughing sickness that sounded horribly like TB.

Later that night Calf Road came to visit. She was married now and had a young daughter—which galled me. After making me suffer so much for marrying Yellow Legs, she was living happily with a brave named Black Coyote, thoroughly enjoying her husband and little girl. At least Madame Black Coyote and I did not have to exchange polite Wasichu greetings. She said nothing. I said nothing. Our eyes never met. I ached to ask Calf Road how she had enjoyed agency life, eating Wasichu beef while I had been in the Spirit World working up my Medicine. But that would not have been very Sheyenna.

My main disappointment was that Spring Grass had not come north with them; she had remained with relatives at the agency, waiting until the grass was up.

We camped on Beaver Creek, beneath Chalk Butte, for the better part of a week, and were joined by Lame Deer's Minniconjous. The combined camps then moved northward, from the headwaters of one creek to the next, looking for game and forage. Bands of No Bows and Blackfoot Lakotas joined us. By the time we left the Powder we had five full camp circles and hundreds of lodges, all headed west, crossing over to the Tongue, going deeper into Lakota Country—away from forts and soldiers, turning our backs on war. I could not have done better if I were walking with the chiefs—personally picking the campsites.

At that moment I figured I needed at least nine months of peace, because I left more than Keeps-the-Fire and Stolen Swan in the Spirit World—I left my menses as well. I had no monthly flow in the Snowblind Moon, which was not unusual. Under the the cold, starved Snowblind Moon my body seemed to hold in its energy. I looked forward to a few days apart during the Moon of Grass Coming up. But the Moon of Grass Coming Up became the Moon When Ponies Shed, and the only change in my body went through was to grow. Enormously, it seemed. My appetite turned ravenous. I ate anything within reach—spring greens, fat prairie dogs, roasted grasshoppers, sweet buffalo tripe. The next moon was the Moon of Making Fat, and if I did not bleed by Sundance time, then I was pregnant for sure.

Nothing was the only person I felt safe sharing my suspicions with, since she took in whatever I said with about equal wonder or indifference. Sitting before the lodge, cutting out leggings, I watched her playing with the Hunkpapa children, telling wide-eyed listeners her simple stories about the Spirit World. Playmates would try to top her with tales about trips to the agency—the ways of Wasichu being every bit as mysterious as the world of ghosts and ancestors. But Nothing would retort that she had a mother who was also a Wasichu. We both knew she had not come out of me, which made for an easy relationship. She called me Mother, without the complication of being half Wasichu herself. I called her daughter, without feeling ultimately responsible for her. A baby seemed bound to change that.

She came begging for cracked corn to feed to some hungry ground squirrels—there was a lot of shelled corn in camp, brought in by agency Lakotas who came to the Tongue looking for meat. I gave her some, casually asking, "Would you like a baby brother or sister?"

Nothing looked up, the corn cupped in her hand, dark eyes giving me the long-distance stare that small ones use on adults. I had always looked right at her, and she had always done the same with me. Her mouth began busily sucking on some sugar sap I had cut her from a box elder.

I hastened to add, "I might have a baby." I tapped my chest and made the sign for pregnant. I wanted her to know Raven was not expecting. And that I meant a human baby; Yellow Legs continued to give her fatherly talks about being sister to the prairie dog and antelope. This was not another ground squirrel on the way.

"You betcha, Ma." Nothing and Yellow Legs were the only people in camp who regularly spoke English with me.

"Really?" I handed her more cracked corn. "You would like a baby brother or sister?"

"Sister." She worked the word around the lump of sugar in her mouth. Turning to feed the squirrels, she reached up and back to pat my chest. First one breast, then the other. "Sister—me." Nothing felt fine about two nursing mothers, as long as I had milk for her too. "A sister," she repeated. "Like you. Blue eyes—yellow hair."

One tall thoughtful order, which I was not sure I could fill. Aside from my rapacious appetite, I felt none of the signs people talked about. I was not sick in the mornings. I craved foods, but not outlandish combinations—it does no good to pine for pickles and cream out on the prairie. Besides, the whole camp was getting fat. West of the Tongue the grass was thick, and the game plentiful, along with wild licorice, sweet fennel, and the first prairie tubers of the year.

The farther west we went, the safer I felt. Women were already saying we were too big to be attacked. It did seem true—*Hetchetu aloh*, as the Lakotas would say. Looking downriver, I saw camp circle after camp circle: brown, white, and yellow tipis filling the bottoms along the river. Next door to us were No Bows and Minniconjous. Beyond them were the Santees and Blackfoot Lakotas, then came the Oglalas and Sheyenna. There had to be better than a thousand warriors in the camp—as many as an honest person could count. And more kept coming from the agencies, many with guns. Not the best guns. But a secondhand Navy Colt or a sawed-off buffalo musket could blow a big hole in your day. You betcha.

I took heart in knowing that the cavalry had to come here looking for us. Sitting Bull would not go seeking out the Wasichu. The grass was long up. The-Bull-Seated-Among-Us could have marched his big encampment straight to the Center of the World and taken on the mining camps; but Lakotas did not make war that way. The biggest war party I saw go out had less than a hundred braves. Minniconjous, No Bows, and Hunkpapas went with White Bull to raid the Wasichu in the Center of the World, coming back with horses. I know, because I got a tough ugly-looking strawberry roan, a gift from Holy Lodge. A real outlaw that she called Rattles Track.

War was at best frivolous amusement. Summer camp was serious business; we had hides to cure and a Sundance coming. For Sitting Bull to go out of his way to fight the Wasichu would be as much giving in as selling *Paha Sapa* for crackers and molasses.

By the time we left the Tongue to cross over to the Rosebud, I was sure there was a baby on the way. At night I lay awake, holding my growing belly, hoping for a dream that would show the new life inside me. And dream I did.

Just before sunup I saw rolling mixed-grass prairie, rippling in the predawn wind. First light spreading over the bluffs turned the bowing leaves

dark green, lead gray, and dull bronze. Wallace stood hip deep in the
bluestem, holding his horse. Beside him was McIntosh, the Scots-Iroquois
who commanded G troop. I saw the Custers: Tom, Boston, James Calhoun,
the General, Libby, and Maggie, a flood of familiar faces. Many looking
worried, some weeped openly. The dream skipped from face to face, until I
realized the whole regiment was drawn up outside Fort Lincoln, saddling up,
parting from their women. Children of the garrison marched alongside the
troopers, waving flag handkerchiefs, beating on tin pans. The General had
a brace of staghounds beside him. At the edge of the prairie he wheeled his
horse about, giving Libby one last hug, kissing her, calling her Bess. His
words rang so clear, I remember them still. "Watch for our return."

Company after company formed into column. The regiment headed
west, with the sunrise at their backs. As they rode into the direction of
darkness and death, the band played a familiar tune, one I had heard roared
out by a full battalion at a dress ball, or sung sweet and soft by ardent young
officers, or slow and sad by trail hands going out on night herd. Calamity had
sung the obscene verses on that hungover morning in the Black Hills:

> If ever I should see the day,
> When Mars will have resigned me,
> Forever more I'll gladly stay,
> With the girl I left behind me.

But this time the regimental column was leaving the band behind, marching away from the Medicine song.

Sunlight burned through rising mist, spilling over the prairie, shining on
pistol butts and carbine barrels, and I saw one of those rare and sudden mi-
rages you see on high plains mornings. Light falling on the column of cavalry was reflected back into the clouds. A second column appeared in the
sky: a ghost column marching west with the real one. In my dream the mirage seemed almost perfect, orderly rows of men riding into the direction of
darkness. Only the column reflected in the clouds was hanging head down,
the way the Lakotas depict dead men drawn on white tanned buffalo hides.

Moon of Making Fat

Jerked awake by the dream, I tossed off my buffalo robes. For once I was alone in the tipi. First light was falling down the smoke hole, and I could smell breakfast smoke, pony droppings, and freshly cropped grass. Getting dressed, I poked my head out of the lodge, looking for Yellow Legs.

A gray sea of tipi ears disappeared into the haze from hundreds of cook fires. Young men were walking up from the wickiups along the river, hoping to breakfast with Hunkpapa relations. They wore loose cloth leggings, new mackinaw blankets and woolen shirts trimmed with whalebone buttons and brasswork. Some carried army carbines. Agency braves were flocking north like swallows, aiming to hunt and to see the Sundance, living in relatives' lodges or sleeping in the small brush wickiups.

Walking a decent distance behind the men was a familiar figure—not Long Hair, but his woman. I stepped out, saying, "I see you, Spring Grass."

"I see you, American Woman."

She looked exactly as I remembered, dark and proud, wearing a bright green dress decorated with big brass disks; silver slides on her leggings still sang as she walked. She too was fresh up from Red Cloud agency, tired of being told she should go south, down to Indian Territory. By now every Sheyenna up north knew the Southern Herd was gone and that only hunger and heartache waited in the home the Wasichu had made for them.

Life on the Rosebud was much more to Spring Grass's liking. She told me she had seen buffalo on the way up from the agency. "Small herds. Not more than a hundred at a time—but everywhere. Not just old bulls, but fat cows and young calves."

I told her about my winter at Fort Lincoln and what had happened on

280

the Staked Plains. Spring Grass was the only other woman I knew who had lived with both the Southern Sheyenna and the 7th cavalry. After listening intently, she asked, "Will Long Hair come here?" Here was the one woman in camp who looked forward to seeing Custer.

So I told her about my latest Medicine dream. Naturally she took it for gospel. Spring Grass was sure I had been an eyewitness to Custer's leave-taking; better than an eyewitness—the eye may lie, but visions do not. She made me go through it in great detail, telling exactly what Custer had done and how he looked, down to his haircut. I said it had been cut short, "Shorter than at his winter camp."

Spring Grass shivered. Cutting his hair was as bad as leaving his band behind. "He is foolishly shedding his Medicine." She was happy to have Libby left behind, but aghast at the tearful goodbye. "War parties leave at night to avoid such scenes. Long Hair has gone off, turning his back to the dawn, with his women wailing. Getting the worst possible omens." I did not need to tell her about the mirage—with the troopers hanging head down as they rode off. Any Sheyenna could already tell that no good would come of such a parting.

A trio of young Bad Faces swaggered past, figuring they cut smart figures with their annuity shirts and Sharps breechloaders. But their show was wasted. Spring Grass and I had our bonnets set on other men—it would take more than a blanket coat and a surplus army rifle to turn our heads.

"I must talk to him," she decided.

"We don't even know he is coming here," I reminded her. There were a dozen good reasons why Custer ought to be headed elsewhere. We were in the westernmost reaches of Lakota Country; coming here meant striking blindly into strange country against unknown numbers.

"He will come," Spring Grass assured me. "The unknown does not scare him."

She was right, of course. I remembered a Fort Lincoln tale about Mc-Clellan's march up the Virginia peninsula. The Yankee army came to a broad stream and none of their slapdash maps told how deep it was. Mc-Clellan was a commander who could easily sit down for a week stewing over a dilemma like this. Fortunately Custer was there. He spurred his horse into the water, stopped in midstream, turned around, and called out, "This is how deep it is, General."

But even if Custer got here, the camp was too big to be attacked. There was bound to be a standoff, maybe even a peace talk. Sitting Bull was ready to talk.

Spring Grass laughed at that notion. "No camp is too big for Long Hair. Not this camp. Not one ten times as big. He does not feel fear like other men." She took hold of my hands, Wasichu fashion. "There will only be a peace talk if we make one."

"We make one?"

"You are Wasichu. Wasichu women have a special Medicine. Long Hair will not fire on you. He has held back when he knew Wasichu women were in our camps." Her idea was for the two of us to ride out between the great war parties. Feathers and lances would face drawn long knives, but we would ride between them in our best buckskin and calico, heads high, the center of every man's attention—an astonishing image.

"We would stop them with our Medicine," she declared. Spring Grass was a chief's daughter, with ten times my self-assurance. "I have ridden ahead of Long Hair before, to speak for him to the Sheyenna. And you are a Jesus person—this is your chance to stop a fight."

Right. Standing up for peace and friendship was the Quaker way—but all I could feel was Medicine Bear's curse pulling tighter. All this talk of war was wildly unfair. The Moon of Making Fat was the best time of year on the high plains, with its long days, short nights, and the summer stretching on ahead. Sundance time was for getting fat and having babies. The grass was thickest, the game most abundant. Everything was extra alive.

Spring Grass dismissed my fears. "We are safest when we trust in ourselves." I never saw anyone as sure of their Medicine as Spring Grass—unless it was the man she loved.

Raven came up carrying the breakfast water and we started a fire. Spring Grass had coffee, making it almost like old times on the Yellowstone. As my sister-wife leaned forward to fan the fire with her Crow's wing, a man walked up—it was her brother, Comes-in-Sight. Without saying a word he placed a gambling stick in front of Raven. The stick was a couple of feet long, painted blue, with three crow feathers attached to it. Then he turned and headed back downriver toward the Sheyenna circle.

Raven admired the stick, placing it where we could see it better. "My brother is holding a feast and horse giveaway." A couple of weeks before, Comes-in-Sight and Young Two Moons had crossed the Yellowstone. Pretending to be Crows, they walked into a Long Knife camp and collected the mounts used by the scouts, stealing thirty ponies from under the sleepy noses of the soldiers. Now the army's Crow scouts were all afoot. The feathered gambling stick was a peace offering from Raven's family, a sign she should come to the feast and contribute food: meat, fry bread, sugar, or coffee. According to backward Sheyenna etiquette she was the one being honored; her importance was acknowledged. She was a useful woman.

Not being Sheyenna, I felt damned insulted. Raven was being invited to work her way back into the family, but no stick had come to me. I was free to sulk in our lodge or follow in Raven's big shadow, welcome—or at least tolerated—because of her.

I started to stake out a green hide, working hard to hide my annoyance. Spring robes are softest, the best for a baby.

"When Hunkpapas do the Sundance the women go out first," Raven observed, "to dance around the Sundance tree, before it is cut and trimmed."

"This is true," I replied. Her discourse on Lakota dance customs seemed really roundabout, even for Raven.

"You should go with them."

"Why so?" I was much too shy to intrude on Medicine rituals.

"Because the sun in summer loves all fruitfulness. And women with children inside them should dance for the living tree."

I stopped, flustered, putting down my awl to keep from tearing the hide. I suppose Raven could count moons as well as I could. Her times apart had come, mine had not.

"Nothing wants a sister." Raven kept working, as smoothly as if we were still discussing Hunkpapa dance etiquette. I felt a surge of affection. For once her patient effort was directed at me, pulling her family together. She went on about how being pregnant in summer meant having a baby in winter—we all knew what that could be like. Spring Grass had lost a baby born in winter, and we had nearly buried Nothing on the Staked Plains. "The Hunkpapas are gracious," Raven decided, "but we should winter with a band where we have sisters and brothers."

I stiffened. Here was the hook. I looked down at the blue-painted stick with its three crow feathers. Picking up the feathered stick, I placed it firmly next to her. "This was given to you, not to me." Too much bad feeling lay between me and the Lakota Eaters.

I got up, found my porcupine tail brush, and went looking for our husband. Breakfast was in full swing at Sitting Bull's big tipi. Mixed Day invited me in. Yellow Legs was sitting on the men's side along with Jack Red Cloud, the son of the Bad Face chief. The-Bull-Seated-Among-Us sat half dressed in the back of his lodge, letting the world come to him.

Jack Red Cloud was praising the breakfast of back ribs and sweet porridge, contrasting it to the poor pickings at the agency. "They give us pig fat, salty enough to choke a coyote—good for nothing but greasing pans and tanning hides." I doubted that Jack Red Cloud had ever tanned a hide or greased a pan, but I believed him about the pig fat. The shelled corn the Bad Faces brought up was mostly fit for horses, or feeding to squirrels. Such swill was supposed to be payment for millions of acres of prime buffalo country—part of our national debt—and the Lakotas were as irate as any bond-holding widow when they found themselves shortchanged. Of course, the agents promised food, much food, and good food—if Red Cloud would just sell *Paha Sapa*.

Jack Red Cloud claimed the last decent feed at the agency had been given by the funny Wasichu who came to dig up the bones of Uncegila, the Mother of Water Monsters—by this he meant Professor O. C. Marsh of Yale, who came looking for fossils. "This funny Wasichu made a big feast, inviting the best men among the Oglalas, giving us plenty of meat and dried apples. So we let him go into the Badlands to dig for bones, mountains of bones"—Jack Red Cloud held his hand high over his head. "Bones so old that they had turned to stone." But what amazed him the most was that the bone collector kept his promises and did not dig for gold as well. "That is very hard for a Wasichu."

Yellow Legs dug into his Medicine bag, coming up with some yellow leaf tobacco, saying it came all the way from the Land Where the Warm Winds Come From and through the Spirit World.

Sitting Bull weighed the dried leaves in his hand. "Good tobacco, like we used to get from the traders. Not the greasy plugs that they give out now. I can feel the Medicine in it." The men made a ritual of crumbling it and preparing to smoke.

Jack Red Cloud had brought newspapers for Sitting Bull's collection. Since traders and squawmen stopped coming to camp, the Strong Heart chief had no one to read his clippings. I dug into the pile, finding them an odd mix—some more than three years old, none very recent. Everyone was having hard winters. In Colorado a prospector named Packer ate five of his fellow miners. Coyote would have chuckled at that solution to unemployment. The Philadelphia Centennial Exposition had opened, and so had the Zoological Gardens—which also made me think of Coyote. I pictured the Exposition: farm products, garish statuary, and gargantuan steam engines swathed in red, white, and blue bunting. Grant had opened the show, shaking innumerable hands—one Wasichu custom that Sitting Bull rather liked. Grant hated it, having a lot more hands to shake.

Amid the Centennial hoopla I saw corset ads and descriptions of color photography, also reviews of yet another school of French painting—"Impressionism"—and reports on Maxwell's work with electricity and magnetism. Some German claimed to have dug up Troy. There was even an account of Professor Marsh's harrowing expedition to the Badlands, bringing back two tons of fossil bones, and tales of angry underfed Indians.

Leafing through, I looked for things that would interest Lakotas. "There are many things in here. New discoveries. New ideas. A man across the Great Water in Grandmother Victoria's land has found that all energy comes from one source."

Sitting Bull said it was good to hear that the Wasichu had found this out, though the Lakotas had known it for some time. He was more impressed when I told him we had added color to our shadow pictures. "The Medicine of the Wasichu is always growing."

I told Sitting Bull that Great Chief Grant would soon retire. "And in the Moon of Changing Seasons we will pick a new Great Chief." Sitting Bull understood Grant's weariness, saying it was hard to be a chief. He too had been successful in war, only to find that peace was not nearly so easy. He asked what the change in leaders might mean for the Lakotas.

The pipe passed. Dust danced in the lanes of sunlight falling down the smoke hole. The men across the fire looked as solemn as the College of Cardinals.

I wanted to be outside, telling my troubles to Yellow Legs, but Sitting Bull needed an answer. This was not winter on the Staked Plains—no one was going to be saved by white lies. Touching the papers to show they were speaking, I told him, "They say that the Wasichu must have the Center of the World." I tried to explain how the government had run out of money and needed the gold at the Center of the World to make more. Neither Sitting Bull nor my husband could see sense in that—the Wasichu had made the Iron Road, the wires that talked, and colored shadow pictures, not to mention French Impressionism; surely they could make their money without digging up *Paha Sapa*. Yellow Legs suggested we make more of the green paper money instead.

I shook my head, saying the Great Chiefs thought the green paper money was no good. Even the white silver money was no good. Only gold would do. It was hopeless to explain sound fiscal policy to savages, especially when you did not believe it yourself. During the War, women had run farms and factories, paid mostly in greenbacks when they were paid at all. Now we had to go back to gold, even if it meant throwing millions out of work or robbing the Lakotas.

Western papers were full of the usual calls for someone's blood to be spilled, saying the Lakotas were sitting on a gold mine and it was the government's job to take it away. The *Yankton Dakotaian* predicted Custer's expedition would pay off the national debt and demanded the army protect the prospectors in *Paha Sapa*—like a burglar who sets up camp in your living room and shouts for a lawyer when you try to throw him out. Local papers were at least honest. Eastern papers piously suggested offering a "fair price"—the new name for lean beef and moldy blankets—then castigated the wild Lakotas for "not keeping the peace." What peace? Newspapers ignored murder and horse thieving by Crows, Northern Snakes, Blackfeet, and other "peaceful tribes." Nor was there anything peaceful about hordes of armed Wasichu marching onto the reservations, taking gold, hides, horses, and anything else that seemed salable—shooting whoever resisted.

Yet the same generals who threw up their hands in helpless confusion when it came to stopping white miners and rustlers said it would be a snap to bring in Sitting Bull and Crazy Horse. Could Wallace be so stupid? Could Custer?

Sick of reading, I got up and left the tipi. As I stood in the sunlight, letting my legs unkink, Yellow Legs came out to join me. Handing him the porcupine-tail brush, I told him we had to talk. He picked up a half-finished saddle and we headed for the benches above the river where the Hunkpapa ponies were grazing, away from the dust and noise of camp. Up on the benches the breezes were cooler, smelling of spring blossoms and horse sweat.

Yellow Legs was a great believer in arranging his life so everything fit together. He was accustomed to working on his saddle up here, sitting on a fold of ground surrounded by ponies: where he could see the form of a horse while he held the leather in his hands. Propping my back against his knees, I had him unbraid my hair, feeling it spill over my shoulders, while I told him all about my dream of Long Hair leaving his camp by the Big Muddy.

"But you saw no one coming here?" He turned his chin toward the line of camps.

"I saw them leaving, headed toward Where the Sun Goes Down."

He began to brush, using long soothing strokes. "This is not some tiny winter camp that can be ridden through at a gallop. They would be fools to come here. The bands have gathered. The grass is up, and the ponies are fat."

Staring out at the immense pony herds—thousands of roans, bays, sorrels, grays, buckskins, paints, and speckled Appaloosas—I had to admit that from where we sat an attack looked almighty stupid. My old pack pony, Carries-the-Lodge, came strolling over. Stolen by Hunkpapas three winters ago on the Yellowstone, Carries-the-Lodge still remembered me. I fished through my pouches and pockets for a reward.

Yellow Legs told me how he had talked to many Lakota Eaters: to Young Two Moons, to Comes-in-Sight, to Ice and Last Bull. "None of them are worried now that they are with the Lakotas." Pausing to work out a knot, he let my hair blow in the breeze. "And none of these men thinks my family is to blame for bad times. Since we left the Lakota Eaters' circle, winters have been worse and buffalo harder to find. Their camp was burned, and their horses run off—all while we were far away. Since we have come back, the Hunkpapas have fed them and the Lakotas are hosting them. An honest man would say that we had little to do with their troubles."

An honest man, yes. But I wondered what Calf Road and the other women would say if Long Hair returned. Yellow Legs too was clearly hinting that we could rejoin the Lakota Eaters circle. He leaned around to fix my part, admiring me, and his work. A smile spread over his face. "The Moon of Making Fat is not a time to worry. It is a time for babies to grow."

Everyone seemed to know my secret. I was too worried to try to be brisk and light about it, telling him outright I was frightened.

"Frightened?" He folded his arms around me.

"Yes, frightened of having no power over my life, or my dreams, or even my body. It is scary to have someone growing inside me, whether I will it or not. It will be a hard thing to have a baby just before winter. It will be a hard thing just to have a baby." I was in no way ready for motherhood.

"Raven will be there."

I nodded, still finding it strange to think of Raven, that big obstacle, as a source of comfort.

"She has had a baby already." He put his hands on my shoulders. "I too am worried. There is not much a man may do about women's Medicine." His part had been done a while back, probably in the Spirit World. "But I have promised a Sundance."

I was shocked. "A Sundance?"

"I promised that if we had no war, and if you had no time apart by the Moon of Making Fat, then I would do the Sundance."

"But you will not hurt yourself." I could not bear to see his flawless chest scarred and ripped. Lakota Sundances are not for the fainthearted.

"I will only dance. To seek a healthy child, and your safety, and for the curse to be lifted. The Great Mystery can do no more for me than that." Suffering at the Sundance was a very private affair. Some braves, like Crazy Horse, never danced. Those who did set their own limits.

"I will need you to assist," he told me. "To add your Medicine." I nodded. The dance was for me. There was no way to say no, any more than I could tell my body to take the baby back.

When we left the Rosebud, it was to go farther west, toward the Little Big Horn, making a dry camp on the divide before descending into the valley of the Greasy Grass. The Little Big Horn was never my favorite campsite. A chill had hung over it ever since we camped there during that last doomed summer with the Lakota Eaters—when we were mourning Medicine Bear and Last Bull shot a Flathead in camp. But at least we were still headed west, away from *Paha Sapa*, the Big Muddy, and Fort Lincoln. I had no desire to be a part of Custer's strategy, or Spring Grass's grand reunion. Maybe I could not outrun the curse, but we'd give it a good gallop.

A cold wind greet us, blowing hard off the snowcapped Big Horns, showing why the Lakotas called them the White Rain Mountains. Here it was, nearly Sundance time, and winter clung stubbornly to their peaks. White flakes flew in my face. First a flurry, then a real snowfall. Unless you have lived on the high plains you could hardly credit snow in June, but it swirled about us, clinging to the grass tops, piling up in powdery drifts. Water froze in our drinking skins and cooking tins. At dusk Yellow Legs and I sat in the tipi, playing with Nothing, teaching her to make cat's cradles out of sinew string. I could hear the Camp Caller going around, saying tomorrow we would head back over the divide toward the Rosebud. Snow in June is not a hard omen to divine for a camp full of Medicine men—it was not yet time to be camping on the Little Big Horn.

Sundance

The Earth is your Grandmother; every step should be a prayer.
—White Buffalo Woman

BY SUNDANCE TIME THE EXCITEMENT AND EXPECTATION OF PREG-nancy should have shone on my face like paint. Instead I was panicked because my life had suddenly become so public. I had lived among the Lakotas and the Lakota Eaters by drawing my Medicine tight around me, relying on camp courtesy. I had held my private *inipi* and gone only to social dances where everyone is invited. But with a baby inside me, there was no holding back. Life had taken hold; I had to throw my Medicine into it and pray.

I had to reach out as well. Without the help of other women I would not have known where to even start. Raven and Spring Grass worked to get me ready; so did Four Robes and Seen-by-the-Nation, who represented the host tribe.

While I prepared for a baby and a Sundance, the camp grew around me, expanding faster than my waistline. The Two Kettles came in, and enough Burnt Thighs to form their own circle. There were even some Hohes as well. Sitting Bull had brought the Hohes and Hunkpapas together last year, a policy that began when he adopted Jumping Bull. I also saw Left Behinds, old-time Sheyenna who wear their dresses tied—not sewn—reminding me of Spirit Worlders. And Oglalas continued to come up from the Red Cloud agency, including Young Black Elk, the shy Medicine boy who had refused to kill squirrels at the Center of the World. Now he carried a gun, a big army Colt given to him by an aunt who lived with the Loafers at Fort Robinson.

This was typically Lakota—a woman living with the Long Knives giving her gun to a boy riding off to join Crazy Horse. If there was to be a fight, women felt both sides ought to be armed. Yellow Legs had a full load of shells for his Medicine gun—a gift from his Wasichu wife.

We set up camp where the valley of the Rosebud widens into a flat grassy oval, a lovely Medicine spot sprinkled with wild rose thickets. Sacred caves and painted rocks looked down on more than a mile of looping tipi circles stretching from the Hunkpapas' Sundance camp to the green bench above the river where the Sheyenna held their Medicine Lodge ritual. Sitting Bull sacrificed a fat buffalo cow, leaving her carcass stretched out on the prairie, legs pointed to the four directions, a gift to the mystery of life and death. Lakotas and Sheyenna do not normally waste meat—even the flesh of the sacred white buffalo is eaten—but The-Bull-Seated-Among-Us was determined to make this Sundance special. This must have pleased Coyote and other Eaters of the Dead.

On the first day Yellow Legs rose early, brushing and braiding my hair, then taking his time painting me, saying, "Among all this summer's pregnant women, I want you to shine." I assured him I would do my best—without actually promising to shine.

Then he turned me over to Raven, and left with the men to find the Sundance tree. I sat beside Sitting Bull's lodge, nervously weaving garlands of spring violets and yellow coneflowers, being coached by Four Robes and Seen-by-the-Nation on how to walk and what to sing. I had to do this whole first day's dance without Yellow Legs's help—men find the Sundance tree, but women bring it down.

The men come howling back to camp, circling their ponies as if they had seen the enemy. Women rose up, walking and riding toward the sunrise gap in the lodge circle, wearing white doeskin dresses with long Lakota fringes. New mothers carried their babies; maidens carried steel axes. I had my arms full of flowers. We chanted and sang all the way to the Holy Tree—a great rustling cottonwood forty feet high. Cottonwoods, whose sawtoothed leaves are shaped like little lodges, are the sacred trees of the plains, giving shade and showing the way to water. Cut their limbs across the grain and you see the veins are spread out like the Morning Star.

Mothers-to-be danced first, for the Sundance is first of all about fruitfulness. I shuffled forward, shy and frightened, my mind on my steps and singing. But once I was beneath the Holy Tree, I felt only the solemnity of the ritual. One pregnant woman among many. As we danced, tiny cottony seeds blew down on us, like snow on a sunny day. The storm of white flakes pleased the Hunkpapas—but reminded me of the June snow flurries that drove us back from the Little Big Horn.

The chiefs followed after the women, doing a victory dance around the tree, led by Black Moon and Sitting Bull. They selected four Hunkpapa braves to count coup on the tree, each coming from a different direction. The one who took first coup stood in the Direction of Death, recounting his many deeds, then struck the tree. One by one of the four braves counted coup, but they did not kill—that was the work of women. Unmarried maidens came forward and chopped at the trunk, the most dangerous task of the day. None of them was supposed to have been with a man; any that had, risked death from the tree or public ridicule if their lover stepped forward.

No one died or was disgraced, and the cottonwood came crashing down in a shower of lodge-shaped leaves. Women gave the tremolo, that undulating cry that I could never twist my tongue and throat into making. Then the maidens used their axes to trim off the Morning Star branches.

Chiefs who were sons of chiefs carried the sacred tree to the Sundance circle, stopping four times to give thanks for the seasons. Once for spring, when the grass comes up. Once for summer, when the world is fat. Once for fall, when the leaves come down. Once for winter, when snow is on the ground.

They stood the log in the center of the great circle formed by the council lodges. Warriors mounted their ponies and formed an even larger circle surrounding the Hunkpapa camp, each man wearing his Medicine shirt and coup feathers, their faces painted for battle. With a yell they lashed their ponies, racing inward toward the tree, clattering through camp, armed only with coup sticks. I saw Yellow Legs flash by wearing his blue breeches and long trailing warbonnet, riding between Rain-in-the-Face and Swift Bear.

The crush was frightful. Horses reared and men wrestled, trying to toss each other out of the saddle. Those who fell picked themselves up and scrambled back into the milling pack, everyone trying to be first to touch the tree—the lucky brave who did could not die in battle between now and the next Sundance. This was why Yellow Legs had been so set on having a stout saddle by Sundance time. Since he had his own bullet Medicine, I suppose he was only in the sham battle for the fun of it.

There was no hope of seeing who won, but from the way the women cheered he must have been a Hunkpapa. The first day's work was done, and that night there were victory feasts. Hunkpapa callers went through the camps, crying, "Come, friends. We have coffee. We have sugar. We have fry bread and buffalo meat. Come feast with us."

On the second day the trimmed log was painted blue, green, yellow, and red, and hung with rawhide lariats. Bound to the top were offerings: tobacco, cherrywood, a red robe, and buffalo hides. Buffalo skulls ringed the base. Women with nursing babies laid them alongside the skulls. Four Robes brought her newborn twins. Raven brought Nothing. Our daughter was not a baby, but she still nursed and this was her first Sundance. Seeing her beside the tall pole reminded me of the Lakota legend that says little girls playing with cottonwood leaves made the first tipis.

The children had their ears pierced by a Medicine man, and there was a great squalling from the babies, but Nothing did not cry out. Raven was pleased, giving her best pony away to a Santee family. This was the first blood rite of the Sundance. Nothing went about like a little warrior, proud that she had shed blood just as Sitting Bull would.

Using the tree as a center pole, men raised the Sundance lodge. Twenty-eight supporting poles formed a great circle, each pole having its own meaning: Two poles stood for the Great Mystery of life and death, two for Grandmother Earth and Grandfather Sky, four for the four directions, four for the four ages of life, seven for the seven rites White Cow Woman gave to the Lakotas, two for the Sun and Moon, one for the Morning Star, one for fire, one for water, one for rock, one for the eagle, one for the buffalo, and one for two-legged people. Together they made twenty-eight: the number of sleeps in a single moon, the number of days in a woman's cycle, the number of ribs in a buffalo, and the number of feathers in Yellow Legs's warbonnet. Setting up the lodge took all day, since each act required a special ritual, though women joked that it took so long because it was done by men—no woman could afford to take all day to pitch her lodge.

That night there was no feasting in our tipi. Yellow Legs began the fasts and sweat baths needed to purify himself for the Sundance. This was his Medicine, but it spilled over onto me. I got very little sleep—just assisting at a Sundance was an endurance contest. I told myself he was doing this for me and for our baby, but the Sheyenna have a way of doing you difficult favors. At first light, I untied my Medicine bag and took out the two remaining cactus buttons. By nightfall I figured my Medicine would be about exhausted. They were all I had to strengthen it.

By sunup the camp Medicine was at fever pitch. The day was perfect for the dance, warm and cloudless. Children dashed about doing their own rituals. The small boys were uncontrollable—at Sundance time they were freed of what little constraint Lakota parents usually imposed. Adults were just supposed to endure it. Boys poked and teased us, making popguns out of ash boughs. One took his little bow and shot a hole in my water bag as I carried water up from the Rosebud, then went whooping off to celebrate his victory over the big blond Wasichu. I could not complain or even scowl at the obnoxious brat without hurting my husband's Medicine. After all, the dancers would suffer much worse.

Yellow Legs meant to do his dance Sheyenna fashion, apart from the Hunkpapas, picking a spot on one of the benches between the main circle and the painted rocks. From there we could see the Sundance lodge, the pony herds, the camps, and the flat grassy bottom, stretching along the river like a shaggy green pool table. He marked his Medicine spot with a buffalo skull, stuffing the eye sockets with sweetgrass and smearing red paint on the bony cheeks. He painted a black line from horns to nose, and a black crescent moon under the left eye socket, and a red sun under the right. I laid my root digger beside the skull, along with an arrow and squares of sod cut from the prairie. Taken together they symbolized the world that fed us.

He proceeded to paint us as well. Here Raven assisted, while Nothing watched gravely. He painted a red circle around his face and a red sun on his chest. Raven helped him cover his torso with hail spots and dragonfly designs. I put a white crescent moon under his left shoulder blade. The effect was properly wild and handsome. Then they went to work on me. My coat of paint was simpler, but no less fantastic. Using my porcupine-tail brush, he parted my hair all to one side, old-time fashion. Raven dipped her hand into a gourd filled with white clay, fat, and water, smearing the mess over my torso and down my legs. Yellow Legs streaked my body paint with his fingernails, except for a white sun circle on my breast.

This quaint piece of prairie Impressionism required that I roll my dress down to my waist and tie my skirt up. When they were done I sat cross-legged on the rise above the camps, wearing nothing but white paint, my bunched-up dress, and a solemn look—mostly naked with half the Lakota nation looking on. Curious children trooped up to see the funny painted Wasichu, laughing at my growing breasts and belly. But we were supposed to endure anything, because the dancers suffered worse.

And they were going through worse, much worse. From where I sat I looked down on the Sundance lodge. Sitting Bull was Chief of the Dancers, assisted by Jumping Bull, his adopted Hohe brother. One Bull was a dancer too, along with a Hunkpapa named White Buffalo who had promised to be pierced. All were painted up. Sitting Bull had his hands and feet stained red and a blue sky stripe across his shoulders. They all walked around the lodge, crying out and offering their pipes to the sky. Then they lay down like dead men.

White Buffalo's assistant pulled up a sizable flap of skin on the dancer's chest, slicing it with a knife. White Buffalo did not wince, though he did call loudly to the Sun and the Great Medicine. As blood gushed out the hole, the assistant pushed a stick the size of a tent peg through, until it came out the other side of the flap. This bit of piercing made my job assisting Yellow Legs seem like a soft assignment. White Buffalo's assistant unbraided the free end of a buffalo-hide lariat hanging from the Sundance tree, tying the lariat strands to the two ends of the stick. The dancer was now tethered to the tree by the stick piercing his chest and could not free himself until his flesh ripped and parted.

Sitting Bull's cutting took the longest. Of all the Lakota men, I felt closest to Sitting Bull—it seemed strange that he should take eager part in this most barbaric rite. But a man's Medicine is his own. Jumping Bull, his Hohe brother, brought out a sharp awl and a knife ground thin and narrow. With these he cut small patches of flesh from Sitting Bull's arm, starting at the right wrist and working his way up to the shoulder, like a woman beading a red sleeve.

Fifty cuts. When Sitting Bull's arm was covered with blood from his neck to his fingertips, Jumping Bull got up and went around to the left side. There he began again at the left wrist. It was eerie to watch Jumping Bull at work—here was a man, born to the Hohe, an enemy tribe, cutting holes in the most powerful Hunkpapa chief, the man who had saved his life and adopted him. War for the Lakotas was very complex and personal.

This torture lasted about as long as it took the sun to travel the width of one of the Sundance poles. Through it all Sitting Bull wailed to the Great Medicine. When the cutting was done the dancers stood up. Yellow Legs stood up too. Drums beat, and the men all began to bob and sway, staring at the sun, blowing on bone whistles. There were other solitary dancers in the throng, but the mass of people just sat and looked on, crooning to the music.

The length of the dance was set by each dancer's stamina. I sat waiting with blankets for those short periods when Yellow Legs would rest. I had a buffalo robe over my shoulders now and there was nothing to do but watch and listen. I thanked the Great Medicine that Yellow Legs was not tearing up his body like White Buffalo and Sitting Bull.

Down in the Sundance circle, White Buffalo was anxious to break free from the Holy Tree. He leaned backward, pulling hard on the rope embedded in his chest. His flesh stood out from his body in grotesque fashion, but would not break. A friend came up and grappled him about the waist, adding his weight to White Buffalo's. Still the flesh would not rip. The friend heaved harder, like a wrestler trying to throw his opponent. Using all his weight, he finally managed to toss White Buffalo to the ground. The rope and stick snapped out of his chest with a sickening twang, flinging gore in a bloody arc. White Buffalo grunted in satisfaction, got up, ordered a pony turned loose for anyone who could catch it, then faced the sun and danced.

Sitting Bull danced all day with his hands dangling. By nightfall the blood on his arms and shoulders was no longer red, but black and matted. Still he did his shuffled dance, staring into the sunset. Yellow Legs shuffled along with the Hunkpapas. In the darkness they would turn about to face the dawn.

This was the real test. It is difficult enough to dance all day with the entire camp looking on, but the dancer could at least draw strength and encouragement from the excited throng. Now they had to dance through the night, with nothing but the beat of drums to hold them up. Each time Yellow Legs lay down I would lie with him, a few inches away so I would not disturb his Medicine.

At first light they were still dancing, bobbing up and down, blowing their bone whistles to greet the day. God, but I was tired. Hungry too. I sang softly to myself. Twice I nearly nodded off. Thinking it would be a hideous disgrace if I passed out from just sitting, I decided to chew one of the cactus buttons. I made a little ritual of scraping it off and putting it in my mouth. Then I sucked and chewed, letting the bitter taste keep me awake.

As the dew dried and the sun rose higher, dancers began to drop out. By noontime, Sitting Bull looked done in, semiconscious, no longer dancing, just swaying to the drumbeat. But he would not lie down. Finally Black Moon, Jumping Bull, and some others stretched him out on the ground. As soon as they touched Sitting Bull, Yellow Legs blew out his plumed whistle and announced, "It is over."

For the Hunkpapas it was far from over. Thousands of people ringed Sitting Bull's prone body, in a perfect pandemonium of wild shouts, weird whistling, and incessant drumming. People fell down before the buffalo skulls, throwing dirt on themselves. A herd of horses was being given away.

Picking myself up, I helped my husband back to the lodge, weaving our way through the Hunkpapas' crazed camp meeting and horse handout. The cactus button filled the scene with wavering colors. Women in white dresses and the nearly naked men seemed to be drenched in paint. Tipis glowed like giant prisms, with rainbows running along their edges. Yellow Legs ended up leading, though I hardly believed he could see after staring down the sun for a day and a half.

I collapsed on the grass floor of our tipi, totally drained. Raven rushed up to attend to our husband hero, helping him to stretch, spoon-feeding him some ghastly blood mush until he fell asleep. No one leaped to attend me.

Nothing came quietly over, crouching beside me, offering to share her fry bread. As I ate, she whispered softly, "I shed blood at the Sundance," referring to the holes in her ears. I said she had indeed, then I curled up, eyes closed and belly full, thinking I was done with the ordeal.

Rainbows flickered behind my eyelids. I had gone for two nights without rest. When you are sleepless that long, what you miss most is dreaming. I dreamed long and hard, but my last dream was the most vivid, crowding out the others.

I was transported back in the Sundance circle. The big Sundance lodge stood bare and empty. Green pine boughs that had smelled so sweet were now scattered about, browning in the sun. The great tipi circles were gone.

Magpies picked through heaps of litter, looking for a meal. Four warriors rode slowly through the deserted tribal circles: proud and tall, nodding eagle feathers in their ruffed-up hair, new-looking carbines lying across their laps. The four braves looked oddly familiar, but very out of place.

Then I realized that I knew them. They were Crows: White-Man-Runs-Him, Goes Ahead, Half-Yellow-Face, and Hairy Moccasin. They had all been at that scalp dance in the Big Horns. I might not have recognized them in real life, but in a dream you just know who people are.

A half-Wasichu came up to join them, wearing canvas pants and a fringed Crow war shirt. It was Mitch Buoyer, Magpie Outside's husband. Beside him was Curly, a light-skinned teenager from Magpie Outside's band. I could not imagine what Mitch and these Crows were doing in the Lakota Sundance camp. There could hardly be a more dangerous place for any of them.

In a second the question was answered. Up the Rosebud came a knot of Rees and a column of cavalry. Leading the Rees was Bloody Knife. Riding with him was the General. He was out of uniform—dressed in buckskins and wearing his flat-topped plains hat—but of course I would have known Custer even in a Snake warbonnet and a sailor's suit. All I had to see were his deep-set eyes and that smart blond mustache. Beside him was Cooke, his big Canadian adjutant. Behind him came his standard bearer, holding aloft the General's personal swallowtail banner—red and blue with white crossed sabers.

Troop after troop filed into the Sundance ring, filling the remains of the Hunkpapa circle with men and horses. Wind whipped away the dust they stirred up. I heard a ghostly bugle sound officer's call.

Wallace appeared. Without any fuss, we became one again, just like in that cold Sibley tent surrounded by the Dakota night. I saw with his eyes and heard through his ears. Godfrey and Calhoun were beside us, my old poker and dancing partners; so were Tom and Boston, also Reno, Benteen, Keogh, and the rest.

The General spoke in quiet tones, careful with each word—not at all the brusque self-confident Custer style. He was explaining, almost appealing. "I am following this trail as far and as fast as I can. I will rely on your judgment, discretion, and loyalty. I turned down General Terry's offer of Gatling guns and a battalion from the Second cavalry, because being just the Seventh, we are in harmony, relying on each other."

Everything felt wrong. The 7th had never been a band of brothers—and Custer was stammering—as if he were taking a step into the unknown and needed unaccustomed support. He claimed the Crows had found fresh tracks, headed upriver. "This is the last bugle call," he told us. "Until we sight the enemy, there will be no reveille, no stable call, no retreat, no taps."

Everyone nodded. Godfrey whispered to Wallace, "Still worried this could be our last fight?"

I yelled, "Yes, yes—it damn well could." But not even Wallace heard me.

Someone passed cold coffee to Wallace. He lifted the cup to his lips, considering—it tasted black and bitter. I felt Wallace's shoulders shrug, his lips move. "It's just a feeling. Can't say where it comes from. The General does not seem himself."

Calhoun spoke up, breaking the mood. "A big camp," he declared. "What beats me is why they stopped so often in such a short space of river. Looks like they camped five or six times in maybe a mile or two."

As usual James Calhoun was making no sense, until I saw that he thought a single band had made all the camp circles, moving a bit upriver each day. The fool knew as much about Lakotas as he did about poker, calling the wickiups "dog houses." I had seen Lakotas do all kinds of crazy things with dogs—talk to them, eat them, pray to them, even dress up in dogskins and bay at the moon—but I never saw a Lakota build Fido a summer wickiup. The hundreds of brush shelters were to house the warriors up from the agencies, the men in cloth shirts carrying hand-me-down army rifles. Calhoun was headed for an unpleasant surprise—but no one moved to correct him. They were the ones who seemed to be sleepwalking.

Mitch came up, with Goes Ahead and the rest of the Crows. I saw the boy Curly standing quietly, arms at his sides. Mitch asked Godfrey, "How many Sioux do you expect to find?"

Godfrey was not sure. "A thousand. Fifteen hundred."

Mitch considered. "Do you think we can whip that many?" The regiment had maybe six hundred troopers.

"Oh, yes," Godfrey replied. Then his natural caution asserted itself. "I guess we can." Godfrey could be awfully sure and unsure at the same time.

Mitch translated, and I saw disbelief on the faces of the Crows. Goes Ahead signed back "Many, many Lakotas," pulling his finger hard and fast across his throat. "Many, many smokes on the Greasy Grass, more fires than stars in the sky, more warriors than we have bullets in our cartridge belts." He plucked at Mitch's gunbelt, to make the meaning clear.

Godfrey wanted to know what the Crows were saying. Mitch smiled wanly, not looking to make trouble. "Goes Ahead says are gonna have one damned big fight."

Calhoun laughed. "Tell 'em to buck up—we'll have Sitting Bull begging for mercy."

A stiff southern wind caught the General's swallowtail standard, blowing it over backward. The banner lay in the dust pointing down the Rosebud toward the Yellowstone, back the way they had come. Careful Godfrey picked up the standard, sticking the staff back in the ground. The wind threw it down again. Determined to ignore the portent, Godfrey righted the staff, boring it tightly into the ground, braced by a bit of sagebrush.

Wallace smiled. "An Indian would say that meant something." Godfrey acted as if he had already forgotten the incident.

I awoke with the bitter taste of dream coffee still in my mouth. For a time I lay there dreading what the dream must mean. There was no mistaking that Custer was coming, bringing Wallace, Mitch, and the regiment right here to the Rosebud.

Looking around, I saw the lodge was empty. My limbs and body were still caked with white clay. Wrapping myself in a blanket, I tottered over to the lodge entrance. Stepping outside was like stepping back into the dream. The Hunkpapa circle was empty. The lodges were gone; blankets and hides were stripped from the wickiups. The great Sundance lodge stood abandoned. Magpies pecked at the litter.

I heard horses snorting behind me. Spinning around, I expected to see Mitch and the Crow wolves. Instead I saw Yellow Legs and Raven bringing in our horses. Nothing rode on her father's war pony.

"I see you, wife." Yellow Legs greeted me cheerfully, as if to remind me who I was. I must have looked alarmingly confused.

"What's happened?" I made a wild circle with my arm, indicating the empty camps.

Yellow Legs pointed his chin upriver. "Lakotas coming up from the agencies saw Long Knives to the south. The camps are moving over the divide onto the Greasy Grass." He was very matter-of-fact, careless in the presence of cavalry.

I was the one totally turned about. I felt like a Contrary. In my dream Custer had been coming upriver from the north, not downriver from the south. Everything was backward. The sun was even in the wrong part of the sky. It took me some time to see that I had slept through an entire afternoon and evening. It was late morning—a day later.

I did not mention the dream. Cavalry coming was apparently no news to anyone. Instead I hurried down to the Rosebud to wash off my paint, wanting to be clean before we struck out over the high waterless divide. By the time I got back, Raven had the lodge down and our camp packed up. My family sat waiting on their ponies, surrounded by cold fire pits, bare drying racks, and the skeletons of wickiups and sweat lodges.

The Lakotas had decamped in a rush. Anything that people did not want was left where it had fallen: broken pots, scraps of blanket, bones, and blunted hatchet blades. Lying upended was a coffee mill—some Hunkpapa had run out of coffee and thrown away the mill. A single scalp whipped atop a pole by the Sundance lodge. It looked white, but I cannot say I inspected it too closely. Scalps never much fascinated me.

As we rode upriver I saw something as sinister as a scalp. Someone had heaped up a ridge of sand in the remains of a sweat lodge. Horseshoe prints were traced in the sand, in a column of twos to mean Long Knives. Above the line of ironshod hoofprints the pictograph had a row of stick figures, heads pointing down to show they were dead.

I asked about the marks. Yellow Legs looked up at the sun, as though he hated to say this in daylight. Then he whispered, "Sitting Bull slept the Medicine sleep at the Sundance. He heard a voice saying, 'I give you these; they have no ears.' Then he saw Long Knives falling head down into camp, like a storm of grasshoppers." There was no need to say more. Sitting Bull's dream was as plain as mine, just a bit more impressionistic—which is what made me a Wasichu and him a Medicine man.

We continued on upriver, turning where the camp trail turned. It was no trick to track the camps over the high divide, even for a novice like me. Thousands of ponies had stamped out a dusty trail a quarter mile wide. So many travois poles had scored the ground that in places it looked like a plowed field.

The Rosebud

We were at their hearths and homes, their Medicine was working well, and they were fighting for all the good God gives anyone to fight for.

—Captain Benteen, 7th Cavalry

I HAD A DRY, DISCOURAGING RIDE UP THE DIVIDE. RATTLERS snaked through the buffalo grass, shaking their tails at our ponies. Near the rock pinnacle called the Crow's Nest was a dead pony, fresh and not yet bloated. As we passed I saw a flap of wings, and an eagle waddled out from behind the torn belly, too glutted to fly. The huge raptor opened his mouth and squawked at us. Yellow Legs, riding with Nothing on his lap, reined in and reached for his revolver. I leaned over and touched his hand to stop him.

He looked at me. "I do not have time to dig a pit and wait all day. This bird is misusing his Medicine, filling himself so he cannot fly. Sitting Bull could make better use of his feathers."

Yellow Legs was constantly concerned with paying back the Hunkpapas, and eagle feathers were always in demand—men who specialized in hunting them had as much standing as a Medicine man or a diligent horse thief. The old-time, ceremonial manner was to wait in a pit baited with raw meat. When an eagle came for the meat the hunter would grab the talons and wring the bird's neck. Modern braves like White Bull shot their eagles with a Winchester—less romantic but more practical.

Saying I did not want to see any killing, I told Yellow Legs about my dream. I omitted mentioning Wallace—merely saying I had seen friends, men who had helped me when I was alone. That covered Mitch and the Crows as well. "Let this bird live. With a baby coming we must be careful."

He holstered his revolver. The miserable eagle hopped after us, screeching and complaining, as if we had meant to steal his rotting pony meat. Yellow Legs smiled at its antics, then looked serious. "During the Sundance I did not sleep the Medicine sleep. Your dreaming grows stronger every day. Once you hardly knew how to use it; now you dream for both of us."

I had not thought that he too might be troubled by the Sundance. Now I saw he had been mulling over his own failure to dream. I wanted to say that I was sorry, but did not know how.

He shrugged off my concern. "You are carrying the baby. Your Medicine will be my Medicine. But I will not always holster my gun."

Nothing sat wide-eyed in his lap, taking in this Medicine talk, acting as if it were all normal. What else was a two-year-old to do? No wonder Sheyenna children grow up strange.

We caught up with the bands on the far side of the divide, a little way down Medicine Dance Creek. Camp Medicine was dry and brittle, as electric as the air before a storm. Women asked if we had seen soldiers. "No," Raven replied. "No smoke. No dust. Nothing." Only in our dreams, I thought, but did not say it.

We all felt safer being in such a big camp, but it meant more work—always moving, looking for game or fresh grass. Lodges went up and down too often. And Sundance feasting had consumed every buffalo rib and antelope steak in camp. Breakfast was whatever we found at the bottom of our parfleches. Four Robes had a huge sack of peanuts, Carolina goober peas, the last of several exotic dishes given them by agency Lakotas. So we sat down and started to crack peanuts. Holy Lodge came over, saying she had to get away from Rattles Track. "This dry weather makes her snappy as a snake."

Sitting under stunted cottonwoods, shelling and eating peanuts, reminded me of a song that Rebel soldiers had taught me and my sisters. Tarheels from the 26th North Carolina regiment had spent the second day at Gettysburg "in reserve" at our farm, playing mouth harps and eating our chickens. I started to sing, translating the words into signs:

> Sittin' by the roadside on a summer's day,
> Chattin' with my messmates, passin' time away,
> Lyin' in the shadow underneath the trees,
> Goodness how delicious, eatin' goober peas.

I had gotten good at signing as I sang, since Lakotas never knew any of the words. Four Robes, Raven, and the others thought the song was funny, so I taught them the chorus. Soon a circle of Hunkpapa and Sheyenna women were singing in passable Wasichu:

Peas! Peas! Peas! Eatin' goober peas!

All the while laughing at my antics.

Yellow Legs rode up, deep in conversation with White Bull and Jack Red Cloud. They were circling the camps, searching for soldiers and generally looking magnificent, their long hair flowing over leather shirts, their bead-work and metal ornaments glistening in the sun. They fit nicely into the next verse:

> *When the horseman passes, the soldiers have a rule*
> *To cry out at their loudest, "Mister, how's yer mule!"*
> *But another pleasure enchantinger than these,*
> *Is wearing out yer grinders, eatin' goober peas!*

The Lakotas hid their laughter behind blankets. It was a fine scandal—not at all the sort of song women sang to passing braves and chiefs' sons. I started on the third verse, to get them to sing the chorus:

> *Just before the battle, the general hears a row.*
> *He says, "The Yanks are comin', I hear their rifles now."*
> *He turns around in wonder, and what you think he sees?*
> *The Georgia Militia—eatin' goober peas!*

The women were ready. But instead of "Peas! Peas! Peas!" we heard the boom, boom, boom of real firing.

Singing stopped. Women stood up. Someone was firing downstream. The sound rolled slowly toward us, like distant thunder on a clear day. Lodges emptied. Women ran to strip the coverings off their tipis, getting ready to flee, sure the shots meant Crows or cavalry.

Word came up the coulee, spreading from lodge to lodge, that scouts had returned saying the valley of the Rosebud was "black with Long Knives." The army was less than a day's ride behind us. Braves with more powder than sense were firing off their guns, working themselves up for a fight.

Callers went around, saying the Council of Chiefs wanted everyone to wait. "Be ready to fight if the camps are attacked." A waste of wind. No mat-ter what the chiefs decided, it was plain that war parties would be going out tonight.

By dinnertime most of the young Hunkpapas were dressed for battle.

White Bull called on Yellow Legs, wearing a warbonnet borrowed from his brother. He had on his private war charm, four Medicine pouches, a buffalo tail, and an eagle feather, as well as a cartridge belt about his waist and a Winchester in his hand: a strange mix of Medicines—the old and the new, the beautiful and the deadly. Sitting Bull was going with the war parties, so White Bull and One Bull were going with their uncle, putting Yellow Legs under heavy obligation to join in. We had ridden Sitting Bull's horses and eaten the Hunkpapas' meat.

Spring Grass came riding up leading a spare pony, a sleek-looking clay-back dun. I told her, "Get down, Spring Grass."

She replied, "Mount up, American Woman. You may use my pony or one of your own."

"Where are we going?"

"To meet Long Hair." She was sure the cavalry on the Rosebud could only be Custer. I admitted I had dreamed as much, seeing Custer at the Sundance camps.

Spring Grass took it for granted that we would ride to greet him. I had no such ambition, and told her so, but she persisted in very un-Sheyenna fashion—the woman could be infernally Wasichu when she wanted. Custer's influence, I suppose; the man did leave his mark, and Spring Grass had been exposed at an impressionable age. "Comes-in-Sight and Young Two Moons are going," she told me, "and Crazy Horse is bringing his Crow Owners. But Long Hair will parley once he sees you." She thought the Medicine of two good women could surely stop a battle, but I didn't see a gopher's chance of us getting between Custer and Crazy Horse.

"You mean to stay in camp?" Yellow Legs asked, sounding surprised. I could sense his war Medicine taking hold.

"Yes, I do. I have a baby coming." I had to keep reminding them—the Sheyenna treated pregnancy as such a natural condition.

"And what if Long Knives come here?"

I opened my mouth to answer, then stopped, seeing what Yellow Legs meant. I could not stay in camp. Not with half the men gone and Custer coming. If the curse caught up with me in a camp stripped of warriors, the results would be too terrible to think about. Any massacre was bound to be blamed on me. I was neatly trapped—the only way to be free of the curse was to ride out and meet it. Crazy Horse would be only too happy if I drew Custer to him.

If I had a dram of sense I would have swooned or claimed the baby was coming, but my sister-wife was already bringing our ponies. Raven too knew I had no choice. Making the best of a bad hand, I tried to act like a hero-ine, saying I would go "for the good of the camps." Courtship has been called "the witty prologue to a very dull play." But my marriage had turned out to be anything but dull. At times it was much too exciting.

Yellow Legs gave me his most solemn assurance he would keep me and the baby from harm. The man took his Medicine seriously and did not make rash promises, but I knew firsthand what a chancy business bullet Medicine was. "Right. But no excuses," I insisted. "I don't want to hear afterward that someone stepped on a skunk or ate fry bread with a fork."

He looked wounded, saying he never made skunk Medicine. Then he set to work, carving a long crooked coup stick, wrapping it with fur, mumbling prayers, and tying on feathers. Raven had Nothing strip down, and we painted protective dragonflies all over her body. Silly as it sounds, it helped. Each dragonfly was a tiny prayer for bullets not to harm this girl. It made us feel less helpless. The family was riding out together, putting all our break- ables in one basket.

We had plenty of time to prepare. War parties don't leave until after dark. Weakened by the Sundance, Sitting Bull had to be helped onto his horse; in no shape to fight, he was merely going along to lend his Medicine. I did not see any of the other big chiefs. White Bull was there. So was Jack Red Cloud, wearing his father's warbonnet. This was a young men's—and young women's—war party. Buffalo-horned hats and animal masks made it feel a lot like Halloween. We were getting dressed in costume, ignoring our elders' warnings, going into the night to play trick or treat with death.

We climbed the divide in pitch-darkness, spattered by black splashes of rain. The roan I was riding was horribly excitable, hard to handle in the dark; I only rode him because he was strong, with plenty of stamina in case I needed to run. I wished for Keeps-the-Fire, or even Stolen Swan. Gradu- ally the clouds lifted, and we rode on under a waning Sundance moon. The men leading us had been over the ground several times already and could have ridden it blindfolded.

At first light we caught up with the Sheyenna and Lakotas led by Crazy Horse. We stopped, unsaddled, and rested our horses. Men freshened up their paint, sang songs, and raised warbonnets to the sunrise, lifting them up four times before putting them on their heads. I took the chance to lie down. Half asleep, I listened to cheerful talk about how many Long Knives we would see, how many Crows, how many Pawnees. I prayed quietly for the whole thing to be a bust. If we saw nothing more dangerous than a sage hen, it was swell by me.

At sunup we remounted. Less than half the men had guns, but there were plenty of bows and glittering lances. Lakota war clubs studded with knife blades looked gruesome in the dawn light. Yellow Legs had on his twenty- eight-feather bonnet and his cavalry leggings, and carried his crooked coup stick—his face painted like a hailstorm under the full moon. Seeing him like this, I understood why men love war so much, parading in all their finery, playing a grand game, whose only admission ticket was being ready to bet your life.

By midmorning we were climbing the bluffs overlooking the Rosebud. Crazy Horse's scouts mounted the slope ahead of us. Men met them at the crest, firing as they came on.

Someone yelled out "Crows," and someone else yelled "Snakes," so I am not sure which they were. So much for Spring Grass's peace talk. I fell back to where Raven and Nothing were, feeling nervous and useless right from the start.

Crazy Horse and his riders chased whoever it was back over the rise. When I reached the top, I saw the forks of the Rosebud below, cutting between the bluffs. This was not the wide bottom where the Sundance circle had stood. Deep ravines and high knolls half hid the river. Using Yellow Legs's field glasses I could see long lines of cavalry and infantry strung out along the bottoms. Between us and them there was a lot of whooping and shooting, as Lakotas and Sheyenna rode against Crows and Northern Snakes. All this enthusiastic gunplay spooked the roan I was riding, and the little beast started bucking like a light boat in a lively sea. Figuring I'd be safer on the ground, I decided to "get down." As I dismounted I saw my first dead man of the day, who looked to be a Lakota.

Crazy Horse led a charge downslope to where the Long Knives waited. Then he turned around and let them chase him back, whooping with amusement. Through the brings-'em-close-glasses I saw White Bull ride down a Snake on a bald-faced sorrel with white stockings, a pretty pony, with red flannel ribbons flapping from neck and tail. White Bull fired twice and crashed into the Snake, counting coup as the man went down. Then White Bull spun about, just ahead of the soldiers. The Snake got up and limped away, but the pretty little sorrel with the white stockings was dead.

Spring Grass stood at my side, telling me to look for Long Hair. I fixed the glasses on the soldiers. The man leading the nearest troop was not a Custer, but it hardly mattered. No one was going to talk to us.

Crazy Horse came up, dismounting to shoot. Yellow Legs joined him. I edged back, fearing the soldiers would ride right over us. But they had more sense. They too dismounted, spreading out, not wanting to be targets for many-firing Medicine guns.

The Lakota Eaters rode up. Young Two Moons and Comes-in-Sight whipped their ponies in circles to get their second wind. Calf Road was there too, with her husband Black Coyote, looking right past me toward the fighting. When the Sheyenna charged, Calf Road rode with them, acting incredibly devil-may-care, even for her. She had no weapon, and must have gone for the pure thrill of charging with the men. The troopers retreated, firing as the Sheyenna came on.

It was clear now that the soldiers would not sweep us off the ridge. Whole lines of infantry and cavalry seemed to be doing not much of anything, standing about, maybe waiting for orders. By now it was well past breakfast, and I fixed myself a sandwich out of marrow paste and fry bread. Strangely the shooting did not disturb my digestion—the baby made me ravenous. Nor was I the only one both hungry and bored of battle. I saw some Lakotas shoot a fleeting buffalo, then get down to butcher and roast the animal, picnicking just out of range of the fight.

A few foolish braves tested their Medicine by riding within range of the soldiers. I saw He Dog, Jack Red Cloud and some Lakota Eaters taking part in these antics. White Shield and Comes-in-Sight crossed in opposite directions before a line of skirmishers. As they parted, Comes-in-Sight's Horse went down, doing a complete somersault, flipping him onto the bare ground. White Shield was riding away from him and did not see.

Through the glasses I watched my brother-in-law stagger to his feet, praying he would get up and run. Taking the reins from his dead horse, he turned to face the bluecoats. Bullets kicked up dust around him. I imagined I could hear his death song.

Without warning a horse and rider raced between Comes-in-Sight and the soldiers. I scrambled to refocus my glasses. The rider wheeled about and came back for Comes-in-Sight. It was Calf Road. Much as I disliked her, I had to think that was one of the bravest things I ever saw, riding unarmed to face that long line of firing men. As her pinto passed at a trot, Comes-in-Sight leaped up behind her. I held my breath. Troopers blazed away, but did not hit so much as a feather.

The gallant pinto carried both brother and sister to safety. Sheyenna cheered and blew their eagle-bone whistles. Raven made the trilling ululation for her sister. Unable to join her, I made myself another sandwich. Pregnancy can be as pitiless as battle.

Calf Road's display was too much for Yellow Legs. He handed me his Medicine gun. "Here, keep this. It will protect you."

"Where are you going?" I stood there, feeling ridiculous holding a marrow sandwich and a rifle.

He gave me a silly smile. "I will be back." Before I could protest, he kicked his pony and headed off downhill, carrying only his new coup stick. Not about to emulate Calf Road and go charging after him, I followed him with the glasses as long as I could, seeing him join up with White Bull. Then both of them disappeared into the dust and gunsmoke. Losing Yellow

Legs scared me. I could not stand it if he did not come back. Or if he came back with Wallace's scalp. Or Mitch's.

Not far off, Sitting Bull sat upright on his horse, yelling encouragement to the younger men. I marveled that the man could even ride after bleeding so much at the Sundance. He was not giving orders, just adding his Medicine. No one was directing this mad display: not Sitting Bull, not Crazy Horse—not Custer.

Lone braves broke cover, plunging down nearly vertical banks, then recovering to take a shot or two at startled troopers. I saw Jack Red Cloud go down, his horse shot from under him. By custom he should have gotten up and calmly removed the dead horse's halter—like Comes-in-Sight had done—showing he was not afraid. Instead he dashed for safety. Crows caught him, whipping him with their quirts and coup sticks. I thought he was dead, but they just stripped off his warbonnet and took his many-firing rifle, satisfied to have embarrassed him.

Nothing demanded a look through the glasses, then complained that she could not see her father. I admitted I could not see him either. Hardly comforting—but I'm sure I was more worried than she was.

The sun had traveled far to the west. Men and horses were played out; braves began to drift back toward camp. At last our men came up out of the dust, walking their horses. Yellow Legs was looking very proud, with a Crow's wolfskin tied to his coup stick, a big fine pelt with the head attached.

Yellow Legs told White Bull, "It has been a long time since I fought the Snakes. I had forgotten what splendid fighters they are."

"They are the best," agreed White Bull—a bit of backhanded boasting, since everyone had seen him lame the Snake on the bald-faced sorrel. He added that the Crows were very dangerous close at hand, not wanting to slight Yellow Legs's captured wolfskin, "but at a distance they shoot as poorly as a Wasichu." No one had a good word to say for the fighting of the Long Knives. They were brave enough, but still did not know how to fight— never counting coup and always needing to be told what to do next.

Besides dismounting that Snake, White Bull had rescued a wounded Sheyenna named Sunrise. Wooden Leg brought back Sunrise's horse and we fixed up a travois. Sunrise himself did not look like he would see sunset. One Bull had likewise saved a Lakota named Rooster. But the rescue that everyone was talking about was Calf Road saving Comes-in-Sight. The Sheyenna were already calling the fight Where-She-Saved-Her-Brother.

Calf Road could have her glory; I was just glad to get Yellow Legs back, happy there had been no massacre. Hundreds of men had fought for half a day, littering the slopes with arrows and spent bullets, but very few bodies. The trophies were mostly like Yellow Legs's wolfskin—warbonnets and weapons, but hardly any body parts. Wooden Leg had a bag of coffee from an army pack. White Shield was showing around a very fine pistol that he had taken off an officer.

They had spotted several old acquaintances among the enemy. Lakotas were sure they had seen Rattler, the great Snake himself, standing over a wounded officer, waving his rattle. Seventy winters and still full of fight, Rattler was renowned for his ruthlessness toward his own people as well as his enemies. To the Hunkpapas he was a greater antagonist than President Grant; certainly they would rather have had his scalp.

Spring Grass kept asking if anyone had seen Long Hair. Yellow Legs laughed, admiring his captured wolfskin. "I rode in among the Long Knives, but I did not see any I knew. They all dress alike, and the dust was so thick we could barely recognize each other."

I told him that in my dream Custer was not dressed in blue, but in buckskins and a white hat.

"No." Yellow Legs had seen no Wasichu looking like that. He added, "I did see a Crow woman in this fight." I could tell he was excited; the story was coming out in bits and pieces, not front-to-back the way a story should be told. "She rode a black mare and wore yellow face paint with a stuffed woodpecker in her hair." I began to feel underdressed in a calico frock and dragonfly paint.

"She was wild and pretty." From the way he smiled I could see he was quite smitten. "When a Crow went down she charged at the Lakotas to save him. She came right at us, waving her coup stick and spitting."

"Spitting?" He seemed to have gotten awfully close to this hussy on horseback.

"Spitting and yelling in Crow. I never saw a woman fight like her. Naturally we fell back. One Lakota came too close and was killed. The Crow woman counted coup on him, then leaped down and took his scalp—very dangerous, but very pretty."

"Makes you want to go crawling into Crow tipis at night," I remarked. I had felt absolutely foolhardy riding out to watch a fight, but Calf Road and this Crow amazon made me look cautious.

Yellow Legs gave my suggestion serious thought, then decided, "No. A beautiful Crow who counts coup and takes scalps is fine to look at, but would no doubt make a difficult wife. I have two wives, which is often one more than I can manage."

"Who knows if she can even cook or sew a moccasin," added Raven. She knew our husband had a fondness for bringing home enemy women who could barely pitch a tipi. White Bull agreed. No man needed a wife so handy with a scalp knife. He had trouble enough with Rattles Track.

We drifted back up the divide, dragging our wounded after us on make-shift travois. None of these warriors thought they were running away. Even the wounded bleeding on the travois figured they had taught the U.S. army a much-needed lesson. A fraction of the camps' warriors had brushed the Long Knives aside like a buffalo tail shooing away flies. Despite my fears—and Medicine Bear's curse—the cavalry had gotten nowhere near the camps.

The Greasy Grass

Custer is at liberty to attack at once—if he deems it prudent—and he will undoubtedly exert himself to get there first and win the laurels for himself and his regiment. We have little hope of being in at the death . . .

—Lieutenant James Bradley, 2nd cavalry

WE DRAGGED SOME OF THE WORST WOUNDED OVER THE DIVIDE and down the dry twisted bed of Medicine Dance Creek, past cutbanks lined with sage and Spanish dagger. We were hauling Sunrise—the Sheyenna that White Bull had pulled out of the press by his wrists—also two Lakotas, both shot through the hips: Rattling Hawk, an Oglala, and a No Bow named She Bear. I could hear them moaning *"Mini,"* Lakota for "water." Warriors streamed back toward the camps shouting that the Long Knives were whipped, trying to encourage them, saying, "The Crows are headed back over the mountains. Snakes are singing their death songs."

Sunrise never made it to camp. He was left wrapped in a blanket for the buzzards, eagles, and Old Man Coyote—who would scatter his bones and return his flesh to the prairie. His soul was already headed for the Spirit World.

When the rest of us arrived, women were already packing up to go down to the Greasy Grass. Only Old She Bear's family stayed behind, to give him a chance to die or recover. I felt sad for Sunrise, She Bear, and anyone who had stopped a bullet. I also felt immense euphoria. The cavalry was last seen "headed south," going away without a massacre or an attack on the camps. We had gotten through the worst of it nearly unscratched. Less than half the camp's warriors had turned back a full regiment, reinforced by Crows, Snakes, and walking soldiers.

Most of us were glad to go back to the full-time business of being Buffalo

Indians. Spring Grass alone complained, saying these Long Knives could not have been led by Custer. Her man would not have hid behind Crows and Snakes. "Long Hair would have come charging up the slopes at the head of his men, sweeping Crazy Horse off the ridge, the way he did on the Day Medicine Bear Did Not Return."

Convinced that even Custer had finally seen reason, I pointed out that Crazy Horse had many more warriors this time. Spring Grass sniffed. "Long Hair does not care about numbers." I thought it was just her pride speaking.

Everyone else was happy to have whipped the cavalry. The sacred Buffalo Hat was brought out and decorated with a fresh scalp. Raven danced before it, waving Yellow Legs's coup stick and Crow wolfskin. But Calf Road led the chorus line, dancing with two rifles, one belonging to her husband and the other to her brother. She and Comes-in-Sight were talking again— a married sister who saved her brother was no longer taboo; she was trusted to be free with her sibling, without fear of inciting incest. Drums pounded and dogs went from lodge to lodge barking for meat, raising the howling that makes an Oglala call a party a "dog ruckus."

I took no part in the victory dance—friendly persuasion is the Quaker way—and Sunday Meeting was no place to learn the steps to a scalp dance or even a fox-trot. Being safe from armed assault was all the victory I needed.

Buffalo herds were sighted west of camp, so we rode off for an old-time buffalo run, returning with ponyloads of meat. I set to work tanning hides, thinking, Here is my new lodge cover. Summer hides are too thin for robes, but are perfect for drying and tanning. I set up a tripod of main poles to hang my hides on and mark where my lodge would be.

Raven planned a round of feasting, intending to invite the Lakota Eaters. I told her it would not aid my digestion to sit down with women who had thrown me away. Raven kept insisting, appealing on Nothing's behalf, saying it would be our daughter's naming feast.

She had me there. Rather than slight Nothing I would sit through a dinner with Calf Road and company. With a new baby coming I had to make extra sure not to hurt Nothing's feelings, these being her last moons as an only child. Right now she was looking forward to the baby, helping me tan rabbit's fur, collecting charms for the cradle bow. I wanted nothing to dampen her enthusiasm.

The naming feast was planned for the fourth day after the fight, the Medicine Day; Raven wanted only welcome omens. She prodded me to make a show of it, helping me make an old-style dress of smoked cowskin, cut from the top of an old lodge cover. The dress did not have a stitch of sewing: Everything was laced, tied, and tasseled. Wearing it would remind people that I had seen the Spirit World—Lakota Eaters could make whatever they wanted of that. The left sleeve was short and open at the top, showing a stretch of bare arm, where Raven painted red slashes to stand for Yellow Legs's coups.

This was a woman's feast—no men came, unless you count Pipe, the Lakota Eaters' man-woman, who was in Raven's quilling sorority. Nothing sat beside her mother, dressed like a little woman in white beaded doeskin, putting on solemn looks and wearing a necklace of sabertooth claws given to me by Spirit Worlders. Girls usually waited until they were five or six before getting a serious name; but having finally hit on a name, Raven refused to wait. "She is a special child, and shows every sign of being able to handle an adult name."

The guests arrived in ones and twos, with bowls in hand. I greeted each woman at the lodge entrance, telling them where to sit. Fat chunks of hump meat and smoked tongues lay cradled in half a boiled buffalo rib cage. Smaller bowls held sweet tripe and marrow bones. Women could see and admire our man's skill with a bow and a buffalo pony.

We stood our daughter up, so everyone would know what a fine child she was. Firelight danced in her dark eyes. It was a grave moment. She was about to lose her baby name forever and get the one she would carry into womanhood. Sheyenna women did not collect and discard names like a Lakota brave. Many carried their adult name throughout their lives.

Raven recited Nothing's story. Told front-to-back, it was impressive; if I had not been with Nothing through most of it, I would have thought it vain boasting. In her first moon the baby girl had left the Yellowstone country and made the long trip to the Center of the World, arriving just as Long Hair blazed the Thieves Road into the *Paha Sapa*. From there she went far to the south, across the Platte, past the Pawnee, Flint, Cimarron, and Canadian. She had camped on the Staked Plains, and in Indian Territory, with People, Kiowas, and Southern Snakes. Her first winter had been bitter—many children had died—but our daughter lived to see the Southern Herd and to follow the buffalo into the Spirit World.

Very few children went on spirit journeys, but Nothing had spent a whole year in the Spirit World, living in the camp circle of old-time People. Only a handful of Medicine women, including myself, could make that claim. Raven did not dwell on the reason for our return—it would be a bad omen to bring up Medicine Bear's curse. Besides, it was Nothing's story Raven was telling, not mine.

And what a story it was. Once I would have dismissed it as extravagant superstition—but if any of these women disbelieved it, they were polite enough to sit on their doubts. I stared at the little girl, thinking about that first day in the Center of the World when I had been enraged at her bare existence. Now I wanted to hug her. But it would have been disrespectful—too Wasichu. This was her moment, not mine.

My sister-wife reminded them that through all these trials and misadventures the girl had borne the plain name of Nothing—that had to change. Anyone who had seen and done so much could not be called Nothing. A chorus of agreement went around the circle.

Raven announced, "She shall be named for the mother who cared for her when she was sick, who cradled her when I could not, and who called for the Southern Herd to save her. From now on my daughter will be American Woman."

I was as stunned as anyone. You could have heard a feather fall in the lodge.

Raven continued in her flat cool way, "Her mother does not need that name. She has the one given to her in the Spirit World. She is E-hyoph'sta, Light-Haired Woman." It was the first time any Lakota Eater had called me that. That triumph alone would have choked me—but it was trivial compared to seeing a little black-eyed girl standing straight in her white deerskin, beaming because she bore my cast-off name.

I pulled my blanket up over my face and cried. Through the tears and blanket I could hear women approving. It was wonderful, strange, and awesome. When I recovered we ate until the lodge was littered with gnawed bones. That night I rolled into my buffalo robe, stuffed taut, wondering how Light-Haired Woman would sleep when she was really huge.

I did not wake until midmorning. The tipi cover was already rolled up, and the air along the Greasy Grass hummed with heat and insects. I heard a horse cropping the grass close at hand. That was strange. Yellow Legs did not usually picket his ponies by the lodge; the last horse that regularly shared my campsites had been Keeps-the-Fire.

I peered out under the rolled-up lodge cover into the bright day. A pinto pony was cropping the yellowing grass, tethered to my three bare tipi poles. He wore a long showy saddle cloth that trailed almost to the ground, trimmed with brass disks and turkey feathers. I sat bolt upright. This was the same little pinto that had danced among the bullets, carrying Calf Road and Comes-in-Sight to safety on the bluffs above the Rosebud.

Raven went about her morning work, oblivious to the pony. Seeing me awake, American Woman ducked under the tipi cover, plopping down on the buffalo robe next to me. "Please, Mama," she begged, mixing English and Sheyenna, "put me on your pinto."

"My pinto?"

"She is yours. Mama said so. She is tied to your tipi poles." Raven was bent over a hide, working on the new lodge cover, steeped in supreme Sheyenna indifference.

I got up, dressed, and put American Woman on the pinto. Seeing how tall she sat, I realized the child knew exactly what horse this was. Our girl had seen the fight Where-She-Saved-Her-Brother. She had stood on the ridge above the Rosebud, protected by painted dragonflies, watching her now-famous aunt ride into a storm of gunfire aboard this pony.

It was harder for me to grasp what the gift meant. In one sense the meaning was as unmistakable as the deep red slashes cut into Keeps-the-Fire's flanks. I would not get an apology, or an explanation. I was getting a good horse and a decorated saddle cloth, no more, no less. Raven stood up and walked over. "This pony has fine lines and looks hardy." She acted as though she had not seen the horse standing there all morning. "Everyone knows she is brave."

I said nothing. Untying the pinto's drag rope, I led our daughter about. Calf Road had passed the deal squarely to me; now I had to call the game. I could ignore the horse—turn her loose, take her back, or give her away— but this gift pony was a *fact*, as sure as my being pregnant. Thanks to the infernal politeness and courtesy of the Sheyenna, I might never know the full story behind the horse. Calf Road could have wounded Keeps-the-Fire, or she could know who did. Or this pinto could be an innocent inducement for me to give up my unfair grudge against her.

I could not storm over to the Sheyenna circle and confront Calf Road, demanding a Wasichu explanation or apology. That is not how to treat a tribal heroine who has just given you a famous pony. I would look worse than Rattles Track, and I knew how people talked behind her back.

I tried mounting him myself—a real pleasure after that outlaw roan I was riding. He was not at all high-strung, the way ponies often are, but was completely self-assured and confident, even with a stranger on his back. I rubbed his neck, talking softly in Sheyenna, so he would not hear a strange tongue as well as having a strange rider—in time I could introduce him to English. Calf Road had trained him well. Comes-in-Sight's sister was not a woman to cheapen a gesture by passing on a poor pony; with her it was all or nothing.

Yellow Legs came up, looking relaxed, leading a trail pony. He too had seen my new mount. We took off together down the Greasy Grass, away from the camps, finding a ford where the water was only a couple of feet deep. Crossing to the western bank, we rode over the big flat bottom where the river bends above Ash Creek. Somewhere up that creek She Bear's people were still waiting to see if he would live or die.

We stopped when we got to an old campsite, the one from three summers before, where Last Bull shot the Flathead. Grass had grown over the rubbish and fire pits, filling the rings of tipi stones—being Sheyenna meant never having to clean up. Our horses cropped the thick bottom grass, and I asked Yellow Legs straight out, "Do you want to go back to the Lakota Eaters?"

He leaned forward, saddle leather creaking. "With the Hunkpapas we live off the generosity of Sitting Bull and his women. He is a bighearted chief, and we have done our best to return his gifts, but it is difficult to stay on as one man's guests, no matter how great a man he is. We are not Hunkpapas."

"Nor am I Sheyenna."

"No, but you have a husband, a sister-wife, and a daughter who are. And you have another child who will be." He reached over, stroking my belly. "Do you want our baby to grow up a vagabond, moving from band to band? Our baby's big sister already speaks a hodgepodge of Sheyenna, Wasichu, and Hunkpapa Lakota, with a touch of Spirit Worlder."

Strange talk for a nomad, but the camp circle is so primary to Buffalo Indians that they hardly consider themselves wanderers. In all the traveling since the Snowblind Moon, from the Powder to the Tongue, to the Rosebud and the Greasy Grass, the Hunkpapas had been constantly "at home." Yellow Legs was saying we too could be at home.

On the way back to camp we found an army breadbox scribbled with charcoal. By now I was used to seeing odd things on the prairie, but Yellow Legs dismounted to examine the smudged markings. "Crows did this," he declared.

"What does it say?" The marks were faint, half erased by wind and rain.

"They say they will be coming for us." What else would Crows have to say? He opened the box. There was dead grass stuffed in the cracks. "And they will be here in summer. When the grass is up." I can't say I took the warning seriously. After all, the Crows had come and gone.

Herds of antelope were grazing where the Big Horn joins the Yellowstone. Back in camp, women had plenty of thin summer robes and wanted antelope hides, which meant turning about and heading down the Greasy Grass. As the guest tribe, the Sheyenna led the whole cavalcade—so everyone else had to wait for them to pick up and march down the line of camps. By now almost all of the Northern Sheyenna had joined us—Big Eaters, Left Behinds, Lakota Eaters, Dirty Moccasin's people—plus many lodges of southerners. Of the thirty-odd war chiefs, only Little Wolf was missing, and his people were expected in any day. Old Bear, Crazy Head, Ice, Buffalo Hat Keeper, and the other old man chiefs headed the parade past the Lakota camps. They led on foot, wrapped in gleaming white robes decorated with pictures of their deeds and coups—turning each man into a walking auto-biography. Last Bull led the Coyote Society. Lame White Man led the Elk Warriors. Crazy Dogs howled and capered. Contraries rode backward. Every-one else rode in quiet dignity, eyes downcast to show respect for the walk-ing chiefs. I saw Spring Grass leading a travois pony with Yellow Bird aboard, also Calf Road and Black Coyote with their daughter. Buffalo warriors in red costumes flickered like points of fire through the dusty mass of ponies, dogs, and People.

Behind them came the Oglalas, then Lame Deer's Minniconjous and Hump's No Bows. Also the Santees, Burnt Thighs, Two Kettles and Black-foot Lakotas—more lodges than I could hope to count—blanketed by the dust from thousands of ponies.

Since the Hunkpapas were the host band, we traveled last, hardly mov-ing at all, shifting over to the west bank to camp beneath the big bluffs that separate Ash Creek from Medicine Tail Coulee. This was no farther than Yellow Legs and I had gone in our morning ride. By now the camp was so huge it took half a day to turn about and change direction.

That night hunters brought back the first antelope slung over their ponies, setting off another round of feasting. Big bonfires lit the Lakota cir-cles, and Callers went around, inviting people to feast and dance. Dressed in our best, we went walking along the water, listening to the Greasy Grass pour over its pebbled bottom. The Lakotas had pitched their great council lodge near the pony ford where Medicine Tail Coulee ran into the river. It was the same spot that I dreamed about on the Staked Plains, picturing Crazy Horse playing cards with 7th cavalry officers. Feeling uneasy, I looked back upstream. Someone was walking slowly away from the excitement, turning his back to the great encampment. The slow limping shuffle was un-mistakable even in twilight. I asked Yellow Legs, "Where is Sitting Bull headed?"

"Up onto the bluffs"—he pointed with his chin—"to make a tobacco of-fering. His old aunt is sick. And he still fears soldiers are headed for the camps."

I watched him go, for as long as it took him to wade the river and dis-appear up one of the dry ravines. Somewhere above was a Medicine knoll where women gathered buffalo beans. In the fading light the bluffs formed an ominous barrier, standing between us and Where the Sun Comes From.

We danced late into the evening, returning by way of the No Bow cir-cle. Feasting was drawing braves from all the camps, and No Bow girls got their pick of dancing partners. Many of the No Bow men were in a bel-ligerent mood—maybe because of the fight, or maybe because the Sheyenna were getting too many of the girls. Whatever the reason, there was an angry tone to the dancing. Word had come down Ash Creek that Old She Bear was sinking fast, leaving his family for the Spirit World. No Bows began to taunt some Blue Clouds who had come with the Sheyenna, calling them interlopers and enemies. Young Two Moons tried patch things up. And Yellow Legs invited the Blue Clouds to leave the No Bow camp and come to our tipi.

By now it was fully dark. Stars blazed down on the Hunkpapa circle. Fires lit the lodges from within like soft pointed lanterns. We took the Blue Clouds in, and Raven tossed dry twigs on the tipi fire, fanning the flames with her crow's wing. When the fire flared up I recognized one of our guests, signing, "I see you, Sage."

The Blue Cloud looked surprised, signing back, "You have seen me before?" Blue Clouds believe in easy relations with women, but I think he was worried about getting too close to some tall Sheyenna's wife, particularly when there were Lakotas in the next camp who already wanted them dead.

I told him, "We met in Stone Calf's camp under the Snowblind Moon in the Winter When the Buffalo Went Away." This was the same Sage who had warned us that the Long Knives at the Sheyenna agency had a paper with names on it. If it were not for him we might never have left Stone Calf's band, never found the Southern Herd, and never followed the buffalo into the Spirit World.

Sage signed they had left their agency at Fort Robinson to steal horses from the Northern Snakes. Instead they had been dragged into camp by Lakotas who thought they were wolves for the Long Knives.

Yellow Legs tried to put the Blue Clouds at ease, saying it was not their fault. "Up in the hills the No Bows have a chief's brother lying wounded and likely to die. And their Caller has been going around saying there will be another fight."

Sage signed that they had heard similar stories in the Sheyenna circle. A dreamer named Box Elder claimed the cavalry would come again, and young warriors had held a Death Dance, swearing they would die in the next fight. I pitied these poor Blue Clouds, who had left Fort Robinson hoping to get horse rich at the expense of the Snakes, and instead had ended up among murderous No Bows, hearing wild tales about Medicine dreams and suicidal battles with the Long Knives.

Sage also had news from his relatives in Indian Territory. No one down south had disappointed me. Stone Calf had brought in his band, along with the two captive girls; and Catherine must have done her best to tell the truth, because Stone Calf was neither hung nor locked away. The army lived up to expectations as well. Sage said there had been a big lineup at Darlington. "The older Wasichu girl went down the line, pointing to the men who had copulated with her." But the officer in charge grew bored with seeing justice done and rounded out his chain gang by picking warriors at random. The result was a riot, followed by a couple more massacres before the Southern Sheyenna were beaten completely into submission.

By the time the Blue Clouds left, our lodge fire had burned down to embers. I lay in the dark next to Yellow Legs. Raven and American Woman breathed softly on the far side of him, so close that I could have reached over and touched them. Owls called in the cottonwoods along the Little Big Horn, and I thought about my three bare tipi poles standing outside, cold and lonely. A tipi is not like a house, but more like a living thing. A lodge cannot stand empty for long—not without fires to warm it and women to tend it, opening the tipi up to the day, closing it to the night, mending its tears, tilting the smoke flaps to keep out wind and rain. Nor can a lodge stand for long outside a camp circle. Soon we would have to go back to the Lakota Eaters camp. The only sort of tipi that stands by itself is a burial lodge.

Falling into Camp

Major Reno was a coward. If we were not commanded by a coward, none of us would have come back.

> —7th cavalry officer, Reno's battalion

A SECURE EUPHORIA CREPT INTO MY PREGNANCY. I SLEPT through the night with nothing worse than a simple dream about being a girl again, in Adams County, sitting on our split-rail fence, my sisters beside me, legs dangling in the July sun. I awoke to summer on the Greasy Grass. The men's side of the tipi was rolled up. Sun slanted in, beating on the fresh grass floor, filling the closed part with hot green smells. Ground squirrels ran back and forth inside my tipi lining. The day was going to be blazing. A fortnight ago it had snowed here, but today you could feel the Moon of Red Cherries coming on.

A Caller was going around, saying we would be moving camp soon. Through the tipi wall I heard Raven talking with another woman, saying in Sheyenna, "Old Four Horns's wife left for the Spirit World last night."

I recognized Calf Road's cool confident reply. She had discreetly waited a day, before following her gift horse with a visit to our camp. Very polite. Very Sheyenna.

But I did not feel like rolling out of my sleeping robe into a conversation with Calf Road. I wanted Yellow Legs to preen and brush me before I greeted anyone—we semi-savages can be very self-indulgent. By my calculations this was the last Sunday in June. Sunday was not a day of rest among the Sheyenna, unless you made it one. Being pregnant meant I had no monthly days apart, no days devoted to myself and my needs—one of the many disadvantages of crowding two lives into a single body.

I lay listening to their conversation, trapped in the tipi. I could not face Calf Road unkempt and unprepared. Nor would I make a big impression

319

lying around all day under a buffalo robe. Raven's habit of starting the day whenever she wished was the second best reason to have my own lodge. Fumbling about, completely disheveled, I grabbed a clean dress and my porcupine-tail brush, feeling like a guilty girl getting ready to slip out under the lodge cover to look for her man.

The problem solved itself. Calf Road finished her visit and left. I should have expected that. She was a married woman with a small child and many things to do—the Sheyenna circle sat some ways downstream and had to move before the other camps could. I just was not that important to Calf Road anymore—thank goodness.

Stepping out the entrance flap, I could see any move was a long way off. Young men were still lying behind the lodges, sleeping off Saturday night on Sunday morning. Yellow Legs was sitting and smoking with Gall, whose people had just arrived. The huge Hunkpapa had missed the fight with the Long Knives. That alone saved it from being a massacre; Gall was a monstrous presence, a born war leader. Right now he looked rather placid, but I hesitated to disturb him.

Yellow Legs looked up, excused himself, and sauntered over, smiling at my condition. When he had me primped and presentable, we bathed together in the swift waters of the Little Big Horn. He teased me for swimming in a dress, asking if I was ashamed of my belly, which was still hardly showing. I replied that men swam in their long trailing breechcloths, when a much shorter cloth would cover all they had to hide.

We dried off on the bank, talking, laughing, and watering our ponies. Yellow Legs was headed for the Oglala circle—"Crazy Horse thinks there are soldiers about, and wants to borrow the brings'-em-close-glasses."

Picking up the pinto's drag rope, I told him I was going to smoke the peace pipe with Calf Road—I was tired of being suspended between two camps. We parted, and I headed for the Hunkpapa circle, with my new pony following me like a big dog, happy for the attention, maybe even knowing he was going to see his former mistress.

Returning to the tipi, I passed Raven setting out to dig prairie turnips upriver, taking American Woman with her. Our daughter strode happily along in her mother's shadow, using her small root digger as a walking stick. Digging promised to be especially hard and dirty today, with the ground baked solid and insects swarming something fierce. I decided to put off any digging until the afternoon, since I could not show up at the Sheyenna camp a sweaty mess, with great wet stains on my dress. Even talking to Calf Road was bound to beat scratching for turnips in the scorching heat.

Ducking into the lodge, I struggled out of my wet dress and into a dry one, a Lakota outfit blazing with beadwork and blood-red crosses. A gift from Four Robes. Dangling alongside the looking glass were Yellow Legs's field glasses. I stared at them. He had specifically mentioned taking them to Crazy Horse. I recognized his cute way of leaving an invitation for me to join him, like the arrow and antelope hoof propped on the trail, showing where the hunting party was headed. We could waste a little time visiting with Crazy Horse and Black Shawl before I hunted up Calf Road.

Putting my new saddle cloth on the pinto, I set off downriver, going by way of the No Bow camp. As I walked, I went over in my mind what I would say—no easy task. It was now past noon, the hottest part of the day had arrived, and the camps seemed fairly deserted. Women worked in the shade of their lodges. Some were taking down their tipis, getting ready to move. Holy Lodge sat scraping an antelope hide. She called out that I had a beautiful horse, asking if I was hungry. "I am always hungry," I called back. "But I am hunting for my husband."

Holy Lodge chuckled, having instant sympathy for any woman with a wandering husband. Her own man, White Bull, had been married nine times and had proposed to many other women, including her younger sister. White Bull had what women wanted and did not mind spreading it about. I had heard his coups counted so many times I could recite them myself. He had touched his enemies seven times, taken two scalps, rescued six comrades under fire, and twice been touched by bullets in battle. He had also stolen forty-five horses, taken two prisoners, twice done the Sundance, killed twenty-three bears, and did not know what liquor tasted like—your model Lakota husband. Yellow Legs could boast a longer string of coups—but he had never killed a bear and had a moderate fondness for Medicine Water.

I asked Holy Lodge how Old She Bear was doing. She looked down. "He is doing badly. His family caught a badger and cut it open so he could see his face in badger's blood. He saw a perfect reflection." A true reflection was the worst thing you could see when making badger Medicine—it meant the face you were wearing was the one you would die with.

Holy Lodge looked toward Ash Creek. "That man may already be lying in his burial lodge." The Greasy Grass was a good place to die. Old Four Horns's wife had died in the night, and we were camped on the spot where Last Bull shot that Flathead. They-Fear-Her's burial scaffold was not far away. And Medicine Bear sat in his pool just downriver.

I looked over Holy Lodge's shoulder and saw another holy lodge. Across the camp circle stood the lodge of the Buffalo Calf Pipe—a tipi so sacred that only the Buffalo Pipe Keeper could enter it. The red claystone pipe was to the Lakotas what the Buffalo Hat and the Sacred Arrows were to the Sheyenna. Wrapped in a purifying bundle of sagebrush, the pipe was the

Lakotas' only physical link with White Cow Woman—who was their Jesus and Mary rolled into one. She had given the Lakotas the Buffalo Pipe and the Seven Rituals, including the Sundance. White Cow Woman had come first to the No Bows, walking naked across the prairie, singing her Medicine song, so now the No Bows were Keepers of the Buffalo Pipe.

Hardly any Wasichu ever saw the pipe—I certainly never did—but I had heard a story of one who smoked it. Two winters ago the No Bows had been camped at the Center of the World. A lot of Long Knives came riding up. A woman told me that Spotted Eagle and Fast Bear invited the Long Knife chief to smoke, getting the Pipe Keeper to bring out the Buffalo Calf Pipe. I cannot say the story is true. But the only Long Knife chief camped at the Center of the World two winters ago was the one the Crows call Son of the Morning Star, and the Sheyenna call Long Hair.

Staring at the Medicine lodge, thinking of Custer and Old She Bear, I saw the air shimmer. A vision hit me, fully awake and on my feet. This was no Medicine dream stealing up in the night, but a picture as clear as day— like when the Wichitas opened up to let in the Southern Herd.

The No Bow circle vanished, wiped away. Instead I saw a single tipi sitting in our old campsite on Ash Creek: Old She Bear's lodge. Death signs were daubed on the tipi cover in wet paint. All around it were the remains of our abandoned camp: cold fire pits, brush wickiups, bones, and rubbish. A ridge of weathered sandstone rose above the cutbank. A trail led up the bluffs.

Once more I was seeing this through someone else's eyes, looking over the ears of a big cavalry mount. The hand that held the reins had a blue soldier's cuff. It took a moment to realize it was Wallace. Reno and McIntosh were with him. So was Bloody Knife, wearing a warbonnet.

A Ree dashed past on horseback, slashing the tipi with his quirt, counting coup on the Lakota lodge. Another Ree raced up and dismounted, stabbing at the tipi with a scalping knife. Running his knife down to the ground, the Ree cut a long slit in the hide cover. He stuck his head inside, then jerked it back. There is no worse battle Medicine than entering a burial lodge; you might as well just climb the scaffold inside and snuggle up to the corpse.

Someone shouted in Crow. Wallace snapped his head about. Mitch was coming up with the Crow scouts. Behind them came Custer, riding a blaze-faced sorrel with white stockings, shouting something encouraging. But I never saw a less encouraged bunch of Rees, clumped by the burial lodge, singing mournful songs, lifting their shirts so their Medicine man could paint their chests. Cavalry troopers filed past. Young, tired faces, sleepy and unshaven, dulled beyond fear. They looked like they had been ridden raw during the night and morning. Rees kept fussing with their paint and singing their death songs. Bloody Knife tightened the chin strap on his warbonnet.

Mitch glanced at the Rees, then rode over to Wallace, saying, "Crows don't want to go either." He motioned with his head toward Ash Creek. "Too many Sioux." Taking on a camp this size was like trying to skin a live grizzly.

Bloody Knife agreed. He lifted his arms to the sun, signing goodbye. "I will miss you when you go down behind the Shining Mountains. I will not see you. I will be headed home." Home did not mean his long lodge by the banks of the Big Muddy. Home meant the Spirit World.

Custer gave Bloody Knife an irritated look, followed by a burst of orders. If the Rees did not want to follow him, fine. They could go with Reno. He would take the Crows. The Rees could watch while he whipped the Sioux.

Wallace heard Mitch singing a drinking ditty under his breath:

> Oh, I don't know, it may be so,
> But it sounds so mighty queer.
> You can tell it to the folks at home,
> But that bullshit don't go here.

Without Crows and Rees the cavalry could barely find their way about, but Custer was dismissing them as though they could not count tipis.

Crows clustered around Mitch to see what he would say. I could feel sweat running down Wallace's body. Mitch made a little speech in Crow, then said his goodbyes to Reno and Wallace. "I'm going with the General." He said it like he did not expect to be back.

Custer was veering off to the right, taking close to half the regiment, including his brothers, Tom and Boston, and James Calhoun. Cooke, Custer's adjutant, came clattering over, saying to Reno, "The General wants you to pitch into them. We will support you with the whole regiment—Keogh too." Like a lot of orders I had heard the General give, this one was sharp and strong, but vague on detail. Where was Reno supposed to pitch in? How and when would he be supported? The whole regiment was certainly not there. I did not see Godfrey, nor Benteen, nor Weir, who was one of Custer's favorites.

Reno and Bloody Knife headed straight down the creek with a hundred-odd troopers and the unenthusiastic Rees. Mitch signaled for the Crows to follow him, climbing the cutbank after Custer. The last ones out the draw set the lonely burial lodge ablaze. Horses stumbled from exhaustion. Ahead Wallace could see the weathered sandstone opening up, and the tops of trees where Ash Creek emptied into the valley of the Greasy Grass. Twisting in his saddle, Wallace stared back at the burning tipi. I could hear Mitch's last words to him, repeating in his head: "It'll be standing room only in hell tonight."

I stood staring at the Medicine Pipe Lodge. The tipi was no longer burning and not alone. The No Bow camp was quiet and peaceful. I wanted to speak, but my throat seized up, as if it dared not break the silence. Holy Lodge was looking at me, no doubt wondering why I had fallen into a speechless trance. I worked my tongue around, but all I could get out was, "They are coming."

Which must have been even more mysterious to Holy Lodge because I said it in English, a language more foreign to her than Prairie Dog. Gathering my scattered senses, I switched to Lakota. "Long Knives are coming."

"So the Caller says." She glanced downriver. "We hope to be gone before they get here." The No Bows could not start out until the Sheyenna were on their way.

I scrambled onto the pinto's back, looking the other way, toward the broad bottom where Ash Creek ran down to the Greasy Grass. The field glasses banged against my breast. Grabbing them up, I fumbled with the focus. A bend in the river blocked my view, but above the timbers I could see a smudge of dust in the air. "No, they are here." I remembered this time to say it in Lakota.

Kicking the pinto, I headed for the Hunkpapa camp, my saddle cloth flapping beneath me. Raven and American Woman were out there, digging turnips in the bottoms. I raced around the Hunkpapa circle, so as not to go crashing among the lodges, raising dust and trampling staked-out hides, like a prairie Paul Revere, babbling warnings in the wrong tongue. I could clearly see the big bottom between the camps and Ash Creek. A small band of Lakotas was crossing the bottom, raising dust, coming into camp. They did not seem to be scared or excited, but they were coming in fast, faster than Lakotas cared to travel with the sun high overhead.

I reined in at our lodge, hoping to find Raven had returned. The tipi was empty. I fumbled again for the glasses. Gall's wives were tanning hides behind their lodge. Plenty Horses came up. Sitting Bull's favorite daughter looked solemn, as if something special had happened. Her hair was cut short, and she had dirt on her face. Then I remembered that Old Four Horns's wife had "left for the Spirit World," making it sound like Plenty Horses's great-aunt was visiting relatives in a remote part of Lakota Country. Which in a way she was. Calmly as I could, I asked if Plenty Horses had seen my sister-wife.

She tilted her head, saying Raven was upriver, digging prairie turnips. I tried to apologize from my desperation, telling her, "An attack is coming."

She looked up at me. "Yes. Father says one could come anytime."

"No"—I shook my head—"not anytime. I mean now."

As I said it, yells and a volley of shots came from upriver. We both looked out over the sunburned bottom. The Lakota band was coming in faster now. Men were circling their horses and firing their rifles, showing they had seen the enemy. Beyond them, about where Ash Creek emptied into the bottomland, the smudge was growing into a towering column of dust, a smoky whirlwind streaming toward us. A cavalry charge was tearing across the bottoms.

Plenty Horses began to scamper from tipi to tipi, shouting at each entrance, "Enemies are here." Women poured out of the lodges, clutching children and bundles, fleeing downriver. Gall's women got up and ran the opposite way, toward the dust and shooting. I spurred my pony after them, thinking they were making some ghastly mistake.

Galloping out onto the bottoms, I saw things were indeed ghastly, but it was no mistake. Farther out, between us and the timbers, children were leading ponies up from the river, right in the path of the rising dust. I reined in and found the field glasses. Gall's women ran ahead of me, yelling and waving their arms.

Children stared up at the dust cloud, then scattered, some running toward camp, others trying to bring in the ponies. Women who had been digging down by the banks were coming up at a run. Behind them, men emerged from the dust, firing as they came on. The lead riders were Lakotas, shooting over their shoulders. At their heels I could clearly see Rees riding and shooting. Cavalry guidons fluttered above the smoke and dust.

Much closer, between me and the Rees, women were trying to bring in the children. I recognized Raven, her badger-tail braids beating on her back as she ran herding children ahead of her. Scanning the faces of the fleeing children, I saw American Woman, back in the pack, her mouth open, her little legs pumping. I knew at once she would never outrun a Ree war pony.

Gall's women got to the children, urging them to run harder, snatching up the smallest. Through the glasses I saw Raven grab up American Woman. "Got her," I shouted. "Now run."

A woman stumbled, dropping the child she was carrying. I groaned. "Get up, get up." She did not get up, but the child did, a small boy. He started to run toward camp. Suddenly he spun about, arms flailing, as if smacked by an invisible fist. He landed in the grass. I realized the women and children were not stumbling; they were being shot down as they ran.

Whipping off the glasses to get a broader look, I saw Raven and American Woman were right in the way of the hard-riding Rees. Yelling "Run,

run," I raised the glasses again. Raven staggered and fell. My stomach gave a horrible heave as she struggled to her knees, still holding our daughter.

Tossing a prayer in the general direction of heaven, I kicked the pinto with my heels, telling him to run. We galloped toward the gunfire, dodging prairie dog holes. I thought, Oh, my God, I am going to be shot, and hunched up, trying to protect my precious belly, guiding the pinto with my knees. Thanks to Calf Road the pony did not need much guidance, seeming to know this business better than I did. I prayed that if a bullet hit, it would be in the leg or shoulder, somewhere that would not harm the baby.

Grass tops flashed beneath my flapping saddle cloth. I passed one of Gall's women crumpled up on the ground and not moving, her body bright with blood. Then I got to Raven and reined in. True to his training, the pinto stopped and stood stock-still, though bullets buzzed about us like little killer bees.

Slipping off the back of my horse, I dropped straight to the ground. Holding on to the drag rope, I crawled through the grass toward Raven, past the body of a boy. He was dead, his chest blown open by a half-inch ball of lead. Another boy sat nearby, badly wounded but refusing to cry.

Raven was down on one knee, her dress a bloody mess, holding American Woman in her arms. American Woman was amazingly unhurt, just screaming, scared senseless. I was scared pretty senseless myself. Bullets clipped the grass tops. I could hear the characteristic zing of cavalry carbines. A firing line of soldiers and Rees was taking long shots at us.

"Take her." Raven shoved American Woman toward me. I gathered up the girl. There was no hope of getting Raven onto the horse. She was slick with blood and bigger than me. I hesitated.

Raven waved me away. She lay down next to the wounded boy who would not cry, pulling the dying child closer to her. I slithered back toward the pony, dragging the screaming American Woman.

My pinto was waiting calm as you please, cropping the grass. Maybe he thought Rees would not shoot a horse they hoped to steal. Crawling around to the far side, I pulled myself and the girl onto his back, losing the saddle cloth in the process. Looping the drag rope around my arm, I gave the pinto his head. He dashed back toward the Hunkpapa camp—a damned smart horse.

We quickly outran the fleeing children and the women urging them on. As the camp came rushing up, I tried to rein in. Hearing heavy hoofbeats behind me, I half turned in my seat and nearly shrieked in fright. A nightmare image bore down on me.

The foremost cavalry trooper was right behind us, growing bigger. He had no saber and had lost his carbine. Like me, he was trying desperately to rein in, yanking at the bit, but his horse had bolted in terror. Horse and rider went roaring past. The man was wild-eyed, his feet planted deep in the stirrups, trying to brake his beast by bodily force. Spittle flew from his open mouth. This blue specter rode screaming past me, disappearing into the mass of Hunkpapa tipis. I never saw him again.

Then I was there myself, plunging into the chaos of the Hunkpapa camp. Dogs dashed and barked. Mothers yelled the names of children. Old men shouted encouragement to the warriors. Bullets splintered the tops of tipi poles and whacked into the lodge covers.

As I neared Sitting Bull's lodge, Four Robes ran by carrying one of her newborn twins—having totally forgotten the other one. I reined in, scared and sweaty, gasping like a mare in labor. I too had left someone behind. Raven was lying out in the shortgrass, shot but not forgotten. Somehow I needed to go back for her, but I did not know what to do with American Woman crying on my lap.

One Bull tore out of Sitting Bull's tipi carrying a bow and stone-headed war club. Sitting Bull limped out behind him, wearing old smoke-tanned leggings trimmed with green porcupine quills and scalp tassels. Sundance scars decorated his arms. He hung his war shield on One Bull, saying to the young man, "Go. Do not be afraid." Sitting Bull had a revolver at his waist and was holding a Winchester carbine. I remember thinking how odd to see a man with two guns sending his nephew off with Stone Age weapons. But to a Lakota, Sitting Bull's Medicine shield was better protection than a brace of Gatling guns.

One Bull rode off waving his war club. Old Four Horns was holding a bow and arrow. Blood covered his legs and arms. I thought the old man had been shot—then remembered that his wife had just died. He had been slashing himself with grief. Now he was riding out to put some arrows in the Rees.

Men helped Sitting Bull mount a blaze-faced black with white stockings, then handed him the reins of another horse. Mixed Day, his mother, was on the led horse. White Bull rode up on a big bay, wearing an old shirt and no paint, but carrying a Winchester. He shouted that he meant to capture a Long Knife's lance—he must have meant a guidon—then he was gone. Swift Bear went with him, waving the Sharps he had gotten off that wolver by the Yellowstone.

Crazy Horse came next, laughing and joking, looking relaxed now that bullets hummed overhead. *Hoka-hey*. He always enjoyed a good day to die. So where was Yellow Legs? Why didn't he come riding up? He had been with

Crazy Horse and must have heard the firing coming from the Hunkpapa circle. Holding tight to American Woman, I called for him, like I did in my
inipi. "I need you."

No answer. How could he not heed me? Raven needed him too, lying out
there on the smoky bottoms. She had been such a force of nature; now she
was shot. For what? For trying to save her daughter.

I sent a second mental summons. No response. Some heap big Medicine
Woman. I had to steel myself to ride back out on the bottoms when the
shooting stopped. Already firing had slackened. It was no longer coming
closer. The whole attack had been gopher-brained from the start—as
doomed as throwing the Light Brigade against those Russian batteries. There
might be some cavalry commanders who could lead exhausted troopers on
a hell-bent-for-leather charge into ten times their number. Major Marcus A.
Reno was not one of them.

The firing continued to fade. Rees and soldiers were retreating into the
timbers. Now I would have to ride out onto the bottoms and look for Raven.
Having seen to his mother, Sitting Bull headed back to cheer on the boys;
I followed, focusing on Yellow Legs, begging for a vision. By now I needed
him immensely. So did Raven. So did American Woman.

I wanted to see Yellow Legs, but the vision I got was of Wallace. He was in
the timbers by the river, a green inferno of noise and smoke. Twigs and
branches clipped by bullets fell like autumn leaves. All around him men
were firing mechanically, chambering rounds, pointing their carbines,
pulling the triggers. But neither Wallace nor I could see anyone to fire at.

Reno was next to Wallace. Bloody Knife was beyond Reno. Their faces
were black with powder, glistening with sweat. I saw no sign of the Custers.
Major Reno was bemoaning that very fact. He wanted to send someone,
anyone, to find the General. A silly suggestion, but when you are being
overwhelmed by hundreds of irate Lakotas you might like to let your commander know. Exactly which part of the battle plan was this? I could not tell
if Reno was drunk or just terrified. It was certainly a terrifying place. Smoke
rolled forward from burning grass and rushes; flames crept behind the smoke.
And behind the flames came the Hunkpapas. Reno had caught a cougar,
without a clue about how to let go.

Suddenly the major yelled for his men to stand to their horses. Reno hastened to obey his own order, falling back through the timbers, leading by example. Wallace went with him.

The nervous, stamping horses were clustered in a Medicine clearing at
the heart of the timbers. Worried horse holders tried to keep the mounts
steady. A hundred or so frightened men stood by their frightened horses.

Wallace stared at Reno. The major was wearing a straw sun hat, looking like some Yankee peddler accidently put in command of the battalion. Wallace kept wondering, where was Custer? Where was the support from "the whole regiment" Cooke had promised?

With a crash and a volley, Lakotas and Sheyenna came storming through the wild roses and buffaloberry thickets, firing and yelling, eager to touch the enemy. Reno's straw hat went flying, carried away by a bullet. He struggled to tie a handkerchief in its place, to keep his hair out of his eyes.

Bloody Knife stood next to Reno. A bullet struck the Arikaree in the forehead, splattering his brains over the major. Feathers from the brave's warbonnet floated down, like bits of bloody snow.

Bloody Knife had always seemed so formidable, the scout who could outshoot Custer. And just like that he was gone, dead, face down on the ground, oozing blood from his forehead. Half of Medicine Bear's curse had been blown out like a candle.

Reno stood there, as shaken as I was, maybe more, mouth open, face flecked with gore, the handkerchief tied around his sweaty brow. "Mount," screamed the major, and he mounted.

Wallace heard him. I heard him. But I doubt that men standing a score of paces away heard him. The major screamed a second order, which sounded like "Dismount." If it was, not even he obeyed. In an instant Reno was off, leading a headlong retreat through the cottonwoods.

Wallace was a half length behind him, riding for his life. Panic was total. Reno could barely give a coherent command. A tiny fraction of the regiment was facing a thousand enraged braves. Branches flashed by, slapping at Wallace. Trees were trying to tear him from the saddle.

With Reno leading, the galloping mob burst out of the gloomy woods into daylight. It was like the crash of the starting gate in a race with death. A cheer went up from the warriors filling the bottoms. Every brave within reach of a pony gave a whoop and holler and mounted up, anxious to cut off the straggling line of troopers. Those who could not mount a horse continued to pour fire into the fleeing column, eager contestants at a carnival shooting gallery.

The soldiers had no hope of reaching Ash Creek. Their tired cavalry mounts ran as though they were plowing through molasses. Warriors on fresh ponies were closer to the finish than they were. Without an order from Reno the frightened troopers turned echelon left, pressed toward the river by the mass of yelling braves. This was the sort of battle that Lakotas loved best, a running fight with a fleeing enemy, better than the grand sham battle around the Sundance tree.

Wallace saw braves slamming their ponies into the American horses, clubbing at the troopers, trying to count coup or wrestle them from the saddle. Men went down. Riderless mounts ran in among the press. There was no rear or flank guard. No turning back for a man in trouble. Troopers emptied their pistols, firing wildly at warriors who had spent their whole lives working on their bullet Medicine. Shooting from the saddle is chancy. Yellow Legs and Crazy Horse never liked to do it in battle. Nor were these troopers trained for it. (Custer once told me that the first time he shot at a running buffalo he hit his own horse in the head.) Six wild shots and a soldier was disarmed. No one could possibly reload. Wallace saw soldiers throwing empty pistols away to get at their single-shot carbines.

Braves came so close Wallace could have touched them with a saber. But he was desperately aware that he did not have a saber. None of the troopers had sabers, or lances, or spiked war clubs, or eight-foot tomahawks, or even tall coup sticks. He saw laughing braves beating at helpless soldiers with pony whips.

Faster than Wallace thought possible the river curved around to cut them off. They were crowded into the pocket where the Greasy Grass bends southward. Less than a furlong ahead was a single-pony ford, where a narrow buffalo trail crossed the river and climbed the bluffs. The banks were ten feet high, the water shoulder deep. Reno gave another useless order, trying to slow the galloping mass of troopers, warriors, and riderless mounts, so everyone might cross in single file. The major might as well have tried to stop a freight train with the flat of his hand. No one obeyed. Terrified troopers crowded behind him. Lakotas drove their ponies right into the river on either side of the fleeing soldiers.

Wallace was one of the first into the water. I felt spray lash his face as he splashed through the ford and up the far bank. Mounting the buffalo trail, he turned to look back, getting a quick look at the burning prairie and the chaos in the narrow ford. The stream behind him was packed with struggling bodies, its slippery banks crumbling under ironshod hoofs. Soldiers and warriors wrestled in the brown churning water. Lakotas shouted "Hownh, Hownh," as they swung their knife-bladed clubs. An officer went over into the water, grabbed the stirrup of a sergeant's horse, and was towed across, only to lose his grip at the far bank and drop back, shot down from across the stream.

Wallace jerked his head around, guiding his horse up the trail. He did not stop until he reached a knoll where the survivors of Reno's command flopped down and began frantically digging rifle pits with knives, belt buckles, and bare hands. Men dug with the fever of repentance, praying aloud as they hacked at Grandmother Earth. A good third of Wallace's troop was gone. McIntosh, his troop commander, had never made it out of the timbers.

Wallace clawed at the packed clay, trying to scrape out a few inches of safety, two thoughts beating back and forth in his brain: Where the hell is Custer? Where's the rest of the regiment?

I felt a horse stumble beneath me and had to catch myself. It was not Wallace's mount, but my new pinto. I was no longer in Wallace's head. I was riding behind Sitting Bull. Smoke from the burning timbers drifted between me and the tops of the Hunkpapa tipis. American Woman had stopped crying. She clung to my lap, looking about. All around us was the wreck left by Reno's attack: abandoned weapons, fallen horses, limp bodies. The only body I recognized was Swift Bear, Crow King's brother, who had nearly shot me on the Yellowstone ages ago. Now his eyes had that death-bright stare.

Braves were stripping dead troopers, looking for guns, ammunition, and tobacco. Young men came riding up, showing off trophies, saying what a great run it had been. "Just like playing Throw-Him-From-the-Horse. Easier than running buffalo."

Sitting Bull told them, "That is good. Now go back. Take nothing from the dead. Let the Long Knives go. It is over." Few heeded him.

I heard a voice cry "Mini." A man was calling for water. He was neither Lakota nor Wasichu, or at least not a white man. It was Isaiah, the interpreter from Fort Rice, who used to visit the Custers' kitchen. The big black man lay on his back, shot in the chest. He had no weapon that I could see, just a coffeepot. It was so like Isaiah to go into a fight carrying coffee fixings. We had sat for hours in Mary's kitchen, drinking coffee and trading stories.

An ancient Hunkpapa woman stood over him, aiming a muzzle-loading musket older than she was. Isaiah kept saying, "Do not shoot me, Grannie. I am dying." The woman was clearly at a loss, having brought her musket out on the bottoms hoping to shoot a Wasichu. Instead she found a man with skin darker than hers, who talked like a Dakota. Seeing us, Isaiah called out, "Friends, do not count coup on me. You have killed me already."

Sitting Bull dismounted, saying not to shoot him. "It is Teat." Unslinging his skin water bag, Sitting Bull poured water into his buffalo-horn cup and held it out to Isaiah. "Teat, why did you come with the Long Knives?"

"I wanted to see this country one last time." He took the cup and sank back.

Suddenly American Woman was struggling in my arms, yelling, "Mama." She said it in English, and I supposed she meant me. When she switched to Sheyenna, I looked up. Raven was limping toward us, leaning on her root digger. She had my fancy saddle cloth wrapped around her middle. Blood soaked one side of it.

Swinging off my pinto, I let American Woman down. She ran to her mother, tears furrowing her dusty cheeks. Raven caught the girl, warning her, "Do not hug, daughter. My rib is broken."

Stripping away the saddle cloth, I knelt and examined the mass of bruise-purple flesh, trying to remember everything Dr. Warren had told me about bullet wounds. It seemed that the ball had struck her in the back, bounced off a rib, and gone out her side. I shuddered. The little ball of lead had made a bloody mess of her side, but it had left her alive, even able to walk.

The old Hunkpapa woman rebound the wound, while I fussed about, asking Raven what I could do for her. My sister-wife stared at me, bleeding like a martyr, with American Woman hanging on her uninjured side. "Where is our husband?" she inquired calmly.

Where was Yellow Legs? I stood fidgeting, shifting from foot to foot. Yellow Legs would know what to do. But where was he?

Leaning on the old woman, Raven told me she had been resting. By which she meant lying and bleeding while bullets zinged overhead—she made it sound like sleeping through chores. "But I must see Yellow Legs."

I started to say I did not know where he was. Before the words were out, I had a sudden, sharp picture of him. He was riding alone, bare-chested and dressed for war, wearing his blue cavalry leggings with the yellow officer's stripes. His face was painted blue and yellow to match the leggings. On his head he wore his bonnet of black-tipped eagle feathers, one feather for each day of a moon. The horse under him looked "borrowed," a big white-faced black stallion with white stockings. Across the animal's withers lay his feathered Henry rifle. He had taken so much time to dress and paint he had missed the fight. Even now he was riding away from the battle, crossing the pony ford where Medicine Tail Coulee runs into the Greasy Grass.

In an instant the vision was gone. Instinctively I looked downriver. All I saw was smoke, and Lakota warriors coming late to the show. But I did not doubt my vision—it was my fourth Medicine dream of the day. (I had not recognized the first warning, my dream of sitting on a rail fence in July, smelling summer primroses—some Medicine woman.) I turned to Raven. "He is crossing at the coulee near the council lodges."

Raven did not ask how I could know this. She simply repeated, "I must see him." Perhaps she only wanted his company, but he was a first-rate healer.

Happy to be of some use, I remounted, vowing to bring Yellow Legs at once. It was no more than a mile or two. Raven needed Yellow Legs, and there was nothing to keep me—Isaiah was dying, and I had no wish to see that. I kicked my pinto into a run; he had his second wind by now, and took off like a live tornado.

Passing the wood where Bloody Knife had been shot, I pictured his proud face exploding. "Sun, I will not see you go down behind the Shining Mountains." The man had certainly called his last card. Half the curse was lifted, and Medicine Bear was no doubt gloating in his watery grave by the Big Horn. But I got no pleasure from it. Bloody Knife had never done anything but good by me. If it had been up to Bloody Knife—or me, for that matter—there would have been no battle. As for the second half of the curse, if Custer had the brains of a buffalo chip he was licking his wounds and headed for Fort Lincoln.

Clattering through the Hunkpapa camp, I found it nearly deserted. The warriors were chasing Reno up the bluffs or stripping the dead. Women had snatched valuables and fled. Only the oldest ones sat waiting by their lodges—too weak to run, ready to die if the Long Knives swept shooting through camp. Meat simmered in abandoned kettles. Tipis had their covers pushed up and thrown over the poles, to make them harder to burn. Dogs and ravens were nosing through the lodges and wickiups, seeing what they could steal before the women returned and order was restored. No disaster is so terrible that someone cannot make a meal out of it.

The Medicine Gun

Custer's Luck! We've got them this time! Caught 'em napping. . . .
As soon as we get through here, we'll go home to our station.
                                        —Custer's last reported words

I TURNED THE PINTO TOWARD THE LITTLE BIG HORN, FINDING
the shallow spot where I had seen Sitting Bull wade the stream. Urging my
pinto in, we splashed across. An empty 7th cavalry canteen went bobbing
by in the current. We mounted the east bank right beneath the bluffs, less
than a mile upstream from Medicine Tail Coulee, where I had seen Yellow
Legs crossing. I pointed the pinto up a dry wash on the south side of the
knoll that overlooks the coulee. From atop the knoll I was bound to spot Yellow Legs; he had been riding slowly, and I had come up from the bottoms as
fast and straight and as my pinto could go.

My Medicine was finally working overtime. Lying atop the knoll, with
his rifle beside him, was Yellow Legs. I nearly burst with relief. The big
white-faced black was with him, lying patiently on his side, silent as a Snake
pony. I gave a joyful little whoop. My husband half turned and signed frantically for me to get down and be quiet—I had come galloping up the draw
making more noise than a band of Flatfoot.

Swinging off the pinto, I tied his drag rope to a twist of sage at the head
of the draw and scrambled over to Yellow Legs, flopping down beside him,
wheezing like a broken bellows—three moons pregnant was no fit time to
be dodging bullets and running races. Before I could tell him about Raven,
he made the sign for silence, pointing his chin down toward the coulee.

"*Jesus,*" I half shouted, giving Yellow Legs a fit.

Wallace should have been lying there beside my husband—it would
have satisfied his curiosity about Custer. Instead of being halfway to Fort
Lincoln, the General and half a battalion of cavalry were coming down the

coulee at a cautious trot, weapons ready, kicking up dust and sending rocks clattering ahead of them. Custer, Mitch, and Cooke rode at the head of the column. The men behind them looked tired. Those farther up, waiting to move, sat heavy in their saddles like sodden grain sacks.

I clung to Yellow Legs's arm, openmouthed, mesmerized by the enormity of what was happening. A quick movement caught my eye. A few men were peeling off, moving fast the other way, fleeing past the straggling line of troopers. Wondering who was showing such remarkable sense, I focused Yellow Legs's glasses, following the fugitives as best I could.

They were the Crow wolves rabbiting away. Curly, Goes Ahead, White-Man-Runs-Him, and the others were headed east, toward birth and sunrise, aiming to live. Bad things were going to happen here and these Crows wanted no part in them. I wished Mitch had been with them. Better yet, the whole column should be turning about and riding away from the camps.

Shots came from down the coulee. I swung the glasses about. A dozen or so warriors were riding back and forth between the Long Knives and the camps, kicking up dust, firing, signaling that they had seen the enemy. A few more had taken cover behind a fold of ground, firing up at the soldiers.

Beyond them I could see the great council lodges, with their Medicine covers stripped off to save them from the Long Knives. Not much else had been done to put the camps in a state of defense. Women and children were fleeing toward the grassy benches, trying to stay out of the fighting. Somewhere behind me, on the bottoms below Ash Creek, there were warriors— two thousand, three thousand, four thousand—more than an honest person could count. But between Custer and the camps there were less than a score of braves. Over a hundred mounted troopers were stumbling down the steep coulee behind the General. A hundred more waited on bay horses atop the ridge, ready to descend.

I could hear the warriors below calling out in Lakota, yelling *"Wica-nonpa,"* which means "Two Bodies." They were calling to Mitch, telling him to turn back. I wanted to shout similar advice, but I was too scared. Mitch was not army. He was half Lakota, and hardly needed to be at the General's side. Mitch's Crows were blood enemies of the Lakotas with losses to avenge, but they had known better than to hang around.

As the cavalry came closer I could hear some of the men singing to raise their spirits:

> *Our hearts so stout have got us fame,*
> *For soon 'tis known from where we came,*
> *Where'er we go they dread the name*
> *Of Garryowen in glory.*

It was Custer's Medicine song, but this time there was no band to bang it out, no Medicine music to freeze his foes. The band had been left behind, along with the Gatling guns—and most of the regiment. All I could see spilling into the coulee were a couple of hundred tired men on tired mounts.

I fixed the brings-'em-close-glasses on Custer. What could the breathtaking idiot be thinking? He was sitting tall in the saddle, in his shirtsleeves and buckskin pants, two British bulldog pistols in his belt, the brim of his white hat pinned back so he could sight his sporting rifle. Was he crazy? Was he scared?

No, the fool was smiling like a genial maniac, that insanely confident Custer smile. He was proud of what he had done. He had struck out alone into the unknown, with his brothers beside him and his regiment behind him, and he had hit pay dirt, just like at *Paha Sapa*. Ahead lay the biggest village the army had ever pitched into—thousands of lodges, an immense pony herd, the sacred Buffalo Hat and Medicine Pipe—with a mere handful of braves left to protect it. God, but it must have looked good to him. It must have looked like Custer's luck.

Even the pretty sorrel he rode seemed to sense the excitement, picking up her feet and prancing as the ground leveled, getting ready for the charge. After all, the warrior on his back was not likely to dither about on a good day to die. Custer rose in his stirrups, turning to the left, right hand on the reins, left hand held high to wave the troopers forward, ready to give the order to go in, sure it would win for him, like it had at Gettysburg, and Yellow Tavern, Woodstock, Brandy Station, and Appomattox, and on the Lodgepole and the Yellowstone. Beside him the bugler put bugle to puckered lips, getting set to blow.

Expecting a trumpet call, I was deafened by the shot. Yellow Legs's no-miss Medicine rifle cracked right next to my head. The slam of the gun shocked me so much that I did not see Custer fall.

When I refocused the glasses Long Hair was down. The Son of the Morning Star was stretched out on the ground beside the feet of his blaze-faced sorrel. Mitch leaped down to help the General. The whole column came to a halt as officers dismounted to attend their wounded chief.

Cooke and Tom Custer lifted the General back onto his sorrel mare, but he slumped forward. Even from where I lay I could tell he was hit hard. His mouth moved, as if trying to give an order. The command stood waiting, horses snorting and fidgeting at the smell of gunsmoke and a strange camp. The firing from below grew louder.

The bugler who had been next to Custer spilled out of his saddle and lay still. No one moved to pick him up. Looking back, I could see more warriors racing down both banks of the Greasy Grass, fierce and confident, fresh from smashing Reno.

The column began to lurch back up the coulee. Their charge was point-less without the commander who had brought them here. It was not a mat-ter of courage—Tom Custer had two Medals of Honor and Myles Keogh, the second in command, was a gallant blade, as brave as they come—but the whole operation had been Custer's folly; without him it had no guiding force. The man who had been driving them toward destruction was hurt or dying, propped up on his big sorrel by his brother.

Mitch started to remount. He was half on his horse when a bullet caught him. He slid backward to fall next to the bugler.

Horrified, I scrambled to my knees to get a better look. Yellow Legs made a frantic "get down" motion—but I had to see. Mitch was alive; I saw him moving on the ground beside the bugler. He rose up on one arm, reaching for his horse's stirrup. The horse shied away, and Mitch sank back, not mov-ing his legs.

More warriors were converging on the ford, most of them Sheyenna. Their camp was just downstream. They had been the last to reach the Reno fight and the first to get to this one. They faced at least three companies re-treating up the coulee; I could see three different colors of horses: bays, sor-rels, and grays. It was a fighting retreat, with the gray-horse troop dismounted and firing steadily to keep the warriors back.

The troops at the top of the coulee, all mounted on bays, rode straight along the hogback toward the high crest overlooking the Sheyenna camp. This withdrawal from the coulee was in no way panicked. It was planned and orderly, smart as you please, really. Keogh and Tom Custer knew their business. They would easily make it to the high ground.

I was mainly concerned for Mitch lying by the ford, where there was no good way for me to get to him. "Lie still," I shouted, though he could never hear me over the gunfire, the beat of hooves, the screams of wounded horses. If he would just lie still the Sheyenna might ride over him. Yellow Legs tugged on my dress, trying to get me to take my own advice.

Then came the charge. Sheyenna swept up the coulee. I saw White Shield and Comes-in-Sight, along with some Lakotas. Most came on low, with guns, bows, or coup sticks ready. The more business-minded had blan-kets out, aiming to scatter and stampede the big cavalry mounts. Yellow Legs kept pulling at my dress hem, pestering me to shut up and stop bounc-ing about. I bent down and grabbed his shoulder, pointing at Mitch with my finger, Wasichu fashion. "That man, Two Bodies, he helped me while I was with the Crows. We must save him if we can."

My husband looked at me as though I were completely daft. I suppose I was half crazy, but it was the sort of silliness a Sheyenna could understand. We dashed over to where his horse lay, running doubled over to keep our heads down. My run was more like a waddle; my belly would not bend the way it used to. Yellow Legs pulled the stallion up and mounted, helping me up behind him. Then he lashed the big black down the gully, leaving my pinto tethered at the head of the draw.

When we reached the bottom of the knoll, the charge had passed Mitch by. He was lying very still. Let him be alive, I thought, seeing that the bugler beside him was stone dead, staring wide-eyed at the high Montana sky. An Oglala rode by doubled over, clinging to his pony with his knees. Snatching up the bugle, he righted himself and went on up the coulee, having a grand time trying to blow a charge.

I slid off the back of Yellow Legs's horse and knelt beside Mitch, feeling his chest. Still breathing. Yellow Legs dismounted. Together we lifted Mitch up, carrying him past the bugler, some way up the knoll, where he would not get trampled. The move must have hurt him, because he moaned dreadfully, clenching his teeth and closing his eyes. Dr. Warren said never move a man with a back injury, but Harvard physicians don't have to face the problem of patients being trampled by angry Lakotas.

Yellow Legs led his horse around to stand between us and the firing, a big black living barrier. The horse did not seem to mind being a shield and began to crop at the grass. After all it was people who were so terribly bent on killing each other. Horses were just here to carry them from one folly to the next.

Mitch stopped groaning and opened his eyes, looking up at me, seeming pretty puzzled. I knelt beside him, saying, "Sarah Kilory—I stayed in your lodge in the Big Horns three summers ago."

"Sacred Blue." Mitch shook his head. "What's an angel like you doing here?"

"You guessed right. I am married to Yellow Legs. Our lodge is just across the river in Sitting Bull's camp. If I can get you there, you will be safe." Mitch was dark-skinned. I figured I could dress him up like a wounded Lakota—or even better, a dead one.

"Sitting Bull?" He tried to crane his neck about, but it pained him to move his spine. From the twisted angle that his feet were at I knew his back was broken. The bullet had done about as much damage as a bullet can that does not kill outright. He sank back, saying, "Where's the General?"

Mitch seemed more concerned about Custer than about his own condition. Most people lying with a bullet in their spine, and in line for a

Hunkpapa haircut might have hard words for the imbecile who got them there. But Custer was a man you either loved or hated. No matter what blunders the General made, or what coups he pulled off, his overblown confidence had people either despising or admiring him. And Mitch was an admirer. If by some miracle Custer escaped this disaster intact, there would surely be people ready to run him for president from his hospital bed, and others who'd happily see him hang.

I glanced back uphill, seeing the mayhem framed by the horse's black-and-white legs. The Sheyenna charge had stalled. They were dismounting, firing from the gullies and bushes. The troopers were higher up, out of sight, but they had to be retreating, drawn by the magnet of higher ground. Atop the ridge they could hope to make some sort of stand. So far they had been making a polished show of it, holding the warriors off handily. They did not even seem to be in much trouble.

"The General is up there somewhere"—I pointed for Mitch's benefit—"but he is hit bad. There is nothing we can do for him." There was nothing anyone could do for Custer that wasn't being done by his brothers and his officers. "You need to worry about you."

Mitch shook his head. "I was dead before the bullet hit me. You say Sitting Bull's here?"

I nodded yes, he was here. So was Crazy Horse, Black Moon, Crow King, Lame White Man, Red Top, Old Bear, Dirty Moccasins, Hump, Spotted Eagle, Runs-the-Enemy . . . the list of war chiefs and band leaders was near endless. But Mitch did not need to know that; he had seen the camp. Mitch had the slim satisfaction of knowing he was right and the General was very badly wrong.

Mitch licked his lips and waved his hand toward where he had gone down. "Please, Mrs. Kilory, get my canteen. Must have fallen off while you were dragging me."

Gall came galloping up with a tomahawk in his hand and a murderous look on his face. I turned my head, not wanting him to see me, not when his family lay slaughtered on the prairie. A horde of Hunkpapas and No Bows were at his heels, along with some Santees, making hideous groaning noises deep in their throats. They disappeared up the north fork of the coulee.

As soon as they passed, I slid downslope to get the canteen. Some Oglalas were riding by, headed up toward the fighting. With them was a pretty young woman, holding her head up and singing:

> Brothers be brave.
> Would you see me taken captive?

No nonsense here about "The Girl I Left Behind Me"—this young woman was riding with them into the firing, carrying a war staff. She was Walking Blanket, who had lost a brother in the Rosebud fight. Rain-in-the-Face came riding behind her, painted yellow and wearing a warbonnet, carrying a stone-headed club and a small blue shield. Like Yellow Legs, Rain never wanted to go into a fight unless he was suitably dressed.

Seeing a canteen on the bugler, I cut the strap and brought it back, trying not to touch the bugler while I was doing it. He was very much dead. Flies swarmed in his open mouth. When I got back to Mitch I unplugged the canteen and held it up to his lips. He drank, sputtered, and shook his head. "Ain't my canteen," he croaked.

"It has water," I replied.

Mitch managed a wan smile. "Did I ask for water? I want my canteen."

I went back and found his canteen, unplugged it, and took a whiff. It was whiskey. This Medicine Water made Mitch a lot happier. He took a long pull and laid back, coughing and grimacing. The drink went down hard, and must have been terrible on his system, not that Mitch was much concerned with his long-term health.

The fighting moved steadily away from us. The sound of shooting faded, though from time to time I heard regular volleys. Aside from the dead bugler, there were few signs of battle. It was all happening higher up. Taking advantage of the quiet, I told Yellow Legs how Raven had been shot—which was why I had come for him in the first place. I felt miserable for not having mentioned my sister-wife sooner, but Custer's attack had made hash out of a lot of people's plans. He let me tell the story straight out, then declared he had to see her.

I knew he had to go, but I could not leave Mitch to be killed and cut up. I said I would sit here until he got back. Yellow Legs gave me his Medicine gun, saying, "This will keep you safe." Then he mounted the big black stallion and dashed off toward the Hunkpapa camp.

Mitch and I were left alone; unless you counted the dead bugler and the Lakotas streaming up the hill shouting "Hoka-hey." It was eerie sitting there on the slope above the coulee with the feathered rifle across my knees, but everyone was far too busy to trifle with a pregnant woman and a backshot Wasichu. Big things were happening up on the bluffs. Even Mitch was mainly concerned with events "up there." He started repeating himself, asking again, "Where is the General?"

Standing up, I could see dust and smoke billowing over the ridge above. Keogh, Calhoun, and Tom Custer had to be making for that high ground, carrying the General with them. Alive or dead, I knew they would not let him go. I told Mitch, "I can't see them, but I know where they are going."

"Where's that?" Strange that he should even care to know, but simple facts must really matter when you are fixing to die.

"To the high ground," I told him. "They are trying to get to the ridgetop to make a stand." If Custer's battalion got to the summit they might be able to hold on until the Lakotas got tired of trying to rub them out.

I sat back down. "Listen, Mitch. Maybe they'll make it, maybe they won't. But I have got to get you to my tipi." I wanted Mitch safe in my lodge, where I could get Sitting Bull to spare him. Mitch was half Lakota, and Sitting Bull was always sparing people.

Mitch shook his head. "I just want to be with the General."

" 'T ain't possible," I told him. "The General is most likely a goner—but I can save you."

He signed for another pull of whiskey. "Nothing to save." He shook his head. "I cannot move my legs. Can't live as a cripple in a Lakota camp, being hauled around on your travois."

"What about Magpie Outside?" I figured somehow I could get him to his wife's camp. The Crows were not that far off. I had made it there once before.

"You go see her." Mitch grinned. "Tell her to get another man, one with legs, like Tom Leforge." His laugh turned into a sputtering cough.

I could see women coming up from the camps, carrying butcher knives and makeshift clubs. They were looking to see if their men were alive, and meaning to get revenge for the dead. Two of them turned and came my way. One was Spring Grass, and the other was her aunt, Black Kettle's sister from Yellow Legs's old village. I was glad to see Spring Grass, feeling sure she would help me. But when I showed her Mitch, she was polite but not much interested. There was only one Wasichu she cared about. "Was Long Hair here?"

I could not bring myself to say that Yellow Legs had shot him. I just turned my chin toward the ridge. "Yes. He must be up there somewhere."

Warriors were beginning to gather around us. Sage, the Blue Cloud, stopped by, along with several Sheyenna. They asked who this dark man in Wasichu clothes was. A Lakota recognized Mitch as Two Bodies. Though they did not say it, I could tell they thought Two Bodies was well overdue for a close-up look at the Spirit World. I told them Mitch was Lakota as well as Wasichu.

A Sheyenna asked dryly which half was Lakota, since it would be a shame to shoot that half. Mitch seemed not to see them. He kept staring at Spring Grass, someone well worth looking at. He wheezed a bit, asking what this mighty pretty woman wanted.

"She wants to see the General. She was his woman down south in Indian Territory."

"Take me too," Mitch demanded.

"No, you need to go to my lodge. Hauling you up there would kill you." It was a ridiculous argument, with braves standing around, hatchets in hand, eager to finish him off.

"I am already done in," he insisted. He *was* looking pretty done in, if not technically dead. "Lay me down by the General."

Spring Grass started to tug at my arm, telling me to come with her and stop wasting time with this half-dead half-Lakota. She had to see if Custer was alive or dead. More women were striding up the coulee with skinning knives in their hands. She was rightly worried about what shape the General might soon be in.

Sitting Bull had come down to the ford. He was calling on everyone to end the fight. "Let them go. Do not disturb the dead." People walked politely around him. There is no Lakota law that says you have to listen to a chief, much less obey him.

Mitch sensed the impatience that Spring Grass was not working hard to hide. "Take me. I want to be with the General."

I nodded slowly, squeezing his hand. "Goodbye, Mitch. You have been nothing but good to me." I gave him some more of the whiskey. I had known Mitch's sense of loyalty was likely to get him killed, but I never expected to see it happen.

He drank, relaxed a bit, closing his eyes, but not saying goodbye. I got up and turned to face Spring Grass, gripping her shoulders. The braves closed in behind me. Mitch mumbled a sarcastic greeting in Lakota. There was a shot. I did not see who did it. When I turned around, Mitch was dead.

A brave had his scalping knife out, but Spring Grass brusquely shooed him away; she was a strong woman, and any warrior should be ashamed of hanging such an easy kill in his belt. Besides, there were hundreds of scalps for the taking up on the bluffs.

I brought my pinto down from the knoll and the two women helped me sling Mitch's body over his back, which the pony did not like, but accepted. Then I led them up the coulee. Spring Grass's face was tight and drawn. Her aunt walked beside her, holding her hand. I wondered if this was the same woman who had presented her to Custer when he had burned Black Kettle's camp on the Lodgepole.

I don't know what I expected to see when we topped the coulee—but what I did see surprised me. It was no massacre. Custer's command, hemmed in and outnumbered, had not been routed or overrun. They were holding the high ground, coolly defending themselves. Despite smoke and confusion,

I could see the troopers nearest to me were dismounted, facing the enemy and firing volleys, trying to drive back the swarming warriors. Farther back, the main mass of the battalion was "in reserve," ready to attack or retreat. Far from being overmatched, most of Custer's men were not even committed to the action.

A desperate situation, but surely not hopeless—not if the swarm of braves could somehow be held back. What made it hell for the troopers was the way the warriors fought. The Long Knives relied on discipline and controlled fire, but the braves had stealth and cunning. A Buffalo Indian fought as a thinking individual, trusting to his own Medicine. Lakotas and Sheyenna were crouching low, snaking through the sagebrush gullies, using every bit of cover. It must have been ghastly for the soldiers on the ridge, under constant fire with barely anyone to shoot back at. The warriors with guns would leap up to shoot, exposing themselves for only a second, like death-dealing jack-in-the-boxes. Those with bows would lie in the grass, arcing their arrows upward to fall among the troopers. War arrows are hideous things, falling silently and hitting without warning, even behind cover. Their flat iron heads were shaped to slide between bones, and gruesome flanges kept them from being easily pulled out. As the braves advanced from bush to bush, I saw scattered blue specks behind them, the bodies of fallen troopers, so few and still compared to the many, many moving warriors.

Not every warrior was in hiding. Through the glasses I saw a lone Sheyenna ride right up to the soldiers' lines, testing his bullet Medicine. He was wearing a warbonnet and a spotted jaguar hide tied to a spotted belt. He circled in front of the dismounted troopers, letting them have a clean shot at him, then he trotted back down the coulee to where some Hunkpapas were gathering their courage. He shook his spotted belt, letting the Lakotas see bullets falling out. Either he had the Medicine or he was a gutsy charlatan who kept spare ammo in his belt.

Most warriors were not pushing their Medicine that much. Some fought in thoroughly Wasichu fashion, huddled together behind a fold in the ground, pouring fire into the troopers with repeating rifles.

The galling fire must have been going on for some time, but the end came in a burst of bloodshed. About two score troopers suddenly mounted up and countercharged, trying to drive the braves back. They surged down the slope—but did not get far. Withering fire forced them to dismount, then fall back, with braves running at their heels. When they regained the firing line, warriors came in with them.

A chaotic hand-to-hand melee erupted, hatchets and lances against pistols and carbines—and once a trooper's seven shots were fired, he had only his clubbed carbine to defend him. Everything hung on that struggle. If the braves could somehow be driven back, the firing line would be restored. If not . . .

At that vital instant a horde of mounted Oglalas and Sheyenna came sweeping up from behind the ridge. The high ground had hidden them until the last moment, so the charge came without warning, like a hawk hitting a mouse. Crazy Horse had brought his braves through the Sheyenna camp, gathering recruits as he went, then crossing the Greasy Grass downstream and coming up the reverse slope—as cool a cavalry maneuver as anyone is likely to see. Officers will claim—in a bit of backhanded boasting—that Lakotas are the finest light cavalry in the world. On a good day with Crazy Horse there, and his Medicine working, it might even be true.

I watched the troopers closest to me panic, caught between Sheyenna and Hunkpapas swarming out of the gullies, and Crazy Horse's riders coming over the ridge. Big bay horses bolted. Troopers turned and fled along the ridge, trying to get to the main mass of the battalion. Howling braves came right behind them, allowing no chance to form a firing line. Fighting spread from left to right along the ridge, pushing the remains of the battalion upslope. Shooting rose to a new crescendo, filling the air with smoke, but the firestorm did not last long. It was over in about the time it takes a patient man to load and light a pipe. Some troopers broke from the main mass, running for the gullies or the river, or just running. They were quickly rubbed out.

Firing tapered off. Through the glasses, I could see soldiers continuing to defend themselves at the top of the ridge, shooting from behind the bodies of their horses. Hundreds of braves, women, and old men had gathered on the heights to witness this last stand by Custer's battalion. Already I could hear parents congratulating the braves, and at the same time holding them back, saying, "Do not return to the fight. You have done plenty. These Long Knives are dead men." After a while, it seemed that only Indians were firing. Braves leaped the barricade of dead horses and rode in jubilant circles, firing into the air and at the prone bodies. It was over.

Slowly the mayhem subsided. Young men and boys were driving horses down the coulee: bays, sorrels, and grays with US stamped on their hips. I could still hear firing, farther away and behind me. Somewhere upriver the battle was still going on, or a new one was starting, Reno and Wallace no doubt, holding out on their hilltop. Maybe Benteen too. I wished them luck.

Spring Grass started pulling on me, saying we had to see what had happened to Long Hair. Still holding my drag rope, I started after her, towing Mitch's body atop my pinto. We walked slowly toward the spot where

Custer's battalion had made its final stand, expecting we'd find the General there.

I was twelve when I first saw dead soldiers. It was the evening of the first day at Gettysburg. Having seen the Rebels march by, and hearing the guns fall silent, my sisters and I thought the battle was done with. We slipped out the bedroom window into the warm July night—a foolish thing to do, but we were used to thinking of the moonlit fields as ours. The soldiers seemed to have gone on, past Gettysburg. We were hoping to find a hat, a shell casing, or some like trophy.

Confederate pickets caught us before we even got to Herr Ridge. They were angry, as surprised and scared as we were, swearing something awful, saying, "Young girls got no business sneaking around at night—not during a battle."

It was news to us that the battle was still going on. Tarheels from Heath's division took us over to where a burial detail was at work, showing us the bodies lined up beside the half-dug graves. The corpses looked like big bundles of rags.

"Bluecoat cavalry did that." They showed us a captured carbine. "They got new repeating rifles—load 'em up, and they will fire all week, faster than a jay ken squawk. You go larkin' around the Yankee lines, and you're sure to be punctured. Yanks don't see in the dark the way we do."

When they found out we were Irish, they told us how much they admired the Irish Brigade's doomed charge at Fredericksburg. "They left their dead not a dozen paces in front of our lines. Cooke's North Carolina brigade gave 'em a cheer, sayin' they showed pluck. Especially fer Yanks." Our captors declared that all Bog Irish were honorary Tarheels.

Eventually they took us home, where Mom scolded us raw and made us fix the hungry men eggs for breakfast. They were almighty grateful. Heath's whole division seemed to be half starved and shoeless. They camped next to our farm for the next couple of days, "in reserve"—eating our chickens while we mended their uniforms, helped them write letters home, and learned the words to "Goober Peas."

On the final day of fighting, Heath's men were thrown into a last vain assault on the Union lines, along with Pickett's Virginia division, brought down from Chambersburg. They were marched barefoot over a mile of open wheatfield that had been mowed to stubble by case shot and bullets—not against Long Knife cavalry, but against two hundred cannon and thousands of Federal rifles. Union troops saw they were about to get some of their own back, chanting to the oncoming Rebs, "Fredericksburg, Fredericksburg . . ."

Heath's men staggered back, carrying close to two thousand wounded and dying, the worst of which ended up at our farm. Their commanders had sent them charging across that wheatfield without making much provision for treating the wounds that would result. But there was no one we could rightly complain to—Heath and all but one of his brigadiers were themselves wounded, killed, or captured. Pickett's division lost every regimental commander and all but one of its field-grade officers.

Both armies decamped, leaving ten dead or wounded soldiers for every man, woman, and child in the town of Gettysburg. We had dying soldiers lying in our parlor with their socks already stitched together, and lines of dead ones in the barn, waiting to be buried. Even with every window thrown wide, our house stank of gangrene and mortification in the July heat—only rain saved us from suffocation. Faint with nausea, I carried water for my mother while she worked among the wounded. When she finished with one man, she would wring blood out of the hem of her dress, then go to the next. Every rug and blanket in the house had to be burned afterward. Patterned carpets I had played over as a child were spattered, then soaked, then gone forever, consumed in a holocaust that I had never thought to see this side of purgatory.

In comparison Custer's dead looked almost peaceful, not moaning, not complaining, just lying on their backs with their arms thrown wide or covering their faces. Farther along the ridge, more bodies piled up. The stink of gunpowder mixed with the summer heat brought back vivid memories of Gettysburg.

Women and warriors were at work, stripping the dead. At the crest of the ridge, I saw one of the most terrible sights of the day. As bad as Mitch dying, or Raven being shot. A soldier, already stripped and naked, leaped up. He had been shamming, playing dead to stay alive. Two women lunged at him, but he grabbed one and used her for a shield. It was a danse macabre—a naked trooper swinging this big woman about, while her girlfriend tried to stab him. Some Hunkpapa braves shouted comic encouragement to the women, nearly busting a gut. Finally, a third woman stabbed him from behind.

Greenbacks were blowing about, dumped out of trousers and waistbands, so many that in places it looked like it had been raining money. Seeing them made me sick and angry. The government claimed greenbacks were unsound and that we had to steal gold out from under the Lakotas—then paid these thirteen-dollar-a-month sacrifices in paper.

The first body I recognized was James Calhoun, lying on a little rise beside a bright pile of spent cartridges, as lucky in battle as he had been at cards. The Lakota who had gotten his gun was still there, calmly going through the glittering shells, looking for live rounds that Calhoun had set close at hand but never got to fire.

Farther on I saw Myles Keogh, lying behind a barricade of dead bay horses, wearing nothing but socks and his medal from the Pope, just like in my fever dream. A hard-drinking Irish gallant, he delighted in dancing and damning the British, but went overseas to vent his anger. He had killed Piedmontese and Confederate Rebels before coming west to try his hand at killing Indians. Now he was lying stripped by Lakotas, who had finally done what Italians and Confederates had failed to do.

I told the warriors going through his belongings that he was a brave man and deserved better than to be scalped.

Personal effects lay scattered about—his watch, gauntlets, and a blood-spattered photo of a woman. A big clayback bay stood beside him, nuzzling the limp body. I recognized Keogh's horse, Comanche—he was badly wounded, with his saddle twisted around, hanging under his belly. Keogh's hand still held the reins, which made the braves loath to take the animal. Stealing horses was one thing; accepting gifts from the dead was another.

We had to go all the way to the end of the ridge before we found the Custers. The first one I came across was Boston, the youngest brother. No Bows stripping his body were incensed because the boy had been carrying a pair of moccasins, beaded on the bottom for a walk in the Spirit World. Loot from a Lakota burial lodge—the absolute worst Medicine you could bring into battle—but I guess a boy from back east would hardly know that. The No Bows wanted to cut him up, but we pointed out he was young and had been punished enough.

Spring Grass kept asking, where was the Wasichu chief? I knew he was sure to be somewhere nearby, and asked her aunt to help me lay Mitch down. I had done what Mitch wanted—no need to worry about his ghost.

A Sheyenna called Spring Grass over, saying, "This is the Long Knife Chief." The body was laying face down, badly cut up and bristling with arrows. Spring Grass asked how the man knew he was the leader. He told her the man had been giving orders and wearing an officer's buckskins. Besides, he had seen a thunderbird mark on the body, and that was the sure sign of a chief.

Spring Grass lifted the head, then let it drop. "No, it is his brother." The Sheyenna was not convinced, trusting more in thunderbird marks than in women's opinions. It was merely Tom Custer's eagle tattoo—the one he had shown to Agnes and me. But the Sheyenna stubbornly insisted that Tom had died bravely, giving orders to the end. As far as the Sheyenna was concerned, this two-time Medal of Honor winner was the bravest man in the 7th cavalry. If he had not actually commanded, it was the War Department's fault.

Then I saw Yellow Legs. Standing there, a living apparition beside his black horse. I dropped my reins and went to him, wanting to grab him, to have him take me home, before I gagged from the heat and decay. By now flies were swarming, thicker than the Lakotas had; the whole hill stank of blood and death.

When I got to my husband, he went down on one knee, pointing with his coup stick. "Here is the man I shot." He was inspecting the hole he had made, like a doctor checking the cause of death. Following each bullet as far as he could was one more thing that made his rifle a Medicine gun.

The General lay on his back, mixed in with his dead troopers. He was no longer smiling, but he seemed perfectly at ease, ice-blue eyes open but not fixed on anything. If he was not happy with what he had done, at least he did not show anger or regret. I swayed a bit, bracing myself on my husband's shoulder.

Yellow Legs looked up. "The second bullet is not mine." He showed me how Custer had been shot in the head, on the left side. Yellow Legs insisted he had hit him in the chest. I have no idea who fired that second bullet. The only thing you can be sure of is Custer did not shoot himself. He was right-handed, and in no condition to do trick shooting once Yellow Legs had put a hole in him. Perhaps one of his own men had done it for him in those last horrific moments. They would do that for a woman; why not for Long Hair?

Spring Grass and her aunt came running over. Taking one look, Spring Grass moaned terribly, then gave a great cry and whipped out her skinning knife, slashing at her limbs.

Warriors looked surprised to see a Sheyenna so vigorously mourning a Long Knife chief, but we explained that he was a relative. Like me, he had married into the tribe, and they ought not scalp him. One of them had started to cut off his fingers—to keep his ghost from harming people—but he stopped what he was doing and walked away.

I held on hard to Yellow Legs, saying I really wanted to go now. Mitch was lying downhill from the General. Bloody Knife too was dead. Medicine Bear's curse was done with. After years of exile and wandering, I could do what I wanted and go where I pleased, without fearing the curse would come following me. I could rejoin the Lakota Eaters. Or even return to the Spirit World if I wished. No giant bear was going to come and chase me out. I never *wanted* things to end this way, but you cannot always have things the way you want them. Coyote and the Staked Plains taught me that.

Yellow Legs stood up, saying, "I made the wound Medicine for Raven, but we will need more wild plum bark and pounded white pine."

I told him I was happy to do for Raven what she had done for Keeps-the-Fire. Such work did not absolutely require a woman—but I was eager to use my newfound freedom and get off this ghastly hill.

Spring Grass kept wailing away. I could not mourn Long Hair the way she was mourning him; I merely bent down and closed his eyes. I was sorry for him, but I was more sorry for Mitch and Bloody Knife, and for American Woman, who had seen her mother shot, and for Gall's family, and for Isaiah. And for Keogh and Calhoun. The list went on and on, stretching all the way back to Yellow Legs's village on the Lodgepole.

Here was the man who had brought death to them and desecration to the Center of the World, lying with his brothers and soldiers around him. On such a grim day it was hard to remember the gentle warrior at Fort Lincoln who loved women, girls, books, and pets; who could be shy and courtly, perching servants' children on his knee and teaching them their letters. All of that was rubbed out by an afternoon full of murder and foolishness.

Spring Grass's aunt bent down, taking a close look at Custer. "This is the one? Who burned Black Kettle's camp? Who smoked with Brave Bear and was warned never to attack the People again?"

She spoke so forcefully, I was not sure it was really a question. All I said was, "Yes, he was warned." Mitch had warned him, Bloody Knife had warned him, so had Brave Bear and Goes Ahead; in our own timid ways Libby and I both warned him—but it took a .44 rimfire to finally convince him.

The woman took out her bone awl and stabbed him once in each ear. Then she stood up. "Now in the Spirit World he will hear better."

We left the soldier in red the way I had first seen him, lying under summer skies in the sunburned Montana grass. As we walked down the hill, leading our horses, a lone brave came ambling up from the river, dripping wet and casually swinging his coup stick. Yellow Legs stared past the oncoming brave, as if he did not mean to see the newcomer.

Being Wasichu, I had to look.

The warrior sauntered by, giving me an evil grin well worthy of Coyote. Three winters had passed since I had seen this brave, but there was no mistaking him. It was Medicine Bear, risen from the river, his Medicine no longer broken, coming cool as you please to count coup on Custer.